THE TRUSTED

A note from the publisher

Dear Reader,

We do things a little differently at *Pantera Press*, what we call
good books doing good things™ .

Our joy in discovering and nurturing talented home-grown writers,
such as John M. Green, and presenting them to story lovers is one part.

Another is our passion for philanthropy and, with *The Trusted*,
we are partnering with Misfit Aid, a unique charity run by surfers.

We chose Misfit Aid because Tori Swyft, *The Trusted*'s main character,
has surfing and surf music rushing through her veins, and that's on top
of her brilliance as a nuclear science PhD and skills as an ex-CIA agent.

Misfit Aid empowers surfers to volunteer and travel to trouble spots
afflicted by natural disaster and poverty, to team up with local partners
and the community on disaster relief projects and local development.
Since it was founded in 2010, Misfit Aid has sent volunteer teams to
Chile, Mexico, Samoa, Fiji and West Timor.

Simply by enjoying *The Trusted*, you'll be contributing to our unique
approach as well as helping this great aid program. We thank you.

If you'd like to do more, please visit www.PanteraPress.com/Donate
where you can personally donate to help Misfit Aid, and discover
more about all the programs *Pantera Press* supports.

And, of course, please enjoy *The Trusted*, the first Tori Swyft thriller.

For news about other books by John M. Green and our other authors,
as well as sample chapters, author interviews and much more,
please visit our website: www.PanteraPress.com

Happy reading,

Alison Green

THE
TRUSTED

JOHN M. GREEN

PanteraPress
great storytelling

PanteraPress
great storytelling

First published in 2013 by Pantera Press Pty Limited
www.PanteraPress.com

Please send all permission queries to:
Pantera Press, P.O. Box 1989 Neutral Bay, NSW 2089 Australia or info@PanteraPress.com

A Cataloguing-in-Publication entry for this book is available from the National Library of Australia.

ISBN 978-1-921997-10-5 (Paperback)
ISBN 978-1-921997-16-7 (Ebook)

Cover and Internal Design: Luke Causby, Blue Cork
Cover Image © moodboard/Corbis
Editor: Kylie Mason
Proofreader: Desanka Vukelich
Author Photo: Courtesy Phil Carrick, *The Australian Financial Review*
Typesetting: Kirby Jones
Printed in Australia: McPherson's Printing Group

Pantera Press policy is to use papers that are natural, renewable and recyclable products made from wood grown in sustainable forests. The logging and manufacturing processes are expected to conform to the environmental regulations of the country of origin.

*In memory of the real Alan Whitehead, with
unbounded thanks, despite the clattering of
midnight milk bottles through his house.*

Other novels by John M. Green
Nowhere Man
Born to Run

'What if a concerted cyber attack brought the whole system down?'

—Michael Wilding, Australian author, *Quadrant*, 2011

'A cyber attack perpetrated by violent extremists could be as destructive as September 11, 2001 ... a cyber Pearl Harbour. Before 9/11, the warning signs were there. We weren't organised. We weren't ready. We cannot let that happen again. This is a pre-9/11 moment.'

—Leon E. Panetta, US Secretary of Defence, 2012

'A single malicious algorithm could turn off the lights, stop airplanes flying, disrupt national financial transaction networks or the electricity grid.'

—David Irvine, ASIO Director-General, 2013

'ELF works to speed up the collapse of industry, to scare the rich, and to undermine the foundations of the state ... Our greatest weapons are imagination and the ability to strike when least expected.'

—Earth Liberation Front, 1997

'Eco-terrorists ... are one of the most serious domestic terrorism threats in the US today ...'

—FBI, 2008

'Over the past century, the most damaging US counterintelligence failures were perpetrated by a trusted insider with ulterior motives ... [including] long-term plants ...'

—The Office of the National Counterintelligence Executive, 2012

'A cornerstone of our risk management is recruiting high-quality people who we then entrust ...'

—Major global corporation, today

PROLOGUE

'SAVING THE PLANET MEANS DESTROYING IT ... to smash industry and technology and finance ... to supplant greed with need. That mission, *our* mission, will take time ... it will be hard ... and it will be lonely. After you walk out of my apartment,' the professor said, again fidgeting with the bolts and chains on his door, 'we will never again communicate. From tonight, your sole objective for the next decade is to devote yourselves to your vocations, to become so valued and respected that you'll ascend to the highest possible echelons. In ten years, you will be chiefs of industry or government, striding as equals if not superiors to the most trusted people there. You will become *the* most trusted. No one will be trusted more than you.'

Professor Mellor flapped back to his chair in his sandals, reached down and, after scraping a match across his heel, lit another cigarette. When he dropped the match into his beer, it hissed in chorus with his wheezy drawback and, as he exhaled, the absurd tendrils of smoke that curled up out of his nostrils

1

like Salvador Dalí moustaches entranced his disciples, almost as much as his plan's raw daring thrilled them.

'Then, my fellow members of 9S,' he said, picking a shred of tobacco off his lip and flicking it aside, 'after those years have quietly passed, and completely out of the blue, each of you will do the unthinkable: you will utterly and completely betray that trust …'

PERCHED UP HIGH in her silvertail nest on the top executive floor, the banker reflected on the professor's challenge ten years earlier. With one exception, she had done everything her guru had asked of her and, having single-mindedly manoeuvred herself into position, her time to act was near.

She peered down at the scruff of demonstrators in the skyscraper's forecourt. After all their noise—their chants and marches and sit-ins—how could they fail to see that protests without action were futile, like tears in a storm?

So, while some still persisted in humping their tatty recycled signs all over New York City, she continued quietly setting the fire for real change. From way up here, where her equally naive colleagues had entrusted her with the keys to the third largest bank in the world, she would soon ignite a voracious inferno.

She wouldn't rob the bank, nor even just gut it. No, she would strangle the entire global financial system, the greedy golden goose that, despite a few hiccups, had been gorging itself at the planet's expense.

She smirked at the idiocy of the protesters. Why occupy Wall Street when you can destroy it from the inside? The tantalising question had driven her for years and, now, after landing her

plum job as the megabank's Global Head of Risk, she would be
able to convert it into a statement, an answer. The answer.

For ten long years of subtle, dedicated and unrelenting
grind, she had clawed her way to the top, elbowing herself into
the very spot where she could make the difference, her own
big bang. Otherwise, why would she bother boring herself
stupid sitting day in and day out on this palatial executive floor
pandering to the interests and the lame jokes of all these smug
fat cats?

The bank showered her, like all the others in its top team,
with money. But seriously, was there a single person on the
planet who needed to rake in $17 million a year? Or own a ritzy
Upper East Side penthouse with eye-popping views? None of
that said anything about who she was; just who she had spent
ten years pretending to be.

To win, she had been playing the long game, living like
them, spending like them and acting like them, but—most
importantly—winning over their absolute trust, even if simply
being around these pin-striped pirates made her want to thrust
her fingers down her throat. For her, purging these hard-to-
shake parasites off the face of the planet would be a triumph.

Code-named Q/1 by Professor Mellor, she had sacrificed her
entire post-doctoral working life, and more, to position herself
for this task, this duty. Yet unlike the protesters down below,
clapping their hands and Kumbaya-ing around their drum
circle, she hadn't wasted one second loitering in city squares
or parks waiting for drooling TV cameras to arrive. Nor had
she once given tedious repetitive lectures about 'us' and 'them'.
What she did was work her butt off to *become* one of them, an
insider, through a vile yet crucial charade.

Those lightweights milling around in the street pictured
themselves as the noble martyrs of the so-called ninety-nine

per cent, the downtrodden masses who were paying the price for the greed of the wealthy, powerful one per cent. But she would show them martyrdom, those grasping Oliver Twists whose own craving was ultimately for more, more, more, even though they and almost everyone else in big cities like this one had too damn much already.

Didn't they see the paradox? At the same time as the planet was haemorrhaging to death, they wanted to slice open more of its precious veins.

But soon, very soon, and whether they liked it or not, her 'less' would be their new 'more'. That was her promise.

And it would be good. Very good.

1

Ten years earlier

THE SUDDEN SHRIEK OF A BEACH shark alarm is typically a trigger for terror, yet most of the people stumbling out of the surf at North Narrabeen were hooting, high-fiving and slapping each other's backs, their feet easy in the foamy fringes of the surf.

The tourists with their eyes red and burning, and their knees still shaking, were gulping in mouthfuls of wave spray, bewildered why everyone else seemed in such high spirits. Blinking the salt from their eyes and with the sun glistening off the shoulders around them, their gazes followed the locals' and landed on a lone board rider way out beyond the break. 'That redhead out there! Is she nuts? Why hasn't she come in?' Looking for a circling fin, they scanned around her but spotted only the waves.

If they'd bothered to read the leaflets the surf club had handed around earlier, they would have been cheering too, not quaking with fear. The siren, on schedule at two pm, was blasting to announce Tori Swyft's fifth annual tribute to her legendary father. The anniversary of surfing icon Mark Swyft's death was always accorded a time-out here. For the pro-surfing world, as well as for locals, Swyfty's death was a double tragedy since his adoring daughter's grief over it had pulled her out of competitive surfing. It was no comfort to them that she turned her obsessive brilliance onto schoolwork, not even when she proved to be a prodigy of the classroom as well as the waves.

But today, Tori would prove that despite restricting her surfing to this once a year event, she still possessed all her old magic.

On her board, Tori heaved up and down on the swells, looking left and right and back, manoeuvring for the right wave. Time had faded the once celebrated freckles that had bridged across her nose and these days her skin had a pasty library pallor. Yet out here alone, she knew that the sea offered her more of a refuge than any building possibly could and her eyes glinted with a frisky sense of homecoming.

The incoming surge felt good and, grabbing her board's rails, she raised her torso and flicked back her hair, flinging a curtain of spray that sparkled like the sequins on her bikini top. The salt on her lips cracked as she grinned, remembering how five years ago—right here—she'd flipped the surfing world on its head when, as a not quite thirteen-year-old, she snatched the Junior World Title away from girls who were five and six years older. When she'd lofted her frontside air on that wedging right-hander, she crushed the event's highest single-wave score. She'd been young, for sure, but none of the other girls she'd been competing against had Swyfty as their personal board shaper, or as their coach ... or as their inspirational dad.

As she readied herself today, Swyfty's fatherly caution—that winning that title would change her life—flashed back to her.

And so did the knowledge that he'd been completely wrong.

Tori's smile dropped. The nightmare from three weeks later— her actual thirteenth birthday, as it happened—was haunting her again. Those long, torturous minutes when Mark fell forward into a wipe out near the bottom of a screaming Alley left, one of Narra's classic waves … and didn't come back up.

The birthday girl had watched it from the beach, helpless. Watched it and felt it.

She adored her famous dad and he adored her. The pair were inseparable, yin and yang. From when she was three or four, whenever Swyfty was out riding or testing one of his boards, she'd be standing with her tiny toes tingling in the foam, imitating him, learning from him, soaking up tips. People frequently commented how father and daughter, both fiery redheads with sinewy, wiry bodies, were so attuned to each other, so alike. Locals would wink and nod to each other as they watched Tori on the sand, her wide innocent eyes fixed on Swyfty and her body rising and dipping and bending and twisting, mirroring his own movements.

When he went under, Tori's eyes bulged. She held her breath, just like he would have to. After she couldn't hold it in any longer, knowing that he couldn't either, she had screamed and started to dart into the surf, but Mark's sister Shaz kept the sobbing, shaking girl back.

From inside her auntie's arms, Tori opened a crack of a wary eye and, as she saw the lifesavers launching their inflatable, an icy despair swept over her and the flecks of silver and gold that normally shimmered in her irises flickered out.

Later, an interminable time later, she shuddered as she saw Swyfty's friends, her friends, lift him limp and lifeless out of the surf, a savage crimson necklace oozing where the fin had gashed his throat.

She broke free of Shaz and ran to him as they laid him on the sand and she prayed, not that she and Swyfty believed in any gods. One after another they breathed into him, breathed for him, pounded his chest, others milling around, screaming for their mate to revive when clearly he wasn't going to.

Many were crying but somehow Tori's eyes couldn't, although her body was shaking and shivering despite the summer heat.

Few children see their father ... their best friend ... die.

That was what changed Tori's life.

2.

IF TORI'S MOTHER HAD BEEN THERE on her thirteenth birthday, the path she followed after Swyfty's death might have been different but, apart from the finger-worn photos, Tori hadn't seen or heard from Caitlin Kaminski since she was two.

According to Swyfty, it was inexplicable. Their world had been perfect until the day Caitlin vanished. His welfare cheque and her waitressing income had been plenty for their long, listless beach days, with Mark hitting the surf while Caitlin played with Tori, who, from the first day she could, scrambled all over the sand stuffing the burnt orange grains into her innocent, burbling mouth.

Swyfty never discovered why Caitlin had left or where she had gone, simply shrugging the thousand times Tori had asked him about it, guessing she must have either got homesick or was hunting better waves. As Tori grew older and got to know that Narrabeen's surf was as good as almost any, she started pestering Swyfty for better answers, since so much more of the story also didn't gel.

When Tori's parents had first hooked up, Mark had only just quit high school for his life on the beach. Caitlin on the other hand, six years older and a Berkeley politics major, was in Australia on a posting for the US State Department. Tori could never understand—no matter how cute a baby Swyfty kept insisting she'd been—why Caitlin, a feisty career bureaucrat by all accounts, had ditched her hard-earned security clearance to have a kid, spend three years as a beach bunny and then slip away into nothingness. There were no good answers, just the aching truth that one morning when Swyfty woke up, Caitlin was not there in the rumpled sheets with him and Tori.

Apart from leaving her child a heartbreaking void of memories, Caitlin bequeathed Tori dual Australian–US citizenship plus, according to the photos, her startling green eyes as well as a love of books that became as deep as her passion for surfing, and helping the girl, much later, to jump whole school years. Her mother's departure also changed Swyfty who, to care for his baby, shucked off his own languid life as a surf bum on welfare to start crafting custom surfboards; boards that, years later, surfers would have killed for and one of which ultimately killed him.

THE ENTIRE BEACH whooped and whistled and cheered when eighteen-year-old Tori started paddling hard, then quickly looked back and, at the right moment, caught the wave. Shouts of *Go, Tori, go!* Mexican-waved down the beach as she got to her feet and ripped in toward the sand. As always, she was riding one of Swyfty's own boards, this time the classic that was usually mounted above the clubhouse bar. The yelling from the beach grew to a roar when, close to shore, she leant forward and triangled her hands and head on the deck ahead of her, kicked her legs back, arcing them upwards into the air and, in her celebrated headstand, glided in to the beach.

Up in the clubhouse, the beers were already being lined up for the annual drinkathon in Swyfty's honour and, behind the bar, hung a famous trio of photos: Tori's first tribute headstand, Swyfty's own headstand the morning before he died, and the third, possibly Australia's first surfboarding photo, a precious heirloom that Manly's surf club had lent for today's event, the sepia-tinged shot of another surfing legend, Tommy Walker, headstanding during the baking summer of 1911/12.

With Tori today a legal drinker for the first time, she aimed to knock back her full share of beers just like Swyfty did after a day out on the waves. Not that she didn't drink already but being legal was a milestone even among her uni friends.

The timing for a booze-up was far from perfect, with her commitment to attend Professor Mellor's secret inner circle that evening, but there was no way she could or would miss the big clubhouse event.

Like Swyfty, Tori felt a connection with nature and she'd become a staunch environmentalist but until Professor Mellor, she had never met one as unswerving or as inspiring, let alone one who also happened to be a world authority in nuclear physics. Loads of her anti-nuke friends pooh-poohed her for it, but she had totally embraced nuclear since, despite its bad rap, she saw it as the scientific discipline with the power to do the most good for the planet in the shortest time.

This professor was unique. Sure, he lashed out against man-made climate change, just like Tori and all her greenie friends, yet Professor Mellor was more than thunder and bile. The first time she'd heard him, Tori remembered something Swyfty used to tell her: *Good intentions change nothing except how you feel about yourself.* That was the thing about Professor Mellor: he wasn't just words, though it took her a little time to discover that.

For weeks Mellor had been quizzing her, puffing his way through packet after packet of cigarettes. She saw it as a trial by cancer but worth every passive wheeze if it helped her persuade her new hero to take a risk on someone so young to approve her doctorate program, and then supervise it.

For Mellor, Tori's youth was irrelevant. To him, she was the final target in a furtive two-year recruitment drive and he needed to be certain about her reliability and as importantly, her potential. As both a leading academic and a vocal environmentalist who often spoke—or rather shouted—at rallies, Mellor had the perfect vantage point to spot activists who could push his carefully honed plan forward.

His first criterion was that they were super-brains so, like Tori, all his targets were PhD students or postdoctoral fellows. But brains were abundant among green campaigners. The sweat was in finding Einsteins with not only the passion but who, for the sake of the planet, would commit to devoting a long decade of hard selfless toil, making sacrifice after sacrifice—if necessary, the ultimate one.

With Tori then an eighteen-year-old prodigy hoping to embark on a nuclear doctorate, once Mellor felt comfortable that she satisfied both his tests, he agreed to supervise her thesis and also invited her to join 'Nine Sisters' or '9S', his very private, exclusive club. After the first of these hush-hush gatherings, she gladly accepted as a secret badge of honour the code-name Mellor gave her: S/14, her surname's initial combined with her rank in order of joining.

9S had been meeting for many months and, as its final
recruit, Tori felt deeply privileged. Professor Mellor had big
ideas, and tonight was the moment they had all been waiting
for, the unveiling of his action plan.

Yet today was also Swyfty's day, so even saving the planet
would have to wait and, besides, she wanted that first legal
drink.

3

PROFESSOR MELLOR SHOOK HIS FIST AND barked, 'Growth is a false god!' His passionate mantras were what had initially drawn Tori Swyft and the other doctoral students, all with code-names like hers, to sit at the guru's feet in the first place.

For Y/6, Yuan Li Ming who was originally from Beijing, Mellor's message was much the same one she had been thrumming under her own breath ever since her father had been arrested and her screams had become voiceless. Here in laid-back Australia, Y/6 could utter her anti-growth heresy aloud, shout it even, and everyone would just keep drinking. Yet back home in China she feared she'd be arrested if they even suspected she thought this way.

The roots of Y/6's cropped black hair prickled her scalp as the memory of her mother's howls returned … as deafening to her now as that day the doors of the black sedan slammed shut on her father's red apron and it whipped and cracked in the dust as the official vehicle sped him away forever. 'Why did he have to complain about the toxins?' her mother had wailed.

Yes, growth was a false god, but it wouldn't be worshipped forever. It couldn't. The Bible's book of Genesis was written for a time like this. For a group like this. 'In the beginning.' Tonight, Y/6's precise role in the professor's plan, everyone's role, would be revealed and, after months of secretly psyching themselves up, it couldn't come too soon.

That might be why the young redhead, S/14, was looking so pale. S/14 had only been to three of these conclaves before but, tonight, when Y/6 noticed that her remarkable green eyes were clouded over with that sickly film, they appeared eerily like the eyes in the piles of dead fish that Y/6's disgraced father had so unwisely protested about.

Y/6 wondered if the tightness in her own chest was also from stress or simply due to the professor's smoke, so she twisted her head away from the rest of the group to steal a puff on her asthma inhaler. As she moved, a drop of cold sweat shivered off her brow and she watched it fall toward the floor as if in slow motion, hoping the ping when it hit the boards wouldn't draw attention to her.

She knew it wasn't the smoke, of course. The professor's unusual spice cigarettes were as much a fixture as his ideology, but tonight the air was also thick with the nervous sweat of anticipation, deadening the scent of burnt popcorn she had forced herself to tolerate. A difficult pleasure.

She didn't understand why someone like Mellor chain-smoked polluting cigarettes. Even so, he was unlike anyone she had known before, especially back in China. For months, she'd sat cross-legged at his feet during these exclusive gatherings, sheepish yet proud she was one of his hand-picked few, deeply inspired even while straining over the metaphors and allegories he painted between puffs, grateful she could take a lead from the other 9S members who didn't realise how lucky they were with English as their first language.

Mellor broke his tirade to take another deep drawback and lolled back his shaved scalp, freckled with age and anger, against the greasy smear on the wall behind his chair.

Professor George Mellor was a man most people would avoid sitting next to on a bus: reeking of tobacco, red veins webbed across the whites of his wild eyes, nose and ears thick with hairs that must have taken refuge there once he started shaving his head, his beard stained and patchy like a ragged carpet in a rundown bar. Yet here she was, thought Y/6. Here they all were. Sitting at his glorious sandaled feet.

Mellor was notorious for his smoking but that wasn't what he would ultimately become famous for, and it wasn't for his academic research either. While his name was right up there with the big guns in his narrow field of hypernuclear physics, nothing in the hundreds of peer-reviewed articles or eight books he'd slaved over would ever launch his face onto a nightly TV news bulletin. Unlike the plan Y/6 expected him to reveal tonight.

His academic work was important, as was her own, but this, what they were here for, was vital. What Mellor was about to unveil in his austere apartment, if the months leading up to tonight were a guide, was guaranteed to get the flashbulbs popping. Even if the old man didn't last long enough to lap it up personally, it would still be his legacy.

Mellor resumed his word spray. 'Some idiot politician— who? I don't care—once said, *Better to have your enemies inside your tent pissing out, than outside the tent pissing in.* But tonight we, the Nine Sisters, will pledge to prove him wrong. We … you … will be on the inside, yet no one will pick us as enemies. From there, we will be a surge of creative destruction within the heart of the industrial-technological complex. We will deaden it but, more than that, we will prevent it from reinventing itself.'

Y/6 and the rest of his hand-picked audience, including S/14, nodded as if they knew where their sage was heading, but they leant even further forward in their hunger to find out. As they did so, Y/6 noticed S/14 looking worse, her face not just pale but now sweaty and starting to go as green as her eyes, which were clamped shut as if she was squeezing their colour out of her pores. Y/6 nudged her to see if she was okay, but S/14 waved her off.

Y/6 wondered if S/14 was experiencing a side effect of the white-noise generator that Mellor had set buzzing in the corner of the room. After he'd lowered the blinds and taped them with aluminium foil to block any laser-activated passive resonance bugs from outside, he'd switched it on in case his earlier sweep had missed some spyware device planted inside the room. Mellor was not just careful, he was paranoid. Because his radical environmentalism would naturally attract enemies all present accepted that secrecy and vigilance for their 9S work were crucial.

While nuclear physics was Mellor's paid work, this was his life's work. He'd researched the strategies of the world's major extremist and espionage networks, from al-Qaeda right back to the infamous Cambridge Five, those bright upper-class students recruited as Soviet communist spies on campus in the 1930s who rose to great rank in the British intelligence services. He especially studied green anarchists, like the radical Earth Liberation Front and the Unabomber, 'Ted' Kaczynski, child prodigy, Harvard graduate and math professor turned recluse and mail-bombing eco-terrorist. In analysing all of these groups and people, Mellor zeroed in on a common fatal flaw and designed his own strategy to overcome it. Consequently, he called 9S a 'notwork' as opposed to a network.

Unlike traditional conspiracies that operated through a secret network with coded communications, clandestine meetings and furtive drops, or gave notice to authorities or made demands, Mellor's notwork would be the exact opposite. How does your enemy infiltrate a group if it has completely ceased to be a group … one that never, ever meets or talks again? How do you tap into emails or phone calls or internet chatrooms if there aren't any? How do you follow a trail if there is none, if they only ever act once, decisively and without warning?

And if, despite his precautions, someone sitting on Mellor's floor tonight was an undercover plant, how could the authorities possibly charge him or his group with anything? No targets had been picked nor were the methods of attack yet known and, to make it even harder for the establishment, no member of 9S would take any action for ten long years. The time lag wasn't merely to create a distance between the members, a smokescreen, it was so everyone could elevate themselves into the perfect positions of power. Until their moment of betrayal, they would each—apart from Mellor himself—be seen as the most solid of citizens.

He'd named his tight little cabal the 'Nine Sisters' even though some were men and there were more than nine. His original plan was to stop at a group of fifteen, not too many and not too few, enough to allow for the inevitable failures or pull-outs. But caution stopped him at thirteen, and after Q/1 and G/3 'dropped out' it was down to eleven, though with S/14 joining he got it back up to twelve.

The actual number of members, even the gender mix, were entirely beside the point, just like with the French eighteenth century *Loge des Neufs Soeurs*, the Masonic Lodge of the Nine Sisters, from which he'd cheekily lifted the name.

It was one of Mellor's little jokes, as his disciples had learned at a prior meeting. Benjamin Franklin and briefly Voltaire had led the original group in Paris, named after the Ancient Greek muses. Their fabled *loge* championed the arts and sciences as the foundation of civilisation, but Mellor viewed things differently, not through such blinkered eyes. Of course, having devoted his own life to science he accepted that back in those days of the so-called Age of Enlightenment science was validly seen as an underpinning of progress, but those optimistic old-world thinkers could never have contemplated the deplorable reality of the late twentieth and early twenty-first centuries, where civilisation had so perverted science that it was now destroying the planet rather than living in harmony with it let alone nurturing it.

Someone had to say stop—to make it stop. Others had tried but failed miserably. Too much was at stake. The planet was at stake. Burning at the stake.

After months of testing his followers' broad commitment in these meetings, Mellor would reveal his plan tonight. And once they pledged themselves to it, also tonight, not only would 9S immediately split up but, following his plan, they would never meet again. They'd never even communicate again, not with him nor each other.

Mellor dropped his cigarette into his home-brewed beer and arced his body forward, resting his elbows on his knees, just below the frayed hemline of his greying shorts. 'Fellow members of 9S, you will strive to complete your doctorates with the highest of accolades, and you will travel and find work wherever in the world your brilliance can take you—into mega-corporations, governments, other universities ...'

Mellor's eyes were ablaze. Despite his protégés being some of the brightest doctorate students, some young, some older, they were entranced, all awed by his ideals, his passion and his charisma. Over many months, by discreetly inviting them one by one into his tight orbit, Mellor not only stroked their egos but bestowed on them a calling far beyond themselves.

He reiterated how crucial was his core defensive strategy, the notwork, and then explained his offensive strategy, that over the next ten years they would doggedly devote themselves to their vocations, becoming so masterful at them that they would become the most respected and trusted chiefs of industry or government. 'If you perform as I know you can, you will become *the* most trusted. No one will be trusted more than you.'

He handed round copies of an extract from a report by the influential CERT Coordination Centre at Carnegie Mellon University. 'You will all read this before you leave tonight. It tells corporations and governments precisely how to spot a covert insider threat ... people like you will be. This is your bible of how *not* to behave. As members of 9S, you will do the exact opposite. Instead, you will be paragons of organisational ethics, culture and cooperation. Thank you kindly, CERT,' he smiled and raised his beer in a toast, ignoring the stub floating in it.

After taking a slurp, he paused to light another of his pre-rolled smokes and took a drag before he reached the part he knew they were on tenterhooks for, all of them except Q/1 and G/3, the two who had left the group and who knew all this already. He looked around, searching their eyes for waverers, but there were none, although S/14 was looking at him through her fingers so he couldn't really tell about her.

'My fellow members of 9S,' he said and, using words he'd practised, told them that their unfailing objective was to betray the trust placed in them in the most imaginative and

spectacular ways, not just to destroy the organisations or
governments they worked for and everyone dealing with them,
but to bring down the financial system, to destroy the food
chain, to freeze transport, to throw a monkeywrench into the
oil and gas industry. To do whatever they could from whatever
heights they'd reached. 'You will do this at a time of your
choosing—what works best for you—but not before November
that year, the northern autumn, so that heading into the dark
of winter you—we—will wreak the most havoc and have the
most impact.'

Y/6 glanced around, careful to move only her eyes and
not her head, not to break the spell. One by one, everyone
seemed as mesmerised, as uplifted, as she was, their eyes glued
to Mellor. Even the old guy, W/12, the soldier who at least
wasn't wearing his stupid uniform tonight, was still sitting
there ramrod straight. Next to her, S/14 moved again, and Y/6
thought she heard her moan. But she wasn't going to let S/14
spoil the moment, and she shut her neighbour out of her mind,
keeping her focus on Mellor.

'To those you work with,' he continued, 'this will be
unthinkable. You will be one of them, or so they will believe.
As you rise in seniority and influence, you will soak up all the
knowledge your organisation has and you will attain the power
to do what needs to be done. You will wear the clothes, you
will talk the talk. You will dine with them, drink with them,
and laugh with them, even if you justly despise them. And then,
my friends, you will start pissing, from *within* your tent. It will
be unexpected. It will be powerful. It will be good. Through
this, Nine Sisters, we—yes, we—will save our planet.'

He raised his glass again and gave them the ritual toast he
ended all his orations with. 'Bring on the winter. *Fiat justitia et
ruant coeli* ... Let justice be done, though the heavens fall!'

Suddenly, S/14 groaned and bent over double, her head almost hitting the floor in front of her. Struggling to her feet, she rushed to the door, one hand tight over her mouth and the other on her stomach. Mellor said nothing. He merely got up to unchain the door and as she rushed out, he shook his head as if she were collateral damage in the war he had just declared.

Ten years later

THIS WAS TORI SWYFT'S FIRST SURF at North Narrabeen's famous bombora in seven years. Originally, she'd left Australia to enrol in a prestigious two-year MBA at Harvard, except it didn't turn out to be the challenge she expected. After blitzing first year almost without trying, then getting jostled by pushy Wall Street bankers desperate to sign her up a year early, she couldn't be fussed even turning up for second year. Instead, she talked herself into a job at the CIA and spent the next six years in various of the world's hot spots, work she found fulfilling as well as meaningful except for the last few stinking months. But that was now over, she reminded herself once again and, with her heart still racing from the surf—or was it the painful memories?—she flipped back the fringe of her dripping red hair, shiny and almost black, placed her board on the sand and lay back on her towel, closing her eyes to Sydney's sharp winter sun.

Having tossed in her CIA security clearance in exchange for a fat wad of piss-off-but-keep-your-mouth-shut money, Tori's far more limited ambitions right now were twofold, reading Proust's *À la Recherche du Temps Perdu*—in the original French—and riding all the waves she could, first these few weeks limbering up at Narra in Sydney, then catching some monsters at Teahupo'o in Tahiti. After that, she had no ideas, but the Agency's pay-out gave her at least a year before she'd even need to think about working again.

An hour earlier, a jet ski had towed her out to paradise, though to non-surfers the towering ten-footers thundering toward the beach were more like a living hell. Shifty peaks, some sucking dry, but Tori had eventually caught a pipe, and it felt awesome to be back here. Maybe, she thought as she wiggled the sand off her toes, she should try punting for another crown and cap off her old junior women's title.

Flat on her back under the cloudless sky, Tori could already feel the sun drilling through the black neoprene of her wetsuit. Sydney was experiencing one of its freak winter heat waves; at least climate change had some advantages. She reached around to her back, unzipped the suit, peeling it down to her waist, and removed her bikini top. On Sydney's northern beaches, going topless was no big deal, but she let loose a smirk as she imagined how her stuffy ex-colleagues at the Agency would react if they saw her, especially her last boss, Martin Davidson, a creep with eyes that wandered where his filthy hands didn't dare.

She twisted open a bottle of luscious sunshine and sniffed the thick coconut aroma, heady from being left to bake in the sun lying on top of her book and, after a pause, she slapped it on. All-over tanning hadn't been so easy working at the CIA, except when she'd been serving in Cuba—but all that was over—and in any case being a fair-skinned redhead meant she always had to find lotions with a strong sun-protection factor.

On her back again with her eyes shut and the surf thundering in her ears, she only vaguely heard the helicopter hovering above the beach and, unaware it was landing a little way up near the lagoon, she missed the glint of sunlight that flashed off the head of a bald, stocky man as he eased himself out of the chopper onto the sand in a three-piece suit, preposterous on any beach let alone this one. Instead, Tori started to think about some of the Proust she'd been reading, the part where the narrator dips a madeleine in a cup of tea triggering a memory of his country home, Combray. Deliberately, she sniffed the kelpy tang in the sea air, and found it worked for her too. There were still good memories here, except for one.

She wiped the lotion off her fingers onto her towel before she ran them back over her book. Proust, she chuckled to herself. Anyone who could write something that so many smart people lied through their teeth that they'd read and enjoyed had to be admired, which was why, now she had the time, she was reading him to decide for herself.

Tori stretched her arms above her head and as she yawned she heard a metallic click, which she thought was her jaw at first. As the clicking came closer she visualised a couple of beers clanking in someone's backpack, but when the sand crunched unnervingly close to her head and she detected a shadow looming over her, she blinked open her eyes and, squinting, looked up.

'Dr Victoria Swyft, good afternoon,' the man said. The sun was behind him so she couldn't make out his face.

No locals had ever called her by that name, and last time she looked she didn't have it tattooed anywhere either. No one left around here knew her by her full birth name let alone that she'd got her doctorate. She'd never made a big deal about it, although the university had, since there were hardly a lot of people who got their PhDs at twenty. Here at Narra she'd always been Tori or Swyfty's girl and, besides, after seven years' absence from Australia, people who had once known might even have forgotten that.

The man's accent was American, in itself hardly unusual as this had been a world surfing hot spot forever, even before the Beach Boys gave it a boost in *Surfin' USA* and, after her time at Harvard, she thought that his way of pronouncing 'afternoon' was a little Bostonian. She caught a whiff of his cologne cutting through both her own coconutty aroma and the salt spray. Her body tensed when she picked it as the same Burberry scent favoured by her slimeball ex-boss at the CIA. What the hell did they want with her now? Her mind scrolled through the faces, but this voice matched none of them. And there was still that damn clicking.

'Enjoying the scenery?' she said, blinking and yanking her towel around herself to cover her breasts before getting to her feet. 'Even in Boston it'd be polite to introduce yourself to a semi-naked woman, wouldn't it, or did you grow up in the Combat Zone?' She meant the city's former red-light district. Tori shifted to put the sun to the side and, when her eyes adjusted, she saw that the odd-looking stranger had been more respectful than she'd imagined. He'd apparently spoken with his back to her to avoid her even thinking he'd been ogling her.

'Okay,' she said, 'you can turn around.'

He was no local, that was clear. Not with that girth and not in those clothes, even if sand had caked over his once highly polished black brogues. His bowtie, barely visible below his cascading double chin, had a blue stripe that echoed the sky but that's where the comparisons ended. His grey three-piece suit was bloated with more material than a stand-up comic's routine. Here on the beach it was as laughable.

As he held out his right hand, she noticed his left was fiddling with gold worry beads. 'I do apologise, most surely,' he said. His words were slow and considered, stuffy and old school. 'Axel Schönberg III, chief executive of SIS from—'

'Boston,' she finished, keeping her hands clasped on her towel, letting his own chubby hand hang there friendless.

'Indeed.'

'How'd you know I was me?' she asked, noticing at least fifty other sunbakers in similar states of undress scattered along the beach and a roughly equal number in the water.

He tapped the rather bulky side arms of his glasses as if that meant something. She assumed it was to give his loose hand something to do rather than let it hang where she'd ignored it. Point one to me, thought Tori, even though she was in no mood for games. 'Look, Mr Schönberg—'

'*Dr* Schönberg, actually. You asked how I knew you were you … my FrensLens,' he said, sliding off his glasses and handing them to Tori. 'Here, try them on.'

'Wow!' she said after putting them on. Text had immediately popped up in her vision just to the side of the man's face: *Dr Axel Schönberg III, heir to the Schönberg meat-packing dynasty, Boston. Born in …* 'What the hell are these?' she said, taking them off as if they might infect her in some way. 'Meat? It says you're a meat baron?'

'They're FrensLens, like I said. A prototype from a client. You go for a drive and they automatically load your route, you look out the window and they tell you the day's weather forecast. You fly over a beach and the facial recognition software scans the faces and identifies Dr Victoria Swyft for you.'

'They're like Google goggles?' said Tori.

'Google schmoogle. These beauties trawl through multiple search engines and social networking sites sucking out then organising the information about the selected face, and then they cross-check against your own data and give you a potted summary of who the face is, where you might have met, all that.'

'That's an invasion of privacy!' she said, waving the glasses back at him.

'That's a problem?'

'Whatever.' She handed the glasses back, perplexed. 'But I don't do social networking,' she said. 'Ever.'

He shrugged. 'Anyone who makes junior world surfing champion at thirteen and completes her PhD by twenty is burdened with a couple of shots of herself scattered around whether she likes it or not.'

'Lucky I was lying face up then.' She saw his face redden from the chins up. 'Look, I know Boston, but I've never heard of you or your meat company ... what was it ... "S" something?'

'SIS.'

'Which stands for what exactly? Schönberg Invades Swyft's privacy?'

His hand moved to his scalp, bald and already beading with sweat, and he gave it a nervous scratch while his other hand clicked his beads.

'Actually, I'd be concerned if you *had* heard of us, Dr Swyft,' he said, his hand dropping back to his side. 'Given the high profile of our clientele—governments, multinationals and ultra-high-net-worths—we maintain a low profile ... No profile, to be truthful. And SIS doesn't stand for anything, not any more—apart from client service.'

'What, er, service brings you here?' she said, suppressing

a snigger for his Bostonian business bullshit. 'A meat market? White slave trade?'

'Dr Swyft, I say this with as much humility as I can bother to muster: at SIS we are the smartest, most trusted and, especially, the most private advisers on this planet.'

'But the glasses said you're a meat mogul?'

His entire body shook as he laughed. 'It's a business my grandfather set up on the side to deflect interest away from SIS. Right from the beginning, no matter how hard we try, we find we can't always keep out of the limelight, so he started an operation so tediously uninspiring that no one would ever think to shine a light on it, but if they did it explains the summer home on Nantucket, the private jet, and all that.'

Tori noticed the helicopter. 'So … you're advisers. Then why bother with me? I don't need any adv—'

'My research pinpointed you as a perfect fit for our firm.'

Despite her discomfort, she had to admit she was a little intrigued, but having come home to escape, to start afresh, his intrusion was irritating her more than it piqued her interest. 'Your research?' she snapped, staring him down. 'About me? What did that—?'

'—tell me? Quite a story, though none will be news to you. A sporting legend at thirteen then, after the shocking blow of losing your father,' he said, without pausing or lowering his eyes from hers as others did when mentioning the tragedy to her face, 'your aunt takes you in, you drop competitive surfing and your physical prowess shifts to the intellectual, which is your far more natural home. You skip whole slabs at high school, yet still make valedictorian at fifteen, almost sixteen—'

'In Australia we call it dux.'

'And I gather you people also smother your toast with a ghastly black sludge.' He visibly shuddered at the merest thought of

Vegemite but, recalling it was made by Kraft, one of his clients, he pushed past it. 'You win scholarship after scholarship, finishing your engineering doctorate by the time you're twenty—'

'Almost twenty-one.'

'Remarkable either way, then you go to Harvard … wait, before that there was a year working at that research facility in, ah—'

'Lucas Heights,' she said, 'in Sydney.'

'That's it, but you win another scholarship—'

'A John Monash Scholarship,' she added, with a pang of guilt.

He shrugged. 'Whatever. And it funds you to attend Harvard Business School, where you top the first year MBA. Yet despite making it as Ford Scholar, you drop out, send the Monash money back—so admirable—but then,' he said, his nose wrinkled as if he'd just caught the stink of a rotten fish, 'you go work a desk at the CIA, of all places.'

'Not just a desk,' she said, her free hand tightening into a fist. 'Where'd you hear about me? From the Agency?'

'Not at first, no. I stumbled across your Swyft Neutronics Model. In my experience, stumbling can be very fruitful.'

And very risky too for someone in his shape, thought Tori. 'You mean my PhD dissertation.' She wiped her forehead with the back of her hand, unsure if the heat in her face was from the sun or from her personal space being trampled on. When she had published her model all those years ago, the nuclear world treated her as a rock star, at least for the brief and wearisome period before she ducked back out of the limelight, where she preferred to stay. Perhaps she did have something in common with this strange man.

Her thesis had been revolutionary, so what they said at the time was true, even if it was embarrassing. Fine-tuning the fuel burn-up inside a power reactor required precise and rapid command of its many control rods, something humans could never hope to achieve alone, but which computer systems made feasible. Tori's model, especially her three ground-breaking algorithms, supercharged the prevailing methods and, with the latest in telemetry as well as the explosive growth in computer processing power becoming an everyday reality, her work allowed the nuclear power industry to take a revolutionary leap in the millisecond-by-millisecond control of the neutronics inside a reactor core. Not only was she responsible for making the Monte Carlo modelling of the billions of interactions between atoms and neutrons inside the core of a nuclear reactor far more accurate and reliable, but for the first time it was economically viable to couple it in commercial applications as a hybrid tool with deterministic neutronics and thermal hydraulics codes.

What she'd done was nirvana for the nuclear power industry, especially because commercial plant operators would be able to squeeze more power out of the same core yet at the same time cut the costs on safety margins. It was like buying a new car with souped-up brakes and handling; you could drive faster yet safer, even right up close to the edge of a cliff.

It took two years for cautious nuclear regulators to approve her model, and the Americans were the first, and as soon as they did the technology houses rushed new products to market integrating her breakthrough into their plant control systems.

'Your work was, still is, brilliant. And yet you made it open source, posting it on the internet for free,' Axel said, his nose wrinkling as if the mere notion of giving away anything valuable was rather unorthodox.

Open-sourcing it had been her supervising professor's idea; for the good of the globe, he'd argued.

'That was our point,' Tori said, retightening her towel, her aggravation simmering. 'Giving it away meant the whole nuclear world could—*would*—take it up. Nuclear power would be cheaper and safer at the same time.'

'According to my research, your model is now built into nearly half the power plants in France, most in the rest of Europe, a good third of US nuclear plants, and a number in Asia, though apparently Fukushima in Japan never quite got around to it. Most impressive, Dr Swyft.'

Tori's feelings were fighting themselves, violation winning but flattery starting to punch its way out of the other corner. 'Dr Schönberg, if your research is so good, why didn't it also tell you I have other plans?' she said, pointing him to the waves.

'Actually, it did, rather obviously, don't you think? It does seem I knew to find you here, after all. But I am rather hoping you'll change your plans. At SIS we make quite the difference. Our work is, er … enthralling. And our remuneration rather generous. You'd even find time between engagements to squeeze in more of this,' he said, his hand sweeping before the surf. 'We do own rather a grand lodge at Teahupo'o, you know.'

Only Tori's travel agent knew she was booked to go surfing there. 'Wha—?' she started, but held her tongue.

He unbuttoned his voluminous jacket and reached inside, extracting a small tablet computer which he handed to her. 'Perhaps you'd be good enough to scan this?'

She moved to avoid the glare on the screen, and started to read. 'You're offering me a directorshi—Shit, how does this thing do that?' The text seemed to scroll up the screen automatically meeting her eyes as they read each line, reversing when she went to re-read a paragraph. Not once did Tori need to touch anything.

'It's got eye-tracking. Makes life so much easier.'

Especially if you have such fat fingers, she noticed, but even so she was impressed. At the CIA, devices like this had annoyingly been above her pay-grade, and while some smartphones came with eye-tracking to keep them switched on when you were looking at them, they didn't scroll like this.

Tori read on and when her proposed pay package scrolled up, she re-read it so many times she started to get dizzy. 'Your terms do seem ... interesting.' Interesting, like a gold brick road. She blinked and added, 'Why do you think I'd accept them, Dr Schönberg?'

'Research, Dr Swyft.' He tapped his nose and the beads clicked below his chins. 'And please call me Axel. Everyone in the firm does.'

He leant over and touched the tablet in the corner of the screen. Another document popped up: a letter from the chief executive of one of the world's largest corporations, coincidently one of the few business leaders that Tori respected. Was it a coincidence? She read it but said nothing.

After a minute, Schönberg spoke. 'So, Dr Swyft?'

'You pay quite, ah, well,' she said, with a light cough. 'And you have a lodge where it seems you already knew I was headed and, as well, your rich and powerful friends say good things about you. But I have no idea what you actually do—what this advice you give is—or what my role would be.'

'True,' he said. 'But before I flesh that out, there's just one little thing I need to know: Why you left the CIA. It was rather sudden, after all.'

Tori was still sore over the circumstances, especially since the Agency claimed to have fired her when the truth was ▮▮▮ ▮▮▮▮▮▮▮, ▮▮▮ ▮▮▮▮ ▮▮ ▮▮▮ ▮▮▮ ▮▮▮▮▮▮▮▮▮. ▮▮▮▮▮▮ ▮▮▮ ▮▮▮▮▮▮ ▮▮▮ ▮▮▮▮▮▮▮ ▮▮ ▮▮▮▮▮▮▮▮▮, ▮▮▮▮▮▮ ▮▮▮▮▮▮▮ ▮▮ ▮▮▮ ▮▮▮▮ ▮▮▮▮ ▮▮▮▮▮ ▮▮▮ ▮▮ ▮▮▮ ▮▮▮▮ ▮▮▮ ▮▮▮▮▮▮▮.* ★

---

* Redacted by the CIA.

'Look, Dr Schönberg, er, Axel,' she said, straining to keep cool. 'If you're as good as you claim, you should know why I left.'

Schönberg smiled, making Tori certain it had been a test; one she had apparently passed. She half expected a gold tooth to glint at her in the sunlight, but there was only another click from his beads and he again offered his hand.

'Subject of course to my answering all your questions satisfactorily, I suspect we may be welcoming you as a director of SIS, Dr Swyft.'

'Maybe,' she said, this time taking his hand and awarding points two and three to him.

5

TORI WAS PINCHING HERSELF. TWO MONTHS ago she was at grave risk of never seeing sunlight again, yet now, after fifteen glorious days' surfing and soaking up the luxuries at SIS's Tahitian hideaway, she was ensconced in her own office in Boston inside the stately period townhouse that SIS called headquarters, and holding down a job that paid more in one week than her shit of a boss at the CIA's Langley complex probably earned in a year. Fuck him, she thought, her lips curling with satisfaction. She was a director, too, of this prestigious firm, prestigious at least to the elite handful who were permitted to know it even existed.

She swivelled her chair toward the sunshine streaming in, and leant back a little to bask in its warmth. The bow window drew her eyes outside through the tangles of ivy winding through the traditional black wrought iron balcony, then south over exclusive Beacon Street, dotted red and brown with the first autumn leaves that were fluttering an escape from their sanctuary opposite in Boston Common.

When Axel had been settling Tori into her office he ran his hands over the oak panelling that lined the walls and proudly pointed out the parquet flooring. 'Those diagonals are Canadian maple. And the inlays are Asian teak and American walnut. Exquisite, don't you think?' She did. The browns were close to Axel's latest bowtie and matching suit. Never trust a man in a brown suit, she'd once heard but, given everything he'd done for her so far, she would ignore the advice in his case.

When her boss was readying himself to leave for another meeting, Tori was still no wiser about what she should start working on, so hesitantly she asked him to give her a steer.

'You're a director,' he answered, emphasising it with a click of his beads. 'Directors direct at SIS, Tori, they're not directed. Not by me, not by anyone.'

Tori started tapping her fingers on her knee under the desk, also oak. All his vague mumbo-jumbo sounded plausible when Axel had said it the first time, but now she was here, as a director of a firm redolent of aristocratic opulence, yet with no clue of what to do.

Axel had seen this insecurity before with his other successful hires. 'Tori, relax. We hired you because of your profile: your DNA is the same as ours ... we all connect dots that most people can't even see.'

'Profile? I didn't sit any psych test.'

'Er, no. But I did get a peek at the one you sat for the CIA.'

This jolted her. She didn't feel affronted, given what she'd already experienced of Axel's research. It wasn't his lack of guile either; she was acclimatising to that, too. What surprised her was that while the click of his damn gold beads got this strange little man access to such utterly private information yet, to him, it was as normal as phoning for pizza with extra mushrooms.

'What did it say, apart from the dots?'

'Psycho-babble mostly. Theirs usually are. There was one titbit … what was it?' He twirled his beads several times around his fingers, somehow without clicking them or twisting them. Tori was starting to hate his beads, unsure if they were simply a foppish eccentricity like his absurd bowties, or an infuriating bit of drama he used for distracting other people's attention. 'Ah yes, I recall,' he said with a little giggle. 'How could I have forgotten it? "Winning the world championship at thirteen," they said, "was the young Swyft's crowning surfing achievement, and she felt that continuing on and risking a loss would dishonour her father's memory … Hence after that, she championed the books rather than the waves." It's a bit romance novelish, don't you think?'

Tori gritted her teeth. Like so much of the Agency insight she'd put up with over the years, this was also drivel. The simple fact was that without her dad to support her, she couldn't bear even the idea of facing the attention that competitive surfing attracted, so she poured her talents inward, into the private world of study.

Axel went on, his face again serious. 'The key points in your profile, to me the thrilling points, were nothing to do with your intellect or your father. What excited me were the high-risk vectors they identified: your free spirit—sassy, they called it—your piercing curiosity and that you're also an infuriating perfectionist. Apparently, together with your physical, ah, prowess, they're the reasons why you were such a good surfer. They're also ultimately why you parted ways with the Agency and, if those brainless idiots had understood the profile in their hands, they would have seen that coming. They're also why you and SIS are a perfect fit.'

He slipped his beads into his pocket and clapped his hands, his chins wobbling just a little. 'Enough of that. Anyone with your capabilities doesn't need me to guide them but, since you asked, I'll give you a nudge. Look over our client list.' Axel had already leaked a few names to her when he was cajoling her to join, an eye-popping who's who of big business and governments. 'It's all on the computer system; restricted, of course, but directors have open access.'

Axel suggested scanning the full list, randomly selecting some and skimming the summaries of the work SIS had done for them. 'Approach it like that, unfiltered and unstructured, and a good idea will eventually pop into your head. Perhaps two, if we're lucky.'

Tori's face paled.

'Tori, it won't happen straight off. It'll be a few days, a month, perhaps even a year. You'll burrow down lots of blind holes but you and those dots will definitely connect one day, most profitably, I'm sure. Apart from the, ah, smarts of our directors, our other big virtue at SIS is our patience.'

Breaking in a new director was no everyday event at SIS, but this roundabout way was how Axel had always done it. It was how his father Axel Jnr had done it and how his grandfather had started the original Schönberg International Services in 1920. When Axel III took over, he formally abbreviated the name to SIS, a simple rebranding since most clients already called it that and no one, apart from clients and of course staff, had ever heard of them.

Axel turned toward the door. 'Spend some time reading the files. Oh, and Francis should be here soon,' he added, referring to the assistant he'd allocated to her.

After Axel left her office, Tori did look through the files. Leaping off the pages were several jobs SIS had done for the fabled Warren Buffett, for decades revered as one of the world's most astute businessmen, the so-called Oracle of Omaha. Yet, if the financial media ever got their paws on these files, their long love affair with Buffett would have pushed them into a ménage à trois with Axel's father and later, Axel. In what seemed to be a perfect partnership, Buffett took the risks and lapped up the glory while SIS, clearly content to feed him a flow of 'his' ideas, collected its many tens of millions in fees, and maintained a happy repeat customer.

It was likewise for Big Tobacco. In the 1950s when Marlboro was struggling to find its market, Axel's grandfather conceived the radical Marlboro Man advertising campaign that shot the brand to iconic status. He'd 'given' the idea to his poker partner, the advertising man Leo Burnett, with Leo taking the glory and SIS minting a handsome royalty.

Then there was Greece, another long-standing though, these days, far less joyous client. A few years back, when Goldman Sachs was publicly pilloried for helping the Mediterranean nation mask its basket-case financial status, SIS had been there too, but hidden in the shadows.

And Rupert Murdoch? Tori flipped through an old file from 1986 on how the Australian media mogul first catapulted himself onto the global stage when, in the dead of night that year, he shifted all his British newspapers to a walled fortress in Wapping, East London, not only sparking a year-long printers' strike but revolutionising the newspaper industry. Axel's father—an old friend of Murdoch's father—had not only hatched that plan but delivered the Wapping site to Murdoch via an offshore trust, one whose connection with SIS was never disclosed, except to Murdoch himself. By July 2011, the British tabloid, *News of the World*, got perilously close to revealing SIS's crucial and historic role and demystifying some of the Murdoch magic, but the media boss shut the paper down the day before it could, under a pretext of dealing with the infamous hacking scandal. When he said, 'We've been let down by people,' he meant it, but not the way everyone thought at the time.

And Apple Inc? Wow, thought Tori. If SIS only owned the patents on that iProduct they'd quietly dreamt up for Steve Jobs.

It went on like this, file after file. Was there anyone rich and famous that SIS didn't give advice to?

If the outside world got a taste of what Tori had been given entrée to, some very big bubbles would be popped.

'D R SWYFT, HI. I'M FRANK CHAUDRY.' He hung back at her office door.

Tori let the luscious caramel voice linger in the air before she turned from the window and waved him in. 'It's Tori, please. Frank Chaudry, did you say? I heard it was Francis?'

'Francis Xavier actually, but I prefer Frank.' To Axel he was Francis, but to everyone else at SIS he was Frank.

Tori pointed to his open-necked shirt. 'No tie?' she asked. 'That's a pretty bold statement around here, with so many of the men wearing Axel look-alike bowties and you an, ah, Englishman to boot.'

'I've got plenty of other affectations, so don't get too excited that I don't share that one.'

As he approached from the doorway, he slid off his jacket, a three-button tweed, and hung it on the back of Tori's visitor's chair before he collapsed back into it, his long legs splayed out like tent ropes primed to hold him against the oncoming wind. He ran

41

his hand over the vast forehead that swept back from his eyebrows like one of the Sydney Opera House sails at night. Despite his rich, plummy British accent, Frank seemed remarkably laid-back, especially compared to the others she'd met here so far.

He had obviously come straight from the airport. His shirt, blue with a faint white stripe, was crumpled but set off his dark skin, and he hadn't shaved. She noticed that both his stubble and the curls on his head lacked a single grey strand. Not bad, she thought, for a guy who'd done almost everything yet was still in his mid-thirties, though she wasn't sure how a Pakistani heritage affected things like hair colour.

'So you're my assistant, Frank. What exactly does that mean around here? Do you take dictation … make cups of tea?'

'Nope, and nope. At SIS, we all do our own typing and get our own drinks. Even Triple-A.'

Tori cocked her head. 'Triple …?'

'Axel. Even he makes his own tea, but in his case it's coffee, decaf.'

'Triple-A?'

Frank explained that was what a few of the more seasoned SISers called the boss, except to his face. Whether it was because he was Axel III, or filthy rich, or due to his triple bypass ten years earlier, he didn't have a clue. 'He was Triple-A when I got here.'

Given his accent, Frank's inclination against conformity was surprising and his straight-talking, dripping-with-honey voice grew on Tori and she idly wondered if there'd been a Pakistani Michelangelo; the more she looked at Frank, the more he looked like a David drizzled with chocolate.

Within twenty minutes, she felt she had him figured out, though she wouldn't have minded Axel's pair of FrensLens glasses to double-check.

From Axel's description, she had expected Frank's strong credentials, but she'd leapt to the wrong stereotype, thinking that he'd slipstreamed into Eton College as the pampered son of some snooty upper-crust Pakistani out of the British Raj, but no. His parents were immigrant factory workers whose bright kid had won a precious King's Scholarship. Later, at Oxford, he'd not only done a double-first in theology and mathematics, which Axel had spoken glowingly to her about, but his aspiration had been to join the priesthood, a goal Axel had described as boyishly errant.

'I hear God is in the numbers,' said Tori, smiling.

Frank's face dropped. 'Yes, I thought so, too. Once.'

Not so common for Pakistanis, Frank's family were Catholics. His nine years at MI6—a different priesthood— included assignments in Iraq, Libya and a year in Australia, though that was after Tori had left for Harvard. After a steep learning curve he had become MI6's chief resident hacker and, by the time he left the Service, his specialty was hacking the hackers, a role he found as stimulating as it was comical. If these guys, he told Tori, had approached their mission with professionalism, they'd really be dangerous as opposed to fly swats. There were exceptions that he tipped his hat to, like the creators of the Conficker worm, and his old chum, 'Fig Jam' Thatcher in New York, but most were kids out for a laugh.

As Frank told her more about himself, though skipping over anything that might be classified, Tori started to shift in her chair, wondering why he was her assistant and it wasn't the other way around.

7

TWO MONTHS LATER, TORI AND FRANK had not only located some dots, they had connected them and then, for three days and long into each night, Axel grilled them on every nuance of how they had done it. Once satisfied, he sent them home to pack and get their passports.

'It's a bit quick, isn't it?' Tori asked as he prodded her to the door.

'Time kills deals,' said Axel, giving her another polite nudge.

The more Tori observed her boss, the more he amazed her. Who'd have guessed the chubby Boston Brahmin would decide to personally pilot his Gulfstream G650 for half of their seven-hour flight from Boston to Rome?

'After all the good work you two have done, I've got to contribute something,' he said, sitting hunched at the controls a few hours later and loving every second, never once offering to give the stick up to Tori or Frank—not even briefly—choosing to forget that both his accomplished employees were also licensed pilots.

SOTIRIS SKYLAKAKIS LOOKED up from his desk which, Axel whispered to Tori, was carved from a single slab of pale cream limestone so large and heavy his 400-foot super yacht *Fun Cool* had to be built around it. Skylakakis slowly put down his knife. '*Yiá sas*, my dear Axel and, I presume, Dr Swyft?' he said, eyeing her up and down. 'The famous Frank … where is he?' he added as an afterthought.

'Halfway to Athens. We can't risk losing time if you give us the green light, so we've got him setting a few things up, to be ready.'

The multibillionaire stood and, with his muscular arms stretched wide in welcome, came out from behind his desk. Meeting powerful men was nothing new to Tori, but she had never tingled like this before and had to stop herself from instinctively licking her lips. From the shots of the bachelor she'd seen dotted all over the web, Tori wasn't sure if the 55-year-old would really be hot or if he'd just been heavily Photoshopped. She could see now that the photos had definitely not been airbrushed: Skylakakis was leanly muscled, more like a thoroughbred than a greyhound, even down to his red Euro trunks. His tan gleamed golden through his white fine cotton T-shirt, and his large, strong mouth showed teeth whiter than the peeled apple he'd been slicing at his desk. And the red swimming trunks? She tried to keep her eyes off them.

He was shorter than Tori expected, closer to her own five-foot-ten, she decided as his eyes held hers. She'd come across one or two other Greeks with fair hair and blue eyes, but his were striking. Under his delicate, almost non-existent eyebrows, his irises were sharp yet seemed to grin with a loosely worn sense of certainty. As Skylakakis approached his guests, he brushed back his blond fringe, more of a wayward curl which, to Tori, made him seem even younger, almost boyish.

His charisma was strangely casual, akin to what CIA people at Langley had said about Presidents Bill Clinton and Barack Obama. She didn't know it, but the last time Clinton stayed over on Skylakakis's yacht, the pair had even shared crude jokes over an ouzo about their mutually celebrated magnetism.

Skylakakis's Eurocopter, a converted military range Cougar AS532-AL, had been waiting for Axel and Tori at Rome's heliport and dropped them on his yacht's helipad only five minutes ago. If Tori had known both his chopper's name, *Gamey Sue*, and his yacht's name, *Fun Cool*, were cocky allusions to the Greek and Italian slang terms *gamísou* and *fanculo*—which broadly meant 'fuck off'—she would have been endeared to the magnate even sooner.

She watched the two men hug. It wasn't so much a polite, faintly distant European hug, but more of a Tony Soprano mafia-style hug with true though guarded affection. After the Greek slapped Axel on the back, he said, 'I'm glad to see you've still got your *begleri*, my friend.'

As he turned to greet her, Tori stiffened. Growing up by the surf, her preferred physical greeting for men in beach gear was high-fiving. She wasn't a huggy person anyway, especially with a hot and rather bulging multibillionaire.

'His beads,' their host said, mistaking her reserve. '*Begleri*. They're a Greek invention.' He took her right hand by her fingers and gently brushed his lips on her tips. 'Hmm,' he sniffed. 'From *begleri* to Bulgari, I think. Do I detect a hint of Bulgari's Jasmine Noir? I am right, yes?'

She nodded but tried not to smile; getting charmed had not been on her agenda, especially once Axel had warned her. Skylakakis's cologne was not one she recognised. It was subtler than Axel's, and she wondered if that slight sweetness was magnolia, but she wasn't going to ask. The Greek's ways with women were as notorious as his parties. An ability to pick a perfume at a single sniff was undoubtedly a handy conversation starter, not that a tycoon needed one, especially if he lived and worked on his own bulletproof yacht with a rocket-launcher-equipped helicopter and a yellow mini-submarine also counted among his many boys' toys.

Skylakakis had never married—something he had in common with Tori's boss—but unlike Axel, the Greek's private life was a public spectacle. It wasn't entirely his own doing, but more from his guests' social networking posts and the gossip magazines that lifted their photos. He could have asked his guests not to take photos, but Tori suspected he preened every time he read he was the world's most eligible bachelor. For a man like him, again was never enough.

His legendary hospitality aboard his yacht meant businesspeople, too, were happy to jump on a plane to come and see him—as she and Axel had—resorting to a videolink or phone only if they were really stuck.

That meant Skylakakis rarely had to waste his own time getting around, even though he had just taken delivery of his new private superjet, a $500 million VIP version of the Airbus A380. The sticker price, according to what Tori had read, was $327 million but he'd spent $170 million fitting it out with the usual billionaire's playthings, including a gold-leaf paintjob, as well as live walls of ferns in the staterooms, corridors and lounges with a turbulence-proof watering system and a strategically placed array of mirrors to bring sunlight to the plants.

With his chopper ready to fly him to the superjet at a moment's notice, the plane could technically be located as far as 770 kilometres away, a near three-hour trip on *Gamey Sue* at full throttle, but his rule was it could never be more than an hour away, with the result that *Fun Cool* generally cruised within 250 kilometres of the nearest shore and his pilots would hop the plane from airport to airport to stay close by. As the world's second richest man for three of the last four years on *Fortune* magazine's rich list, living aboard his yacht not only insulated him against being a personal tax resident of any country, there were also obviously big security benefits, and a helipad that converted into a full basketball court when the urge for a game took hold was understandably convenient.

'Axel,' said Skylakakis, looking up from Tori's hand, 'you never mentioned that Dr Swyft was so—'

She cut him off. 'Please, Mr Skylakakis, it's Tori,' she said, removing her fingers from his.

'Of course,' he said, but alarmed her by taking her hand back again. 'And I am Sotiris, though I prefer Soti.' He bowed. 'Now, before we get down to, er, business I suggest you get out of those travel clothes and—' he checked his watch, '—in half an hour we'll meet on the aft sundeck for some canapés and cocktails, and we can talk. You have intrigued me, my friends, so I'm looking forward to ... what did you call it, Axel ... your little idea?'

'Tori's little idea.'

'Even better,' Soti said, moving his hand to the small of Tori's back, not feeling the shiver going up her spine, and guiding her and Axel to the door. '*Ta léme*, see you soon.'

'*YAMAS!* CHEERS!' SAID their host, holding up his glass and clinking it off each of his guests'. Tori noticed that with hers it was less of a tap and more of a touch but maybe, she thought, she was falling victim to the Sotiris Skylakakis media hype. 'These are my special Greek mojitos,' he continued. 'Who needs rum when you have Metaxa? It's far better with limes and mint leaves.'

To the super-rich, Tori realised, good taste is simply what tastes good. Or what tastes good to them. She wasn't usually big on mojitos, not even this one made from the deep coppery liquor from one of the fifty Cristal de Sèvres decanters of AEN Metaxa that Axel had given Soti for his fiftieth birthday, paying 1,000 euros apiece. To some, mixing this pricey nectar with ice, let alone muddled limes, sugar, lemon juice and mint leaves would be sacrilege. But not to Soti and Axel.

Out on the sundeck, the curved white lounge was so close to the yacht's infinity pool that Soti could lounge back and still stretch his feet on the pink marble coping. Tori could have too, but she was working. His legs were hairless and his flowing white toga—silk, she assumed—fell open on a hairless chest. That might explain his lack of eyebrows, she thought, or maybe it was all-over laser treatment.

Axel, sitting between them, was in a suit and bowtie as always, but the crushed white linen looked like he had flown in it all the way from Boston even though Soti's valet had only just pressed it for him.

Like Tori and Axel, Soti had also used the half-hour interval to change, though he had limited his effort to exchanging his T-shirt for the toga and his red swimming trunks for an equally skimpy black pair, shorts that Tori felt were in fine taste around a pool, but not in a business meeting, no matter how well cut. Tori worked hard to keep her eyes up, trying to meet Soti's, until she noticed his own drifting down over her body.

Her satin jumpsuits—tonight, her black one—were slinky but she'd never thought of them as sexy, more as practical, which was why she always threw in a couple of them when she was travelling light. Self-consciously, she brushed the folds flat and hunched her shoulders a little, but when Soti's eye-dropping became a wink she zipped it up to her neck, hardly expecting that her increased modesty would only make her more of a challenge for him. The wisp of breeze off the water didn't help either, so faint it did nothing to cool her frisson or the light sheen brushing pink over her cheeks.

Soti raised his glass again, keeping it up for so long that Tori felt compelled to clink it with hers across Axel's lap. She forced a smile, but said nothing and now avoiding Soti's eyes as well as his shorts, she looked over his shoulder to the horizon past Corsica where the golden pink clouds were firing up to a luminous deep coral, almost a match for the glowing tip of his cigarette as he took a drag.

'Alright, Tori,' he said, exhaling the smoke in five small rings he tried to link into an Olympic symbol, 'what's your little idea?'

At last, she thought; it was back to business. When she had first unveiled the plan to Axel, she already knew the details inside out. By then, she and Frank had spent weeks working night and day, at first alone and then as they refined it, with an increasingly fat wallet of consultants, experts on both US and Greek law, covering tax, corporate, trademark and constitutional issues, as well as a clutch of international real estate advisers. She'd hesitated hiring them all but, as Frank reminded her, connecting dots as scattered as these needed more than a pencil and since SIS directors automatically had a discretionary budget of up to a million dollars for dishing out on advisers, Axel clearly expected her to spend it.

As she cleared her throat, she reminded herself of Axel's advice on how to present the idea to their rather unusual client. When she and Frank had shown Axel the detailed pack of slides they'd prepared, he tossed them over his shoulder. 'No disrespect,' he'd said, 'but on Soti's yacht, he only does chats, not presentations. If he buys the idea, he'll get his people to bury into the detail. And don't hit him square in the eyes with it. Bring him round slowly. Take time. For him, business is social. Oh, and be prepared to be teased. It's an annoying habit of his but, provided you know your subject, like you do, it'll be harmless.'

Tori sat forward as far as she could, avoiding the embrace of the squelchy white leather. 'Mr Skylak—'

'It's Soti, remember?'

'Soti, yes.' Bring him round slowly, she reminded herself. 'The two things you love most in the world are?'

He ashed his cigarette in his hand and rubbed it on his leg, then took a slurp of AEN Metaxa straight from the decanter. 'Dear lady, I ask what your idea is and you answer my question with a question? What are you … a Greek? Perhaps a Jew?'

Tori took a deep breath and shrugged, holding back that her mother, as far as she'd discovered, had in fact been half Irish-Jewish and half Polish-Catholic.

Soti laughed. 'Okay. The two things? Apart from my good friend Axel here?' He patted Axel's leg.

Tori was relieved her boss was sitting between them, certain it would have been her leg under Soti's hand otherwise. 'Ah, yes. Apart from Axel.'

'And apart from beautiful women, such as yourself?'

'Mr Skylak—'

He held up his finger.

'Sorry … Soti.'

'Thank you,' he laughed again. 'Well … I suppose the two things are my beloved Greece and, as Axel will attest, my mother Helena, rest her soul.'

But Axel spluttered. 'And if you weren't being so *aneilikrinís*?' he said.

'*Aneilikrinís?*' asked Tori.

'Disingenuous,' Axel translated. 'Your mother, Soti? Tori, you need to know that the only reason Soti attended his mother's funeral was to make sure the old witch was dead.'

Tori gasped and snatched for her drink, hideous though it was.

'Relax, my dear,' said Soti, stopping her by reaching across Axel for her arm. 'My dear mother—and by that I don't mean adored, I mean costly—was a nagging, grasping woman. Even with the flawless English she picked up as the American ambassador's whore, she never once saw the irony when she called me a son of a bitch, so forget my, ah, little joke at her expense. So, to answer your question truthfully, the two things I love most are first, as I said, my beautiful country—sadly bankrupted by morons, thieves and bankers—and second, my business, which performs rather better.'

Tori managed to draw her arm away from him, although the tingling remained. 'Perfect.'

What the general public saw in Soti was mostly the playboy, and clearly he played up to it. They were aware he controlled Delphi Inc, the mammoth technology empire he founded, but were clueless that Delphi's success came from supplying its highly specialised components to almost all the big names in telecommunications, information technology and computers. Without Delphi's innovations packed inside them, virtually all the computer products from firms like Apple, Sony, Samsung, Toshiba, Dell and IBM would be half as good and twice as expensive, but they had the brand names with the relatively unknown Delphi as their silent partner.

Since the Greek billionaire's first *Time* magazine interview years earlier, his technology conglomerate had snuck up and overtaken its rivals to become the world's leading provider of basic computing grunt. Delphi shares were publicly traded on the NASDAQ exchange and on a good day its market value sat at around $350 billion, not as big as Apple on a similar day but far bigger than Google and Microsoft and, to Soti's special delight, Delphi had also shot right past his chief adversary Larry Ellison's Oracle.

In interviews Tori had seen, Soti denied he had an obsession with Oracle, even though he'd named his own company 'Delphi', after the hillside location where, as the centre of the ancient world, the famous oracle issued her cryptic prophecies.

Soti had actually started up his Delphi in Silicon Valley, the centre of the modern tech world, straight after he graduated from MIT and then, while his business was still small enough to avoid the glare of US tax officials, he migrated it to Bermuda. His connection to Greece was mostly spiritual and, like many Greeks, paying tax there had never featured high on his agenda.

These days, his tangled corporate structure had Ólympos Inc, his private holding company, sitting right on top of Delphi. From poring through SIS's confidential files, Tori knew that both Ólympos and Delphi had recently been redomiciled away from Bermuda and that Axel had elegantly tweaked the structure so that the private part of Soti's empire no longer had any fixed abode, just like its owner, helping to avoid prying eyes and more tax officials.

In turn, Soti's private company, Ólympos, had negotiated an unusual business arrangement with Delphi, the public trading arm, with the result that Delphi was mostly an empty shell, a front, despite its monstrous size. Under the arrangement, Delphi employed hardly any staff and owned almost no assets. All the products and services it sold were licensed under trademarks and patents that were actually owned by Ólympos, which also provided the thousands of people Delphi needed under a juicy management contract. Ólympos even rented out to Delphi all the offices and factories it occupied worldwide.

Through his private Ólympos, Soti had effectively wangled access, legally, to the billions that the public had invested into Delphi without having to loosen his tight grip on control. To cap it off, Soti owned—through Ólympos—a defensive twenty-per cent stake in Delphi, but that was cleverly structured—again by Axel—so it was worth far more, valued at almost a third of Delphi's market value simply because Axel had made them voting shares whereas the bulk of the remaining stock carried no rights to vote, not even on a change to the board of directors. So today, Soti's shares in Delphi were worth a cool US$100 billion and generated dividends for him of $3 billion a year, but even that was on top of the far bigger management fees that Ólympos sucked out of Delphi for all the services it provided.

Tori continued, 'Your business is in great shape, Soti.'

'And he hasn't even launched FrensLens yet,' said Axel.

Soti leant across Axel towards Tori, 'Do you know what they are?'

'Axel showed me the trial pair you gave him.'

When Soti's face darkened and he sat up straight and tightened his toga around him, Tori feared she had said the wrong thing, but she needn't have worried.

'Axel,' said Soti, 'I meant to tell you earlier, your banker friends from Goldman Sachs flew here yesterday, making a pitch to raise outside capital for FrensLens. They want to IPO it as a separate business and, get this, they've put a value on it of $20 billion, give or take, even in this crappy market.'

'They're full of crap themselves, so why are you surprised?' said Axel, taking a sip of his mojito.

'FrensLens isn't worth that?' asked Tori.

'It's easily worth twice as much,' said Axel matter-of-factly.

'Okay,' said Tori, deciding to bring them back to her plan. 'Your business is in first-class shape, Soti, but Greece?'

'My *Elláda*? She is, to use the crass but evocative English word, fucked, but that's hardly news. What is this anyway, Tori? Twenty Questions? You're starting to sound like one of Axel's philosopher bullshitters from his precious Age of Enlightenment.' He paused. 'But then again, none of them would've looked quite as stunning.'

8

STRANGELY, TORI HAD DREAMT UP HER 'little idea' only after she'd heard about Axel's obsession with the Enlightenment philosophers.

Her introduction to it had not come from Axel, but over beer and pizza at what had become Tori and her assistant's regular dinner haunt, when Frank quietly told her that their boss's thesis at Yale had been on this influential group—principally Voltaire, Rousseau, Hume, Locke and Smith. He went on to regale her with some of the stories about the firm's collection of antiquarian books, many of them first editions from the Enlightenment, and quite a few signed by the masters themselves.

SIS's elite clients and its tiny staff revered the rare chances they got to view the library of these gilt-embossed books, all kept under such high security in the climate-controlled basement that Frank stressed—looking warily around the pizzeria as he said it—how outside that cloistered world, knowledge of the collection was non-existent, even among scholars.

Axel's grandfather, he explained, had launched the collection in 1929 with a Gutenberg Bible, a snap purchase from a famous New Yorker inconvenienced by the market crash. Sixteen years later, Axel Jnr upstaged his father by pouncing on a more valuable Gutenberg—printed on vellum and with its original fifteenth-century bindings intact—courtesy of a German military officer's fire sale of what he claimed were 'his' assets before he fled to Argentina. But when Axel III took over the business, while he appreciated both the Goots, as he called them, what drew him down to SIS's basement almost every day he was in Boston were his acquisitions from three centuries later.

'Soti,' Axel said, puffing a cigar over a candle, 'the Enlightenment was—'

'Axel, Axel, Axel. You and your damned Enlightenment! Do you think civilisation only started when that effete bunch of French and Scottish—'

Axel jumped in, 'No one denies the prior place of Aristotle and Plato—'

'What is this, a business proposal or a history lesson? Can we get on with it? The chef is doing his savoury soufflés and they don't wait for any man—or woman,' he said, cracking a weak smile at Tori but clearly irritated.

'Soti, take another sip of your mojito and just listen for one more minute,' said Axel, shoving a cigar into his mouth and taking his client's arm. 'The Enlightenment spawned revolutions: France, America, even your *Elláda*. It splintered empires, gave birth to the modern nation-state, led to a resurgence of the arts and sciences and it even had a commercial spillover, the industrial revolution, but—'

Soti raised his eyes to the sky. 'Do I need this lecture?'

Axel stood up to stretch his legs and wandered over to the handrails on the portside, muttering, 'You most certainly do,' though too quiet for Soti or Tori to hear. He gripped the rails and raised his own eyes to the heavens. The clouds calmed him, the puffs and brushstrokes of pinks and reds and oranges across the sky recalling for him his latest art acquisition, an abstract painting by De Kooning.

'Soti,' Tori said calmly, 'Axel's simply trying to make a point … that most of the risky new ventures in the industrial revolution couldn't rustle up finance—'

'So what's new about that?' Soti said, his impatience not cooling any.

'What was new,' said Axel turning back around, 'was how they solved that problem—'

'And I care?'

'You should. The only way to invest in these high-risk entrepreneurial ventures … steam engines, electricity, railroads, batteries, photographs, typewriters, sewing machines … Do you want me to go on?' Axel asked, when Soti threw his head back and strummed his fingers on his legs.

'Not really, no.'

Whenever Axel came to the Enlightenment, he got fired up. 'Until the 1850s,' he pressed on, 'the partnership was the main legal structure available to all these brilliant inventors for raising the capital they needed, but it was flawed … The investors, their partners, had to put everything else they owned at risk because of unlimited partnership liability, so lots of them shied away. The solution was one of the greatest unsung inventions of that era, the limited liability joint stock company. That simple change threw endless fuel into the oven of innovation and, as these new-fangled corporations grew, then merged, grew some more, merged yet again … they spread outside their home countries to become huge multinationals … growing even more … until today, when a few have even surpassed the might

of some of the political and military empires, and become
empires themselv—'

Soti struck his forehead with his hand. 'What? Like Ólympos
and Delphi? I get it. You've come here to break up my empire!
Are you two fucking crazy?'

Axel took the cigar from his mouth and spat out a fragment
of leaf. 'Quite the reverse. Tori's delicious notion is that you
will be the first *corporate* empire that takes the inevitable next
leap in progress. Soti, my friend, you're going to buy a country.
In fact, you're going to *become* a country.'

'Greece? A corpocracy? Holy fuck!'

'If you must put it that way.'

'SO YOU'RE TALKING about a reverse takeover,' Soti noted
after he calmed a little and heard Tori explain that he would 'sell'
his private holding company Ólympos to the Greek government
in effect for control of the country.

'Why would they agree?'

'Because they've got no choice,' said Tori. 'Without this
deal, they limp along with ongoing austerity if not bankruptcy.
But with this deal ...,' and she explained how, as well as giving
an immediate boost to the world's confidence in Greece, Soti
would launch Greece into a new era of growth and prosperity.
He would become a national hero, personally dragging his
country out of its economic swamp, and in return the Greeks
would willingly hand him the same firm reins for the country
that he had so successfully held in building his business.

'But what about one teensy little detail ... that Greece hasn't
got a spare $200 billion to pay me for Ólympos, let alone to do
any fucking thing else?'

Tori explained that Greece would give Soti a twenty-year IOU in the form of a sovereign bond, paying him interest at two per cent, a bargain-basement rate Greece hadn't seen for years and would easily afford.

'What is this ... loans for thrones? You're kidding, right?' said Soti, almost shouting. 'You think I'd hand over the keys to my company today in return for some *skaténio* promise to pay me my money back in twenty years, if I'm lucky, and toss me a measly two per cent in the meantime?'

Tori stayed calm. 'The beauty of this is that Ólympos returns to Ólympos; you move the whole of your empire to Athens and operate it as a full arm of the Greek state—'

'You are truly fucking insane. Those lazy, blood-sucking *gamóto* will destroy what I've spent my whole life building!' replied Soti. Now he was definitely shouting.

'Soti, let her finish,' Axel said. 'Tori already told you that you'd be completely in control, exactly as you are now.'

'The deal hinges,' Tori continued, 'on the parliament electing you president of the Republic, and not just any president, but one with a special commission to run Ólympos as his priority in the national interest. Nothing changes except—'

'Are you serious? First you want me to give them all I've built for some ... some shitty scrap of twenty-year paper, and you really think they'll appoint me, a business tycoon, as leader of the country? They'll do that the day after they tell the British Museum they can have the rest of the Parthenon, the parts that bastard Lord Elgin didn't steal.'

'Italy elected Silvio Berlusconi—'

'And dumped him! Although,' said Soti, his lip curling a little, 'his bunga bunga parties were truly something.'

'Okay, bad example. What about America putting burger queen Isabel Diaz into the White House? Or New York City?

They voted in Michael Bloomberg as mayor, and he's a financial data king. This does happen, Soti.'

Soti pulled at his chin, and Tori paused.

'Me as president, hmm,' he said. After a moment, he swirled his finger, signalling Tori to go on and listened intently to how she had designed it so he, uniquely, had the power to flick a magic switch, instantly turning his battered, cottage-industry country into the twenty-first century's new Silicon Valley so the real Delphi could once again take its place as the centre of the world.

The shift would trigger an invasion of highly skilled technology workers, a boost to the country's schools and universities, as well as its service industries, an unparalleled building and construction boom, an explosion in manufacturing and productivity and it would also rake in billions in foreign exchange, after which Greece could look back and laugh at its past financial crisis.

As outrageous as Tori's *Rebuilding Greece 20-20-20 Plan* was, its mechanics were simple enough. In return for Soti swapping his empire—all of Ólympos plus its control of Delphi—for the twenty-year bond, he and Ólympos would be granted an immediate tax holiday for the same period as well as rent-free leases over the thousands of hectares of currently 'useless' land that Greece had up for sale for years but that no one had come forward to buy.

Soti would commit to building the Ólympos Technopolis, as Tori called it: a sprawling new technology city, with state-of-the-art design, materials, structure and communications. The entire project—offices and factories as well as apartment buildings and houses—would pay itself off in the first ten years alone, and would be handed back to Greece for free at the end of the lease.

If Greece agreed to the plan, Ólympos would encourage at least half of its 80,000 employees worldwide to move progressively to Greece, by launching Tori's second plan, her *10-10-10 Incentive*: a pay hike of ten per cent, a similar cut in the personal tax rate, and ten years of cheap housing inside the Technopolis.

Of course, Greece was lumbered with laws that needed changing to implement all this but, according to the high-powered legal team Tori and Frank had worked the idea through with, it was all possible if the country's parliament had the resolve to go ahead, and that, she said, depended on the public response.

The key to the public getting behind the deal, she argued, was that Soti was Greek himself and would be seen as a true patriot. Not only would he get to continue running and building his corporate empire, but as head of state of the new Greece he would save his beloved country and simultaneously block the politicians, pen–pushers and black marketeers who'd helped wreck it in the first place from doing it again.

Soti's ego was working overtime as he started thinking about the possibilities.

'If that's not enough, my friend,' said Axel, 'Tori's pièce de résistance, or however you say that in Greek, is that the delightful wand of sovereign immunity gets waved over Ólympos once it becomes a formal arm of the Greek state.'

'Whoa!' Soti never smiled when anyone mentioned the European Union's looming anti-trust probe into Ólympos's aggressive competitive practices, but he was all teeth now. Suddenly he stood, let his toga slip off his shoulders and shouted, '*Gia tin Elláda re gamóto!* For Greece, dammit!' And dived into the pool.

He hardly made a splash. He'd make the real one later.

9

IN LOS ANGELES, THE BRASS NAMEPLATE shone under the rising sun but inside the Bel Air immunology clinic, the receptionist took a dim view of the two men who had just entered.

'I'm sorry, sir, but Dr Fenton is—Hey, stop!' The receptionist flew out of her seat to block the door to the doctor's surgery. 'You can't go in there!' With her boss's list of patients straddling Hollywood and Silicon Valley, she wasn't getting fired, not in her first week, not ever, if she could help it.

'See this LAPD badge, ma'am?' said the detective as he flipped his holder open, moving his medallion under the lights so it glinted at her. 'It says, and I quote, Detective Jerry Rourke, Homicide, can go any-goddamn-where he pleases. Pretty amazing, huh? Now, ma'am, please step aside.'

'Detective, do you have a warra—?'

Rourke ignored her. Wised up from his sessions downtown with Dr Fenton's last receptionist, including the precise location

63

of the doorlock switch, he punched the switch and pushed past the new receptionist, swinging open the heavy cedar door into Dr Fenton's plush suite.

He couldn't help letting out a whistle. Rourke had barged into some ritzy offices in his day, but this one had more swank than Hilary in *Million Dollar Baby*.

An art connoisseur himself—though his pay packet only let him stretch to admiring, not buying—the detective stopped as cold as if he'd taken a right hook from the screen print of Muhammad Ali that was now staring him square in the eyes. It was his all-time favourite Andy Warhol. One had sold for $9 million at Christie's back in 2007 and, tossing in the frame for free, it came to six grand per square inch. To Detective Rourke, auction catalogues were art porn, as close as he could normally get to salivating over the real thing.

The doctor's room was huge, more like a gallery than a surgery. At a glance, Rourke recognised most of the other works too, but his eyes stopped again when he saw one of Giacometti's nobbly, spindly *Walking Men*. The investigation had already told him that Dr Fenton was a money machine, but a sculpture by Giacometti? It had to be a fake, which made him wonder if they all were.

Rourke's entry into Fenton's office caught the doctor out, quietly reading in a high-backed armchair in the corner. The book looked heavy, some sort of medical tome, Rourke guessed. Fenton's head had been nestled against one of the chair's wings but as he looked up, the smile dropped from his face, and he realised the intruder wasn't his receptionist. 'What—who the hell are you?'

'A fellow art lover.' Rourke pasted on his own smile.

'Oh?' said Fenton, catching his secretary frantically signalling him from behind the stranger just as a second man entered.

These men weren't dressed like any of Fenton's usual patients. He guessed the drab grey suits oozing off their bodies probably cost less than one of his patients' neckties, not that many of them wore ties. And their shoes! Shoes spoke a lot about their wearer and Fenton always checked them out. These, both pairs, looked as scuffed as the fishing boat Fenton had chartered last week in Maine when he hooked those tautog and striper. As they got closer, the men smelled as bad, too. Sweaty. Salty. But of street salt, not sea salt. And burgers. They'd definitely just had burgers. 'You're an art lover?' said the doctor, raising a confused eyebrow, unsure whether he should be snooty or scared.

'Yeah, but I'm also Detective Rourke, LAPD. This is my partner, Detective Briggs. Nice Giacometti you've got there, doc, or should I say a nice fake? You wouldn't have bought it from, ah, what was his name … the Count of something?' Rourke was recalling scraps of a story he'd read that a German, posing as the Count of Waldstein, had been sentenced a while back to nine years' prison for possessing fake Giacomettis, a thousand of them.

Fenton froze. The irony. Getting sprung for the art, when he'd been guilty of so much worse. He'd known the risks when he'd bought his 'Giacometti' at a hotel near Frankfurt's airport but without risk there was no reward, as one of his happily deceased banker patients used to crap on about. What a blowhard that guy had been! So easy to spout about risk and reward when you still got your bonuses, even after the taxpayer was forced to bail you out of a mess you created yourself! But the guy had been right about risk, and Fenton had taken a risk on the fakes in the hope that a façade of showy success would help him attract his desired list of über-rich patients much faster than his ability ever would have alone. Fenton did have the ability, he knew that, but as F/7 in the Nine Sisters he wasn't blessed with the luxury of time.

Rourke saw Fenton's hands balling a little under his book but his time was short, too. Any moment the media he'd given a heads up to would be jostling outside. 'Dr Fenton, we're not here about the sculpture.' He waved his hand at the walls. 'Or the paintings.'

Fenton closed the book and leant forward to place it on the floor at his feet, closing his eyes as if it would help him work out his next move. It must be about the patients, he decided. He had always risked exposure and arrest, so that wasn't what was worrying him; it was the timing. Once Professor Mellor's sixty-sixth birthday ticked over, not very far off now, he would have been proudly volunteering what he'd done, telling the whole world in fact. That was part of the pact that he and the others had made with Mellor, what their cheeky guru had dubbed their public 'Environmental Impact Statements'.

They'd all be vilified, Mellor had made that plain to them, and they'd face certain imprisonment, if not worse, depending on where they lived, but the planet needed martyrdom like theirs. As beacons for other passionate people worried about the planet, their Environmental Impact Statements, and the radical actions they'd reveal, would create a surge of support as people realised that the damage could not just be stopped, it could be reversed. The Nine Sisters wouldn't be a wake-up call, but a call to arms.

But now, all F/7's remaining patients—especially, damn it, his final and most juicy target—would be put on alert. He'd saved her, one of the world's wealthiest philanthropists, as his spectacular last hit.

He was sickened every time he read about her in the media. The wide-eyed dupe had so far dished out half a billion of her dollars trying to help eradicate malaria, when to Fenton the virulent disease had a purpose; it was one of the planet's natural ways to say 'enough'. To cleanse itself. The rich bitch's arrogance in getting in nature's way disgusted him and, every time she'd come in for a consultation, he struggled not to show his loathing for her.

Rourke walked over and placed one hand on the doctor's shoulder, his other sliding a warrant out of his inside jacket pocket.

When Fenton looked up at Rourke's partner holding out a set of handcuffs, he couldn't stop his lower lip from starting to quiver, though both cops misunderstood why.

He needed to buy time to see if he could somehow complete his mission. 'You know I'm a respected immunologist? If some of my patients die—?'

'Wilbur Mark Fenton, I'm placing you under arrest for just that—for the murder of Steven Paul Jobs, David Neil Mortinsen and six others named in this warrant. You have the right to remain silent. Anything you say …'

Rourke completed his standard arrest warning, then went on, 'We all die, Fenton, but—' he waved the warrant, '—your job was to try to save these people, not kill them. Instead of giving your patients the immunosuppressants they needed after their transplants, you gave them worthless placebos. You guaranteed their deaths, in the meantime causing viral infections, respiratory failure, in some cases full organ rejection. Steve Jobs was a genius, Dr Fenton, a man changing the world, yet because of you, he died well before his time, before he could complete his mission.'

Fenton didn't smell burgers any more. His own lunch had been filet mignon, cooked rare but now, sprayed all over his lap, it didn't smell so good.

10

AS TORI WALKED PAST THE TV in her suite, the welcome screen was still boasting how the yacht *Fun Cool* delivered 673 channels from all over the world. She stopped and settled for the first one she could find that was broadcasting in English, then unzipped her black jumpsuit and stepped out of it, dropping it to the floor and, after turning up the TV's volume, went into the bathroom to get ready for bed. There, she was surprised to see another TV, this one glowing out at her from behind the vanity mirror and showing the same channel. All she noticed in her bathroom earlier when she'd freshened up for cocktails and dinner was the array of soaps, shampoos and colognes, the usual hotel-type knickknacks, although all of it was monogrammed *Fun Cool*, even the tissues. It was, she decided, a bit over the top unless perhaps Soti suffered from some bizarre strain of amnesia where he woke up every morning needing to be reminded where he was. From what she'd read of his exploits, maybe there was a tinge of truth in that.

Three minutes later, if she'd been applying her mascara instead of removing it, she might have poked her eye when the newsreader announced the dramatic revelation about the death of Steve Jobs back in October 2011. According to Los Angeles police, the iconic co-founder and former CEO of the computing giant Apple—and as Tori knew, a once loyal SIS client—had not simply died from his cancer, as previously reported, but had been murdered. Information had just come to light that the respiratory complications that killed him had been induced.

As Tori's mind started swirling, wondering who could have done that and why, the report began to elaborate, explaining this was the work of a serial killer with police discovering seven other victims so far. Like Jobs, all of them were rich and all were either Silicon Valley aristocracy or bankers. Worse, the killer was a doctor. Their doctor. 'Doctor to the rich and famous,' said the newsreader. *Doctor Death*, Tori couldn't help herself thinking.

Snatching up the phone in her bathroom, she immediately called Axel's suite but his phone was already engaged. Presumably he'd heard the news too, so she tore into her living room to watch the drama unfolding on the bigger screen, in time to see the cameras rolling on LAPD detectives as they escorted this medical monster out through the front doors of his clinic, his arms pulled back and his cuffed hands behind him.

She sat back on the sofa, luckily not the kind of leather that bare skin sticks to, but when the doctor paused at the top of the stairs and squinted into the sun at the cameras it kindled a glimmer out of her past, a distant familiarity, but whatever it was flew off as quickly as it had come. Where were the FrensLenses when she needed them?

She pricked up her ears for the doctor's name, but didn't have to wait long before the newsbar started sweeping across the bottom of the screen: *LAPD arrests celebrity doctor on serial killer charges … for murder of Apple's Steve Jobs and seven other patients … Dr Wilbur Mark Fenton of Bel Air …*

Wilbur Fenton? Or Mark Fenton? Either way, his name didn't ring any bells. But his face? They said he was a specialist immunologist with an exclusive clinic in Bel Air, but that didn't help her zero in either.

Tori had been to Los Angeles four times, once surfing with her father when she was twelve, twice when she worked at the Agency, and once when she visited trying to track down her mother, but she had never come across any Dr Wilbur Mark Fenton. So what was that fleeting memory? She squeezed her eyes shut trying to think, but it was as successful as trying to catch smoke between her fingers. If only she had one of Proust's madeleines.

Unhooking her bra and slipping out of her underwear, she took herself back into the bathroom. Despite having long ago quit her life in sports, she had always worked out. Not bad, she thought, looking into the mirror as she sashayed in, until the TV's images started competing with her reflection and it freaked her out a little, so she flicked it off.

Then in the quiet, and with her hands on her hips, she swivelled left and right a couple of times and a light curl of contentment came to the corner of her mouth.

But it didn't last and Dr Fenton flew back into her head. It bugged her that she had come across him. Somewhere. She wondered if the rhythm of brushing her teeth might help her think, and she picked up the tube of paste. As she brushed, it tasted a little like the limes in the mojitos that Soti had been mixing.

When her doorbell buzzed, she spat out the paste and wiped her mouth on a towel, for some reason avoiding the monogram.

PROFESSOR GEORGE MELLOR slumped in front of his TV. Draped over his lap was a scratchy picnic rug, its stripes as faded as his memory and its old man odour as sour as his spleen. He sat silently as the screen showed the cop pushing down on Wilbur Fenton's head, guiding the doctor into the back seat of the police vehicle.

Fenton's final step in earning his medical specialty had been a stint working in Australia under a prominent local immunologist, one with an international reputation. Fenton had met Mellor at a rally and, after a few meetings where it was clear they saw things eye to eye, Mellor invited him to join the Nine Sisters as F/7.

A cigarette stub hung from the furrow in Mellor's lip, its fire long gone just like his own. These days Mellor's eyes were dull, seemingly unfocused, and his face was devoid of even a tic of emotion, not pain nor pleasure, nor even today the slightest shake of disapproval that F/7 had launched himself too early.

According to the LAPD, even though Fenton's patients included movie stars, rock singers and other celebrities as well as an array of high-powered business people, his victims were almost exclusively technology industrialists, six powerful people at the very top of major internet, computing and communications firms, and two bankers who financed them.

If he'd been listening, Mellor would have heard that some media commentators had already branded Fenton as the iKiller or, for those who refused to be hooked by Apple's marketing machine, the eKiller. Regardless of the tag, no one could grasp how a doctor, especially such a celebrated one, could kill his own patients, let alone so callously and deliberately cause them such pain.

Fenton wasn't helping either. He was refusing point blank to utter a single word to the police about his crimes or his motive. That time was almost, but not yet, ripe.

11

OVER THE NEXT TWENTY-FOUR HOURS, Soti's helicopter *Gamey Sue* ran a shuttle from Rome airport, bringing five of the six members of his executive committee onto the yacht as their flights arrived from various parts of the world. While Tori's plan had passed all of Soti's tests, he explained that without his top team's input he would take no action. He might overrule them—Soti did that often enough—but he always asked for their opinions.

Simone Lucas was missing from the team. The feisty Texan, head of IT security and also the product champion for FrensLens, was onboard the *Polar Majesty* enjoying a rare vacation, an Antarctic cruise with her partner. Except for the fact that their ship wasn't due at its next port for six days, Simone—as loyal and dedicated a lieutenant as Soti could ever hope for—would have cut her trip short without blinking, and even Athena would have been relaxed about it since she knew Simone's work drill better than anyone. When Simone had

72

joined Soti's top team five years ago, which was how the two women met, Athena had been one of his personal assistants, the one normally trusted to make his 'Soti's really sorry, but ...' calls, like the one Simone had just received, interrupting their vacation.

Simone beamed herself into Soti's boardroom, located on one of *Fun Cool*'s lower decks. Being at the end of a staticky satellite phone was far from ideal, not least because she was opposed to the deal as soon as Tori laid it out for them.

'Soti,' Simone crackled through the loud speaker, 'you'd be putting yourself at the whim of some hokey parliament and a bunch of blockhead bankers whose only claim to fame is that not only did they do their best to fuck up the entire global economy and still get paid, but they convinced the same brainless world to peel them off even more money so they could fuck it up some more. You want to be at the mercy of pricks like that? Really?'

His other five executives ranged from sceptical to equally opposed, but with Tori and Axel helping them tease out every microdetail, all the executives were eventually won over, including Simone. That took two long days, which would have been exhausting for Tori even without Soti's continuous flirting, something none of his executives, or even Axel, seemed to notice.

Soti then flew in Ólympos's lawyers to sprinkle their holy water over the plan. Axel had already sat through a full review from SIS's legal team before leaving Boston, so he was satisfied the plan was legally robust; it was why he'd been confident enough to send Frank straight on to Athens, to prepare a secure operations suite in the city's prestigious Hotel Grande Bretagne. Not only did the hotel have the city's best communications facilities, it was only steps across historic Syntagma Square from the Greek Parliament, a few minutes by car to the Prime

Minister's office and so, apart from its proximity to police tossing the occasional cylinder of tear gas into the Square to break up protests, it was an ideal base for negotiations with government.

Soti's executive team might have only taken two days to get comfortable with the deal, but the lawyers took a further four. 'Why wouldn't they?' asked Axel, spinning his beads round his finger as they watched *Gamey Sue* lift off for the second time that afternoon carrying away the rest of Soti's management and legal advisers. 'They're flown in to work on board the most splendid yacht sailing the Mediterranean with champagne running on a spigot and they get to charge through the nose for the pleasure? I'm shocked they didn't take a full week.'

'Their time sheets will say they did,' laughed Soti as he turned to Tori. 'Congratulations, Dr Swyft. I propose we celebrate tonight now that your little idea has become such a big one and,' he added, 'we do love big ones, don't we?'

THAT NIGHT, AFTER a six-course degustation dinner personally cooked by Rome's latest culinary sensation, the city's newest Michelin 3-star chef, and Tori wasn't sure how many glasses of wine—but thankfully no mojitos—she was finally back in her suite getting ready for bed. She leant into the bathroom mirror and just as she was about to remove her make-up, her doorbell rang.

'It's me,' he said through the door, not even pretending to whisper. It was his yacht, so why would he? He hadn't kept his voice down any of the other nights he'd come, though he had been a little sheepish each time she'd opened her door a crack and sent him off, politely bidding him good night.

· Unhurried and purposeful, she continued at the mirror but when he buzzed again she took another moment to take in her body and smiled. This time on her way to the door she stopped at her desk, opened her music library on her laptop and selected *Blasket Islands*, one of her favourite tracks from The Break, and wifi'd it through her suite's sound system. She paused for another moment, steadying herself for that first grand rhythmic musical sweep of crashing Irish ocean swells and, as always, couldn't stop her body from her ankles right up rolling and tingling with the cymbals. Her eyes closed and she stood there swaying, feeling the force of the surf through her and over her. She leant to pick up her jumpsuit—tonight it had been her cobalt blue one—and slip it back on but, halfway down, as she felt her breasts pulse with their loosened confidence, she changed her mind and straightened up.

'Soti,' she smiled, pulling her door open wide and surprising him. Here was a man who wanted for nothing yet couldn't stop his eyes or his Adam's apple from wantonly yo-yoing over her bare skin, a man who assumed only half-correctly that her goosebumps were for him.

She stood there, her eyes dark and green like the brooding musical waves she felt washing over her, and he stepped inside and over her crumple of blue satin still on the floor. She touched the door closed with her toe, her hands pushing the white robe off his shoulders, leaving them to rest there but holding herself back as if reserve was only natural for two people entirely naked apart from his usual skimpy swim shorts.

A drop of saliva bubbled at the corner of Tori's mouth and she watched him watching her as she slowly licked it away. By the time she reached inside his trunks, his eyes were mesmerised by her, by the rhythm shuddering through her body and transmitted to his own by her hand.

'Hairless … and all over,' she said, her voice quiet, a little gravelly. 'So smooth,' she added, bobbing a little to apply her tongue to his pecs. 'And a little salty,' she said, looking up at him.

He placed a finger beneath her chin and, raising her head back up, he sucked on her lower lip but she drew back.

When Tori decided to play, it was always her choice and by her rules. He was indeed the lord of the manor here, but she had already shown he wouldn't be snatching any traditional *droit du seigneur*. All week so far, she'd been scrupulous not to mix business with pleasure especially on her first job. She'd resisted his flirting even though it was enticing, but now the lawyers and everyone else had signed off and she had clearly proved her worth to him, she would allow him to prove his worth to her.

'Come,' she smiled, swivelled around toward her bedroom and, keeping her hand busy where it was, she pulled him along behind her.

WITH ONE HAND she tickled his balls and, for the third time that night, she lowered herself back onto him, this time leaning forward to kiss his eyes.

'Mar-ry me, Doc-tor Swyft,' he said, mouthing one syllable on each of her strokes up and down.

'I didn't think you were the marrying kind,' she smiled, flicking back her hair and increasing her rhythm.

'The funny thing is I wasn't, not until now,' he said and rubbed his nose against one of her nipples before taking it in his mouth and rolling it around in his tongue.

'That's good, Soti, because … hmm, that's *really* good. Where was I? Ah yes … The thing is, I don't believe in premarital sex … oh, that is so very good! … so your proposal, though very sweet, is just a little too late.'

His mouth released her and he blinked up at her, 'You mean my dream … the house with the white picket fence … it's fucked?'

'Perfectly.' She said it long and languorously and slowly slid herself up to his tip. She held herself there, squeezing him in wave after wave, and looked down on him as his eyes rolled back and he writhed in their shared rapture.

12.

TOM MAJOR LIVED IN A POSTCARD. With the spring sun peeking over Auckland's horizon, Waitemata Harbour was starting to glitter like the obsidian glass it was named after. He hit the sand on Half Moon Bay, exhilarated by the simple press of white grains through his toes. He carried his surf ski with just two fingers, its Kevlar shell almost as light as his mood.

Tom always launched here, a one-minute stroll from his Auckland home, though he was a bit later than usual. He loved the slurp when he slipped the hull into the cool water, the sibilant scrape when the carbon-fibre foil of his paddle pushed him off the sand, the whoosh from the first stroke forward. Today he was headed to his Ngati Tama Te Ra people's *taonga*, their treasure, at Motukorea or Browns Island. With no wind to fight against, it would take him thirtyish well-paced minutes to get to his landing spot when he'd make his ritual quick run up the side of the cinder cone to its rim before scuttling back down to hop back on his surf ski and paddle home. What a way to start the day, he thought—as if he needed reminding.

At this point in his life, Tom Major could afford to live anywhere. It had been a tough call: his hometown versus Sydney, where he had earned his doctorate and won his first job. Vancouver had got close, and even Cape Town, but Auckland won.

As chief software architect of Sofdox Inc, Tom Major was responsible for creating as well as managing the product that the firm's stellar growth was built on so he felt entitled to park himself where he liked even if Sofdox headquarters were just south of San Francisco, in Silicon Valley. Coincidentally, the head office was twenty minutes from the other Half Moon Bay, where he would go paddling whenever he could slip away from his visits to head office, which these days was one tedious week out of three. Until Isabel Diaz had won the White House, these two tranquil Half Moon Bays on opposite sides of the planet made Tom whole but, since her elevation to the presidency, the sleepy American bay had become a teeming tourist Mecca, with busloads of rubberneckers pouring in daily, demanding that the short-order cooks at the BBB diner there flip their burgers just like the president used to when she worked there as a runaway fifteen-year-old. Tom had no more against President Diaz than any other president apart from this shrine to her past ruining yet another refuge.

His personal investment in Sofdox stock options had grown close to $200 million.

On top of his stock options, he had his house in Auckland and, a four-hour bike ride away, his wholly organic farm on Kaipara Bay near Kaukapakapa. Out of everything he owned or did, the farm, biking and kayaking were all he truly cared about, which was lucky since he knew that the value of his Sofdox stock options—and just about everything else on the stock market—would be plummeting pretty soon, assuming things went to plan. His Nine Sisters plan.

He paused his paddling as he neared the mouth of Hauraki Gulf to take a swig from his bottle, water that he had drizzled himself out of his farm's natural spring. Life was good, and soon it would get even better.

When he had joined Sofdox, it was just another start-up trying to ape somebody else; in their case, it was Adobe Systems, the software house that way back had pioneered the revolutionary PDF, the portable document format. Because of Tom, Sofdox had now leapfrogged all its competitors, including Adobe. Just three months ago, *Fortune* magazine had published its annual list of the world's most admired companies, citing Sofdox as number one in computer software and hailing Dr Tom Major as software designer of the decade. Little did they know.

Tom was close to achieving all his goals and, as he wiped his hand across his mouth and sat bobbing on the harbour, he wondered about the other members of Nine Sisters and whether any of them had managed to insinuate themselves as deeply inside their tents as he had managed to.

Tom had spearheaded Sofdox's most profitable products so everyone, from the board and chief executive down, had learnt to tolerate his tyrannical outbursts about design and quality control. 'Apple put up with Steve Jobs and he was a brilliant asshole too, right?' the exasperated CEO had said to his board only last week, after Tom let fly with yet another of his famous tantrums.

Both Tom Major and Steve Jobs had been instrumental in building their companies, but there was one crucial difference between them: Tom was also going to destroy his.

Tom was so entrenched as Sofdox's creative software genius that no one touched a single line of code without his say-so.

This was especially helpful when it came to one chunk of code. Tom's sub_10009S120 code lay dormant and unseen, embedded inside every Sofdox PDF, ebook and all other digital documents made with Sofdox software. Over the last twelve months Sofdox had become the world's pre-eminent 'digital paper' platform, with the marketing department boasting that most computer devices on the planet had now viewed at least one Sofdox PDF or ebook. For Tom Major's purposes—as Nine Sisters member M/9—just one viewing was plenty.

The genius of sub_10009S120 was that it didn't do anything by itself, nor did its sister code sub_10009S0C, but as the yin to the other's yang, when they were put together they morphed into an intelligent, malicious payload.

Tom had hidden the sister code inside the official Sofdox update he would soon be authorising. Millions of unsuspecting users would receive the standard update message and, coming from the world's most admired software company and carrying all the verifying certificates under the sun, they would unthinkingly download it, just as they had got into the habit of doing with every other bimonthly update over the last year. Once they clicked 'install', the standard program would, as always, first check what operating system managed the device, such as Apple's OS X or Microsoft's Windows, and then it would deliver the appropriate update version.

When it did, the new string of code would track down sub_10009S120, stick itself onto it and the newly created Siamese twins, swathed in a wrap that made them look as innocent and natural as a baby asleep in its mother's arms, would nuzzle into the host device's BIOS or EFI for a seven-day snooze to await a worldwide take-up of the update. After that, his twins would wake up, switch off all the inbuilt mechanical cooling fans on their host devices and simultaneously trick the heat sensors into ignoring the rising temperature. The silicon in the chips would melt, as would the connections, and because the computers didn't sense anything was wrong, there'd be no automatic shutdowns and no alerts to the users. Tom's babies would destroy the millions of devices that sheltered them, frying their hard drives and everything on them: all the data, the files, and even the software. Permanently.

For battery-run laptops or tablet devices, his twins would also let out a little cry to the microcontrollers that monitored battery voltage, perturbing their work so that they'd under-report, duping the batteries into overcharging themselves until they exploded. Tom Major's babies would die, needless to say, but like him and his fortune, everyone had to make sacrifices for the greater good.

Three years ago, Major had won Sofdox's Good Citizen Award for his altruistic plan for the company to distribute all its software for free to essential services, to organisations like airlines, shipping lines, train companies, and to hospitals and medical services, to police and corrective services departments, and especially to 'our boys' in the military. If only they'd worked out why! He laughed so much, his surf ski rocked from side to side.

A history buff too, Tom knew of the fire that razed the library in Alexandria, once hailed as the repository of all the ancient world's knowledge. Now, with companies, governments and libraries all over the world having gone digital at least to some extent, whether for cost or convenience, and some already completely digital, he and his twins would get to burn down the new Alexandria, remotely and with ease.

The cheap, efficient technology that everyone naively embraced to supplant print books and hard copy files with electronic ones would virtually obliterate knowledge, or at least ready access to it. But to Tom Major, such regress was progress.

13

THE LONDON REFUSE COMPANY HAD JUST won a Lord Mayor's Clean City Award but this London alleyway was not one of their pin-up sites. Locals always covered their noses and sped past its dim entrance, the stench hanging like the corpse they feared was rotting in the darkness.

Deep inside, crouched on a mattress of damp newspapers and flattened, mouldy boxes, the gaunt, unshaven man lit a match and held it under the spoon shaking in his other hand. His ginger hair was as wild as the fire that once burned within him. His blue eyes, once as sharp as the filthy syringe by his side, were distant and unfocused, like he'd forgotten what he was searching for. *Home is where the heart is* popped into his head. He didn't need to look around his latest home to know the homily was crap. The Ozzie had no idea where he'd left his heart, or his head, not any more. It certainly wasn't here, among these boxes and dumpsters and shit—and not all of it dogshit. Or in this dope.

Oscar Philips had been his name. Oscar Philips. It should have been Dr Oscar Philips. Fuck it. And he'd once been called—what was it?—P/8. No, it was fucking Phi/8, because that cunt of a professor who was supposed to give him his doctorate but didn't—for some reason he couldn't remember—insisted on giving him a code name by using the Greek letter for the F sound—Phi as in Philips—and not using the P, the first letter of his surname, like the bald bastard did with everybody-fucking-else in his, er, sister-thingy. What was that jerk-off slime's name, anyway? Philips couldn't recall that either and now the question came up, he didn't want to.

He hadn't been Oscar Philips for a long time. 'The Ozzie' was what everyone called him now, not that there were very many who saw enough of him to call him anything. The local cops, they'd seen him a bit. And his dealer's toughs, whose fists and boots he knew better than his own.

But nothing would hurt The Ozzie anymore, he thought, as the flame gave off the smell of a birthday party candle, and the powder started bubbling into liquid heaven.

14

A T THE ROME HELIPORT, TORI AND Axel
stepped out of *Gamey Sue*. Heads bowed, they scurried
out from under the rotor blades and over to the
terminal where they'd find their limousine transfer to Axel's jet
to take them on their next leg, to Athens. Crossing the tarmac
with the cool wind from the rotors pushing from behind them,
Tori felt she was living a dream. Only a few months ago she was
swirling in a CIA nightmare with her world crashing down yet
now, not only did a delicious and new hunk have the hots for
her—even if Soti's suburban white picket fence proposal had
been in jest, thank goodness—but far more critically, she was
about to execute the most audacious deal in history. On top
of that, she reminded herself, while she'd had some help, the
idea itself was entirely her own. She looked sideways at Axel,
about to thank him for his trust and for Frank, and for his loose
million dollars she'd been free to spend on advisers, but her boss
got in first.

'I can't wait for step two,' he said, happily waving his newest recruit through the revolving doors.

If Tori was a seer, she'd have realised that Axel was mentally patting his own back—for his masterstroke in hiring her—and overjoyed that if her proposal won over the Greek Prime Minister at the meeting they'd set for later that morning, SIS would be well on the way to a fee that would monster its entire earnings for the whole of the last decade. Oh, and he was mindful that they might also rescue Greece, a long-standing client, from choking on a sickness of its own making.

When the pair of them had been through this heliport last week, the place was almost empty, but today scrums of businesspeople were huddled over laptops, tablet computers and newspapers, or standing alone near windows engaging with their mobile phones. Now that people could send text messages and play games on them, read emails, check the weather or update their social networking page, who actually needed them for mere talking? One man sitting alone in a neat blue suit with his briefcase temporarily chained to the railing behind him was reading a book that Tori guessed, from the flame-red Cyrillic scrawl and the gory image that dripped off its front cover, was a Russian or Slavic pot-boiler. A clutch of Italian high government officials, judging by the uniformed chauffeurs standing around them, had commandeered the central lounges, and were leaning back laughing and gesticulating as if they had solved that nation's economic woes over breakfast and were looking forward to a liquid lunch of a bottle or three of Borolo. For a split second, Tori felt an urge to race over to them and share her plan to rescue Greece, and possibly Europe, but her long-practised discretion outvoted her vanity.

Tori expected their chauffeur to be waiting in the terminal but instead Axel's pilot was stiffly positioned under the green *uscita di emergenza* sign, with the sun streaming through the doors onto the golden epaulettes on his starched white shoulders. When their eyes met, his head tipped a welcome, sharp and detached. Tori wondered what was troubling him. On the trip over from Boston, he had been friendly and relaxed—and why not, since his boss had done most of the flying?—but as they got closer to him, Tori saw his pursed lips and furrowed brows. He again nodded, to her, but with Axel he leant down and put his arm around his shoulders and took him aside, whispering, Tori felt, a little conspiratorially. When Axel glanced back at Tori, with a smile on his lips but not, she noticed, in his eyes, she was sure of it. His eyes were now small and concentrated, just like his pilot's. Something was wrong; perhaps the pilot had heard some tittle-tattle about her night with Soti.

Or maybe it was more serious … that while they'd been on the chopper and out of phone contact, Frank had rung through some bad news from Athens? She took out her phone and saw she'd had two missed calls, both with their caller IDs blocked. Was Soti trying to ring through that he'd changed his mind about the deal … or her? Or was it simply that Axel's Gulfstream had a mechanical problem?

From the tightness starting to squeeze Axel's flabby face and the way he was clenching a fist and rolling one of his *begleri* between his other thumb and forefinger, Tori was growing certain it was about the Greek deal … that it had been pulled. That two months of day and night work and now, after the last week, close to two million in advisers' fees had been flushed down the toilet. Shit, she thought, Axel will rue ever hiring me.

He peeled himself out from under the pilot's arm and came back over to her, his face no less stern.

'Axel—' she began.

'I've got to make a call,' was all he said before he swung around to go outside, leaving her to stew. She was about to ask the captain what the problem was but, seeing his arms folded and his hands rubbing his elbows, she knew it would be fruitless.

Suddenly hungry, or so she thought, she wandered over to the food stand and ran her eye over the fare but none of it grabbed her, not even the focaccia with her favourite toppings, bufala mozzarella, basil and tomato. While she was making a decision, her mobile phone jangled, the ringtone sounding louder and more shrill than usual. Despite it being a blocked number, again, she answered it.

'Listen, Tori,' said Frank. Instantly, she knew it was important if he wasn't using his own phone; if he didn't want to create a record of him having called her. 'I probably shouldn't say … Okay, a buddy at Six just gave me a heads-up—the guy we had dinner with in Boston?' It had been during her first week at SIS, and Frank's former MI6 colleague, stir crazy for curry and beer and banter about football, had snuck out of the executive junket at the Harvard Kennedy School that Britain's security service had sent him over from London to attend. 'He's back at Legoland,' Frank said, meaning Six's headquarters in London, 'and he's heard some chatter that a problem has popped up with your PhD thesis.'

Tori's head jerked so suddenly it almost knocked the phone out of her hand. 'What would *they* care about my thesis, let alone at … at what? At seven am in London?' she said. 'Besides, I published it years ago. And … and why the hell would he be telling you?'

'I was best man at his wedding, remember? And he was worried that, er, me being seen with you right now might not be so, er, positive for my reputation.' *Give her a fucking wide berth*, was actually how the British spook had expressed it when shouting down the phone at Frank.

'What the—?' she started just as Axel tapped her on the shoulder.

'Tori,' he said, 'we seem to have a problem. Quite a biggie, I fear.'

15

OUTSIDE, THE MORNING SUN WAS PEEPING through a stand of poplars, scattering slats of golden light and black shadows across their path as Axel bustled Tori away from the terminal building toward the sanctuary of their waiting limousine. The sunlight flickering into Tori's eyes gave her an uncomfortable premonition: a squabble of photographers snapping at her while she peered back at them through prison bars. There were no cameras here, yet she looked around just the same.

They reached the car, the same dark Bahamas blue Maybach 62S that had ferried them here last time. Axel held his finger up, signalling to the chauffeur not to get out for them, and instead both rear doors slowly swung open and Axel and Tori slid inside, with the doors silently self-closing after them.

'Axel—'

'One moment,' he said, leaning over to the centre console and pressing buttons. Tori's seat started to recline and her footrest rose. 'Sorry, wrong switch,' he said, correcting her seat and eventually raising the electric privacy screen to separate the driver as well as closing the side and rear curtains. When the privacy screen was fully up, the clear glass blinked and became opaque. Axel opened the cigar humidor, but thought better of it, and pressed the intercom to tell the chauffeur, in English, not to drive away until their pilot arrived with their luggage. 'Yes, sir,' he replied, also in English.

Axel switched off the intercom. 'Tori, there's quite a storm brewing.'

She knew he didn't mean the weather and thought about mentioning what Frank had told her but held her tongue.

'And it seems you are smack in its eye because your doctorate algorithms contain a flaw—'

'That's not possib—'

'Tori, half to two-thirds of the world's major nuclear plants, as you know, have installed core protection and rod control systems with your model integrated into their brain.'

'But my work was supervised by leading experts and, after I opensourced it, it was peer-reviewed to death … and then after that, it passed every regulatory check you could think of, in Europe, the US—'

'True, but everyone seems to be ignoring all that. The instant problem is that in—' he pulled his sleeve back and looked at his watch, '—in about thirty-six hours, all US nuclear power plants will be placed on shut-down alert if they haven't—'

'Because of my work?'

'In short? Quite probably. Look, what I've been told is that two days ago the operators in a plant in the midwest suddenly saw their rod control systems going haywire. Most of the instruments showed everything as within tolerance, yet others signalled a problem. When the operators instituted the requisite safety checks nothing actually seemed to be wrong, so they assumed that a few of the meters were simply faulty. Still operating within the mandated safety window, they replaced those components with spares yet the malfunction kept repeating. Normally, that would have tripped a scram, an automatic shutdown, but the control rods didn't budge, not even an inch let alone move themselves into the core as they should have, so the operators had to launch a manual shutdown. The long and the short of their analysis so far is that there are three possibilities for what caused this, and your model is the favourite.'

'Suddenly, and after all these years?'

'I'm told that the Nuclear Regulatory Commission is contemplating a directive mandating that all US plants that are fitted out with these components immediately replace them pending an investigation. The only thing holding them back is the little problem that the spares didn't work either. The NRC's not willing to risk plants running blind, so the worry is that if the only safe solution is installing completely new rod control systems—'

'That could take weeks, maybe months.'

'Exactly. They've alerted the Brits and the French, too, and probably the Chinese. I didn't hear about the Russians. If this isn't solved pronto, it could get seriously out of control. With winter around the corner across the northern hemisphere—' Axel ran his hand back over his scalp, and briefly closed his eyes. Tori had seen this manoeuvre with her old boss. It was like a tell in a poker game, and both times it had meant bad news was going to get worse. 'Tori, there's talk they might have to go even further … ordering full shutdowns of all plants operating with control systems that are based on your model.'

'Hell!'

'It will be a lot colder than hell for a lot of people if they do that,' said Axel, 'but you're right, it will get very hot for you.'

'What do you—?'

'Tori, like it or not, this is the situation. A certain Dr Victoria Swyft has suddenly become the NRC's most wanted person to speak to, and Homeland Security and your, ah, friends at the CIA have also got involved. If it's your model at fault, and not something else, the big question they'll be asking is whether this was accidental or intentional. That sort of thing.'

'Intentional? Jesus!' As she said it, something from her distant past suddenly flew past her, but she couldn't catch it … for the second time this week, which was especially niggling for someone with such a strong memory.

'Tori,' said Axel, shaking her arm, 'you're going to have to give this your complete attention.'

'Huh? Right.' She nodded. 'But the timing,' she mumbled, still trying to hook the fleeting thought.

'You mean Greece? Tori, you can't be anywhere near that transaction, or near SIS either … not until you clear this up.'

'What?' Tori stared at him, her eyes searching his. 'I'm fired?'

She forced herself to breathe in the enclosed space, but with the stuffy leather car smell, Axel's usual lashings of woody cologne and the perfume wafting from the atomiser fixed to the rear console, a wave of nausea was welling in the base of her stomach, something that rarely happened to her.

'Consider it more of an annulment,' said Axel, stretching his pudgy fingers out and staring at his nails. 'If anyone asks, Tori, you've never worked for us.'

'But—'

'Hear me out. When this blows over, you'll be back at SIS as if it had never happened, but I'm afraid that SIS doesn't do notoriety.'

'So meanwhile, what? I'm hung out to dry and … you … you milk the Greek deal?'

'Tori,' he said, about to rest his hand reassuringly on hers until he pulled it back at the last moment and twisted around to face her. 'You mustn't think so ill of me. If the Greek deal goes ahead, your contribution will be well rewarded whether you still, ah, work for me or not. You've already broken the back of it with Soti.'

An unwanted image of her night alone with the billionaire leapt into her head but she instantly shook it off. 'My *contribution*? Axel, it was my damn—'

'—idea? Absolutely. But until this is over, I'm allocating another director to work on it. I'll have to tell Soti the truth of course, or at least a version of it.'

She coughed and said, 'I'd, er, prefer it if I could do that,' even though she wasn't sure that was really wise.

Axel picked up on her wavering. 'I think not, Tori. Better you don't speak to him right now. And while we, ah, never hired you, be assured you won't be fending this off on your own. Regardless of your, ah, rather suddenly retrospective disemployment, you are still *unofficially* part of the SIS family and I expect to have you back when this blows over. So meanwhile, you'll have whatever resources you need. My plane, for example, is at your service if I'm not using it. Just tell me what you want and if I can arrange it, it's yours.'

Finally he did place his hand on hers but when he felt her shaking, he quickly removed it as if she was on fire. Axel was not comfortable with emotions unless they were about money or his library. 'Tori, if anyone asks about our relationship, tell them I'm thinking of investing in, ah, the surfwear sector. Firms like, ah, Billabong and Quiksilver, or are they just brands? Whatever. But you … you're privately consulting to me on it, as my surfing expert. Who knows, maybe I *will* have a fling in that direction. I could look quite dashing in a wet suit.'

16

ON THE FLIGHT TO ATHENS, BOTH Axel's pilot and co-pilot sat at the controls while he spent the entire trip on the phone, though only one of the calls concerned the crucial meeting in the Greek capital later that morning, a private audience with the latest Prime Minister. This one—an old school friend of Soti's—had been in office for only two months. By the time the plane was in descent, and in spite of it being the middle of the night in the US, Axel had gleaned from his various contacts that Tori's name had leapt to the top of both the NRC's and Homeland Security's critical-meet lists.

He filled her in on everything he'd heard, and even as they touched down he kept swinging his beads rhythmically, like a pendulum, something she wondered if he'd be allowed to do on a commercial flight.

This was moving too fast for Tori. Axel had extraordinary sources, for sure, but if she was so sought-after, why hadn't someone, apart from Frank, called her? Her question was answered when her phone rang.

From his first word—'Swyft'—she knew it was her old boss from the CIA, Martin Davidson. She put the phone on loudspeaker so Axel could listen in knowing how important it was to keep her current boss onside, even if temporarily she'd stopped working for him. 'It's one-fucking-thirty in the goddamn morning where I am,' said Davidson, 'and here we are again with you causing me big trouble.'

She knew she needed to keep her disgust for Davidson compartmentalised, but even the memory of the man's tomahawk face and his leaden mind made it hard to stop her stomach churning. 'Because?' she asked. Keeping her comments tight was the best way she knew to stop her overreacting.

'You've heard about this NRC thing, right?'

'I have, yes. And Homeland Security.'

'Well, the Agency isn't gonna risk some civilian pen-pushers blabbing to a TV camera or some Congressional committee how a former CIA officer compromised a third of the nation's nuclear plants.'

'Because I haven't, right?' She glanced at Axel, who nodded, but she wasn't sure how much he believed her.

'Swyft, that's a matter of conjecture from what I'm hearing.'

She wasn't going to take him on again, not over this, at least not with the CIA knowing more than she did at this point. 'And you propose?'

'You're in Athens—'

'How'd you—?' She stopped herself; of course he would know. They knew her phone number, and tracking a cell wasn't even spy school 101, it was more like pre-school. 'Yes, and I've just touched down.'

'We're setting up a videolink. Can you get to our embassy?'

'I'll do it from the, er, airport,' she looked at Axel, circling her finger in the air to indicate she meant she'd do it from the plane, and he gave her a thumbs up. She didn't want to mention that she was with him and equally, until she knew exactly what was going on, she wasn't going to put herself inside any place covered by US jurisdiction. For getting a job with the CIA, her dual citizenship had been handy but for remaining at liberty her Australian passport—and some of the others she'd acquired— might be handier.

'But—'

'Don't worry, I'll make sure it's encrypted. I haven't forgotten everything you taught me.' She knew Axel cloaked himself in as much security as any government agency, if only to keep what he knew away from them until he was happy for them to know it. 'Give me twenty minutes.'

As they taxied toward the private jet terminal, Axel popped up the credenza between them and poured her a glass of the Macallan from a Lalique decanter. 'And here,' he said, also handing her his trial pair of FrensLens, 'these might be handy.'

She wasn't sure if he meant the whisky or the glasses, so she took both. The whisky stung her eyes before it hit her throat; at least that was her excuse for the tear that briefly welled there.

Axel left Tori on board to take the call, but only after surreptitiously setting up the 'Record' feature so he could skim through the whole thing himself later. Not that he didn't trust her.

Tori locked the camera at her end so it would only transmit her face and not reveal she was sitting inside a luxurious private jet. Before he'd left, Axel had set up his decoy router so that while Langley already knew that Tori was in Athens, they wouldn't know exactly where since her location would shift every five minutes—somewhat annoying if they tried to track her down.

In turn, the room at CIA headquarters she was beamed into was an internal one, similar to those she'd sat in many times with giant wall monitors for oversighting small overseas operations or surveillance by drones. Judging by the half-empty paper coffee cups and water bottles and the briefing notes strewn over the table, the nine people in the room must have already been in there for at least an hour and, given her experience of the air conditioning there, she even felt the stuffiness, so the fact that everyone was wearing their jackets was hardly a welcoming sign, especially at 1.30 am their time, well, closer to two now.

She didn't recognise any of the faces at first, except for her old boss's, and assumed the grin on that weasel bastard's face was from his newfound schadenfreude, taking real pleasure in her latest misfortune, not least because her sudden exit a few months earlier had so stifled his career prospects.

All these people knew who she was, but at this time of night they were hardly going to dwell on long introductions and social chit-chat so, to level the playing field, Tori popped on the pair of FrensLens. As she scanned across the faces, four of the people, including Davidson, had nothing show up on the FrensLens. A long career in clandestine services did have some privacy value, she thought. Moving along, there was a man from Homeland Security, Alan Whitehead, apparently head of the Office of Operations Command, plus his chief of staff. Quite a dump of personal background started scrolling up on her lenses about Whitehead, but she kept her eyes moving, deciding to come back to him later if she needed to.

Judith Dunn from the Nuclear Regulatory Commission was next, and her sidekick.

The only other woman in the room was Concetta Pittorino, deputy director of the CIA's Directorate of Science and Technology. Tori remembered her induction, when the DS&T people brought along some of the whizzbang gadgetry they were famous for, explaining DS&T was the CIA's version of Q in the James Bond movies. Briefly, she wondered if they had anything like FrensLens.

Pittorino surprised Tori by introducing herself in a deep Southern drawl.

Tori knew from her years working at the CIA that TV-show impersonations of the Agency's upper echelons, especially its women, were way off the more humdrum reality, and while Pittorino may have spoken with an unexpected twang and had a Masters from MIT, she looked very Main Street ordinary. She fitted none of the popular stereotypes. She wasn't young and drop-dead gorgeous, nor was she a severe, greying spinster. And though head of DS&T, she wasn't a white-coated boffin peering through thick Coke-bottle glasses either. The deputy director looked to be in her late forties; her olive complexion and an apparent disdain for make-up would have made Tori hesitant about her age, except she read that she was fifty-five. Pittorino could easily have passed for a cost accountant working in the back office of one of the Big Four accounting firms. Her black hair was pulled back, but not so tight it denied her a hint of femininity and it still allowed her dark eyes to show their softness, perhaps a kindness, though Tori suspected that was her own wishful thinking. A pin through Pittorino's bun had a simple yellow and white flower motif, a daisy Tori guessed, not a Stars and Stripes like the one waving from her old boss's lapel. That smirking shit, she remembered, never bothered to wear it when she worked for him; he was protesting a bit too much, she guessed.

Pittorino's suit was beige, one she could have bought off-the-rack at any department store a few seasons back when it might still have been fashionable, and the tan shirt under her jacket had such a prim high neckline that it made Tori instantly think of Cate Blanchett playing a stiff queen in *Elizabeth: The Golden Age.*

The man on Pittorino's left handed her a tablet computer and she paused to read it.

After a minute, she clasped her hands on the desk in front of her, showing off a neat manicure with clear polish and a simple gold wedding band—Tori already knew she was married to a university administrator. In fact, she was overwhelmed at the detail she was seeing about Pittorino, but if she'd had time to Google her, she would have readily found most of it in a single local-girl-makes-good article which *The Atlanta Journal-Constitution* had posted online when Pittorino landed her current job. Even so, these FrensLens were good. Highly specific, instant web trawling; hands-free name-surfing.

Pittorino cleared her throat and swallowed, her Adam's apple unusually prominent for a woman. 'No time for pleasantries, Dr Swyft,' she said, tilting her head as if apologising for skipping the introductions. 'So let's get down to it, okay? The way I hear it, y'all fucked the Agency before, and it sure looks like y'all are gonna do it all over again, with your fancy-pants Swyft Neutronics Model about to scare the livin' bejesus out of the American people, if not somethin' far worse, by sendin' half of this country's nuke plants into a tailspin.'

'Half the *world's* plants, ma'am,' said Tori's former boss, only dropping his sneer when the deputy director shot a stare at him so icy it froze his tongue to the roof of his mouth.

The venom hit Tori hard, but she let Pittorino continue. 'I hear tell you're a greenie, Dr Swyft?'

'I made that plain to the Agency when you hired me.'

'A greenie who works in the nucular industry?' She pronounced 'nuclear' the same way as a former US President. 'Not too many greenies do that, eh?'

'You're wrong on two counts, ma'am. I haven't worked in the industry for years but many people who care for the planet do work in the nuc—'

'Whatever. But what if there was a greenie who was only pretendin' to like nucular—'

'Pretending? Director Pittorino, nuclear is the cheapest, safest, greenest power around—'

'Yadda, yadda, Dr Swyft. You don't think I don't know the mantra? As I was sayin', a greenie who pretends to like nucular but secretly tries to destroy it, and in the process kills hundreds of thousands of innocent people, screws up whole economies ... an eco-terrorist, young lady. Perhaps a wave-pumpin', tree-huggin' gal like you?'

By the end of the call, Tori had volunteered to work with the combined technical team being scrabbled together. What choice did she have? At the very least she wasn't going to give that bastard Davidson a reason to go around waving his flag pin and saying, 'I told you so' about her.

When Pittorino asked Tori to work from the embassy in Athens, she replied that since she was staying with a wealthy friend with a good communications set up, she'd work from there and, before she could be asked any more questions, she terminated the link.

As she slid into the limo Axel had arranged to wait for her, Tori phoned Frank, asking him to get the hotel to urgently set up a large video screen in her suite and to patch it into the telecommunications world through another decoy router.

ORDINARILY, TORI WOULD have been open-mouthed at the opulence of her suite, even though she wasn't a fan of the chandeliers, the antique armoires or the heavy cream and taupe silks and damasks. The private balcony was also wasted on her, today anyway. Its sweeping views of the Acropolis, the Parthenon and Syntagma Square would have to wait, but either way, the Grande Bretagne was some hotel.

Axel and Frank had just left her suite for their meeting with the Greek Prime Minister. Axel had wanted a last-minute briefing since Tori wouldn't be joining them and even though Pittorino had insisted the US operation was 'classified', Tori was desperate for every friend she could get so ignored the restriction, giving her boss and her assistant a complete blow-by-blow, spelling out all the allegations against her, and unwittingly reconfirming Axel's trust both in her and in his judgment. After all, he had already linked into the plane's system using a remote connection and skimmed through his own recording of the call, just in case.

Tori needed to prove the accusations against both her and her model were wrong. She wasn't worried that Axel mightn't let her back into SIS; that was her least concern. What haunted her was the image that had popped into her head back at the heliport: peering through prison bars.

With the suite's balcony doors closed, the drapes pulled tight, and the chandeliers and table lamps extinguished, there was nothing in the room—or outside—to distract her, apart from the irksome open phone line she had been forced to agree to. Except for that intrusion, she would have been playing her *Church of the*

Open Sky album. It would have been blaring at her, bombarding her. For Tori, The Break produced some of the best surf rock since The Atlantics released *Bombora*. Whenever she got in a mental hole, but couldn't swing to a beach for some surfing to clear her head, surf instrumentals were her next resort. The brainwave for her doctorate, she remembered, came with her dad's favourite, The Surfaris' *Wipe Out* playing over and over. Its maniacal laugh, its rolling drum breaks, the cymbals like monster waves crashing down on her head. She'd kept the same track on repeat for six days with nothing else allowed to intrude her mind space. Just The Surfaris and her equations. It was as if her father, her coach, her mentor was there mocking her, daring her. Pushing her.

But today, as much as immersing herself in a sea of rock would help her think, she was forced to put up with the NRC's Judith Dunn chattering on the line. Tori sat cross-legged on the sofa, her shoes on the floor beneath the glass-topped table, and her eyes spellbound as she projected the thousands and thousands of lines of equations, code and data onto the video screen, the same image appearing simultaneously thousands of miles away over a similar military-grade high-encryption line onto screens in a sealed-off section in the Agency's research facility near Langley. Dr Dunn, at Tori's virtual elbow as she trawled the data, was on the open line to talk things through. Since there hadn't been time for Dunn to fly back to the NRC's emergency technical centre in Tennessee, she and her team were working through the night out of the CIA facility.

What Dunn had got streaming for Tori was a complete dump of the inner workings of one of the two faulty nuclear plant components. At first, after so many years away from this, Tori felt it was like reacquainting herself with Ancient Greek, and with so many sigmas, omegas and deltas in the code it even looked like it.

When she had told Frank she wanted 'large', she hadn't expected a screen that would take up half her sitting room wall, but it was perfect. She zoomed the display so the characters and symbols were about two inches high. They cut through the darkness, the green glow they washed over the room like a wave that had dumped her—like she was swimming under the data.

At first, it was overwhelming and she was struggling for air, drowning. Her model was in there; she could see it was the code's foundation, hardly a surprise given how frequently and freely her work had been cut and pasted into nuclear plant systems once the NRC had given its formal okay all those years ago.

What Tori was trying to find was nothing. If nothing was out of whack, then she would be in the clear, she could get back to the Greek deal, and it would be up to one of the other teams running in parallel to discover the cause of the problem, hopefully something prosaic, like quality control people mistakenly letting a small batch of components out of the production line with, say, a scratched slice of silicon on their chips.

As the data continued to spill over her, it all started to come back. She rose from the bottom and started to swim with it, getting the feel of its current, exactly how she felt when she was writing it. Maybe she didn't need the music.

It was years since Tori had even bothered opening her model. Once she'd opensourced it and then got hit, first by the onslaught of academic attack dressed up as peer review, then by the regulatory inquisition, she had promised herself she would never look at it again. She tried her hand working in nuclear research at the Lucas Heights facility in outer Sydney— the work nothing to do with her thesis—but even that was too close for her. She needed something completely different, which was when she won a John Monash Scholarship to do a Harvard MBA. Topping first year and simultaneously her own

who-gives-a-fuck threshold, she ditched Harvard for the CIA
without even taking a single second-year class.

Despite the hour in Virginia, the urgency of their work and
Pittorino's crude belligerence, Dunn was treating Tori with kid
gloves. To Dunn, Tori was still an industry legend who had, as
a twenty-year-old genius, changed everything. Plus Dunn was
a staunch innocent-till-proven-guilty woman and, like Tori,
she was a greenie who believed in nuclear, so Pittorino was
hardly her pin-up.

Back when Tori released her model, Dunn's then boss had sat
hunched over it for three days and nights straight, periodically
shouting whoops of amazement, astonishment and delight. He
even missed his daughter's debutante ball. After the third day,
he jumped up on the top of a lab bench, his hair as wild as
Einstein's, his face unshaven, his lab coat stained with cola and
nachos, and proclaimed, 'She's the new Boltzmann.' While the
nineteenth-century physicist Ludwig Boltzmann had created
the basic equations for non-equilibrium statistical mechanics,
Tori had taken his work to an extraordinary new level. Dunn's
boss, an academically inclined romantic who retired last year,
had even briefly debated nominating Tori for a Nobel Prize.

But after four hours of Tori and Dunn's team finding nothing
but headaches, Dunn's impatience started to overtake her
respect. 'This is hopeless,' she said. 'I'm gonna run a compare,'
a sophisticated program that would run Tori's model side by
side against the faulty component's version so they could easily
highlight the differences.

17

THE COMPARE PROGRAM HAD A TORRENT
of data to chug through and, even though it was
running on DS&T's supercomputers, it took two hours
to finish.

'Stripping out the componentry complications,' Dunn told
her, 'we're seeing your model, sigma for sigma, omega for omega.'

For the whole two hours, Tori had not stopped scouring the
data on the screen. But it was only then that she noticed it: a
chunk of perfectly innocent-looking code buried deep inside
the model—very deep—and what caught her eye was that it
wasn't in her 'handwriting'. It was perfectly understandable but
if she'd written it, it would have been expressed differently, in
both mathematical grammar and style. It was similar to how
some people say *whom* yet others *who*, and how some stubbornly
refuse to begin sentences with *and* or *but*.

'Dr Dunn,' she said, the exhilaration lifting her voice. 'Take
a look there.' With the electronic pointer, she circled a squiggle

of light around the relevant lines on her screen so Dunn would
see exactly what Tori saw. 'It's a differential scattering kernel …
like mine. But see when it's normalised, the integration is
changed, yet it doesn't seem to be linked in anywhere. It's just
sitting there, like an island, unconnected to anything. And look,
the active scattering kernel is fine. So why would someone put
this there?'

Dunn said nothing but knew, as Tori did, that the compare
program had shown this very piece of code to have been inside
her original model; that Tori looked to have put it there.

Over the next hour, they found two other floaters, as Tori
was describing them. Superficially they were clones of key
sections of the model but each had a crucial element changed,
and they weren't linked to anything. After that, for another
thirty minutes, and thousands of miles apart, they scrolled back
and forth through the code, talking through what they were
seeing, until suddenly one of Dunn's technicians screamed out,
'There! At the foot of the screen. It's a trail. Shit, these floaters
are all working together and backdooring themselves inside the
neutron transport equation.'

As soon as he said it, Tori saw it too.

They hadn't found nothing. This was something. *The* thing.
And it was inside of—part of—Tori's original model.

Yet she'd never seen it before. 'Holy—' she said, her mind
working faster than the others in stepping through what it was
doing. 'It's designed to override the model and spit out a state of
normal, regardless of what is really happening inside the plant.
It means that operators won't have a clue what's really going
on inside their reactors … With this, plant control becomes
a roll of the dice … And there—' she pointed to another
section of code, '—see that … it's a random date generator with
a … what's that? Shit, it's a *not before* date … The day before

yesterday … the day the plant went down. Jesus, this has been set up so it can launch anytime now, in any plant that—'

Tori stopped and stared at the screen.

'Dr Swyft, I have to ask,' said Dunn while scratching a note to her colleague to alert the head of the NRC, as well as Alan Whitehead from Homeland Security, and Concetta Pittorino at the CIA, 'why the hell did you put this inside your model?'

'That's just it … I didn't,' she whispered, her spine tingling as if a spirit had just entered her body.

18

TO TORI, IT WAS OBVIOUS FROM the way the rogue code had been written that it wasn't her work, but try telling that to Pittorino, let alone Davidson and his ilk, or Whitehead at Homeland Security. Only sophisticated mathematicians would grasp something so subtle, and none of them was either a mathematician or, in her opinion, particularly sophisticated. Dunn and her NRC people were different, and with them Tori at least had a chance. 'Dr Dunn, I'm telling you this isn't mine. Someone's inserted the damn thing there and made it look—'

'Sorry, Dr Swyft. I acknowledge it's got a different swing to it, but how do you explain that it was there when you posted it open-source. We ran the compare program, remember?'

Tori hadn't visited her old website for years, so called it up to view it and, yes, the malicious code was sitting there just as Dunn had told her. But how? She'd set up the site so people could only copy but not alter what she'd put there. She hadn't written this code, nor had she posted it, yet there it was.

'Wait, I need to check something else.' She called up the website for her university's library, got through to the section where doctoral theses were accessible, and clicked on the link.

It didn't work. Dammit.

The sweat was running down her back and the room, still in darkness except for the flashes of green data swirling down the big screen and the light from her laptop, was closing in on her.

She tried again. The spinning wheel kept spinning …

After a further long thirty seconds, she was in, typed her university student number and clicked open her original thesis, heading straight for the Appendix where the key components of her model were laid out … page after page of equations and code. She flipped and flipped until she found it.

The rogue code was there too. Fuck!

Someone had clearly doctored this, but who? Why?

Her heart was pounding, the noise in her ears blocking out everything else. She didn't even notice her legs, still crossed beneath her, had gone numb. She stared at her thesis for what seemed like minutes, as if she was hoping it would itself reveal what was happening.

'Dr Swyft, are you still there?' said Dunn, another phone ringing somewhere behind her. 'You were checking something?'

Tori's eyes were locked on her old work, trying to replay writing to. She even started to hum *Wipe Out* and imagined herself back in her old room, visualising the details—down to the surfboard she kept in the corner, one of her father's—to see if it were remotely possible this could have crept in somehow, that she could possibly have done this. She'd done it but somehow forgot? How was that possible? There was something here, something gnawing at the raw edges of her memory.

'Dr Swyft?'

'Give me a minute,' she said, still staring. The code was there, in her thesis, it was on her old site, and it was in the componentry. To any fair-minded observer—anyone but Tori—all the evidence pointed to a single conclusion: that a decade ago, she had buried a malicious code in her model intending it to end up deep inside many of the world's nuclear plants. A greenie who secretly hated *nucular*, as Pittorino had insinuated. Except that it wasn't true.

This was no accident. No glitch. It couldn't have just popped out of her head and wormed its way in here all those years ago without her remembering. This had clearly been designed so the control instrumentation would show everything in the plant was normal, hunky-dory, even when it wasn't—preventing the normal safety mechanisms from moving the control rods back into the core. In most cases, by the time the operators realised their reactor was running out of control, it would be too late. The midwest plant was just lucky, it seemed, or had outstanding operators.

This had been specifically created, she was sure, to hurt the nuclear industry by causing real damage to nuclear plants. Or maybe only to damage one, and when people realised there was a risk that all these plants could run amok without anyone knowing, it would trigger a public panic and eventually a global nuclear scare. Not only would authorities shut the plants down, they might need to shut down the entire industry, to give it a final hurrah. The French would be the worst hit, with eighty per cent of their power from nuclear. The country would have to buy power coming from Germany, if their neighbour had enough capacity, far less likely after the Fukushima disaster, when Germany had started switching off its own nuclear. The price of electricity in France and other affected countries would skyrocket and for many it would become unaffordable, even if they could get access to it. The looming winter would bring thousands of deaths. Tori suddenly felt cold.

This *wasn't* her work. She *didn't* write this.

'Dr Swyft?'

'Not yet,' she snapped back.

Tori clicked open the Properties on her thesis document— the typical place to find the name of its creator and the date they last modified it—and waves of both delight and fear dumped over her. There! Proof.

In black and white, it was there. The thesis, or this distorted rendering of it, was created almost two years *after* she'd actually written the original and posted it on the web. This carried her name but the date on it was the clincher.

She turned her head back to the speakerphone. 'Dr Dunn. Judith. Someone's tampered with my work. Two years after I submitted it—just before the NRC gave it regulatory blessing— someone snuck in and amended the copy of my thesis on file with the university, and I imagine they did the same thing to the website post, and it was that one, the wrong one, that the whole industry has copied.'

The only copies that Tori still had access to herself were these: the one at the university and the other on her old website. She hadn't intended it that way, but it was how it played out after her laptop was stolen. Shit, she remembered: it went missing not long after she submitted her work for regulatory approvals.

But wait, she thought, a sliver of relief trying to extract itself. What about the version of the model that the NRC itself worked on and ultimately approved? They'd gone over her work line by line. In fact, so had all those resentful academics who'd tried kicking the twenty-year-old in the guts during their spiteful so-called peer review. There'd be countless copies of her real model out there.

'Judith, what about the NRC's archives? They'll prove what I'm saying. My original model … what you guys signed off on … it won't have any of this in it.'

Dunn was quick to answer, since the same idea had already occurred to her. 'Dr Swyft. Tori. I've already called for it to be pulled in from our archives but that won't make a zot of difference to whether you did this or not. Even if your original model was clean—which is highly likely or we wouldn't have approved it—what's to say you didn't fiddle with these other documents afterwards, knowing that once we gave it our okay the component makers would go straight to the source, in other words, to you?'

How could Tori prove a negative—that she hadn't contrived this as an elaborate ploy, a premeditated blind, so that today, years later, she could demurely flutter her lashes and protest that someone else had done it? Pittorino would eat her alive. Davidson would annihilate her. Axel would definitely let her go down.

'In any case, assuming it wasn't you, we still need your help trawling through the, ah, doctored model to make sure we remove the dirty bits without creating any new glitches, so we can issue an endorsed clean version. Your old model in our files might do the trick for us, as you say, but nobody knows this model like you. It would be a sign of your, ah, good faith.'

'Judith, you're right but I need some thinking space before the good faith.'

'Tori, it's already close to noon here. We've all been working non-stop through the night—'

'I know. Sorry, Judith, but I'll have to call you back.' And she terminated the call. She slammed her fist into the sofa. The problem wasn't the nuclear crisis. That was over, to Tori anyway. All the NRC would need to do is get the component suppliers to issue a patch with her untainted model in it. The problem that flummoxed her was who had done this. To her. She sat in the dark, dazed. The green numbers and symbols from the screen ran down her face where the tears would have been if she had let them fall.

With a focused intensity, she pored over every symbol, every nuance in the formulas and eventually found another floater though, no matter where she looked, she couldn't see this one being linked to anything else. It was a loner and, weirdly, it reminded her of a graffiti tag, the stylised signatures kids spray on the sides of buses and subway carriages:

$9\Sigma: (\Phi/8 >> (\Sigma/14, \emptyset))$

She wasn't sure what it meant, but it had to mean something.

She was just about to reach for a sip of water when an explosion outside shook her window, and her. She heard a distant tinkle that, if the thick curtains had been open, she might have recognised as shattering glass from a car or a shop window. Sirens cut the air as the rhythmic chants of an approaching crowd wafted up to her. She knew the local alphabet—what student of mathematics didn't?—as well as enough of the language to safely order keftedakia and souvlaki in a seedy Plaka café, even baklava, but that was about all. Even if she could understand Greek, from up here on the seventh floor she wouldn't have been able to make out their demands, so she shut the disturbance out of her mind and focused on the floating code, the tag. Given the variety of choices in science speak, $9\Sigma: (\Phi/8 >> (\Sigma/14, \emptyset))$ could mean almost anything.

Sigma (Σ), she knew, was not merely the eighteenth letter in the Greek alphabet, equivalent to S, but it was also the number 200 and the scientific notation for adding up a bunch of numbers.

To confuse things even more, in its lower case form, it represented what she knew as the Stefan–Boltzmann constant, that the total energy a black body radiates per unit surface area in unit time is proportional to the fourth power of the thermodynamic temperature. Which of Σ's meanings was the right one?

At least the colon (:) in the tag only had two options: *extends over* or *such that*.

Phi (Φ) on the other hand was another doozie. As well as the twenty-first letter, the Greek equivalent to F, or Ph, it also represented both 500 and 500,000, and more, it could be the Golden Rule, as well as Euler's totient, and—which was how Tori was most familiar with it—a probability density or distribution function.

The $>>$ was easy, she thought, meaning *much greater than*.

And $\emptyset$ was a diameter symbol, but it could also mean *an empty set*.

With all these variants, parsing this into something meaningful could take her days. Unless she patched together a mix-and-match program. She was about to do precisely that when Frank started banging at her door.

What the hell does he want, she wondered, annoyed at the intrusion, the explosion outside having slipped her mind. 'Tori,' shouted Frank through her door. 'Open up.'

She got to her feet but, forgetting her pins and needles, she stumbled and, as if in slow motion, she saw the hard edge of the glass-topped table with the upside-down reflection of the equation fast looming up at her.

TORI'S HEAD THROBBED like a muffled drum, with a jarring *tic-tic* in the background crawling under her skin. She cracked open an eye, trying to take in her surroundings, and the bright foggy light blinded her. Through her squint, it looked like smoke yet the only odour was like alcoholic warm butter … whisky. She blinked a few times to clear the haze and adjusted herself back on the sofa cushions.

'Axel, could you possibly put those damn clicking things away,' she said. 'It's my head?' She touched it near where it ached and noticed the plastic texture of a Band-Aid, or whatever Greeks called them.

'Certainly,' Axel said, pocketing the worry beads, and he walked over to the remaining window and pulled those curtains back too, bringing in the soft flush of the hotel's exterior lights.

Tori took the tumbler Frank was holding out for her, but even the clink of its ice cubes made her wince. 'You were banging on my door. Did the meeting go badly?'

'Just the opposite. The PM is onside, but there's still a way to go. No, it was a bit of excitement downstairs we wanted to warn you about. A demonstration. Happened just after we got back.'

She forced a weak smile but, when she felt it pull on the sticking plaster, she let it go. 'I can't hear anything down there now, or is that just me?'

'The police moved them on,' said Axel, looking down into Syntagma Square, which was still spotlighted and barricaded, but empty apart from placards, bottles, picks and assorted backpacks and T-shirts littering the marble paving. 'You, on the other hand, had a little fall and luckily our resident master-of-all-trades here had his key to your suite and managed to fix you up nicely. Quite a talent.'

Frank moved in close and looked into her eyes. 'Follow my finger,' he said, his honey-soaked voice calming her as he moved his finger from one side of her nose to the other and back again.

'This isn't *Catch-22* is it?' Tori asked, trying not to smile.

'Where I say that I see the double of whatever you show me?'

He shook his head, happy to smile himself. Her eyes were fine. 'Sorry, but I have to check for concussion. What's your name? And don't give me Yossarian.' He turned to Axel. 'That's the character in *Catch*—'

'I know,' Axel snapped. 'I'm not completely stuck in the eighteenth century.'

'Hell-o,' said Tori, getting their attention back. 'My name is Tori Swyft ... Doc-tor Victoria Swyft to my dear friends at the CIA,' she said in a Southern drawl, doing her best to imitate Concetta Pittorino, unaware Axel knew exactly whom she was mimicking.

He smiled. 'Sounds like our old Tori is back, eh, Francis?'

'Not so fast, Axel. Okay, Tori, where were you born?'

'Sydney.'

'Who's the current Prime Minister of Australia?'

Her face sagged. 'Oh, Jesus!' she said, but the others could see her reaction was from scorn, not amnesia.

'That's close enough.' Frank laughed. 'And the President of the United States?'

'Isabel Diaz.'

'Right. What was your doctoral thesis about?'

'It's a neutronics model,' said Tori, her eyes starting to glaze, and then suddenly she sat upright, her eyes as wide and clear as her conscience, her whisky spilling out of her glass over her lap. 'Axel, Frank. Someone's trying to set me up, and ... I've just worked out who it is.'

19

TORI QUICKLY FILLED THEM IN ON how bad things were looking for her with the NRC people, and how she was sure that by now the CIA and Homeland Security would also have been briefed. She left nothing out, but this time everything was news to Axel.

'This formula—this tag—up on the screen, it's a boast,' she said from the sofa, and with the electronic pointer she circled it and read it to them aloud, '$9\Sigma: (\Phi/8 >> (\Sigma/14, \emptyset))$. It could mean a million things, but here's how I'm reading it, and I'm sure it's right. 9Σ translates into 9S, which I'm reading as an abbreviation for Nine Sisters.'

Axel's face, under the weight of what Tori had explained, was even doughier than normal, but she'd unwittingly given him a frisson about his beloved Enlightenment and his cheeks flushed with a little pink, 'Like Benjamin Franklin's Masonic lodge in Paris?'

'Yes, but nowhere near as benign,' said Tori. 'Let me go on.

Next, the colon. That means *extends over*. The $\Phi/8$ is what it sounds like, Phi/8. The $\Sigma/14$ is similar, S/14. And the $\emptyset$ means *an empty set*, but let's say it means *an empty suit*. So here goes my translation ... oh, and you have to read the stuff in brackets first ... *Phi/8 is much greater than S/14, who is an empty suit, and the Nine Sisters extends over both of them.* Gentlemen, I'm the empty suit. I'm S/14. The person who did this was Phi/8. He did this to prove he was better than me, which the arrogant shit might really be, given what he's achieved.'

20

AXEL INSISTED THE TRIO MOVE CAMP to his Presidential Suite on the fourth floor. Tori's wasn't exactly cramped, not even with the massive screen in it but, despite opening the windows, the rank salty odour from the hours she'd been sweating in there plus the bowls of nuts and half-empty coffee cups was a little oppressive for her boss's apparently sensitive nose. Once his suite's dedicated butler opened Axel's door for them, Tori entered a suite bigger than any apartment she had ever rented, its wall-to-wall lavishness so grand it belittled her own. On reflection, grand was too slight a word. It was three times bigger than hers yet it quietly spoke with the same restrained flare of classic opulence and refined elegance, though with so much more of it that most Greeks—even those still holding jobs and pensions—would hungrily press their noses up against the windows to check it out, if only they could stretch up to this floor.

For Tori its stateliness evoked SIS's Boston headquarters—the sweep of leafy panel mouldings on the walls, the rich symmetrical inlay in the polished parquetry floors—and she couldn't help run her fingers over one of the velvet armchairs, at first leaving a trail in the plush pile before she quickly smoothed over it with the back of her hand.

In one of Frank's many calls to her while she'd been on Soti's yacht with Axel, he had confided that when he had first arrived here to set everything up, he had also checked out the Royal Suite for Axel. At twice the size of the Presidential it also boasted an antique Bösendorfer grand piano. But he panned it, he'd joked, 'So, for once, Axel will have to rough it', though he didn't tell her the real reason, to avoid Axel insisting that Frank play Beethoven's Fifth Symphony when they had guests. Frank loved the symphony despite the advertising industry molesting it as a jingle or, in the seventies, that it had become a tacky disco hit. No, it was simply that he was done being Axel's ivory-tinkling party trick, so he had 'downgraded' their boss to the piano-less Presidential Suite.

What he hadn't told Tori was that for the last nine days, while she and Axel were on Soti's yacht breathing the crisp, clear sea air and he felt stuck in polluted, depressed Athens, he took the uplifting liberty of road-testing the Presidential Suite himself. At $12,500 a night, plus tax, it was, he felt, the least he could do to check that his boss would be sleeping on a comfortable mattress. He also extensively checked out the room service menu, justifying it to himself like he was an emperor's food taster. For a man whose parents were Pakistani immigrant factory workers, the white-gloved waiters lifting the polished silver domes into the air in a synchronised flourish was a delightful touch, especially when they revealed hamburgers and fries—served on separate plates, of course.

Tonight, the Presidential Suite butler drizzled some lightly bubbling Krug into Axel's and Frank's champagne flutes. Tori passed, even though the yeasty aroma with, as Axel blathered on, its hints of apples and honey did get her salivating. She passed too on the small blinis and the pot of beluga caviar. The two men, led by Axel, dug their silver spoons right in but she was in no celebratory mood and waited for the butler to leave.

'Tori, you have to admit that what you've told us sounds, ah, far-fetched. That some lunatic professor hornswoggled a bunch of you into falling for his environmentalist clap-trap to become his radical secret agents,' said Axel, shaking his head as he took another mouthful of caviar and let his eyes roll back in delight.

'We weren't supposed to be agents. The whole idea was that we *didn't* report to him, or to *anyone*; we didn't take orders. We were simply charged with finding something big to do, getting ourselves into the right positions, and then doing it. I was S/14. And there was Phi/8 … Philips. Yes, Oscar bloody Philips. He was also working in my field, and he was a total shit. Look, I'd forgotten about the whole thing until now. I'd only been to three, no four meetings. I was a starry-eyed eighteen-year-old …'

'An unusually smart one,' said Frank, mirroring the scepticism that Tori was sure to face from those back in the US still waiting to hear from her.

'True that,' she said in Agency-speak, trying to make light of it for a reason that made no sense other than her exhaustion, but neither Frank nor Axel laughed. 'Look, even prodigies play with dolls and swoon over movie stars, okay? My professor was a tremendously charismatic man, a bit of a father figure too, I guess. Something I had maybe been searching for? When he took me under his wing, it was huge for me. The last Nine Sisters meeting I went to turned out to be their last. He was supposed to unveil the big plan for saving the planet, but I was, er, sick, really sick and had the sweats, cramps, headaches … I couldn't think, I wasn't really listening, and I ended up racing

outside to … to you know … in the bushes. I didn't have
the guts to go back inside and I skulked back to my room in
college.'

She saw Axel starting to swing his beads again, with
continuous 360-degree swirls, a sign, she felt sure, that he was
showing both agitation and disbelief. 'Look, Axel, it's all true,'
she said. 'But the next day, when I went to Professor Mellor's
office to apologise, he was fine with it, surprisingly. I'd fretted
all night over how dismissive he'd be, that he might even
withdraw from supervising my doctorate, but he was really
considerate, asking if I was okay, how I felt, all that. I remember
him taking me out back—he was a chain smoker—and as we
hung around near the bins, he asked what I'd thought of his
plan, but he was laughing it off like it was all a joke. My mind
wasn't all that clear on what had happened the night before—
okay, to be honest I hadn't been sick, I was drunk—but I did
remember the weird conspiracy thing, the *notwork* concept I
just told you about? How we were supposed to focus on our
careers and infiltrate the highest levels and then turn the whole
world to shit ten years later. Yeah, it's all coming back … we
were supposed to wait ten years and then start "pissing from
inside the tent",' she said, putting the phrase in air quotes with
her fingers. 'That's what he'd said. Anyhow, that next day he
continued to chuckle, telling me it had all been an experiment
in group behaviour that he'd agreed to set up for some mate
of his in the Psychology department and that a few of us,
though not all of us—certainly not me—were in on the scam.
I remember thinking it was pretty unethical, but Mellor wasn't
your average rule-abiding academic and at the time, frankly,
that was why I was attracted to him.'

The two men glanced at each other. 'Attracted?' asked
Frank.

'Not physically, hell no. I'd have rather taken a poke in the eye with a stick than one from him,' she said, her mouth twisting with disgust like she was trying to bite off her own ear. 'Let's just say his whole body smelled like a walking ashtray. No, what drew me in was his mind and his ideas, and his oratory.'

'What then?'

'Well, he told me that after I'd, er, run out of the meeting he'd told them all the truth and by way of amends to everyone, he'd pulled out a mess of beers—his home-brew—and they all sat around and got drunk themselves. From the way he said it, he'd obviously worked out I wasn't really just sick with gastro. Anyhow, after that, I never saw any of the others again apart from Mellor, who stayed on as my supervisor, and unfortunately Philips, who Mellor was also supervising, so the Nine Sisters never crossed my mind again. Until tonight.'

'You never thought this experiment thing was a bit strange? You didn't ask Philips about it?'

'I was plenty pissed about it, but I kept it to myself. I really did want to do my bit to save the planet and I thought this was going to be it, you know, my life's calling kind of thing.' She turned to Frank. 'Like becoming a priest.'

'Or not,' he said, and turned away.

'And this Philips?' prodded Axel.

'Wait! I did ask him. I remember now. I really despised that guy. He was always out to prove he was better than everyone else, especially me, like we were always in a competition, for goodness' sake. Carried a huge chip. Anyway, I was lined up behind him in the cafeteria a few days later. There was one portion of the spaghetti bolognaise left and he asked me if I wanted it, which I did, so he asked the server for it—I thought he was asking for me, turning over a new leaf—but he put it on his own tray and said, "Bad luck", the little shit.

I laughed it off even though I was fuming inside and, to show I didn't care, I asked what he thought about Mellor pulling back the curtains on the Nine Sisters thing and revealing it was all a fake. But he couldn't resist and looked down his nose at me like I was a piece of crap and told me how he was one of the inner circle who Mellor had let in on the truth that it was a psych experiment, and that as far as he was concerned everything went to plan … apart from me racing outside like a little girl. That's what he'd said … "like a little girl". I had more questions but after that I dropped them and avoided the creep as much as I could.'

As she rambled, Tori doubted her colleagues would believe her story. She wouldn't have. Their faces were hard and opaque, like the marble table Axel had left his champagne glass sitting on. The bronze sculpture of a discus thrower next to it represented how she felt. She'd thrown out her story and, her stomach tight and her lungs empty, she waited to see if it landed over the line. Neither of the men spoke.

The strain ruptured when Axel's phone rang. It was the Prime Minister's office, he mouthed. 'Tomorrow, sure. At noon? We'll be there.' He hung up. 'We're on, chaps. What time will Henry be here, Francis?'

Henry Harvey was the director of SIS, who Axel had briefed on the Greek deal that morning to step in to replace Tori. 'He should land around six am,' Frank answered. 'So there'll be plenty of time to brief him on today's meeting with the PM before a ten o'clocker. He's bringing reinforcements, as you asked: Paul and Stephanie.'

'Good, we'll get to the deal later. So Tori, this Nine Sisters meeting when you were, ah, sick,' Axel said.

'Drunk.'

'Yes, when was it?'

Tori was already pallid, but her skin got even whiter. 'Ten years ago.'

'And now you're thinking it was no psych experiment, right? No play-acting.'

Tori threw up her hands. It was obvious that a bunch of people she once vaguely knew were out there set to unleash their own individual versions of Armageddon onto an unsuspecting planet. She might have foiled Oscar Philips' plan in time, only just, but she didn't even have a clue anymore who the others were let alone what they were plotting. Suddenly, she looked at her two colleagues, moving from one pair of dark, piercing eyes to the other and back, searching for what they were really thinking. 'You both think I'm talking crap, don't you? That I really did this ... that my story's an elaborate smokescreen?'

Axel started to swing his beads so they twirled around his finger, then swung them the other way to unwrap them and he kept repeating it so it became hypnotic. 'The thought had crossed my mind,' he said, his brows furrowing. Tori had found Axel was similar to her in one respect: when confronted with a choice between conspiracy and something simple like a stuff-up, he'd choose the simple answer every time. The problem was that this time, Tori was the simple answer. 'And Tori your, ah, Langley friends will certainly want to explore that possibility,' he said, avoiding her question.

'Well, I'm inclined to believe you,' said Frank, picking up his champagne in salute but not smiling.

She would have preferred it if Frank had completely believed her, but she knew an inclination was the best she'd get, for the moment.

'Axel,' said Frank, 'if Tori's suspicions are correct, this is ... I don't know ... massive. Tori, you'll have to run a real gauntlet on this ... to convince the Agency and whoever else to track this Mellor down, to find out who all these others are and, if they're active, to stop them. That'll be no mean feat.'

'I know,' she said, still looking at Axel, waiting for his response. If he didn't believe her, she had no hope that Pittorino would, let alone any of the others. And Martin Davidson wouldn't believe her even if she managed to persuade his damned poster boy George W. Bush to give her a character reference, which was not going to happen either.

Axel continued to rhythmically swing his beads. 'What did this Philips look like?' he asked.

For a full minute Tori was silent as she searched her memory for the snippets of detail. Frank knew not to speak. It was a key to successful interrogation and, as he had discovered at SIS, to good business negotiation too.

Tori pressed the fingers of both hands into her scalp, surprised by how greasy her hair was yet unaware she'd been making the same gesture repeatedly while on the lengthy call to Dunn. 'Axel, I'm sorry,' she said. 'Apart from his pinprick devious eyes, I've put him out of my head. There's nothing. Just those eyes, always tight and shifty, like a slit-eyed cat, and permanently bloodshot so I used to think they were scarlet. But that's all. His eyes.'

'Excellent,' said Axel, surprising both of the others. 'I'm inclined your way too.' The chances were that a liar would have concocted a much more detailed portrait to satisfy Axel's question. Being able to recall only a single feature, like her detail about the spaghetti bolognaise, and especially such a remarkably different one, had the ring of truth about it. It wasn't proof, but it gave Axel the confidence to lean her way, as did the small matter that she was a walking ideas machine who had already proved she had the potential to earn him an even bigger fortune.

He suggested she call Dunn at the NRC and ask her to reassemble all the others so as to avoid Chinese whispers. 'And give Dunn something. Tell her it was Oscar Philips.'

While they waited for Dunn to call back with a time, the two men finished their champagne and caviar. Tori was still in no mood for either. Axel got the butler to bring in coffees, an espresso for Tori, and she dropped in more sugar lumps than usual. Worn out already, she knew the long day was hardly over.

Before the butler left, Axel asked for a second decaf cappuccino for himself—he didn't like waiting and he was a quick drinker—and only after the door closed did he continue. 'Hopefully Pittorino and the others will believe you about these ... what would you call them ... neo-Luddites, I suppose. Yes, even the Enlightenment had its dark side.'

'You're far too kind to these ... these bastards,' said Frank, getting up a bit of steam, not really thinking how Tori might react, having herself been a follower. 'The Luddites in the Industrial Revolution ... mostly they rampaged inside a few factories, smashing the new-fangled machines they feared were about to rip their jobs and their food away. They didn't aim to kill industries or, like that Unabomber guy, people. Okay, there were a few deaths, but they were the exceptions. So don't flatter this crackpot Mellor and his Nine Sisters whackjobs as modern-day Luddites. They're out-and-out terrorists, Axel. Eco-terrorists on a potentially giant scale, depending where they ended up, and using cyber-terror tools. Global suicide bombers equipped with brains, status, computers and money. And better clothes.'

'Point taken. Assuming some of them are still out there and committed.'

'Well, Philips is!' said Tori.

'True,' Axel replied, momentarily holding his beads in his hand as he considered the thought. 'Or he was. But if you tell the CIA and Homeland Security this—' he paused to search for the right word, '—this story, I doubt they will believe it, let alone do anything about it. You are their sole person of interest and whatever you say will be seen as deflection.'

She knew he was right.

'And the more pervasive and complex you paint this conspiracy, the more likely they won't believe you.'

'So fucking Mellor wins and I lose,' she mumbled and took a sip of her coffee. She winced at the taste; she'd put in one sugar too many.

The three sat there quietly as it all sank in. Frank eventually broke the silence. 'Tori, where's Mellor now? Where's Philips? You mightn't recall any of the other names but those two are a start, and finding them will help clear your name and maybe lead to the others. Where do we look for them?'

Axel's phone rang again. This time it was Soti Skylakakis phoning for an update and as Axel started speaking, he carried his coffee into the suite's dining room and tried to fit himself into one of the carving chairs but found it too narrow for his girth, and moved across to the armless dining chair next to it.

Tori told Frank she didn't have a clue where Philips or Mellor might be, since she'd completely lost touch after she was awarded her doctorate. Once she'd opensourced her work— which was actually Mellor's idea, not hers—the professor never again replied to her calls or emails, something she'd thought weird at first but rationalised as him being preoccupied with some grand new theory. As to Philips, she had been only too glad to escape his constant sarcasm and backbiting.

Frank grabbed his laptop out of his briefcase, connected to the hotel's wifi and checked out her old university's website.

First he tried for Philips, but he couldn't find a reference to an Oscar Philips anywhere, and there was certainly no doctoral thesis listed for him.

'He must be listed there. He would have finished the year after me, two years after, tops.'

'Nope. No Philipses around then, not with one L or with two. Are you sure he finished?'

She shrugged. 'I guess I can't be. Pittorino will say he never existed, I bet.'

'Cross that bridge when you have to. Besides, the university records will prove it, one way or the other. I could hack them now, but I think that's a lower priority.' Next he tried for Mellor, who was certainly listed, but they saw he was now an emeritus professor with no classes and, it seemed, no office or contact details either.

'He's retired, I'd say,' said Axel, who'd wandered back and was looking over Frank's shoulder. Having seen the university administration's number at the top of the webpage, he'd already tapped it into his cell phone.

'Axel! It's the middle of the night in Sydney.' Axel was like a few others she'd met. When they were awake, they expected everyone else to be. That had been Davidson's approach when she worked for him, no matter where she'd been stationed and, with the protocol that she could never switch off her phone, the bastard abused it frequently.

At that moment, the doorbell rang and the butler entered with Axel's second coffee, and left just as quickly.

Frank ignored the interruption and typed 'Professor George Mellor' into his search engine and, after correcting the search tag to eliminate all the entries for a professor of atmospherics at Princeton with the same name, he flicked through the search pages, all with links to the correct Mellor's old books and articles and a few environmental speeches, but turning up not a single clue as to where he might be today. It was only when he got to the sixth page of the entries that he spied one, in Italian, that looked like it might have potential. It was a newspaper article from Venice's *Il Gazzettino* and was only six months old.

Tori was good with languages but Italian was not her strongest suit. 'Click on the "translate this page" link,' she suggested.

'Francis *is* a "translate this page" link,' said Axel. 'His Italian is flawless. He was going to be a priest, remember?'

Frank started skim-reading the piece for them. 'It's an interview with someone called Dr Alison Emilio-Mellor. She's an art historian working out of the Peggy Guggenheim Collection in Venice. It says she's the—Yes! She's the daughter of a famous Australian nuclear physicist. *Our* physicist! Bingo! Emilio must be her husband's name. Shit, she's a doctor. Do you think—'

'Forget it,' Tori snapped. 'What harm could an art historian do? Drop a potion into the acqua minerale to make every visitor suddenly swoon over Jackson Pollock's paint droppings? Axel, I've been to that museum, in case you're wondering. Besides,' she added, 'I met the daughter once, in Mellor's office, and she definitely wasn't in the Nine Sisters.'

This time it was Tori's phone that rang. It was Judith Dunn and she was calling to say that the group had assembled and was ready for the videolink.

They left the laptop open and Tori and Frank ran out and up the stairs to take the call on the big screen in her suite. The idea was that Axel and Frank would watch unseen from the side. Axel meanwhile took the elevator. Urgency was urgency, but the only exercise Axel stretched to was pulling a cork out of a bottle of fine wine if the sommelier wasn't around, or shaving a truffle over some runny eggs. Shortly after, he joined Frank in Tori's suite, out of view of the camera. The screen was still blank and while they waited, he noticed that the maids had fluffed up the cushions since they were last here. In fact, they'd cleaned the entire room and the stuffiness was gone even though they'd closed all the windows. Axel sniffed, smelling the fresh roses a full moment before they caught his eye. When they did he almost swooned at the petals, the same deep orange as the smouldering hearts of the embers of oak he recalled from childhood winters in Nantucket.

He leant across and pulled one of the buds, first closing his eyes as he inhaled its bouquet. He broke off most of its stem and slipped it into his lapel, then glanced into the gilt-edged mirror, enjoying the effect of how his black linen suit set off the fiery orange.

21

TORI WAS ALREADY ON THE SOFA, but not cross-legged as this time she would be on camera. With Frank and Axel watching from the side, she patted down her hair and fiddled with the buttons on her blouse. She hadn't noticed before but the silk fabric was almost an identical shade of beige to the brocade on the sofa and an absurd image came to her of her head, on camera, seeming to hover in space. She grabbed the black cardigan that housekeeping had neatly folded over the back of the sofa and slipped it on, then reached across to the coffee table, picked up the Grande Bretagne notepad and tossed it over to the other side of the room. She didn't want anything to identify where she was. 'At a rich friend's', that was how she'd left it, and the furnishings easily gave that impression. She leant over to pick up the pair of FrensLens she'd also left on the table, and absent-mindedly started to flip them around by one of their arms, a little like Axel's bead habit though quieter. Axel coughed, and she looked up to see his loose features contorted into what she guessed was a gripe about harming the valuable item, so she stopped twirling them and popped them on.

The screen snapped to life with not even a tizz of static snow. The image was razor sharp. Those at Langley were in the same room as before and yes, it was the same group, just as she'd asked Dunn to arrange. While she didn't know the names of all of them, since her FrensLens had nothing to say about the Agency people apart from Concetta Pittorino from DS&T, there was Dunn as well as Alan Whitehead from the Department of Homeland Security, plus their sidekicks.

While the image was perfect the sound was non-existent. There was nothing, not even a crackle or a hiss and, as far as she could tell from the gesticulations at the other end, it was worse for them, which was obvious when Tori repeatedly waved her arms about saying, 'Hello, hello, can you hear me?' and got zero recognition.

As she waited for the connection to recalibrate and fix itself, Tori focused her Frenslens on Alan Whitehead, taking the time to find out if his credentials before his Homeland Security role were anywhere near as impressive as Pittorino's, or Pitbull as she was now privately calling her. There was something familiar about Whitehead, perhaps the way he carried his head, tilting it slightly to the side despite his ramrod back, but she assumed it was simply because she'd seen him before, during the videolink she'd taken from Axel's jet. The FrensLens was scrolling a stunning resume for Whitehead, a relief to Tori since it suggested he was the perfect guy to be working on this. He'd only held his current post for a year, as head of DHS's Office of Operations Command, but what he'd done before that wowed her:

While assigned to the Office of the Assistant Secretary for Global Strategic Affairs, Counter Weapons of Mass

Destruction, Dr Whitehead served as senior advisor providing policy oversight of the Department of Defense's Foreign Consequence Management program, and had responsibility for force development and force management policy for DoD's chemical, biological, radiological, and nuclear capabilities. In addition, when Dr Whitehead was stationed in ▓▓▓▓▓▓ ▓▓▓▓▓▓▓▓▓▓▓▓ ▓▓▓▓▓▓▓▓ ▓▓▓▓▓▓▓ ▓▓▓▓▓▓▓.*

That covered only the surface. The guy was a superhero. He'd even worked on operations to protect the President, the current one, and though Tori was no political junkie—if anything she was a political cynic—she was an unabashed admirer of President Diaz, instantly making her a fan of Whitehead's as well. What sort of background gets you into all that? she pondered, thinking back to her own and where that had got her—or rather, not got her.

The FrensLens reeled off that not only was Whitehead married but they were quite a power couple: his wife was the Global Head of Risk for EuropaNational, the global banking giant that, despite its name, was these days headquartered in New York City. Whitehead, born in North Carolina, earned his Bachelor of Science from Duke over twenty-five years ago, then got his Master of Public Administration from Wharton, and nine years ago he was awarded his Doctorate in Strategic Studies, after being sponsored into his PhD through a joint program of the US and Australian governments.

Suddenly, a sense of disquiet pinched the base of Tori's spine and started working its way up, pressing in tight over each of her vertebra, one by one.

---

* Dr Whitehead's role and the country where he performed it has been redacted by the CIA, despite this being publicly available information.

His doctorate was from the University of NSW in Sydney. Where Tori did hers. Where Mellor taught.

Whitehead got his doctorate there just over nine years ago. Almost ten.

There was a military man, she now recalled, in the Nine Sisters—an older guy. He'd joined not long before her. At her third meeting, her second last, he freaked everyone out when he showed up in his swanky dress uniform. He'd made an excuse that he'd come from some kind of ceremony and didn't have time to change into civvies and, after all the nervous jokes about him being a plant—initially half jokes—she remembered how dumb he looked when he sat on the floor with the rest of them, cross-legged and rifle-straight in his immaculately creased whites and gold braid epaulettes and his cap balanced on his knee.

It was coming back to her. Mellor had made some wisecrack pun about *White in whites* or *White-something in whites*. Yes, his name was definitely White related. Shit! It had to be the same guy. Alan Whitehead was W/whatever in the Nine Sisters. Wait. He was W/12; she remembered now that he'd joined not long before her.

'What's up?' whispered Frank as he watched her body go rigid. The video still wasn't working, but a quiet word was the cautious approach, especially with Pittorino now standing with her legs aggressively apart, one hand on the table, the other stabbing a finger toward the camera and her mouth so wide, screaming presumably, that even in Athens they could see she needed dental work. If Pittorino had anything to do with it, the connection was only moments away.

Tori didn't answer, but looked over toward Frank, a frozen look of terror on her face. 'Tori?' he pressed, stepping forward a little but Axel held him back.

'Whitehead. From DHS.' She pointed, almost in a daze. 'He was in the Nine Sisters. He was W/12.'

Axel blew out his breath so hard that his cheeks shook and his lips brrred. 'He can't be. He's a direct nominee of President Diaz.'

'And why's she beyond being conned after what happened with her own husband?' Tori asked.

'Or,' suggested Axel, 'you could be wildly wrong.'

She took off the pair of FrensLens and tossed them to him. 'See for yourself. Whitehead got his doctorate in Australia at the right time and the right place, and it triggered my memory. There *was* a military guy in the group with White in his name, like Whitehead or Whitely, something like that. And that guy did that same thing with his head that this Whitehead does, that cutesy incline to the side. It's him! It's definitely him. Christ, what the hell do I do? I can't risk telling them now, with him sitting there. It'll—'

'—give him a chance to cover up,' Frank said.

'Or give you credibility,' said Axel. 'If he was there, like you say, but he dropped out like you did, then he'd support your claims.'

The screen started to crackle, with intermittent sentence scraps coming through into the suite. Frank signalled to Tori to quickly get up and follow him and he led her and Axel into the bedroom where he shut the door behind them. 'There's another possible outcome,' he said.

'I know,' said Axel, rubbing his temple, his fingers pressing deeply into the fleshy hollow. With his beads safely in his pocket where they couldn't make a noise, his hands had to do something to help him think. 'If you're right about Whitehead, we'd be playing Russian roulette.' Tori breathed a deep sigh of relief when she noticed him say 'we' and not 'you'. She might not have Axel with her one hundred per cent, but he was still giving her the benefit of his doubt. He continued, 'If you say even a word about the Nine Sisters or about Mellor or Philips, you'd be … I don't want to be melodramatic, but you could be—'

'—signing my own death warrant?'

Axel nodded.

'Fuck! Oh sorry, I didn't mean to swea—'

'Right now, you're definitely allowed a fuck moment,' said Axel, and he placed his hand on her shoulder, though only for a second. He was not one for the touchy-feelies.

'You could tell Pittorino offline,' Frank suggested, but Axel instantly disagreed.

'Are you joking? Think about it. The word of an embittered nobody—sorry, Tori—who after being booted out of the CIA—'

'I resigned.'

'To them, they fired you. Anyway, the say-so of a vengeful nobody kicked out of the CIA who only months later tries to destroy the world's nuclear industry single-handedly, versus one of the most respected people in the current Administration, someone with a stellar career, a lifetime of civil service who has worked faithfully under three presidents from both sides of politics. No. We can't tell Pittorino either. We can't tell anybody. Not yet.'

'So when?' asked Tori, but Frank spoke over her, 'What about my mates at MI6?'

'My dear chap,' said Axel imitating his employee's syrupy British plum, 'from what I hear, they already think your head is ruled by a certain appendage of yours, so I don't think asking them to help your latest damsel in distress is a good idea.'

Tori spoke through the fingers she'd pressed to her face. 'What the hell am I going to do?'

'You pull the plug,' which is exactly what Axel proceeded to do, opening the bedroom door, edging over to the back of the screen so as not to be seen. He yanked the screen's power plug out of its wall socket and the line cable out of the secure satellite modem that Frank had brought from Boston. Given the political and market sensitivity of the Greek deal, Frank had brought a mini-armoury of communications devices with him so they could be both self-sufficient and secure.

'Damn technology,' Axel said, pulling a large black silk handkerchief out of his pocket and wiping his hands and mopping his brow. His handkerchiefs always matched his suit. 'All this gadgetry never works when you really need it.' He saw his colleagues were startled. 'What's wrong with you?' he said, refolding the cloth. 'The videolink hasn't worked so far for—what?—ten or fifteen minutes of trying, so they'll be none the wiser if it completely drops out, and it'll buy us time to work out our next moves.'

He also phoned the hotel operator. '*Milás Angliká?* ... You do speak English? Excellent. Listen, we are now going to sleep, so please put a "do not disturb" on this phone. No matter how important anyone says their call is, take a message but don't put them through. Yes? Thank you. *Efharistó.*'

'They don't know I'm staying here,' said Tori. 'Dunn asked me where I was before and I fudged it.'

'They could have tracked your cell again.'

As if on cue, Tori's phone rang with the caller ID showing Martin Davidson, her old boss, but before she could answer it Frank grabbed it from her and seeing it was a phone where you couldn't remove the battery, he quickly switched it to airplane mode, and then turned it off completely. 'Like Axel said, damn technology.' He opened his briefcase and Tori saw three phones he'd slipped into the pockets before they left Boston. 'Here, this is one of my burners, untraceable. It's now yours.' He took it out and tossed it to her.

22

'**M**ELLOR IS INDEED THE KEY TO this,' agreed Axel. 'So, yes, you need to get to his daughter in Venice.' He was making some calculations on the small computer he had pulled out from inside his capacious jacket. SISers often joked how Axel's tailor must have a sideline making bespoke magician's costumes, and that one day their boss would pull out a rabbit instead of the endless paraphernalia he habitually seemed to transfer from suit to suit. Axel never carried a briefcase; perhaps because he used his suits, and his employees, as substitutes. 'Tori, if you want to take my jet to Venice, it's yours. It's just sitting here doing nothing in Athens anyway. It'll take around … wait a minute … yes, flying time here to Venice is around two hours, give or take. I suggest you leave tonight, before your, ah, Langley friends work out exactly where in Athens you are, if they haven't already. That reminds me—'

He put his computer on the table and took out his cell phone. 'Markos, *yia sou*! A little favour my old friend. You know we've booked our suites at your wonderful hotel under the name ... what was it, Francis? Yes, Angelo Benedetti, that's it. Given the sensitivity of the, ah, matter we are all working on, can you make sure the hotel's lips are completely sealed? It would be ruinous for our deal ... Why do I ask? Some pesky journalists might have picked up a rumour. You know, they'll call the hotel and pretend to be some official or other wanting to know more ... Exactly ... Excellent. By the way, my chalet in Val d'Isère? There's a few weeks free this winter if you'd like to take your wife and children again ... Of, course. Think nothing of it. My kisses to Antheia.'

Tori wondered why Axel would be so revealing or accommodating to a hotel employee until he turned back and, reaching inside his jacket to place his phone there, explained it. 'Markos is an old, dear friend. As well as the senior partner of the Greek law firm working with the PM on this—and several deals with us in the past—he's also chairman of the company that owns this hotel. He'll make sure that even if they did track your phone here they'll get nothing from the hotel staff. But back to Venice ... you should overnight there. In my usual suite at the Cip, of course.'

He looked up, his eyes beaming. It wasn't his favourite hotel in the world—that was on an island he owned, through a non-traceable trust of course—but the Hotel Cipriani came close. 'That way you could get a push on this and visit the professor's daughter first thing in the morning.'

He sensed a reluctance from Tori to accept his generosity but, to Axel, it wasn't a kindness, merely a business decision. The sooner he knew one way or the other about her, the better and the safer it would be for SIS. 'Flying commercial from Athens is a bad idea; there's nothing direct. The quickest is via Rome,' he said picking up his tablet computer again, 'and the next one doesn't leave till … yes, 6.55 am tomorrow, and it's four and a half hours with the Rome layover … so you'd get to Venice at 10.30 am allowing for the hour's time difference.'

'An hour's difference? A decade, more likely,' Frank chuckled.

'But which way?' said Tori, now breaking into a laugh herself, though a nervous one. They only had one lead, one possible step forward, but she knew—they all knew—it could easily take them nowhere. Mellor's daughter might not have a clue where her eccentric and difficult father was. It wasn't beyond the pale that she could be estranged from him, given how difficult Tori knew him to be. Even if his daughter was in touch with him, she might still refuse to speak to them. Anything was possible.

Axel was heading to the door. 'By the way, if you do fly to Venice, Francis should go too, to be a help and such.'

And to report back, no doubt, Tori decided.

'You don't mind, Francis?' Axel added almost as an afterthought, not expecting an answer.

Frank and Tori spoke over each other.

'But the Greek deal?'

'The meetings tomorrow?'

Axel waved them both off. 'We're not seeing the PM again until noon and you said Henry and the other SISers are getting into Athens at six, so there's plenty of time, especially if I chat to them while they're in the air tonight. So don't worry about it. Your little deal is safe with me. I have done one or two big ones myself, you know.' He left the suite before they could argue any more.

Tori and Frank spent ten minutes on the sofa tossing around the cover story for speaking to Mellor's daughter tonight, assuming they managed to get through to her, but when the door buzzed the pair instantly stiffened and looked sideways at each other. Axel? Housekeeping? Someone sent by the CIA or, worse, Whitehead?

They heard the door unlock and just as it started to open, Tori back-flipped over the top of the sofa onto the floor behind, crouching low and unseen, and Frank rose to his feet ready to confront or at least divert the intruder. He almost laughed, but suppressed it as a cough, when he saw it was only the butler from Axel's Presidential Suite bringing the coffees and pastries their gracious boss had apparently decided they needed.

Embarrassed, Tori stood up, talking loudly about how she'd dropped her earring back there, but the aged butler merely nodded as he set down the tray and turned, leaving what he thought were two young lovers alone.

Seeing the cakes, Tori realised she hadn't eaten anything all day apart from nuts and snacks from the minibar, so she sat back down and devoured two of the baklava and one of the kataife almost without speaking, a better way, she decided, to get a sugar hit than extra lumps in her coffee. As she took bite after bite, the honey syrup drizzling down her fingers, she let Frank do most of the talking and note-taking and she mainly grunted and jabbed approval. She licked her fingers for the final time and drained the last of her coffee.

The two of them went over the script top to tail and when they were satisfied, Frank placed the notes in front of him and, using the burner phone, dialled the Guggenheim. His handwriting, even though he'd written it in block letters, wasn't as clear to read as he would have liked, not after Tori's finger-pointing had splattered it with translucent rings, making the ink run a little.

It was close to six pm in Venice, but the museum operator was still answering. As Frank started speaking in his perfect

Italian, Tori suddenly leant over, ripped the phone away from him and stabbed her finger on the 'end call' button.

He looked at the phone in her hand, then at her. 'Why the hell did you—?'

'What were we thinking?' she said. 'We can't speak to her by phone.'

'But I told you it's a burner, non-traceable, and I wasn't going to mention your name. We agreed on that, so why—?'

'We should have seen it before. We were in too much of a panic, I suppose, but—'

Just at that moment, Axel burst through the door, or at least his butler used his master key again and burst it open for him.

'Don't phone that woman!' Axel shouted. His face was red and sweating, his eyes bulging and his chest heaving. He had tried to phone through but the operator had politely but firmly refused, explaining there was a do not disturb request on Tori's room and that it would be worth more than her job to disobey it.

'What's with the two of you?' said Frank, throwing his hands in the air and looking as muddled as his parents' native Punjab when the British Raj decided to partition the province right across its middle. But suddenly he slapped his forehead. 'Oh, hell. I get it. If she tells Mellor someone's asking after him, at the very moment he's picked as ripe for his group's actions—'

'—he'll vanish,' said Tori and Axel simultaneously.

The safest course, they all agreed, was for Tori and Frank to confront Mellor's daughter face-to-face and unannounced.

23

AXEL'S USUAL SUITE AT THE CIPRIANI was already occupied. When he phoned Gigi, the hotel's general manager on his direct line, it seemed to Tori there was no one her boss didn't know personally but, despite Axel's cajoling, even Gigi wouldn't contemplate downgrading a certain Texan oil man and his, shall we say, young niece merely to squeeze in a couple of Axel's closest friends on their 'honeymoon jaunt' through Europe.

In truth, Tori and Frank were relieved. They weren't going to have time to revel in the little luxuries that Axel had been rattling off to them one after the other, like the Jacuzzi spa in the suite's private garden and the exclusive use of a *motoscafo* that not only would pick them up at Marco Polo airport but zoom them and their bags across the lagoon and, thirty minutes later, discreetly drop them at their own dock at the end of their garden. For their needs, a plain vanilla water taxi would be plenty and, if they had time and if the early November weather permitted, the hotel pool—heated and half-Olympic-size—would be fine, too.

Axel winked cheekily as he gave their names to Gigi: Mr and Mrs Francis Chaudry. Despite that, he tried for a two-bedroom suite but even in these last days before the hotel's mid-November shutdown for winter, all the two-bedders were also booked. Of what was left, when Tori hesitantly put up her hand for the poolside junior suite which, at $2,500 per night would not exactly be slumming, Axel noticed the crinkle of concern in her eyes. The expenses were mounting.

Tori had scored a decent payout from the CIA—one of the many things about her that continued to gall Martin Davidson—but she knew even that tidy bundle wasn't going to last long if she started spending it at this rate—on ritzy hotels, jets and whatever expenses she and Frank would need to clock up—and while her pay at SIS was stellar if she took into account her potential bonus, she hadn't actually earned one yet, plus there was the added impediment that only this morning Axel had retrospectively disemployed her.

'Tori, don't worry about the costs,' said Axel. 'The jet's on me. What's a bit of fuel between friends? And consider the rest a credit against your bonus for the Greek deal, assuming,' he laughed, 'that I don't screw it up for you, and that you clear all this up so we can hire you back again.'

'And if you do, or you can't?' she asked.

Axel suddenly seemed preoccupied with a loose thread on his shoulder and spent an age trying to pick it off.

IN TORI'S LAST minutes at the Agency, Martin Davidson smugly held out his hand to take back the various fake passports he had authorised during her six-year stint, documents 'from' ~~Cambodia, Belarus, Guatemala, Iceland Myanmar~~ and ~~Rwanda~~ *

'As a civilian, Swyft,' he'd said, 'you'll just have to manage on your legit US passport and, if you really have to, your one from Down Under. Given the facts, you're damn lucky Uncle Sam hasn't grabbed his back, and you can be sure as shootin' I suggested he do just that.'

For Tori, travelling incognito had become an addictive freedom and, when it started looking likely that she and the CIA would be parting company, she splashed out on a few spare identity documents from a dealer she'd met and used several times when she was stationed in Havana, Cuba. Now, with the significant chance that the nuclear plant debacle would leak into the media before it got fixed, and the risk that Davidson would have leapt forward to spearhead the search for her personally, she took the precaution when leaving Athens of using her Russian passport and, on arriving in Venice, of using her French one. The fact she was Josette Duchamps and not Mrs Francis Chaudry when Gigi himself checked them in at the Cipriani didn't even raise an eyebrow, nor did the couple's lack of wedding rings.

Frank had been quietly tickled by Tori's first passport switch so, as soon as they boarded Axel's plane and the steward disappeared into the galley to collect some snacks, he flicked open a hidden compartment in his briefcase and pulled out his own array of identity papers, spreading them before her like playing cards. 'I see you, and raise you,' he joked.

'Yeah, but who's looking for you?' Tori said. 'Victoria Swyft, on the other hand, is probably not the ideal name for me to be using right now. Have a look,' and she handed him the burner

---

* The CIA has redacted the names of the countries for which Tori Swyft held Agency-issued passports.

smartphone she'd been using and he read the news report she'd just found.

(REUTERS) WASHINGTON, DC: WED. 12.20 pm EST
US NUCLEAR ALERT

Many of the nation's nuclear plants are under threat of imminent shutdown due to a recently discovered bug in standard control systems, according to sources close to the Nuclear Regulatory Commission.

'Even though we hear it's a minor fault,' said Magda Black, from advocacy group *Nukes Aren't Us*, 'plants could become dangerously unstable if it remains uncorrected.' The flaw is claimed to be inside a mathematical algorithm approved by the NRC and used in at least one third of US nuclear plants.

The algorithm, once considered groundbreaking, was developed by an Australian scientist, Dr Victoria Swyft, who worked until recently for the State Department. Neither the State Department nor Dr Swyft have been available …

AT ONE AM Tori finally locked the hotel room door behind them, and she fell back on the king bed exhausted, with Frank likewise but taking the couch. The pair hadn't slept a wink on the plane, and though they'd contemplated getting stuck into Axel's scotch and the steward had fussed over an elaborate menu, they'd settled on cheese and biscuits and, over endless glasses of mineral water, spent an hour reframing their line of attack with Mellor's daughter. Once they'd landed on one, Frank cracked his knuckles ready for some hacking. 'Just like the good old days,' he said, his eyes smiling even more than his mouth.

To find Mellor's latest whereabouts, he tried getting into the employee records at the University of NSW, but their security was tighter than his jeans and he gave up, at least for now. He knew he could crack it eventually; he'd infiltrated NASA, twice for goodness' sake, and even the US Department of Defence, joyously making them think he was a Chinese hacker. So no tin pot university at the other end of the world was going to stop him—but there wasn't time to keep trying, especially since the plane's satellite connection kept dropping out, despite the money Axel had pumped into his communications system.

The Peggy Guggenheim museum in Venice was another story and he broke into their records after a mere ten minutes, digging out Dr Emilio-Mellor's current home address, her original employment application and assorted bits and pieces about her. She'd been working at the museum for eight years, and six years before that had a stint at the Museum of Modern Art in New York. 'She married an Italian just before she applied … yes, Emilio is her husband's surname. Sorry, he *was* her husband. They divorced two years ago.'

'I can read the screen too, you know.'

The best news was that Dr Emilio-Mellor's apartment happened to be on La Giudecca Island and, according to Google Maps, it was only over one bridge and a few minutes' stroll from the Cipriani Hotel.

THE GUGGENHEIM'S DAILY opening time was ten so, wanting to find Dr Emilio-Mellor at home, they arrived at her building, a deep terracotta-red five-storey block on Calle del l'Albero, at eight am.

'You didn't need the scarf.' Frank laughed as they lurked in the shadows of a rust-coloured building opposite. 'Your hair would have blended right in.'

'Maybe, but given how chilly it is compared to Athens, I'm glad I got it.' Both were in jeans and sweatshirts but Tori had covered her head with a black scarf she'd bought at the hotel boutique, which Gigi had arranged to be opened up early for her. Apart from wanting the warmth, she wasn't keen to stand out, hanging around down in the street while Frank was busy telling his well-crafted lies upstairs.

As he crossed the narrow street and went through the garden to the front door, Tori leant back against the building opposite mock-reading the Italian-language newspaper they'd also picked up at the hotel. For Frank, deactivating the buzzer entry was swifter work than he'd planned since it was broken, so he simply pushed the front door open and took the stairs two at a time to the third floor, taking care not to ruffle the lavish bouquet of red rose buds he was hoping would disarm Dr Emilio-Mellor's suspicions when an unexpected tall dark stranger turned up at her door. The hotel, Tori had told him when she removed the flowers from one of the vases in their suite, wouldn't mind. It was better than stealing bathrobes.

They'd cobbled together a story that Frank was trying to locate his own father, a tale they hoped would resonate with Mellor's daughter.

Standing at her door, he told her how he'd lost touch with his father years ago, after he remarried. His father's new wife was a Venetian woman he'd met in London and they both moved here, leaving Frank, still hurting from his mother's suicide a year earlier, to fend for himself on his scholarship to Oxford.

Oxford was the only truth in his story. Frank told her that after the marriage, he and his dad had become estranged but now, with kids of his own—and pointing into the crack in the door a wallet photo he'd got off the internet and printed at the hotel— he explained how keen he was for his kids to get to know their grandad, and vice-versa. He'd had an address—Dr Emilio-Mellor's—but his father had never once replied to his letters so he'd flown here to find him. He knew, he said, that turning up like this was an incredible intrusion, for which he apologised but, with a tear welling in his eye, he explained it was his last desperate hope for tracking down his father. For his kids.

Unsure of what did the trick with Mellor's daughter—the bunch of roses, his hangdog expression as he told his emotional fable, or his deep, buttery voice that today he slurped with an extra helping of smooth Italian mocha—Frank mentally punched the air when she unlatched her door chain and held it open for him to enter.

It was obvious from her accent that she was not a native, but she wasn't offended when he pretended to guess she was Australian and offered to speak in English. However, she preferred the language of her adopted country, she told him. The truth was that the light cadences of the dark-skinned Londoner's accent, as perfect as any newsreader from a Roman radio station, reminded her of her former husband and, surprisingly, she told him as much. Despite Frank being taller and darker than Silvio—she pointed to a wedding photo on a table near the door—there was something about Frank, not just his caramelly voice or his poise, that made her flutter when he spoke. Or perhaps, he wondered, it was her loneliness, living with someone who wasn't there. Frank didn't know how close he was to the truth.

The L-shaped room was an ordered, utilitarian space with nothing out of place, in fact very little to put in place, not quite spartan but certainly austere, and the almost sickening reek of tobacco that was thick in the air only added to the weight of a sadness he sensed hanging there. Outside, a cloud passed and the breaking sun flashed a glint on the plate of cakes on the table by the window. 'I'm sorry,' he said, noticing the setting. 'I've interrupted your breakfast.'

'Please,' she indicated, suggesting he take one of the six high-backed chairs he suspected were rarely used, except by her. 'I could use the company,' she said, her inflection hopeful though without the confidence to be insistent. 'Espresso?'

'Perfetto.'

It wasn't a small room; it only felt and smelt oppressive. In the other arm of the L was a heavy three-seater sofa and two matching armchairs, their weary velour seat cushions once a chirpy orange but now sagging from years of conversations that had long ago exhausted themselves. The two rugs sprawled over the limestone floor tiles were oriental in style, but the brilliance of the reds and whites was no more either. The brown and beige striped wallpaper was the only wall covering, the room devoid of photographs, apart from the one near the door. There was no art either which, at first, Frank found odd in the home of an art historian, so he wondered if perhaps she kept her home as a refuge from work, her private space where work never intruded. It was, to Frank, an odd approach since he imagined someone steeped in the art world would hardly consider it a chore and would prefer to be always bathed in art, enveloped by it, reminded of it. As he took in the blank walls, he tried to put himself in her shoes, thinking how he'd feel working day in and day out among paintings by Picasso and Chagall and Kandinsky, and sculptures by Moore and Calder and Arps, and suddenly the idea came to him that maybe the empty walls and bare mantelpieces were an artistic statement themselves, like that piano piece by composer John Cage he once forced himself to sit through in the Albert Hall, three movements performed without a single note being played. Maybe her apartment was her solace. An oasis of calm. Or was it, he wondered, a symptom of a woman throwing up her hands in depressed resignation, a sign that on her mundane paypacket nothing could be gratifying compared to what surrounded her at work?

After she brewed his coffee and as he continued to embellish his story, she took his flowers and arranged them in a striking rectangular glass vase that she brought out from the kitchen. It was out of place here, though its strident red, yellow and blue sides reminded Frank of something but he couldn't think what.

She noticed his quizzical look and interrupted his story. 'I work at the Peggy Guggenheim Collection. Do you know it?' He said he'd heard of it but had never been there. 'The vase is from the shop there. It's a tribute to Piet Mondrian, a Dutch painter,' she said, setting it on the sill overlooking the street. She opened the window and noticed an unfamiliar woman in a black headscarf down below and on the opposite side of the street, speculating to herself that the poor soul was probably mourning a lost parent or a lover. Or maybe she was one of the new Muslim families, so not mourning at all. Why the woman was reading her paper in the shade when she could sit in the morning sun on a stoop opposite flashed into her mind, but Frank continued to unfold the rest of his story and as his rich, resonant voice melted her question away, she joined him at the table without noticing a thin cord that dangled from the woman's ear and snaked its way into her jeans pocket.

For Frank, the light cool breeze brushing over the roses he'd brought was a welcome respite from the stink of old furniture and stale tobacco, which even the rich aroma of the fresh coffee had done little to mask.

'Fathers can make life very tough. Take my own,' she laughed, a little too nervously, passing him the plate of pastries that her Rembrandt figure and her flabby arm suggested was a regular highlight of her mornings. 'A brilliant, brilliant man and,' she sighed, taking a cake herself and shaking off the crumbs to join those already scattered on her plate, 'an extremely difficult and complex one. But sadly that was long ago.' She tapped the cake with her index finger and took a bite.

'He's dead?' Frank said, hoping she hadn't heard the dread in his voice.

She chewed methodically then swallowed, and took a sip of her coffee to wash it down. 'Oh, no,' she said slowly and purposefully, her eyes seeming to look over his shoulder. 'Nothing is ever quite so simple with my father.' Her expression was wistful, as if she were looking at an old family photograph that wasn't there but which still brought back painful memories of a lost childhood. 'For a dazzling mind, like his, dementia is a far worse fate.'

'For the family too, I venture,' Frank said, realising it wasn't the past she'd been contemplating, but her present.

'These days he's an empty shell. Gets out of bed, goes into his office and sits there all day. Hardly speaks. Occasionally calls out for my mother. Never mentions me … never even recognises me. It's like I don't exist. Maybe for this version of him I have never existed. It's very … hard, let me tell you.' Her chin quivered ever so slightly and as her hands moved under the table, Frank noticed her jaw tighten in an attempt at self-control. He could almost feel her hands, unseen, rubbing her legs, squeezing out her tension. She looked at him and blinked, as if seeing him for the first time. 'I rarely exist for him any more, but he babbles on about his sisters. But the thing is … he never had any sisters! He calls out for *them*, but never, never for me.'

Frank, trying to stay calm, nonchalant, passed her his napkin and she wiped her eye. 'Sisters?' he said.

'It's strange.' She rose from the table and left the room for the kitchen again and this time Frank leant over to peek past her down the corridor, guessing from the number of doors he thought he saw in the darkness that this was a three-bedroom apartment. A moment later she was back with a tissue and blew her nose. 'Out of the blue, he'll start ranting about his make-believe sisters. And then he'll start waffling on in mathematical formulas. M this, W that. All letters and numbers, like highways—A4, M6, that sort of thing. I have absolutely no idea what he's prattling on about, but then I never did. What would an art historian know about physics and mathematics except their physical representation? I've always wondered if all that came from something he was working on, a project.

'So many times,' she added, 'I've been tempted to sift through his papers, you know, to see if I can find something, anything, to help me draw a real conversation out of him, but frankly I wouldn't know what I was looking at even if it was staring me in the face. I'm sorry … I'm going on a bit, and to a total stranger, too, yet you really are such a comf—'

'No, really,' said Frank, placing his hand on hers across the table, and lightly squeezing it. 'Sometimes it's easier to talk to someone you don't know, to get things off your chest.' He felt a little guilty when she drew a quick breath. It had been quite a while since manipulating emotions was his day job, standard fare at MI6.

She took a napkin to her eye and dabbed it again. 'You know, my husband and I decorated a room for Dad so it would look like his office—one of the doctors had suggested it—and we set him up in it with all the old papers and books the university had boxed up for me. We were hoping it might prompt some memories out of him or even just a bit of his old spark. At the beginning, it helped a little but lately it's been downhill and, frankly, now I think it's a complete waste of time.'

'His papers,' said Frank and, to mask his excitement, he pretended to take a sip from his cup, careful to avoid the bitter black sludge lurking at the base. He looked up. 'So where is he? Still in Australia?'

'I wish!' she said, a blush suddenly colouring her face, but she quickly added, 'I shouldn't have said that. No, he's in there.' She pointed toward the closed doors down the corridor. 'With my mother gone years ago, I'm all he's got left. I am his whole family now. Apart from his stupid made-up sisters. I just don't get that. Who'd invent a family?'

Frank would have loved to tell her, to make her feel better about herself, but he simply raised an eyebrow and shook his head, as if in sympathy.

'Three years ago,' she continued, 'when his university wouldn't put up with him any more, my husband and I brought him here from Australia. My job pays well enough and so did Silvio's, but not so well that we could afford one of those care homes back in Sydney, or here either. My friends told me how they're an endless sinkhole for money but, frankly, I wish I'd ignored them and found the cash, even borrowed it; I might still be married. The three of us, in this apartment ... it was a debacle. Anyway, that's another story. So, Dad's got his bedroom and now his office.'

'My neighbour in London?' said Frank. 'She has her mother living with her. Alzheimer's,' he shook his head again. 'But there's an aunt who comes in during the day while she's at work. How do you cope, with being at the museum? How does he handle you not being here?'

'I've got my angel,' she said, pointing up to the ceiling.

'An angel?' he said, pushing his chair back a little.

'Not a real one,' she laughed weakly. It was an embarrassed laugh. 'It's Signora della Scalla. She's one floor up and pops in to check on him for me. I can't even get back for lunch since I'm always stuck at the museum giving lunchtime lectures.'

'So he gets a routine. I gather that's very important.'

'Routine? Oh yes! My father has always had people running around for him, doing what he wants, when he wants … I'm sorry. I shouldn't have said—'

'It's fine, truly.'

'Thank you,' she sniffed. 'She's a gem, you know. Signora della Scalla, I mean. Every day, I give him breakfast at seven, then bathe him. He usually goes back to bed, but sometimes he sits in his office while I have my own breakfast, alone in peace. That's where he is now, in his office, smoking his damn cigarettes. I'm sure you can smell them. Why am I telling you all this? You seem so … It's hard for me, you know. I get on the *vaporetto* every morning to go across the lagoon to work and the other passengers avoid sitting next to me because my clothes reek, just from being here. And the cost, Mother of God! He has no idea how expensive cigarettes are these days. He's such a chain smoker he lights his next cigarette with his last, and look at those burn holes in my rug!'

'Well, your neighbour must be a blessing,' he said, trying to redirect the conversation back to their daily routines.

'Oh yes. An angel, like I said. I make his lunch before I leave for work, but she feeds it to him and takes him to the bathroom—all that. She comes in from noon to two, every day except weekends, and puts him to bed before she leaves. He usually sleeps till I get home. Frankly, I don't know what I'd do without her.'

You'd probably have a life, thought Tori as she listened in on her earpiece.

AS DR EMILIO-MELLOR said goodbye and closed her door on him, Frank's face hung low, despondent, using his genuine sympathy for her plight to evoke the frustration he would have naturally felt when this turned out to be a dead-end for finding his own 'father'. He reached the staircase and said aloud, 'Coming down,' not that he needed to and, before descending, extracted his phone from his top pocket and switched it off.

In the street, Tori removed her earpiece, folded her newspaper and immediately began strolling to the corner. Frank would catch up with her, but in case Mellor's daughter was looking out her window they didn't want her to see them together. While walking, Tori checked her watch and, yes, there was an age before Emilio-Mellor would be leaving to catch her ferry. They'd bet on her being a regular on the 9.28 am Linea 2 *vaporetto* from the nearby wharf at Redentore. Before they left the hotel, they'd checked the online timetable for Actv, the local ferry company, and calculated that the art historian's two-stop ride would take her six minutes to cross the Giudecca canal to the Zattere stop and then, according to Google Maps, she'd have a brisk nine-minute walk across the Dorsoduro district to the museum, with a spare quarter hour before opening time. With the museum closing its doors at six in the evenings, she was unlikely to be back home before 6.30 pm, which at this time of year would be well after dark. So, Tori thought, with Signora della Scala coming in from twelve to two and Mellor having a nap afterwards, 2.30 pm seemed to be the perfect time for a surprise visit. She assumed Frank would think the same.

BACK IN THEIR room, they found a message to phone Axel. Other people would have left the message on one of their mobiles, but Axel was not other people. They'd intended to call him anyway, to check on how he was faring with the new deal team.

He mentioned to them, almost in passing, that US Embassy people had visited the Grande Bretagne while he and Henry Harvey were off with the PM but that his friend, Markos, had done a good job; not one of the hotel staff had even blinked at recognition when shown a photograph of Tori across the counter.

Axel kept that part of their conversation out of earshot of the new SIS arrivals. They did know about the 'nuclear problem' as Axel had taken to describing it, but not that Tori and Frank were in Venice, or why. Axel had decided that the fewer people aware of Tori's whereabouts the better, since what was at risk was not mere information but the safety of two of his best employees. So despite being uncomfortable about misleading Henry, he asked Tori and Frank to pretend they were on the jet heading back to the US.

They spent the next hour on the phone with Axel and the others bouncing around a neat tax twist that Henry had dreamt up to sweeten the deal for Greece without costing Soti Skylakakis a cent. It was such a good idea and seemed so obvious that Tori wondered how she and Frank had missed it. Unlike her experience at the CIA when someone came up with a new idea, Henry wasn't crowing about it. It was just his expected contribution, to prove he was no free-rider coming in on Tori's slipstream. It was another example for Tori of how Axel seemed to attract quality acts, something she had been looking pretty close to, she reminded herself, until she unwittingly brought scandal to SIS's door.

Despite the messiness of avoiding a videocall with Langley before leaving Athens, she'd done it knowing that the NRC could easily work on it without her, bringing together whatever tools they needed to repair her model and avert a nuclear shutdown. She'd told Judith Dunn virtually everything she could anyway, and Dunn was a very capable woman. Even so, not taking the call, let alone vanishing, didn't look good. But the truth was that apart from revealing her suspicions about Alan Whitehead, she could do nothing more to help them and, as she'd teased out with Axel and Frank several times, it was way too risky lighting the Whitehead fuse without incontrovertible evidence, precisely what she was hoping to get out of Mellor.

Now the morning clouds had cleared, she looked out through their terrace doors and private garden to the glistening hotel pool. With time to kill until after two o'clock, Tori and Frank took turns using the bathroom to change into their swimwear then raced each other outside to take a plunge. They'd expected the water to be even more bracing than the ambient air but kept at 29 degrees all year round, as the sign said, it was like diving under a cosy blanket.

The pair raced each other freestyle for lap honours and after Tori had won, three times and by several body lengths, they left the thirty-two-metre pool and dripped their way over to the two sun lounges reserved for them on the terrace outside their suite's garden. The sun had taken the nip off the air and, to the other guests and staff, they behaved exactly like the married couple they were supposed to be, in other words, barely talking between the catnaps and the non-alcoholic margaritas. They would have liked to try Bellinis, the hotel's signature drink but, with the tasks ahead of them, alcohol was out of the question.

Throwing a glance sideways at Frank, Tori had to admit that semi-naked he didn't look half bad either. Her reaction gave her mixed feelings since, with him working for her, she needed their relationship to stay professional. She was going to keep it that way too, she told herself—not like with Soti—even despite becoming more and more uncomfortably partial to how Frank's chest hair slithered its way down his taut abdomen and roped its way into his board shorts.

She took a deep breath and closed her eyes, fully aware that it wasn't only the salt around the rim of her margarita glass that was making her salivate.

24

PICKING A LOCK WAS A HANDY yet simple
tradecraft skill that both Tori and Frank had collected in
their separate days in the field, so en route to Dr Emilio-
Mellor's apartment they tossed for who would take today's
honour. It wasn't an actual coin toss but an app Tori had found
on the burner phone while they had been sunning themselves
around the pool, and she made the flip while they talked to each
other through their earpieces, with Frank trailing her by around
fifty metres. As she turned into Calle del l'Albero ahead of him,
this time wearing a russet-coloured scarf in case anyone had
noticed her before, Frank called heads.

'You've rigged it,' she laughed. 'The pool's my domain, but
the flip of a coin is yours.'

However, it wasn't much of a victory since, at the top of the
stairs as she waited for him, the shank of a key blinked up at her
from under the doormat, reflecting what little light there was
in the corridor. As she bent to pick it up, courtesy of Signora

della Scalla she presumed, an unpleasant yet familiar whiff of cigarettes crept out from under the door. It smelled of burnt popcorn and, to Tori, it was like Proust's madeleines again, the smell instantly taking her mind back to Mellor's office in Sydney, recalling the day he lied to her about the 'sham' psych experiment.

She peered through the darkness to check she wasn't being observed then took the key and unlocked the door, edging it open and thankful that it didn't creak. The light bursting into the corridor from inside was as intense as the tobacco smell that swamped her—now strong and astringent. Tori, her eyes wincing and stinging, held her breath and stepped in. The apartment was exactly as Frank had described it. Though the windows were closed, the shutters were open and the afternoon sun drenched and heated the room, exacerbating the foul odour. Remembering how Mellor hardly ever took a step without a roll-your-own stuck to his lip and threads of smoke curling into his and everyone else's eyes, she guessed he must have had quite a few of his cigarettes before he'd gone back to bed.

The lunch dishes were draining on the kitchen sink, a tea towel bone dry to her touch hanging pointlessly off a thin rail. The only sound she could hear was the occasional drip of the tap and Frank, she assumed, padding up the stairs.

He closed the door behind him and whispered, 'I thought I won the toss?'

'You did.' But she held up the key before placing it near the door where they'd see it on their way out. She didn't replace it under the mat outside in case Signora della Scalla got a whim to pop back while they were still inside. It was better to have her worrying she'd misplaced it than take the risk of her discovering them.

Dr Emilio-Mellor's budget extended to cigarettes but not to laying carpet runners down the corridor, so they removed their shoes and Tori stood behind Frank to place both pairs inside his backpack. 'Done,' she said as she zipped it closed.

As they progressed down the passageway, the reek got worse and Tori tapped Frank on the shoulder just clear of his bag strap, her eyes watering and her face twisted. He shrugged an I-told-you-so then pointed to the scattered lines of dropped cigarette ash on the floor and, stepping over them, slowly inched open the first door after the kitchen.

With its shutters closed, the room they guessed was Dr Emilio-Mellor's bedroom was in darkness and, rather than switch on the light, Tori flicked on a torch app on her phone to reveal a room that was ascetic even compared to the living room. The three pieces of furniture stood separately, unfriendly and alone: a narrow one-door wardrobe, the craze of cracks in its veneer—possibly rosewood—giving Tori the impression of a painting she once saw of dried-up creeks in the Pilbara; a two-drawer maple dresser topped with two combs, a hand mirror and a hairbrush so completely devoid of any strands of hair she wondered if it was ever used; and a lumpy-looking barely double bed with a red chintz spread, positioned directly below a framed print of the Sacred Heart of Jesus, His head temporarily bathed in the divine light illuminated by Tori's torch.

Frank carefully opened the room next door and the strong, sour pong of smoke and age that billowed out onto them was almost sickening. The curtain and shutters were open, but again not the windows, and Tori could see from the butts overflowing from the ashtray onto the floor that Mellor no longer smoked rollies. In this room, there was no holy picture, though she would have been surprised if there had been since Mellor ranted against religion almost as much as he did about growth. The bed was a single and emerging from under the sickly greenish-yellow bedspread was the back of a man's head, mostly bald but a few of the scabs were open and weeping. 'Perhaps Signora della Scala isn't quite the angel that the daughter says,' Tori whispered.

Frank closed the door as silently as he'd opened it, and the pair moved onto the last room, the one before the bathroom. It was also bright and stinking of cigarettes and, to Tori, it did have the look of Mellor's old office. Pushed up against one wall, under a large framed photograph of an empty stretch of highway, sat two grey steel filing cabinets similar to those she remembered pressing her back up against when she was arguing with him back at the university. The desk was a little smaller than his old one but, even so, it was covered with the familiar tottering piles of papers with a small clearing for his computer. Two walls were taken up by bookshelves, stacked from floor to ceiling with volumes of all thicknesses and colours, and with every available nook stuffed with even more academic papers.

But there was something different. It was the dust. There was no hive of active genius buzzing here, no feverish pace of discovery or debate. It was a relic, perhaps a tomb. At best an homage. For the first time, Tori thought she understood why a still life was also called a *nature morte*.

The framed photograph above the filing cabinets echoed the sense of decay in the room, the hollowing out of a once frenetic life full of passions about things that mattered. It was a shot taken across the grey expanse of an empty highway in the middle of nowhere, and was absent any signs of life. No trucks laden with cattle or fresh oranges whizzing by on their way to market, not even any evidence of them. No papers being scattered by the wind, no skid marks or tyre ruts, just thick rivers of sun cracks carving through the blacktop and breaking up the painted lines, just as they would continue to do for hundreds more miles.

Tori and Frank had no idea where to find what they were looking for, nor indeed what they were looking for, but they split up the room between them, Tori taking the filing cabinets and Frank the desk including Mellor's computer. They decided they'd scurry through the bookshelves last if they had time, and if not, tomorrow was always a possibility though an undesirable one, even if it meant they'd get in a night at the Cipriani and they'd actually sleep for eight hours. Time was short.

'THANK GOD FOR dementia,' said Tori to Frank's astonishment after their first hour inside Mellor's office. 'Here, read this,' and she passed him a legal-looking document entitled 'Last Will and Testament', and pointed to the relevant clause:

> I direct my daughter, Alison Mellor, who is executor and trustee of my Will, immediately on my death to destroy without exception all my personal and academic papers, files, computers, disks and my effects in whatever form, including my artwork ('My Work'). I note that I have also left a Living Will where my said executor and trustee is instructed to do likewise on my sixty-sixth (66th) birthday if I am alive on that date yet, due to my mental or physical incapacity, I am unable to destroy My Work myself at that time or ask for it to be done.

'Hang on,' said Frank, sitting at Mellor's computer, his bag at his feet, laboriously searching through the data files looking for anything relevant. He tried to access the internet but there was no connection. Dr Emilio-Mellor hadn't gone quite as far as getting an internet connection when replicating her father's office. They guessed she must do all her searching and emailing on her phone or at work, so Frank drew out his own phone, visited Wikipedia and found Mellor's bio. 'He had his sixty-sixth birthday three days ago.'

'Huh? That's the date Oscar Philips set as his activate-not-before-date inside my nuclear model. I knew Mellor had an ego, but this? The Nine Sisters spend ten years scattered all over the world preparing to do his dirty work, while he sits back waiting for them to come back, bowing and scraping, to his crazy majesty bearing their wicked deeds as a series of worshipful birthday presents? Really?'

'Maybe he saw it as his gift to the world? Anyhow, what we should be thanking God for isn't his dementia, but his daughter. Either she hasn't got a clue about his Living Will or, if she does, she decided to ignore it.'

'I'm guessing the latter.' Tori took the Will from Frank and slipped it back in its place in the filing cabinet drawer. 'This room, she told you, was her only hope of unlocking his brain. Destroy what's here and she destroys any hope of ever seeing even a spark of her father. If we're right, it means that we're not wasting our time. If Mellor wanted all this destroyed, then the key is right here.'

'I'm not so sure. Martyrdom is quite the rage these days, if you haven't noticed. When your life's dream is dragging the modern world back to your more primitive version of utopia—a new Dark Age to anyone rational—wouldn't you want to grab all the credit you could muster?'

'You might,' said Tori, 'or you might be paranoid about someone stumbling over the details beforehand and stopping you, like a depressed daughter going through the papers of her demented, or dead, genius of a father to work out which bits to save for posterity. Imagine it. She's in here, trying to find something good to hang on to other than this wretched swamp she's living in, but instead she discovers he was a terrorist mastermind, an anarchic architect of destruction on an unprecedented scale.'

Frank's eyes jumped all over the room. 'All we've got to do is find the fucker, whatever it is.'

'And preferably this afternoon.' Tori tapped her watch. 'If his birthday was the trigger, it means the rest of the sisterhood are set to launch their separate bombs any time now, so we don't have much ti—'

Both of them froze. From outside the door, the sound was brief but sharp, like a twig snapping but rougher, like a chafing or an abrasion.

'It's a match. He's awake and he's out there.' Frank sprang out of his chair and dropped to his knees. 'Under here,' he said, crawling under the desk. Tori closed the filing cabinet drawer and wriggled under with him. A minute later, they heard a toilet flush. Crouched low, they waited, then watched the handle turn and the door swing open, revealing a stooped old man, slow and erratic in his movements, like an ancient timepiece winding itself down.

Mellor had to be somewhere inside that body, she thought, but this was not the man she knew, despite the cigarette stuck to his lip and the tendrils of smoke framing his face. His charisma, his vitality, his energy, they were nowhere to be seen. There wasn't even a skerrick of them. This fossil of a man's shoulders were hunched and tired, not proud and angry. It made him seem inconsequential, which would have horrified the younger Mellor. His head was no longer shaven but the hairs were so sparse it might have been, and his beard, once a forest of rage,

was a patch of prickly grey wisps, some matted by the ooze from
the scabs he'd recently picked. The fire once in his eyes had long
sputtered out and, to Tori, his irises were almost blank as he
stared into the room looking for something but seeing nothing—
thankfully not the two people skulking under his desk.

His legs akimbo, he stood with his fly zip undone and his
penis hanging out. A few drips of urine, then a stream, fell
toward the floor, hitting one of his feet then with a quick pshht,
dissolving the ember of ash he had only just dropped there. His
trademark sandals were gone, and he was wearing socks, new
ones, it seemed. Perhaps a birthday present from his daughter.
They were cobalt blue, though one was now slightly darker as
it absorbed the wetness.

'Fuck it,' Mellor said. 'Fuck *them!*' he shouted, as if to a
crowd. He took a step into the room, and his visitors tensed,
knowing that if he sat at the desk, his feet would find them
even if his eyes hadn't. But instead, he reached for the door
handle and pulled it closed.

Tori turned an ear forward to listen for his footfalls on the
stone tiles in the corridor but heard nothing, wondering if he
was still at the door or if he had shuffled back to bed or perhaps
to the bathroom again. Then a thought struck her. 'His Will!'
she said to Frank. 'Of all his prized possessions, why would
he tell his daughter, an art historian, to destroy his artwork?
What artwork does he have, anyway? There was nothing in his
bedroom … The highway photo,' she whispered, pointing to
the wall, and when she looked up at it, and really looked at it,
she added, 'Fuck.'

Frank stared at it for a moment and saw it, too. 'Well, blow
me—'

'Not likely,' she smiled. 'But let's check it out anyway.' They
scrambled out from under the desk, and Tori unhooked the

frame from the wall. To the right of the picture, almost out of the frame but a hint of it just visible, was the segment of the classic highway sign for America's fabled Route 66 that they'd both seen.

'Clever. We launch after my sixty-sixth birthday,' said Frank, 'and Route 66 tells us how.'

'Or maybe it tells us who.' Tori pointed to some pencil marks at the foot of the photo. 'Does that look like the letters GRM to you? They're his initials, George Rawfolds Mellor.' She flipped it over to look on the back, but there was nothing except brown paper backing and tape, and the hanging chain. She cut down the sides of the tape with her nail and stripped off the backing, then lifted the photo out of the frame to see if there was anything on the back, but there wasn't. So she replaced it as best she could, found some tape on his desk and slapped it on to hold it together, then hung it back on the wall and walked over to the window.

Down on the street below a man, probably in his seventies, was riding a rickety bicycle. If the window had been open she might have heard the rusty rattling of the chains on the paving stones. He stopped where a small girl was sitting on a step playing with her dolls. In greeting, he raised his beret, a rather bizarre green tartan, then wiped his brow and undid his maroon cardigan to cool off as if he'd just completed a sprint. Every time the girl giggled he snapped one of his trouser suspenders and she'd giggle again, and finally he took something out of his pocket for her, patted her on her head, and continued on his way.

As Tori turned back into the room, she and Frank spoke at the same time: 'Stegas!'

Steganography, as they both knew, was the science of hiding secrets in plain sight, like the age-old spy ploy of sending a seemingly bland postcard where the first letter of each alternate word spelled out the real message. With modern software, it could be done with images—perhaps a highway photo—and with far more security and sophistication. The first time Tori had come across steganography was at the CIA when monitoring an aviation fan-site her boss, Davidson, had suspected was a front for al-Qaeda. Annoyingly, the shit had been right since what she'd found, buried inside a seemingly innocent photo of a fleet of F-22 Raptor aircraft mid-flight, was the complete text of a 121-page terrorist manual with the blueprints of the subways they were proposing to blast apart.

For security experts, steganography won out over cryptography. Instead of creating an expensive and bothersome encryption algorithm, where the encryption raised a red flag by its mere existence—either because it was a mess of gibberish that clearly needed unscrambling, or because it obviously required a key to unlock it—steganographers simply buried the secret in a place the unsuspecting eye wouldn't, or couldn't, go looking for it.

The shot Tori had found that first time—four fighter jets in flight formation—had looked totally innocuous yet the pixels concealed a step-by-step plan to blow up the London Tube and New York City's Subway.

Tori and Frank's hunch was that the photograph on Mellor's wall was more than an ode to a crumbling highway, that it was a stega with some of its pixels subtly altered from the original in ways their eyes couldn't detect, perhaps the merest of shifts in the shades of grey in one of the many road cracks. The trick would be to find the differences from the original, and therefore to also find the original.

Frank jumped back into the chair and buried inside Mellor's computer to see if he could find a steganography program loaded on it. A few minutes later, he let out a chuckle. 'If it's here, the bastard's hidden that too. He's probably renamed it "Esoteric Paper on a Boring Topic No one Could Give a Shit About", or something else similarly banal.' Even though Mellor's machine wasn't internet-connected, at least it had wifi and Bluetooth connections, so Frank piggybacked into the internet, using his own phone as a hotspot modem, and located and then downloaded a proprietary stega finder which, after it searched the computer, found what he was hoping for.

'Beautiful,' he said, 'and yep, he's given it a dummy name, the "k-eigenvalue", whatever that is. And what's more, I've picked up a few digital versions of the highway shot. Hopefully one will be the original and another the stega.'

'Does the program let you de-stega them?'

'Fingers crossed.' While the program was running, he checked the properties of the image files, telling Tori, 'He created these on first November ten years ago. How about that for foresight?'

'Or ego.'

Frank shook his head. 'Damn! It won't do it.' He reached down to his bag and pulled out a black device hardly bigger than his phone. With a short cable sticking out of it, Tori recognised it as a portable external disk drive. Earlier, she had suggested they buy one in the hotel's business centre, but her trusty assistant had simply patted his bag, as if an SIS director's assistant would ever travel without one. Now, plugging it into a USB-port on Mellor's computer, he downloaded the professor's entire hard drive onto it.

'My little baby's got a terabyte of capacity and his disk is only using—' he checked, '—twenty per cent of that. I'll copy everything and we'll work on it back at the hotel, so we can't be interrupted.' While the data was transferring, Tori used

Frank's phone to take photos of the room, the highway shot,
and Mellor's Will.

Five minutes later, they slipped their shoes back on, Frank threw his backpack over his shoulder, Tori wound her scarf over her head, and they escaped the apartment, sliding Signora della Scalla's key back under the mat as they left.

25

IN SHANGHAI, YUAN LI MING OPENED up the
treasured portrait she had secreted on her computer's hard
drive. With it shot ten years ago, she wondered about Professor
Mellor and what he looked like today … how he was … if he'd
ever visited China. She'd never once tried to find out, strictly
obeying his veto not just against contact but against anything
that could trip their enemies into discovering and thwarting their
mission. She had thought of web-searching for him countless
times, but her paranoia always cut in with China notorious for
electronic eavesdropping. Self-discipline was second nature to Li
Ming. She prided herself on it.

There he was, at that Sydney rally where she'd first fallen for
his ideas and her camera had captured him in full flight, the spit
of his rage flying over her and the other people cheering him
from the front row. After printing the photo, for the first time,
she folded it neatly and slipped it into her shirt pocket, close to
her heart.

She logged into the control system and sat quietly for ten minutes, in awe of the technological marvel she'd helped to create: China's burgeoning fast train network, a key piece of the infrastructure greasing the nation's growth and its rapid urbanisation. It was true, and remarkable, that China's more recent policies and leaders had helped lift hundreds of millions of citizens out of abject poverty but, as Professor Mellor had asked all those years ago, at what cost to an ailing planet?

By tomorrow, all that would stop. She would see to that, and she raised her glass of water in a final respectful toast to her idol, her mentor. Checking no one was in earshot, she smiled and said, 'Bring on the winter! *Fiat justitia et ruant coeli,*' confident that none of her colleagues would know the Latin for 'Let justice be done, though the heavens fall'.

Li Ming picked up her pen and scrawled 'Y/6' on her season train ticket, and popped it too into her pocket, her heart thumping—not with fear but with pride for what she would soon be doing.

26

AFTER ANOTHER ROUND OF SUCCESSFUL TALKS with the Greek PM, Axel and the rest of his team were back in the Grande Bretagne Hotel toasting their progress with an iced bottle of Krug, the 1995 vintage. Axel held the flute of lightly golden champagne to his nose and inhaled, long and loud, with his eyes closed. He licked his lips in anticipation. 'Ah, don't you love how that pistachio and lemony zest work together?'

Henry Harvey's nose for wines was as sharp as one of his boss's annoying beads were round, but he nodded all the same. To Henry, champagne was a girly drink, not half as satisfying as swilling a pint of draught beer in a noisy bar where you got to toss your peanut shells on the floor. Brought up in the Bronx, Henry felt that if you craved a yeasty aroma, why tickle your nose when you could punch it? But he went along with Axel's rituals. The boss might be wrong about alcohol, but he was right about almost everything else.

Axel and Henry were going over the day's progress to agree their next steps ahead of giving their update to Soti Skylakakis. It was clear that if the negotiations kept moving as rapidly as they had so far, Soti would need to come to Athens for the signing and the announcement. The new Prime Minister and Soti were old friends and, while Axel felt it his duty to make his daily debrief, it was obvious that Soti had a back channel that was already feeding him the information.

When Tori and Frank called in, with the phones at each end on speaker, Henry and the wider deal team still had no idea that their two colleagues were in Venice so, to avoid risking a slip up, Axel excused himself to take their call privately from the sitting room off his bedroom. Once he closed the door, he bubbled over, regaling them with the tale of how, only an hour earlier, the PM's team had green-lighted them to move to the next delicate stage. 'And the latest from Venice?' he added, almost as an afterthought.

'Mellor is here. Physically I mean, but mentally he's in ga-ga land,' said Tori. 'Dementia, apparently. So personally, he's going to be useless to us, but we've been through his computer and—'

Frank held up his hand. 'If you don't mind?'

Tori stopped and smiled. It was Frank who'd found the material, plus Axel saw him as entirely trustworthy and objective, virtues she could only hope he'd see in her again sometime soon. Frank explained that after they'd got back to the hotel, they spent two hours trying to decipher Mellor's stega. They hadn't completely succeeded, he said, but they'd opened a crack, showing that the image concealed a list of people's names with matching codenames. The difficulty was that the lists were corrupted, with random letters missing. Tori, for example was V--tor-a S-yft: S/-4. Frank had used the decoding program he'd copied from Mellor's computer but, for a reason he couldn't fathom, it kept throwing out these errors time after time. 'So Axel, we've got corroborative evidence,' Frank continued. 'It's definitely not just Tori's *word* now, and the facts stack up pretty much like she told us. Her name, or rather V-double space-T-O-R-space-A followed by S-space-YFT,' he spelled it out, 'is there as is S-slash-space-4.' He looked down the list. 'And there's an O-space-C-space-R which I take as Oscar followed by PH-space-LI-space-S. So Oscar Philips is there too.'

Axel interrupted: 'I'm completely lost here, with all this space-space stuff you're saying.'

'Hang on, I'll email you the list as best we've got it.'

A moment later, Axel received it. 'I can see it, yes ... Oscar Philips.'

'Yes, and like Tori said, there's also M-space-A-double space-R, then first name A-space-A-space—'

'Hmm? Major Alan Whitehead? Maybe. I suppose he had to be a major once.'

'Go with us on this, okay? Unless two people of that name and rank were doing a doctorate in Sydney ten years ago, it's definitely the guy from Homeland Security. And as national head of ops command today, he's no mere minion.'

If Tori didn't know Axel, she would have thought the phone had clicked off, but she guessed the silence was simply him swinging his beads while he contemplated the possibilities. She raised her finger as if requesting an okay, and Frank nodded a yes. 'Axel,' she said, 'I've filled in the blanks for all these names as best I could from memory and we've done some quick web searches of the ones—'

'The ones you *think* are the ones,' said Axel, sounding annoyed. 'To make accusations of this magnitude, this gravity, we'll need a lot more than guesswork, Tori.'

'Axel, this is moving fast. As well as Oscar Philips, another one's gone active: Dr eKiller? Remember him from last week? The doctor arrested in LA for murderi—'

'Steve Jobs?'

'Yes, him,' said Tori. 'He's the seventh name on the list in front of you. If you fill in the blanks, it's got to be Wilbur Fenton, right? When I saw the newsflash last week, I thought he looked vaguely familiar, but I couldn't … Anyway, Fenton is F/7. Surely we've got enough to—'

'Enough? These are snippets. You certainly don't have enough to point the finger—to slander Whitehead. For heaven's sake, he's an American hero. He's devoted his life to serving the public interest. Besides, if it is the same Whitehead, and I'll grant you it looks that way, what if he's still active? If you warn him … As I said yesterday, I don't like the possibilities … for you … or, when I think about it, for all of us.' Axel shuddered.

They debated the next moves for twenty minutes and settled on Tori trying for a one-on-one call with Concetta Pittorino. The CIA didn't enjoy working with other agencies at the best of times, so maybe the old rivalries might let Tori jam her foot in the door. By the time Tori got through to Martin Davidson to arrange it, it was eight pm in Venice and two pm in Langley. She was using the hotel phone but had routed the call through a dummy landline number in Athens to misdirect her location, and had fixed it so Frank and Axel could eavesdrop via their own computers.

Tori kicked off by first asking Davidson how Judith Dunn and her nuclear team were progressing, but her former boss blasted her for going to ground. When, during a short breather in his tirade, she asked for the solo call with Pittorino, he blew up again. 'With you just two signatures away from becomin' America's Most Wanted for fuckin' over the country's nuke power plants, why the fuck should Pittorino want to pander to you in a one-on-fuckin'-one? You kiddin' me?'

Davidson might like to 'entertain' women who worked for him in a gas-guzzling six-cylinder but to Tori, the guy had a one-cylinder mind. 'Listen, Davidson, my nuclear model was perfect, not a single thing wrong with it. The NRC approved it, don't forget, so don't throw that down at my feet. I already told Dunn who did it, who framed me ...'

'Yeah, some mark called Oscar Philips, blah, blah. Swyft, those NRC tech-heads might eat your crap but I don't. Not me, not Pittorino. We looked into your Oscar fuckin' Philips, and the guy's a stale donut, a zero. He dropped out without finishing his doctorate. Fuckin' vanished off the face of the planet until two years ago when he turned up on the sheets, in London, charged with snatch and grabs, petty break-ins and, whadya know, a drug bust. That's a messed-up mind, not a genius master-fuckin'-mind.'

'He was a slimy bastard, for sure, given what he's done to frame me, but he didn't have an exclusive on slime, eh, Davidson?'

'Hey! Listen to m—'

'No, you listen. I've got something to give Pittorino and if I can't get to her—'

'What? You'll go public? Bullshit! Not with the story I'll background the media with and, let me tell you, that will be one big fuckin' thrill.'

She held her breath, her mind flooding and her gut churning with all the reasons she so viscerally despised this man. 'Davidson, I'll phone you back in ten minutes. Meanwhile you tell Pittorino what I told you. If you haven't done it by the time I call back, just remember a certain video in a certain safe.'

'You wouldn't! You fuckin' despicable slut. You—'

And you? she thought. Your parents said you could be anything so you became a prick. But what she said in fact was, 'I'll call back in ten,' and hung up, fuming. Frank and Axel, who'd heard it all, stayed silent while she calmed herself, both men knowing better than to ask.

'He called me a—!' she said, unable to bring herself to repeat the slur, but her eyes were fierce, and cold. 'I need some water.' Frank went to get a bottle from the minibar and when he turned back, Tori had torn off her top and dropped her jeans, stripping down to her underwear—black lace, he couldn't help but notice—and she was already pushing open the doors to their garden that led to the hotel's pool terrace. Leaving him holding the bottle of Perrier, she ran outside and dived into the pool. Strictly speaking, the pool's opening hours ended at seven pm, but by the time the agitated bar attendant got Tori's attention, she was already walking up the steps at the shallow end so he handed her a towel, trying hard not to ogle through the soaking lace.

TORI WAS DRAPED in a sumptuous hotel bathrobe when she dialled Davidson, precisely ten minutes later. 'Swyft,' he said, 'I got you Pittorino but you better have somethin' big or you're as fucked as a Bangkok whore.'

'Is that your sister you're talking about?'

He clicked her through so fast she didn't hear his response, nor did she care to.

'Swyft, your little nucular escapade is keepin' me and about five thousand other people across the world sweatin' night and day,' said the deputy director, 'so I'm not in no mood for a fireside chat just because it suits you. I want answers and we'll start with this … if you claim to be so blameless of settin' off this shitstorm, why're you playin' so hard to get?'

As Pittorino was speaking, Tori heard a cough on the line, and thinking it was Frank she cast a dirty look over at him. He was listening in via an earpiece, but his face showed alarm, not guilt, and Axel's face, which she could see live through a window on her computer screen, was similarly startled.

'I'm not playing at anything, ma'am,' said Tori, 'but it seems like you are. I requested this call as strictly one to one. You and me alone. Who's there with you—Davidson?'

'It's me, Al Whitehead from Homeland Security,' said a soft male voice, an indeterminate middle-American accent melded together from years flitting around the corridors of power in various cities and countries. 'I would have introduced myself yesterday, though I didn't get the chance but, Dr Swyft, I think we may already have met … a long time ago. What you don't know is that I've been given overall responsibility for this operation, coordinating the CIA, the NRC and everyone else involved. So whatever you wanted to tell the deputy director privately you can tell me. But frankly, given how serious this is looking for you, I suggest we do that in person, so why don't you put your skates on and bring yourself in. I've had people at the embassy in Athens waiting since yesterday to, er, assist you.'

'We've already met?' said Tori playing for time, and unsure if Whitehead's admission was good news or bad. 'Where was that?' Pretending she didn't know couldn't hurt her, she decided on the fly, and his answer would give a good hint of where he really stood. If he admitted to having been in the Nine Sisters, her world would look a lot rosier than if he hid it.

'We did our doctorates at the same university.'

So far so good, she thought.

'But where we met was during what turned out to be a rather stupid psych experiment, quite an unethical one in my opinion.'

Was that good or bad? She didn't have a clue. Mellor could easily have fooled Whitehead with the same blind he'd used with her—in which case she could safely unburden herself on Whitehead. But she was edgy; there was a risk he was using it as a cover, like that bastard Oscar Philips had. Thinking quickly, she decided it was safer to assume the worst. 'Dr Whitehead, I'm struggling to recall. All the drama over my thesis has crowded out my memory of pretty much everything else from back then, and my mind's not registering you either, I'm sorry.' That way, he'd be less likely to regard her as a threat. 'You don't think you've got me mixed up with someone else?'

'No, ma'am.'

'Well look, I was calling the deputy director to offer some proof that I'm clean, that a man called Oscar Philips set me up. He was at the university, too, but I doubt you would have known him,' she lied.

'Your proof?'

She explained the formula she'd found and what it meant, though being careful not to mention anything about the overarching Nine Sisters reference or Mellor. Whitehead responded by repeating what Davidson had already told her about Philips' slide into crime and drugs, then Pittorino butted in, the derision in her voice biting as she noted how simply expedient it was for Tori to have found a scapegoat who was unable to defend himself.

'Your story's 'bout as flaky as my momma's pie crust, Swyft,' said Pittorino. 'I think y'all should do as Dr Whitehead here has suggested and pop yourself over to our embassy.'

'I would if it helped, ma'am, but I don't think either of you even wants to believe me. Thanks for your kind offer of hospitality but I'll pass on it, for now. When I've got more proof, I'll let you know. Meanwhile, Dr Dunn and the NRC are quite capable of fixing the nuclear glitch before it does any real harm so—'

'Swyft, you don't know what you're up agains—'

'I know it better than you think. *Ciao*, as they say,' she said, hanging up.

'Tori,' said Axel immediately over their open line, 'You were supposed to be here in Athens. The Greeks don't say *ciao*.'

She looked at Frank. 'Shit.'

27

RUSSIAN PASSPORTS WERE HANDY WHEN AXEL'S plane landed them in Saint-Petersburg the next morning. Tori and Frank had spent almost the entire night beforehand in their suite at the Cipriani trying to crack perfection out of the stegas. Frank had scoured the drive he'd copied from Mellor's computer but, despite everything he tried, all the names were corrupted to some degree, and some more than others. The one Tori could reconstruct with the highest level of certainty was Vasily Yevtushenko. It wasn't much of a stretch from V-sil- Y-vt-sh-nko and she recalled the name almost straight off, and how the first time they'd met she'd asked if he was related to the famous Russian poet, which he wasn't.

While Tori's primary reason for using her Russian passport was to avoid detection, Frank's was the purely pragmatic one, to get into Russia without a prearranged visa. His passport was in a family name he'd carefully selected from the South Asians who'd come to Russia as traders in the eighteenth century. From past experience, officious bureaucrats poked around a little less with this name than when MI6 had sent him to Moscow the first time named awkwardly as a blue-blood Russian.

Tori stood on the pavement outside the lime-green mansion that housed Yevtushenko's enterprise, NuAgeCloud Systems and, showing more nerves than normal, she looked back over her shoulder across the river to the *Letniy Sad*, the Summer Garden, and then back up the street to the café where she'd left Frank holed up. They had come here via a very circuitous route—two cabs, the subway, and a stroll through the park— so they were fairly sure they hadn't been followed, but both knew they could take nothing for granted. Tori adjusted her jacket and, in the reflection from the mirror-polished stainless steel rotating doors, she checked one last time that no stray red strands were sneaking out from under the wig. She'd had it fitted an hour ago in a salon on the Fontanki Embankment before she took the last cab ride, as a blonde.

She knew that she was about to take a massive risk. Yevtushenko was as powerful as he was wealthy and, since no multibillionaire would likely grant an immediate meeting to a stranger turning up out of thin air, she had no choice but to chance her arm. She took a breath and pushed against the door to go inside, and the segment of space she stood in started to circle its way around. But midway it stopped. She pushed, yet it wouldn't budge. She pushed backwards but it was the same. The doors were sheet steel, so she couldn't see ahead or behind. Her heart started to race, and she began to breathe deeply, to calm herself. Relax, she told herself. Don't panic. She was about to speak to Frank over the phone line she had open to him, but decided not to, aware even the doors could be bugged. Since it was the main entrance and exit, she knew it wouldn't stay locked like this for long, but what began to worry her was the thought of who she might find waiting to greet her when the door swung around again. Russian thugs, maybe. She closed her eyes for a few seconds, then pasted on as bright a smile as possible, and looked up to check if there was a camera looking down on her—and there was. She waved at it, and seconds later the doors started rotating again of their own accord. They spilled her out into the lobby, a soulless, largely empty expanse of white plaster and concrete that some minimalist architect had probably charged Vasily a maximalist fortune to design. There were no musclemen waiting to greet her.

Striding across to the reception desk as if nothing had happened, she kept telling herself that being entombed inside an airless steel cell was nothing, an event that probably happened all the time in Russia. 'I am here for Dr Vasily Yevtushenko,' she said in Russian. 'Please tell him I bring greetings from our mutual friend, Professor George Mellor, with a personal message about the health of his nine sisters.' It wasn't perfect, but between Tori and Frank's rudimentary knowledge and some translation software, it was passable.

They'd chosen a personal message as the approach to most likely get her through even the most officious assistant and, if Russia's technology titan did drop everything to see her after this very specific message, it would most likely signal that he was indeed an active sister. If he had dropped out of the group, as she and Frank had considered, he would hardly disrupt his schedule just because some old university chum had popped in for an idle chat. The worry, as Frank had said, was that rather than turn her away, he might deputise his security people to lean on her and discover why a loony green anarchist was visiting him ten years into the plan. One way or another, his response would tell them what they needed to know, and that was a risk

Tori was willing to take, with Frank recording everything via the open phone line in case they needed evidence.

The receptionist pointed Tori to one of the ludicrous stainless steel lounges while he placed a call and passed on the message. Three minutes later, with Tori's head buried in a Russian magazine she pretended to be engrossed by, the receptionist came over, ushered her through a metal detector and into an elevator, pressing his security card against the button for the top floor and watched the doors close on her. The lift walls inside were also stainless steel. It wasn't a comfortable feeling as the lift jerked upwards.

When the doors hissed open at the top, again everything was pure white, except for the shock of orange on the tall, lanky woman whose head was entirely shaved and who was wearing a skimpy tangerine dress. It was so tight-fitting it sucked the colour and whatever personality she might once have had out of her face, making her seem as vacuous as a department store mannequin with eyes as starved of expression as her body seemed of nutrition. She didn't speak a word, saving her tongue, Tori imagined, for her wealthy boss. The woman simply swivelled on her orange stilettos and click-clacked as she led Tori down a corridor, her prance more attuned to the catwalk at the Moscow Fashion Show, where Yevtushenko had 'discovered' her six months ago.

At the far end of the long white-walled corridor, Tori spied the hot pink leather sofa she'd seen pictured repeatedly in the articles about Yevtushenko that she'd devoured while flying here, but halfway down the hallway, Miss Praying Mantis turned hard left into another corridor and into a windowless but still white room. Tori chose the seat closest to the trio of wall outlets that she spied low down on the skirting board and as she moved to sit there, a waiter, his shoes, jeans and T-shirt all black—as was his complexion—carried in a tea set.

It was the classic Lomonosov Imperial cobalt net design inspired by the private dinner services of Catherine the Great, but rather than the famous blue-on-white this was black-on-white, an exclusive edition the Saint-Petersburg porcelain company had made specially for Yevtushenko, their city's famous son. The waiter poured her a steaming cup and she took a slice of lemon when he offered it. When he left, leaving the tray behind, she fumbled her teaspoon and it fell to the floor.

She had barely risen from picking it up when Yevtushenko flew into the room and closed the door behind him. He was the same man she remembered from university but slimmer, now bald and his face surprisingly untrammelled after a decade of ripping out his competitors' throats. Botox perhaps? '*Kto ty?*' he asked as he sat, not noticing the flush in her face.

Tori chose to answer in English. 'Who am I? You don't recognise me? Professor Mellor gave me the name S/14,' she said, staring directly into his eyes, which were as black as the pattern on the tea set. 'You, I recall, were Y/2.'

He slowly poured himself a cup while he put his words together. 'Ah, that little foray with radical environmentalism. We were so young and naive, weren't we?' His accent was as Queen's English as Frank's, but his tone harsher, more clipped. He certainly had none of the dark throaty Russian Ls, his Ws were perfect—'we' was *we*, not *vee*—and his Ths were excellent, so 'that' was *that*, not *zat*.

'Young, yes, but naive? Surely you still share those ideals?'

'What? Go forth and be successful, piss out from inside the tent … that was Mellor's mantra, wasn't it?' Seeing her nod, he continued, 'But, my dear … S/14, you said? When you work as hard as I have to pitch your own tent, when you shape and cut the cloth with your own two hands, it destroys your urge to destroy. Instead, you realise you are a creator, that you are yourself reshaping the world, a better world, and in a different more constructive way. But you still haven't answered my question. You are?'

'Dr Victoria Swyft.'

'Your name, it is familiar.'

'Of course. From our Nine Sisters meetings.'

He didn't answer immediately, his glare making her feel like a thoroughbred mare he was considering bidding for at auction to enhance the bloodlines in his stud farm. 'You had a different hair colour back then. Ginger perhaps, or red?'

'And you may have lost your hair,' she forced a laugh, 'but you have retained a good memory.'

'It pays dividends. Ah yes, I saw your name mentioned this morning, did I not? In the news?'

Tori's explanation about the news reports swayed from the truth. 'You should never believe everything you read, I'm sure you know that. But it's because of that I'm here—to warn you. Mellor told us never to communicate, never, but recently he broke his own rule and contacted me as soon as he discovered a mole, one of our Nine Sisters, the one who got me into this pickle with the nuclear authorities.'

'You persisted with Mellor's fanciful plan?' Yevtushenko hit his forehead with an open palm, but there was something about the slap and in his chuckle that told Tori it was not sincere. His expression was incredulous but his eyes were not; if anything, they were apprehensive, as if his mind was ticking over at full pace.

'You didn't stick with it?' she asked in response, and raised her cup to her lips.

'An absurd question. I'm afraid we have no more to talk about, Dr Swyft.'

She put the cup down without taking a sip. 'Then why did Professor Mellor ask me to come here, to warn you?'

Yevtushenko stood and pushed back his chair. 'You will have to ask him that. In my case, I have no wish to get my organisation or myself embroiled in whatever quagmire you have created for yourself. *Do svidaniya*, goodbye.'

WHEN TORI LEFT the building, she slipped into a recessed doorway in a side alley and, opening her bag, swapped her blonde wig for a black beanie, tucked in her hair and reversed her jacket, showing the green side instead of the yellow. She then strolled to the café to sit with Frank, who was busy with his laptop. He looked up as she entered.

'Nice hat! I'm in, by the way, so great work,' he said, popping a small bobal'ki biscuit into his mouth.

'What did you think?' she asked.

He'd heard the whole conversation over the open line, and had already emailed the recording to Axel. While their boss was broadly supportive, Frank worried he would go out on a limb only so far, and not merely because of his weight. 'In one way,' Frank said, not looking up from his screen and continuing to tap, 'it was worse than a fizzer. Pure denial from the Russian, versus a fake confession from you.'

'I had to take that risk or I'd get nothing.'

'Yet you "confessed" and we still got nothing. Unless I get somewhere with this—' he nodded toward his screen, '—the Russian might even turn out to be genuine. It is hard, I'm being honest, to think he'd destroy a multibillion-dollar personal empire he's worked so hard all these years to build from scratch.'

Having not even tasted the tea she'd been offered earlier, she ordered one now. 'Did he have me dragged off in handcuffs?' she asked. 'No. And why not? He'd seen the news reports, so he knows there are questions about what I did, or was supposed to have done. I admitted as much, right? But did he express outrage? Did he call his security people? No. He simply said fuck off!'

'Granted,' Frank said, continuing to focus on his screen, 'but you could have been a lunatic or a journalist ... Much the same thing, I suppose.' He looked up but saw that Tori wasn't smiling. 'Okay, hang on ... here's something.'

The tiny transmitting sniffer that Tori had inserted into the wall outlet when she'd dropped her spoon had been Frank's spike into the heart of the NuAgeCloud computer network. The device was high frequency but low range, the reason they needed to stay so close to it. He'd been running a program he'd first created at MI6, and even before Tori had left the building he had hacked himself into the network and was searching for Yevtushenko's own computer, so they could eavesdrop on what the former Sister would do once Tori had departed.

'Got him! Now let's see if we can perch quietly on his shoulder ...'

USING THE NAME Aubrey Williamsburgh, Yevtushenko logged into a widely used free email service, and typed a message:

Kenny, my dear chap,
A change of plan. I'm bringing forward my move by a month, likely in a few days. Fingers crossed you've ironed out those bugs in the solar spring pumps? Very excited

to be coming finally after all our prep. Hope the fish are jumping and all that. Will miss Oxford and London, but as you know, old chap, Y/2 Island is my dream come true. As usual, not a word. Don't want to alert the nosy tax boys and girls, what?

Yours,

Aubrey.

PS: I'm bringing you a case of Pétrus. I know how you like French merlot. It's the heavenly 2000 vintage, by the way.

Yevtushenko's email account page was set up to routinely display the first three lines of each message, allowing Tori and Frank to skim every one on the screen. It was clear that in this guise as a wealthy, reclusive and tax-dodging British businessman, Yevtushenko had been shuffling money—buckets of it—through a mysterious labyrinth of offshore accounts so he could develop a remote, uninhabited South Pacific island into his entirely self-sufficient, off-the-radar refuge, though its precise location wasn't mentioned in anything that Frank had seen so far.

'He's doing a runner,' Tori said, feeling vindicated yet petrified. 'So he's got to be planning something—'

'—big,' Frank finished the sentence. 'He *is* actually going to destroy what he built,' he added, shaking his head and clearly surprised. 'Billions poured down the drain. Well, blow m— sorry … *goodness* me,' he said, taking his fingers off his keyboard long enough to rub his chin. 'The question for us is how is he going to do it?'

Frank opened a screen window using a technique where he could, unseen by a target, scan the directories on their computer. 'Well, one thing, he's a pilot like Axel. See there?' He pointed to a file and clicked it open. 'He's got a Gulfstream too, and hey, Axel will love this: it's "only" a G450!'

'Can we forget the boys' toys? Look,' she said, 'in that other window ... That's a link into his Cloud's control system, isn't it?'

'Shit, I've got to be quick.'

CLOUD COMPUTING WAS the rage both for cost-conscious businesses as well as budget-busted governments. As computers had become more powerful, as the storage demands of data increased, as customers demanded service at the snap of a finger, as security risks accelerated, many businesses were reaching breaking point with their ballooning spend on information technology and their mushrooming IT staff numbers.

But using the Cloud was like renting a virtual warehouse that came with a factory for all of an organisation's data and processing. If a business or a government department suddenly needed more processing capacity, more software or even more data staff, it would take less effort than choosing the wine at lunch to simply dial it all up over the internet from Cloud services like Yevtushenko's, and for a relatively small fee.

Going to the Cloud was akin to moving into a floor of a giant ready-made office building, sharing the entire infrastructure and facilities, saving massive amounts of time and money compared to designing, constructing, funding and running your own. In the Cloud, customers paid only for what they used, outlaying mere cents per hour or per gigabyte of data worked on. Firms were moving away from running their IT themselves, instead buying data and processing from shared data centres like Yevtushenko's, just like buying their electricity off the power grid. No longer did they need their own service and storage, or service teams, nor did they need to worry about upgrades. That was all done for them by their Cloud provider.

The cost savings were massive and, importantly, customers thought they were getting better security than if they did it themselves since, typically, Cloud suppliers spent far more on protection than any one customer would even think of doing for itself.

On the plane to Russia, Tori had been reading up on Yevtushenko's Cloud business, and saw one cynic had told *Bloomberg News*, 'He's not doing it out of goodwill. He's got no choice with Clouds being such juicy targets for hackers. Think about it: instead of some team in China working 24/7 for weeks on how to hack into a Sony or a General Motors or the Department of Transport, if they hack into Yevtushenko's Cloud they get not just one, but hundreds of organisations to play havoc with. For the hacker, the Cloud is heaven on earth.'

While some of Yevtushenko's toughest competitors in the Cloud world were big names like Amazon, Google, Microsoft, Apple, IBM and Salesforce, with more popping up all the time, his NuAgeCloud was certainly no pipsqueak. He was already hosting the critical data and networks for 308 of Eastern Europe's major industrial giants—including a good number of the empires owned by the Russian oligarchs, plus he was winning contract after contract from the Russian government, the latest from the Federal Tax Service. He was even about to subcontract for Microsoft in Russia, and last week Amazon and Google had started talking to him.

In the last two years he'd also made a big push to expand into Western Europe. The turning point was when the London Tube signed on as a customer. Paris's Métro followed suit, then National Grid, the UK's main power supplier, and, since then, other European companies had come flocking in. The economic quagmire that Europe was still trudging through meant more and more cost-cutting, with the result that when suppliers like NuAgeCloud promised top security and top speed but rock-bottom pricing, the decision to shift a firm's critical information systems off its own expensive, creaking proprietary systems was instantly attractive.

YEVTUSHENKO HAD OPENED an innocuously named file called 'New York apartment', which as well as some photographs, contained a strand of numbers and text that ran over six lines. Frank quickly placed his fingers on several keys at once and captured an exact image of them, sending it to his desktop. 'Bet you that's his password. Yep.' He smiled. Yevtushenko copied and pasted the strand into the password section of the login box. Frank took another screenshot.

'Now what's this? Looks like a top-level directory of all the data he's got stored in his Cloud, by country and then by client. Take the UK—there's London's Tube, the Metropolitan Police Service, National Grid, Royal London Hospital, St George's Hospital … woo! It goes on and on. This guy's Cloud is everywhere.'

'Jesus, see that?' Tori pointed. 'It looks like … he's adding in a command, to go active at midnight tonight … It's to drip-feed the data belonging to all these clients onto some website. Shit, he's going to leak addresses, credit card numbers, passwords, hospital records, criminal records. Can you scroll down a bit more?' she said and, as he did, the two of them cracked an uneasy laugh. The website that Yevtushenko was planning to post all this highly sensitive data to was named EverythingYouWantedToKnowAboutEverybodyElse.com. 'I doubt Scotland Yard will see that as funny,' said Tori.

'I doubt anyone whose data's going to be leaked will.'

They quickly looked around to see if anyone had noticed their suddenly animated conversation, but they were in the clear; the waiter was behind the counter chatting on the phone and examining the fingernails on his free hand while the only other customer was focused on his own laptop and, judging by the jiggling from his head and the tinny sound they could just make out, he was listening to music, if you could call it that, through his earphones.

'This is huge,' said Frank, taking another screenshot. 'He leaks sensitive customer data and by doing that vaporises his entire business. Not only that, it will push Cloud computing back by years. Who'd entrust a Cloud with their critical data after this?'

'Sure, it's big, but it's not big enough. Okay, confidential data will be posted so anyone can see it, and he'll probably have some rolling clone sites that it will automatically spill over to when the authorities try to close it down. So while this is big, it isn't Mellor big. A bit of fraud, lots of squealing, tons of inconvenience with people having to change passwords and get new credit cards, blah, blah. But I doubt that's Yevtushenko's game.'

'How right you are, Tori. Look there.' He pointed. 'He's gone into the operating system and he's inserting a new command … Hell, it's a crash and burn. He's going to crash his entire Cloud *and* destroy all the data, all the software, everything that's on the servers … Wait. He's setting a start time for six am tomorrow, just a second …' He took another screenshot. 'He's giving himself time to morph himself into Aubrey Williamsburgh, get to his island or well on the way and vanish before he brings down the whole shooting match. If he succeeds, the whole world will be looking for someone who no longer exists. He's bringing winter on the world and he gets to lie in the sun on some luxury island.'

In their research on Yevtushenko, they'd found that in the last two years, his company's new business growth had skyrocketed, mostly through controversial long-term contracts won from some of Europe's major transport systems, power networks and a smattering of emergency services, such as hospitals and police forces. The markets had feted NuAgeCloud, almost quadrupling its stock price as a reward for wiping its competitors out of the game. The Russian had been aggressively shaving his margins by claiming efficiencies his competitors protested simply weren't possible with current technology. But real or not, his promises were seductive, especially to European governments in their various degrees of financial distress. Bedrock costs combined with superior services were huge trophies for politicians facing re-election in the face of skin and bone austerity budgets, even with rival Cloud operators going on the record claiming that Yevtushenko had to be losing money on these deals, lots of it. His stock price soared even higher as antsy pension funds, desperate for returns in a virtually zero-interest world, scoured the globe for places to put their billions in loose change.

One disgruntled rival had indiscreetly posted: 'London Tube would've been crazy not to take NuAge's offer. They get all their data storage, drive systems, computer power and tech support at a tenth of their current cost, which is about a third of where we pitched to them, and for us to do even that our backs were so close to the wall the paint stuck! The Russkis can't possibly be running a sustainable business model at these prices. They're an accident waiting to happen, for sure.'

When that was quoted on *Bloomberg News*, NuAgeCloud's stock price rose a further five per cent.

Tori remembered one of her dad's sayings: *If it seems too good to be true, it probably is.* 'It's obvious,' she told Frank, lifting her head from the computer screen they were sitting over.

'Yevtushenko never had any intention of running a long-term profitable business. He wanted to suck in as many cost-conscious clients and greedy investors in the shortest possible time, then destroy them.'

'Havoc. Hospitals down all over Europe, the London Tube *and* the Paris Métro ... airports—which ones? It was Heathrow and Rome, wasn't it? Paris, Moscow, Munich, all without power and gas. No central command for the cops to keep order. Holy shit!'

'What about backups? Surely—'

'Are you reading his mind?' Straight after Yevtushenko had closed out of the control system, they watched him typing: R-e-d-u-n-d-a-n-c-y.

A link popped up taking Yevtushenko, and them, to a site that displayed a map showing four backup servers located across Europe and the US: mirror sites in Edinburgh, Marseille and Moscow as well as Boise in Idaho; the spread in geography and time zones clearly one of the big clinchers for so many of the government agencies, and indeed the cost-conscious corporations for giving their business to NuAgeCloud. For the critical systems they were responsible for, and their business continuity and disaster recovery plans, the clients knew they needed loads of redundancy. If disaster struck one site, whether a natural one like an earthquake or human intervention like terrorists, NuAgeCloud had a mirror site ready to spring into action for them, minimising the downtime and the inconvenience, let alone the risk. Where NuAgeCloud beat its rivals hands down was it offered four complete mirror backup sites as part of its package at no extra cost. No one else did that. 'The benefits from our Cloud are stratospheric,' was NuAge's latest marketing tagline.

But offering and delivering, as Tori and Frank were seeing, were quite different things. With Frank continuing to save screenshots, they watched Yevtushenko click on the backup sites, one by one, each time inserting a crash and burn command inside its control system which he set for six am the following day.

'So not only does Europe screech to a halt, but for anyone who believed his bullshit and didn't keep their own disaster recovery centres running, there'll be nowhere to restore from to make an easy migration to another Cloud provider. It'll be months ...'

'Chaos. This is exactly what Mellor wanted. Each Nine Sisters meeting I went to ended with the toast, "Bring on the winter! *Fiat justitia et ruant coeli.*"'

'I know it,' said Frank, his Eton education showing. 'Let justice be done, though the heavens fall.'

Both of them felt the chill even with the café door closed.

28

CHINA'S EARLY TOLL WAS 8,243 PEOPLE dead and another 11,583 critically injured with at least one of their limbs severed or crushed and horrific burns, and there were tens of thousands more with lesser wounds. To rescuers and volunteers rushing to the multiple crash scenes, if the faces of the dead frozen in terror and the wrenching sight of those alive screaming or quietly sobbing were not bad enough, the raw, base stench would stay inside their nostrils and mouths, and nightmares, for years. Acidic, burning flesh, smouldering seating, blood splattered everywhere, mixing with vomit and other bodily fluids. It was hard for the rescuers not to let loose themselves, and many did.

Earlier, at 5.45 pm Chinese central standard time, sixty-three fast trains carrying an average of 500 passengers each simultaneously lost control. Fifteen trains screeched to a stop, neither their drivers nor operations command able to re-engage them. The other forty-eight, positioned at short,

201

highly calibrated but normally safe distances behind them on the same lines, continued to move, racing towards them at over 300 kilometres per hour, accelerating to maximum speed and, within a few minutes, the first wave careened headlong into the rear of the stalled trains. Within another ten minutes, it was the same again for the trains behind them. And again.

Carriages jack-knifed into the air, others dangled from bridges. Body parts and backpacks floated in the lakes and rivers below, though the TV helicopters that had raced to the scenes only showed close-ups of broken dolls and fluffy toys encrusted with blood. Tunnels were infernos unable to be extinguished, hell on earth, but for those passengers trapped inside, at least death came quickly.

Despite frantic calls from panicked drivers and passengers to the control centre, to police and other emergency services, to family, not a thing could be done to stop the oncoming trains. The network operations chief on duty was a man who Yuan Li Ming had once had respect for, before he'd touched her. She knew he would be on duty tonight; it was the reason she chose it.

The chief's wife was a passenger on one of the trains. She had texted him only thirty minutes earlier as it was leaving the station. Her next text, that her train had strangely ground to a stop between stations, came only a second after he saw it on his control panel.

When the terrifying possibility of what might be happening became plain to him from his wall bank of video screens, he slammed on the kill switches for each line on the network— his wife's line first—to cut all the trains still running to a dead stop, but he didn't know that Yuan Li Ming had overridden them.

It was as if he'd done nothing. The failsafe failed.

He threw the power switch for the whole network but that too ignored him.

Impotent, he watched the horror on his screens and, as it unfolded, he could do nothing but scream and scratch the skin off his face. Between his fingers he opened one eye and watched his wife's train, the image taken from the one racing up to it from behind. He saw them hit. The screen went black and a short message briefly appeared on it, signed by Li Ming: 'Hands-free, Mr Yu.'

The bitch, he screamed. Was she totally mad? He'd done nothing to her. It was only a touch, and he'd meant it to be endearing, fatherly, but that stupid Li Ming hadn't seen it that way. Everyone knew that he loved his wife.

His dead wife.

When he looked up again, through tears, the screen had changed and, to his partial relief, the notice of his shame had been removed. In its place, on all the screens, was another message but it wasn't in Chinese so he couldn't follow it.

The China dream is a nightmare.
Fiat justitia et ruant coeli.
We, Nine Sisters, reclaim the planet for itself.
It is sad yet necessary that people die so our planet can live.
Yuan Li Ming,
Y/6,
Member of Nine Sisters.

Almost immediately across the huge nation, authorities shut down every other train, no matter if it was a fast train or not. All over the country, long lines of crowded carriages were stranded, on bridges, in the middle of fields, inside tunnels, and millions and millions of frustrated commuters started crowding stations, streets, bus terminals, taxi ranks, unable to get home or to their factory night shifts.

As concerned train passengers got texts on their phones about what was happening elsewhere, the panic mounted. If they couldn't force the doors open, they smashed through them using whatever they could to escape the trains in desperate fear that theirs, too, was a sitting duck. Roadways and expressways, clogged at the best of times, became virtual car parks as people who would normally commute by train took to the roads.

China ground to a halt. And that was before anyone outside the control room knew of Li Ming's message, apart from the handful who had seen her social media post before they took it down.

29

TORI NOTICED THE SWEAT BEADING ON Frank's normally cool forehead. As soon as Yevtushenko had exited his mirror sites, Frank was inside his hidden browser window trying to log back in as the Russian himself, to try to reverse the tycoon's countdowns for both the data leak and the crash and burns. But the password he'd copied wasn't working.

'Yevtushenko's good,' said Frank. 'He must have used a once-only. Shit, Tori, with the limited grunt on this laptop, it'll take me hours to crack the codes to get back in—assuming I don't set off an alert while I'm at it. Listen, I know you won't like this, but I think we've got no choice …'

She held up her hand. 'Yeah, maybe.' She knew that despite the Whitehead risk, Frank was going to argue that opening this up to Langley and Homeland Security was the best hope of averting a crisis he had already described to her as cataclysmic. 'Let's talk to Axel first,' she said as she threw down more than enough roubles to pay for their drinks and cakes, then flew out of the café to hail a taxi while Frank packed up his computer and assorted paraphernalia. By the time they got to Axel's plane, it was around two pm in Saint-Petersburg, though only eleven am in Athens and they got Axel at the hotel since the negotiations that day were scheduled to recommence just after lunch.

They heard Axel put down his silverware. After listening to them in silence, he voiced the same opinion as Frank. 'Tori, this is too … you … we … we simply can't sit on this, or try to fix it ourselves. You won't want to hear this but—'

'I've got to take a chance on Whitehead?'

'Correct.'

Tori already had enjoyed a taste of Axel's extraordinary contacts. 'Can't you get me in above his head?' she asked. Not everyone's boss was on first-name terms with a Soti Skylakakis or a Bill Gates, let alone the last four US presidents including the incumbent.

'I could,' he said, drawing it out slowly, which she hoped meant he was considering it, but her optimism was short-lived. 'But I won't. Tori, that would be an exposure I can't afford. I hope you understand.'

Frank interrupted, 'I could go to my friends at—'

'—MI6?' said Axel. 'You could, but it's better—for SIS, anyhow—if Tori front runs on this.'

'In case it all turns to shit.' She said it without any spleen. It was a simple statement of the obvious.

'Exactly,' said Axel, glad she understood. Tori thought she detected a whirring in the air, as if he was swinging his beads in the background. 'Tori, I suggest you call Pittorino and Whitehead—get them on the phone together—but tell them everything. Frank and I will listen in, like before. Given what's involved here, they'll have to go multiagency on this, and immediately. They'll call in Frank's former employer in London, they'll need to get the FSB in on it, too,' he said, referring to Russia's post Cold War successor to the KGB. 'But wait, I'd rather you two weren't in their country when the FSB finds out about this. So don't make the call until you get the plane up and you're well out of Russian airspace. I've still got plenty of time here.'

'So we fly back to Athens?' asked Frank.

'Forget Athens,' said Axel. 'Everything's in hand here. Tori needs to be in Washington, to offer them everything, to prove her bona fides.'

'And me?' asked Frank.

'And you, too.'

THE PLANE WAS queuing for flight clearance for what seemed an age but within an hour of talking to Axel they'd cleared the Gulf of Finland and, when they were approaching the coast of Sweden, they placed the call. That it was only seven am in Washington was a good thing as far as Tori was concerned. If her former colleagues swung into action, they had eight hours before Yevtushenko's Cloud started leaking—at midnight, Saint-Petersburg-time—and a further six before it completely burst.

She phoned Davidson but before he could start screaming, she gave him a number, told him to get Whitehead and Pittorino to call her on it, and hung up. Until she knew what reaction they'd have, Tori didn't want them to know where she was, so once again the number was a router, though this time it would divert the callers to the plane's central phone hub, where Tori and Frank were ready to pick up, with an automatic piggyback linking Axel in Athens.

It was no surprise that Pittorino started out furious. 'Swyft, with what else is going on around here, and at seven in the damn mornin', I don't feel like another one of your little tizzies,' she said. 'Are you gonna hang up on us again, or what? Hey, Davidson, where are those danishes? And coffee!'

Whitehead was joined in from Homeland Security, but today he was located in their New York office. 'Morning, Dr Swyft, or whatever time it is wherever you are.' He clearly had his team running a trace on the line and knew it was being routed, although not to where.

'Actually, it's afternoon. Listen, we don't have a lot of time for pleasantr—'

'Indeed we don't, not with everything else.'

'That's not my intentio—'

'Fine,' said Whitehead. 'So listen up. Dunn and her team at NRC have made a patch to fix the nuke bug. It means the instrument makers don't have to manufacture replacement components and install them, and since they can do it overnight, that means no plant shutdowns, no public panics—which right now is mighty convenient—and it saves weeks of delay and probably millions in costs.'

'I'm delighted to hear that, sir, but—'

'It gets better—for you anyway, Swyft. Dunn has also confirmed that the NRC's archives back you up. What you originally gave them was one hundred per cent clean. As well as that, our forensics have trawled both the webpage you opensourced and the university's thesis records and while it's clear both were corrupted, they found scraps of code referring to Phi/8, so our working hypothesis is that the perpetrator was Oscar Philips, like you said. So what have you got for us?'

'Hmm,' said Tori, and she drummed her fingers on the

plane's table. 'If that's your working hypothesis, your non-working hypothesis must be that it was me, right?'

'Your good friend Davidson's arguin' just that,' said Pittorino. 'He says you could easily have planted those scraps, as red herrings to throw us off your trail.'

Whitehead cut back in. 'But for the moment we're discounting that.'

'Listen, Swyft, we're kinda busy here so if you're tryin' to be helpful, like you say, tell us where you are right now.'

Tori told them the truth, and that she'd land in Virginia in about eight hours, at around three pm. 'But Dr Whitehead, let me reciprocate with some discounting on my own part. You said we met at university—'

'Do we really have to discuss your sorority parties?' asked Pittorino.

'We do.' Tori glanced at Frank, and mouthed *Here goes*. 'For a short time,' she said, 'Dr Whitehead and I were both starry-eyed members of a radical environmentalist group, under the awe of a certain Professor George Mellor. Am I correct, Dr Whitehead?'

'Well, you might have been under his awe,' said Whitehead, suddenly speaking calmly and slowly, but it wasn't slow like he was trying to buy time to concoct a story, it was more an exasperated confidence about his position. 'I thought I dealt with this yesterday when I said I was conned into being a pawn in a psychology experiment, a most unethical one. I assumed you were the same.'

'Whoa, stop there. What the hell is this?'

'Director Pittorino,' said Tori, 'this is why I've been playing so hard to get. Dr Whitehead and I attended meetings of what superficially—'

'Swyft, let me,' said Whitehead. 'Concetta, while I was doing my doctorate in Sydney, sponsored by the State Department I might add, I attended a few meetings of an extremist deep-green group, posing as an acolyte. I wasn't there because I held their views, or because I was, er, awed. It was simply meat for my thesis. My topic was on new directions in anarcho-terrorism. I'd been a minor player in the investigative team that nabbed the Unabomber in '96, but after 9/11 when the focus switched almost totally to al-Qaeda, I decided to dig elsewhere, into what the intelligence community had stupidly allowed to become white space, all the homegrown neo-Luddite whackjobs out there—people who passionately believed the Unabomber was right and who were still taking up arms in the same struggle. Eco-terrorists. To cut a long story short, this little group in Sydney was run by a very charismatic science professor—charismatic in a weird way—but when he folded the group, suddenly, he told me—and I assumed you, Swyft—that it was because we'd been ignorant patsies for one of his buddies in the psych department and the university authorities had just shut down the experiment for being totally unethical, like I said. But my question, Swyft, now you remind me of all that, is that I had a good reason for being there, but what was yours?'

On the pad in front of her, Tori scrawled *Believable so far, but I'm not 100%*. When she swung it around for Frank to read it, he gave her a thumbs-up in agreement. 'Me?' she said. 'I wanted to make a difference to the planet, the same reason I was doing my doctorate in nuclear, to help guarantee it was safe, and thus the work I did on my protocol.'

'Which,' said Pittorino, 'almost lit a global safety hell-fire.'

'Ironically, yes, but as Dr Whitehead said, your working hypothesis is that it wasn't my doing.'

'Swyft, until I hear more, I'm not so sure if that hypothesis is the right one, so get on with your story about this here group, but make it quick, okay?'

IN ATHENS, WHILE Axel was listening to the call, he briefly wondered why Pittorino and Whitehead were so pressed for time. But he didn't let the thought stop his silver fork from cutting into his foie gras and delicately laying the slice of soft caramelised heaven on his tongue. As he let the flavours dissolve, his eyes rolled back, almost in orgasmic delight. Food, good food, helped him think. He briefly panicked, double-checking that his phone was on mute; it wouldn't do if the others heard such moans of delight.

The TV in the corner finally caught his eye. For the last fifteen minutes it had been silently broadcasting dramatic aerial shots of train wrecks, but he was only registering them now. Twisted, mangled, burning, smoking wrecks. Lots of them. The newsbar scrolling along the bottom of the TV screen said that Europe's stock markets, already open, had started another kind of bloodbath, a financial one. Commodity markets were also plummeting, unsurprising given the headline that just flashed up: 'Fast train disaster … big hit to China growth'. He put down his fork and checked his tablet computer, and saw it was alive with news about the crisis.

If this was as big as it looked, it could finish the Greek deal, he thought, and every other deal SIS was working on. If China's growth stalled, it could wreck any hope that countries like Greece would come out of purgatory. It was a body blow to an already limping global financial system. And to think that Yevtushenko's plan could launch on top of this. He pushed his foie gras away and sent Tori and Frank a text message in case they hadn't heard about it. But once it was sent, he relented, and pulled his delicacy back to him.

TORI ACCEPTED THE bottle of water that Frank handed her and took a sip, then continued. 'The group was called Nine

Sisters and its leader, like Dr Whitehead said, was inspirational, at least the eighteen-year-old I then was thought so, but he was also the professor who ended up supervising my doctorat—'

Pittorino interrupted. 'Say again. What did you just call the group?'

'Nine Sisters? It was named after a Masonic Lodge in Paris that Benjamin Franklin and Voltaire were membe—'

'Holy shit,' said Pittorino. 'Al,' she said to Whitehead, 'I haven't had a chance to tell you … the intel only came through just before this call … but our analysts have just turned up two links to that name, one in LA and—'

'Wilbur Fenton?' asked Tori. 'The guy the media's calling Dr eKiller?'

'How in blazes d'you know that?'

'He was in Nine Sisters at the same time as us and so, by the way, was Oscar Philips.'

'Why didn't you—?'

'Deputy director, you do know that I specifically asked Davidson to set up yesterday's call as a one on one between you and me, right? I did have a good reason for that: namely to tell you that Nine Sisters was where I first came across Dr Whitehead, *and* Fenton, *and* Philips. My, er, working hypothesis was that Dr Whitehead might not have been so much a pawn, as he puts it, but a sleeper like the other two. So frankly, when you both ambushed me on the call, I panicked.'

Pittorino exploded. 'Do you realise who you're talkin' abou—'

This time, Whitehead interrupted. 'Cool it, Concetta. Anyone in Swyft's shoes would rightly have concerns. But I've explained my involvement. So, Swyft, keep talking. Where does this go?'

'Where—?' Tori started, but she paused as Frank pointed her to Axel's message. 'Where was the other link?' she asked. 'You said there were two, LA and somewhere else.'

'Huh?' said Pittorino, still taking in what Tori had been saying. 'China.'

'Not the fast trains?' said both Tori and Whitehead at the same time.

'Yes, the trains. Jesus, Swyft are you sayin' Fenton, the trains, your nuke bug, they're all connected?'

'Fenton, yes, the nuclear bug, yes, but what's the link to the trains?'

Tori heard a rustling of paper as Pittorino pulled a sheet in front of her. 'Before the Chinese government took it down, we captured a post on a popular Chinese social media site, a suicide note. By a woman named ... Yuan Li Ming. She ring any bells?'

Neither Tori nor Whitehead responded.

'She wrote it from her phone, while she was sitting on a train ... just before it crashed. It translates like this: "Growth is a false god. The China dream is a nightmare. China can't continue expanding at ... blah, blah ... without doing irreparable damage, not just to China's environment but the entire planet. Every individual we lift out of poverty inches the nation and the world further toward their certain death. I have been honoured to be head of rail systems integrity for," and she names one of the large rail companies and then continues: "The high-pressure rollout of the fast trains is the key to China's rapid urbanisation and industrialisation—cheap, fast transport allowing workers ... blah, blah ... The blah, blahs are mine, okay? This Yuan Li Ming woman, she really goes on and on ... Where was I? Yes, here it is ... For the sake of our planet, this must stop. I have worked hard to give myself the power to stop it, and I will stop it. Today. Now. This I do in the name of the Nine Sisters. I am on board one of our trains as I post this. I and other people must die, so our planet can live." She then adds … added … something in Latin …'

Again Tori and Whitehead spoke together: '*Fiat justitia et ruant coeli*. Let justice be done, though the heavens fall.'

'Holy Jesus! What the hell is this? Whitehead? You sure got a helluvalot of explainin' to do.'

'Before he does, ma'am, the actual reason for my call is that while this is clearly bad already, it's about to get way, way worse. There's the trains for sure, but there's also what I've discovered in Venice and Saint-Petersburg …'

Without mentioning the assistance she'd had from Frank and Axel, Tori raced through a description of Nine Sisters, of Mellor, what she'd found on his computer and the results so far of the steganography decoding. She was about to give them her dump on Yevtushenko. 'I'm emailing the stegas to you right now … just a second … done. Now, what I found in Saint-Petersburg—'

'You got all this on your lonesome, Swyft?'

'I worked for the Agency for six years, ma'am, and—'

'Swyft, stop there please,' said Whitehead. 'Concetta, with what started out as benign turning toxic, and clearly a question mark hanging over my head, I've just buzzed my deputy to join us on this call. John, say hi to CIA Deputy Director Pittorino and Dr Tori Swyft.'

'John Weiss here, folks. I'm in Washington. What's the situation?'

'Weiss,' said Whitehead, 'I'm stepping aside temporarily—'

'From the nuke op?'

'It's not just a nuke op anymore, so I'm stepping aside from the op *and* my job. Until the Director of DHS says differently, Weiss, you're in charge of it all.'

'Excuse me, sir?'

'I'll explain it all to you later, but it's in nobody's interests, least of all mine, if I hear what Dr Swyft is about to tell us. And time may be short, so you need to take charge and get the team cracking. Hang on a moment—' The others heard footsteps as Whitehead went to his door. 'Right. I've called Ed Petrie into the room here with me. Concetta, Ed's our station manager here in Ops Command in New York.'

'Ah ... what's the deal, sir?' said the new voice the others presumed was Ed Petrie.

'Weiss, I'm giving my access pass and my cell phone to Ed.'

Those listening heard the card slide across the desk and then something heavier.

'But, sir, what's this all abo—?'

'Just take 'em, Ed. Now Weiss, I want you to suspend my security clearances immediately and likewise initiate password changes cutting off all my access to the network. Freeze my email accounts and set Forensics on them. My phone calls too. And here ... Weiss, Concetta, I've written down for Ed my private email account with login and password, not that you don't have it on my file already. And Weiss, fix me up with a polygraph test. The sooner I can clear myself, the better. Meanwhile, I'll sit outside twiddling my thumbs in the anteroom.'

30

'SOFTWARE KING ARRESTED IN WETSUIT', shouted the headline on *The New Zealand Herald*'s website.

At dawn today on Waitemata Harbour, police plucked one of New Zealand's wealthiest men from his pricey Kevlar kayak to arrest him on 17 counts of tax fraud. Dr Tom Major, currently being held in custody at Auckland's Mount Eden Corrections Facility, is chief software engineer at Sofdox, the world's most admired software company …

As Tom Major sat hunched over in the prison cell, his head in his hands, he couldn't believe this. It wasn't just the indignity of being caught, let alone how and where, it was the timing. Today was set to be the day. *His* day. *The* day. The day he'd worked ten years for as M/9. The day he had chosen to activate his Nine

Sisters plan and launch his software bomb that, in a week's time, would wipe millions of computers clean and explode millions of others.

At least there was one silver lining: the prison guards were stupid enough to promise him that once all their paperwork was finalised, they'd give him access to a computer. He only needed one. Any one. And he didn't need it for long.

31

AFTER TORI AND FRANK HAD SPENT three of the next four hours on the jet's phone to Langley and Washington—made longer by the occasional call drop-outs—the steward laid out a far more sumptuous meal than either of them felt like eating. It wasn't just that the stock markets that were open had already gone into a swan dive and so it seemed vaguely obscene, it was more that what Tori really wanted was sleep. But her mind was still buzzing and it needed comfort food, good solid carbs to trick it into slumber, so the pasta starter was perfect.

On the call, Weiss had proved competent, though initially lacking Whitehead's poise, fairly reasonable for a guy thrust unprepared into the hot seat, a boiling one at that. For Frank, the clincher that Weiss was a winner was when Tori revealed the crisis that Yevtushenko's time bombs presented. Weiss was unruffled. He acted, and acted fast. He was no tight-faced bureaucrat worried about covering his butt. By then, he'd already assembled a small team around him and rather than delegate something so important, he interrupted the call, picked up another secure phone and direct dialled his peer in Russia's Federal Security Service, the FSB. Weiss and Uri Golovanov were clearly on first-name terms and in impeccable Russian— far better than Frank's or Tori's—he brought Uri succinctly and completely into the loop. Simultaneously one of his team sent through the screenshots of Yevtushenko's computer, and when Uri was looking at them, Weiss coolly suggested, according to Frank's attempt at translation, that the FSB had little time, and needed their best code-crackers marshalled for immediate raids on Yevtushenko's Saint-Petersburg headquarters as well as his Cloud servers in Moscow.

After the line had dropped out the first time, just after Whitehead had disqualified himself, and before she explained about NuAgeCloud, Tori reconnected and volunteered the plane's direct satellite number in case it happened again. It did, several times, and each time Weiss called back on the new line.

The plane's communications were good, but not perfect for sending documents or data. While Frank had successfully emailed—in Tori's name—the screenshots of Yevtushenko's computer, sending the stegas for decoding had proved more problematic. The emails kept bouncing back. He tried uploading them to Homeland Security's secure FTP site, but they arrived even more corrupted than when he'd sent them, so with the list of names being so short, a mere fourteen of them, Tori spelled them out over the phone, blanks and all.

She put down her fork and spoon and checked her watch; there were still five hours before the leaks phase of Yevtushenko's plan was due to start. She and Frank briefly debated checking their own banks, to see if they used NuAgeCloud, but decided not to bother. 'If that happens, it'll be the least of our problems,' said Tori. Plus, Weiss had already directed his people to block the website Yevtushenko had set up to spill the leaked data, EverythingYouWantedToKnowAboutEverybodyElse.com, so unless the Russian had also set up a backup they didn't know about, his leaks wouldn't be very effective.

Clinking their glasses—a French merlot—for the third time, or maybe the fourth, they both got a giggle over how Pittorino got so pissed when, after Weiss had alerted Russia's FSB, he also called in the FBI. For the CIA chief, this was a rat act, despite it being obvious that Weiss had no other choice given that securing the NuAgeCloud facility in Boise, Idaho, was a domestic operation and so outside the Agency's mandate. Weiss had also placed a call to Maria Channells, the head of MI5 in London. He put her on high alert, pointing her to Yevtushenko's Edinburgh backup site. He followed it with a call to France's internal security service, the DCRI, to secure NuAgeCloud's servers in Marseille.

That was the moment Axel chose to quietly leave the call for his meeting with the Greeks, though he couldn't help wondering if, given the ructions in the markets already, the deal discussions were still worth persisting with. But then, in his long experience, markets had short memories.

Weiss had already allocated one of his key people to work with the FBI on the op in Boise, and another as linkman to coordinate with all the other US domestic agencies that he would progressively bring in. Weiss wasn't an inter-agency tug-of-war player, like some of her former colleagues at the CIA. He simply stepped up, knowing that Tori's information—plus what he'd now got from Pittorino—meant the various agencies needed to act immediately and together or he'd risk catastrophic and rolling systems collapses—power, transport, banking, hospitals, police—first across Eastern Europe, then Western Europe and eventually the US. His job was protecting the US but, on the information he had so far, Europe was the Nine Sisters' likely back door entry, and he would do whatever he could to keep it securely barricaded. Outside of a still very small group, no one knew that Nine Sisters linked the Fenton murders, the nuclear mess and the China crisis, and now there was Yevtushenko. Despite the need to start bringing numerous others into the loop, Weiss was trying hard to keep a lid on it. Panic was his second-worst enemy, the Nine Sisters themselves being his first.

Weiss instantly accepted Pittorino's offer of a team to work on tracking down the other 9S members. Tori had done her best to plumb the depths of her memory, offering guesses of the actual members' names as well as what she could recall of their disciplines of study, and the Agency was now trying to cross-check those as best they could against the doctoral graduation lists for the period at the three key Sydney universities. No one was concerned that it was the middle of the night in Sydney; Pittorino's people had their ways, as Tori and Frank knew from personal experience, both having once been junior analysts.

The Russians were no slouches either. Just over an hour after speaking to Uri Golovanov for the first time, Weiss read out a message that the FSB had run simultaneous surprise raids in Moscow and Saint-Petersburg, aiming to arrest Yevtushenko only to discover he'd left not just his building, but Russia. Not only had he vanished, but more amazingly, so had his jet. Ten minutes before Weiss's call, it had already escaped Russian airspace. The flight plan it had logged in was to Moscow yet after takeoff it had headed west, not southeast and fifteen minutes later its identity blip completely disappeared off the screens, no longer showing up on any of the international air traffic systems.

'Damn that guy,' said Weiss, frustrated though with a tinge of respect. 'What can't he do? Relocating the Bermuda Triangle up to the Baltic wouldn't have been easy.'

It was the only time Pittorino had laughed. 'Yeah, and he didn't ask us for permission, either … after all, the Triangle's supposed to be our little baby.'

Once the call had finished, and the pasta dishes cleared away, Tori and Frank tossed for who would take the first shower, getting to wash off the pressure of the last few days under the sprays of steaming hot water courtesy of Axel's luxurious marble bathroom. According to the steward, showers weren't even optional extras for Gulfstream G650s, but that hadn't stopped Axel. Frank won the toss, and by the time he came out towelling his hair, and garbed in the standard evening wear on Axel's plane—fresh silk pyjamas—Tori's head was already on the table.

ONCE TORI HAD showered and changed and after another glass of red, Frank started to look even more disturbingly good to her than usual, with the gold silk rubbing against his smooth, dark skin. She put down her merlot and asked the steward to remove it, with the lame excuse, 'It'll stop me sleeping.'

'And me from working on Mellor's hard drive,' said Frank smiling, handing him the bottle. Tori hoped that if he'd noticed her blush, he'd think it was the shower, or the wine but, either way, he made no show of it, and was more preoccupied that he should use the remaining four hours in the air to find a better program to decode the stegas, and possibly something to give further colour to Tori's story about the Nine Sisters. On that score, he'd found nothing so far, but he was hoping to stumble across a manifesto, a speech, anything while Tori was sleeping. His plan was that after dropping Tori in Virginia with the hard drive, the stegas and whatever else he may have found, he and the plane would head straight back to Athens.

The plane's phone rang. Tori and Frank shot worried glances at each other since the display that popped up on the comms screen puzzled them, showing that this call was routing in via the decoy number they'd first given to Langley, not the direct number they'd since given to Weiss and Pittorino. It meant this wasn't the CIA or DHS, and it was unlikely to be Axel since he would still be with the Greeks.

When Tori and Frank slipped on their headsets, the voice they heard was Alan Whitehead's. He was calling from a secure phone, he said, with a favour to ask.

They'd already agreed over dinner that the fact Whitehead had suspended himself *before* Tori had given her data dump was at least some evidence he deserved the benefit of the doubt. Weiss seemed to share their opinion since, when he told Tori and Pittorino that Whitehead had cleared the polygraph test, she could hear the relief in his voice. Weiss clearly respected— and liked—his boss and was stressed not just by the events he had to step up to, but also the prospect that his role model might no longer be one.

'Tori,' said Whitehead, 'I apologise for calling. I know it's irregular and if you feel you need to report this to Weiss, please go ahead, I'll understand. But after you hear me out, I hope you won't.'

'I'm listening, Dr Whitehead.'

'Please, in the circumstances I'd prefer it if you called me Al.'

'I could call you W/12,' she said, smiling at Frank for support but he sternly shook his head at her. He was right; this was no time for levity. 'Sorry, I guess that's not funny, er, Al.'

He let it slide. 'Tori, I wasn't on the call when you gave them your stega with the list of Nine Sisters members, but can you tell me if there was a Margy Quando on it?'

'It's not a name I remember, Al, but wait a second.' She got up to grab her list from the console at the other end of the cabin. Her headphones were wireless so she didn't need to remove them and as she walked back, she ran her eye down the list. 'The closest I've got is,' and she spelled it out, 'first name, M-space-R-G-space, then the surname, Q-double space-N-space-O. It could be a Margy Quando.'

Why Tori didn't know the name was because, Whitehead said, Margy had left the group just before Tori had joined. 'I wasn't entirely truthful before, Tori. My real reason for joining Nine Sisters was I was dating Margy and I tagged along with her, but when I found out what it really was, I persuaded her to quit while I stuck with it, for my research, like I said.'

'And why are you risking Weiss's ire to call me up and tell me this?'

'Because ... well ... Margy is my wife.'

'Whoa!'

Whitehead explained that Margy was the global head of risk for EuropaNational, the international banking giant hailing from Paris but now headquartered in New York. Tori had read only a week ago, while on Soti's yacht, rumours that EuropaNational and the smaller Citigroup were discussing a merger.

Whitehead continued: 'I know she's clean, but I've still got the national interest to consider, to make absolutely certain of it no matter whose wife she is.'

'So why ring me and not Weiss?'

'Tori, I don't know what you found out in Russia—and please don't tell me—but if there's even a hint that Margy's a Nine Sisters sleeper—which she isn't—her job, her whole career is finished. No bank would ever hire her again. Worse, until she was cleared, it would throw her bank in turmoil, putting it at great risk in these skittish markets we're in. Think of the chatter. It could cause a run on the bank and given its size, the whole financial system could ... Look, Tori, all I really want to do is protect my wife and stop an unjustified banking crisis. I know Weiss. He's good and he will get to her, but it will take him time—'

'Time?'

'For starters, Margy hasn't gone by the name Quando for almost ten years. It was her husband's name from her first marriage. She was midway through her divorce when she met me and when she got it, she switched back to her maiden name, Bernardo, and that's what she's gone by ever since. But Tori, for goodness' sake, she'd left Nine Sisters before you even joined it.'

'I hear you, Al, but what can I do?'

'Divert your flight to New York and go see her ... help me prove she's clean. That way, you can give Weiss the whole package before he even gets an inkling about her. Please?'

'But Weiss and Pittorino are expecting me in—'

'Find a reason.'

Frank was writing furiously on a sheet of paper. *Why can't he get the proof himself? Why ask you?*

She nodded and asked Whitehead outright.

'How would that look on the nightly news, Tori? Suspended government official tries to concoct alibi for his own wife? No way. Look, I passed the polygraph and all—I don't know if you heard?—but clearly I'm conflicted. I need someone totally objective on this, not someone blinded by emotion like me. I also need a person with discretion, who won't blab until she's done the work and has the answer either way. Look, if Margy is a sleeper—which she isn't—then you tell Weiss, end of story. No complaints from me ... only deep, deep grief.'

Tori excused herself as she put him on hold to discuss it with Frank. 'This guy's incredible,' said Frank. 'He's stepped down from his job, and he's still putting the national interest above his own wife.'

'But if she is a sleeper then her just knowing about his suspension ... the investigation ... it would be a go-sign, a warning she should move to action. Shit!'

She reopened the line. 'Al, have you told your wife about your suspension, about any of this?'

'Not a word. Look, to be honest, I wasn't thinking straight at first and I did make a mistake and try to call her but, thank God, I didn't get through. Turns out she's in some heavy board meeting. Her assistant said the President was even involved so—'

'Wouldn't he always be involved in a board meeti—'

'Not the bank president. Her, the US President.'

Frank scratched on the paper again: *Mega-merger rumours true???* Tori shrugged, at first not caring, but her mind started whirring, wondering if there was an angle for SIS there, with Citi and EuropaNational both being major lenders to Greece as well as to Soti Skylakakis's empire. But she parked that thought; if the Nine Sisters weren't stopped, there would be no Greek deal. There'd be nothing.

'Tori, clearly I can't be anywhere near Margy, near anybody, until this is over. If I had managed to get through to her and Weiss found out, especially since I hadn't fessed up that she's on the list, she'd be finished.'

'And so would you.'

'Right, but this way there's a hope. That's all I'm asking.'

'Al, where are you calling from?'

He told her he was on a burner phone, calling from the balcony of his apartment, the penthouse he shared with Margy when he was in New York.

Tori went on hold again and debated with Frank, who was strongly in favour of doing what Whitehead had asked. 'The guy's whole world is falling apart yet he hasn't once moaned about his own predicament, just the country and his wife. He's a patriot. Let's at least give him something back.'

She went back online. 'Al, we'll do it.'

'Thank y—Did you say we?'

'Sorry, I should have introduced my colleague, Frank Chaudry. He helped me get the stegas and the screenshots, er, other stuff. He's ex-MI6 so he does have a few useful skills, despite the accent.'

Frank wrote on the sheet again: *And he looks extremely hot in silk pyjamas!* Tori grinned back, but took the pen and scratched it out, unsure if Frank was making a joke or had actually read her mind.

'Dr Whitehead, Chaudry here. We'll use the rest of our flight to work up a plan. How long is this board meeting set to run for, do you know?'

'Gayle—Margy's assistant—said it was set to be an all-nighter, that I shouldn't expect Margy back at the apartment if I was planning on being in New York tonight. I didn't tell Gayle where I was by the way, and last time I spoke to Margy was yesterday when I was still in Washington.'

'What message did you leave for your wife?'

'Actually, I asked Gayle not to tell her I called, that she had enough on her plate and that I'd be seeing her on the weekend anyway. We've got tickets for the ballet on Saturday.'

'Great,' said Tori. 'We may want to run some of our thoughts past you, so call us back, say, at two pm your time, that's an hour before we're due to land, and by then we'll have worked out why we suddenly need to be in New York.'

32

AT 3.50 PM, TORI'S CAB PULLED UP at the Avenue of the Americas entrance for The Skewer, the name a disparaging public had given to EuropaNational's preposterous stainless steel and glass New York headquarters, a tower designed for a CEO who happily squandered other people's money to stroke his ego. The edifice was supposed to evoke a spindle, like what old-school bank managers in green visors once spiked their memos and messages with. *The New York Times* had slammed it, saying the only spike evident must have been in the board's water jugs when they lost their minds and signed off on the expensive eyesore and, on *The Daily Show with Jon Stewart*, the host kept parodying EuropaNational as 'the bank that looks how it makes you feel'.

Axel's pilot had landed Tori and Frank in New York a half-hour early at 2.30 pm. The pilot's mother, Tori had lied to Weiss not long before, had just had a stroke, the reason she had to detour via New York and wait for him for a couple of hours.

So, with Teterboro Airport's private jet terminal just over the George Washington Bridge, Weiss had one of his New York people waiting for her at the foot of the airstairs, where she handed over the stegas as well as the copy of Mellor's hard drive.

With all the work to be done on the stegas and on Yevtushenko's Cloud, Weiss knew his team would be buried so he wasn't fussed about a delay with Tori, especially since the NRC's Judith Dunn had vouched that Tori had already done everything she could to help build the patch for her neutronics model.

Leaving the airport and on the way to visit Whitehead's wife, Tori had made three stops. The first was together with Frank in SoHo, at what turned out to be a paradoxically opulent penthouse spanning the top floor of a musty, abandoned-looking apartment building, where they'd come to pick up a supply of tiny earbud transmitter/receivers and an array of other equipment they suspected might be handy.

The windows facing the street were boarded up and the exterior brown paint was peeling so badly that a sheet of it, as large as the trunk of the rust-bucket car raised up on bricks at the kerb, landed near Tori's feet while they waited at the joyless front door. Frank phoned their arrival—there was no security pad, not even a bell behind the cold steel chain slung back and forth across the locked entrance. As the door clicked and swung itself inwards, Frank ducked under the chain and Tori followed, stomping on the paint, and cracking it into a hundred pieces that fluttered momentarily into the air as the door slammed shut behind them. From inside the industrial-sized goods elevator slowly clanging its way up to the top floor, Tori noticed the strange windows that Frank had warned her about. The dealer they were visiting—from Frank's colourful description, an eccentric Brit called Thatcher—had installed electric one-way glass that from the outside was coated so it looked like boards but also had a state-of-the-art heat frequency nullifier so that heat-detecting drones, spy choppers or prying satellites would never detect a skerrick of light or a breath of heat escaping from his apparently deserted but in truth palatial pad. As far as the authorities were concerned, Thatcher's home and headquarters, his mission control, was an empty floor in a derelict building in a seedy part of SoHo.

When they entered the apartment they were greeted by a rather solid man whose abundant girth was garbed in a tailored tuxedo and a wing tip-collared white shirt, all chiming in nicely with his swanky furnishings, leather chesterfields, drooping chandeliers and oriental rugs. His brogues were so highly polished Tori wondered if the cream he used on them was the same as what he obviously plastered onto the few luckless strands left on his head; the aroma floating after him was pleasant—half coconut, half bubble gum—a little like the surf wax she used to use. Thatcher caught Tori's quizzical look, and shrugged, 'My dear, one simply cannot know who might drop in on one unexpectedly, can one?'

He pronounced 'drop' as *dwop* in that eccentrically upper-class British manner, and his formality, together with his pinched adenoidal voice and his vague air of someone habitually lost in thought somewhat threw Tori, but Frank had vouched for him as a highly trusted friend he'd scrapped with all through Eton and Oxford, as well as someone he'd shared numerous momentous hacks with over the many years since.

Hacker circles boasted black hats and white hats but, despite Thatcher's lack of hair, he decried hats of any kind and chose to be known after one of his favourite delicacies, Fig Jam, unaware that his resentful hacker rivals would see it as aptly short for Fuck I'm Good, Just Ask Me.

He leant forward and, as best he could, tried to wrap his arms around Frank and give him a squeeze. 'My dear Chowders, how very good to welcome you and your colleague into my humble abode.' Humble? And Chowders? Tori guessed it was a British public school thing, wondering how Frank would take it if she called him by that nickname in future, but she decided to stick to Frank or Chaudry.

When Thatcher was fumbling inside one of his vaults searching for some of the equipment, Frank whispered that the last time he'd been here, Thatcher had confessed to him about owning twelve tuxedos, his ambition being to possess an even twenty of them. Each suit was in a different black cloth: superfine wool, silk, mohair, cashmere, and almost every combination possible. On that earlier occasion, Frank had sneaked a peek inside Thatcher's closet, which was more of an expansive dressing room, and apart from the rows of black jackets and separated pants, there were three racks of starched white shirts hung airily, an inch or two between each 'so they can breathe', as Thatcher commented when he caught his friend poking his nose there, adding, 'One can never have enough of a good thing, what?'

Thatcher was also a stickler for grammar and spelling as Tori would discover, even in short text messages. No LOLs and URs for him, and as she scanned his penthouse, there were no hacker clichés of old pizza boxes spilling over his desk and floor either, although there was a strange musty odour hanging in the air. It wasn't unfamiliar, but she couldn't place it.

If she had not been too embarrassed to ask, Thatcher would have rushed to answer the question by opening his fridge to let her inhale the heavenly aroma of the black truffles that FedEx had delivered to him only that morning from Batlow in Australia's Snowy Mountains. For his fussy nose, these were a musty sniff ahead of the even more expensive truffles he used to import from France.

To Tori, Thatcher seemed like a younger and British version of Axel. His massive oak dining table was already set hospitably for three, with Georg Jensen silverware and Baccarat crystal glassware at one end, evidencing his gallantry as much as his passion that meals were to be savoured not wolfed.

The two old school chums had much to catch up on and since Tori wouldn't need Frank for an hour or more, she excused herself from the feast their host had whipped up, and left him behind heading off to the meatpacking district, her next stop. There she collected her freshly-minted ID and the 'official' letter she'd ordered in another call from the plane. This dealer was her own contact, one she'd used twice when she worked for the Agency, mostly because his work was better than theirs, yet another irritant that scratched Davidson the wrong way about her.

Bloomingdale's was her third stop, to get herself into character, a role that required both grim stiffness and gravitas: Chief Auditor, Serious Fraud in New York's Department of Financial Services. The NY DFS was feared in banking circles after it lashed out, labelling the respected Standard Chartered Bank a 'rogue institution' in 2012 for allegedly hiding $250 billion in transactions tied to Iran in breach of the US's sanctions against that country, a claim that almost instantly wiped $17 billion off the bank's market value.

When Whitehead had first suggested that cover to her, what immediately popped into Tori's head was an image of the dismal, soulless ex-model in Saint-Petersburg who escorted her to Yevtushenko. She couldn't shake the picture for the whole trip to Bloomies, but by the time she got there she decided that her own manufactured don't-fuck-with-me persona would never wear orange at work, instead settling for a severe two-piece kohl-black suit and four-inch black patent stilettos.

Since not even Whitehead had been able to cut through EuropaNational's red tape to extract his own wife out of a board meeting, his ingenious way to guarantee immediate access to her was by faking a surprise official audit from one of the bank's panoply of regulators, in particular this one. Even in a board meeting, opening a sealed envelope marked *Urgent, Private & Confidential* from the NY DFS pressing for an immediate face-to-face over 'disquieting' rumours of sanctions breaches with Iran would send a shiver up any risk officer's spine, especially after the Standard Chartered Bank affair, and even more so if her own bank was in the last delicate throes of negotiations on a politically sensitive mega-merger.

As Tori rode the elevator to the eighty-fifth floor of The Skewer she stretched herself tall, tightening her face muscles in different combinations, and continuing to check out her various 'looks' in the mirrored steel doors, but as soon as they slid open she almost cracked up. Tori had heard about this, but she never expected to see it, not from up here. One of the clinchers for the bank's board to sign off on this absurd structure was its promised 360-degree panorama out to the horizon. The problem, which she was desperately trying not to smirk about, was that something in the design or materials of the towering metallic spike attracted clouds to hug it, just above the eightieth floor, which meant that from the ground it often looked like it was piercing a puff ball, but up here you were in a total whiteout, unable to see a thing from this senior executive floor.

Instead, the lack of view concentrated a visitor's eyes on the interior, shimmering with wealth, power and influence. The décor, hard and harsh, was a tasteless clash of contemporary against French Regency, the flouncing and flamboyant style that so symbolised aristocratic excess to the eighteenth-century French population that, even after Louis XVI toned it down, they still guillotined him. These bankers, thought Tori, had as little a sense of history as they had of style.

A profusion of gilded rococo swirls and stucco shells bounced back at her from the highly polished stainless steel walls, ceiling and window frames, made all the brighter from the light reflecting off the clouds outside. The clouds were starting to thin and, with the early-November sun already setting, the predominant colours infusing them were gold and orange, making it seem as if the rococo elements were exploding all over the walls. The effect was of a jarring opulence, a theatre of the absurd—like Tori's general opinion of the banking world—but as she neared the windows, and the clouds suddenly started parting, it was strangely uplifting, almost literally, since the stainless steel ceilings and zinc floors that mirrored the sky gave the impression there was nothing above her, that she was floating on the remaining wisps.

It was ethereal, until she brought herself back down to earth by realising that this exhilarating sense of invincibility, of immortality, was precisely the wrong sensation to create for people in charge of trillions of dollars of other people's money.

She stood there pondering this for six minutes before Margy Bernardo came to greet her, long enough for Bernardo's assistant, Gayle, to have checked that the pushy Chief Auditor Victoria Swyft was indeed who she said she was. Gayle's call to her usual contact at the NY DFS was brief, courtesy of Frank, who was enjoying some truffled roast beef at Thatcher's while still staying on cue. After Tori had left them, Thatcher let Frank use his array of equipment to hack into EuropaNational's switchboard, locate Gayle's extension on the network—easy since Whitehead had told them the number—and when Gayle dialled out to the NY DFS as they expected she would, it was Frank who, swallowing quickly, answered her call. After she asked him where her usual contact Paul MacDonnell was, Frank explained that Paul had gone home with a stomach bug and yes, Victoria Swyft was Chief Auditor, Serious Fraud. He added, 'Paul asked me to call you, actually, but I got tied up in a meeting with the Superintendent and only just got free. Sorry. Listen,' he added, 'do your boss a favour and let her know that Swyft would eat her own children if she had any.'

When Margy Bernardo eventually strode across the floor and offered her hand to her uninvited visitor, Tori ignored it instead reaching up to fix Bernardo's suit jacket. 'Your collar was up. Can't have that, can we?' It was also the perfect place to secrete one of the tiny GPS tracking devices Thatcher had supplied her with.

As Bernardo led the way to the meeting room and passed the reception desk, she again tried to be hospitable, asking if Tori wanted anything to drink. 'No gratuities under our new rules,' Tori replied. 'I imposed 'em, so I gotta stick to 'em, right?' She laughed. Her Australian accent was naturally somewhat Americanised after living here for so long, but Tori tried to Aussie it up even more.

Bernardo shrugged and ordered a cappuccino for herself from the receptionist and continued into the room. As Tori walked beside her, she observed her host even outdid the images that she and Frank had seen on the web when they decided she and Whitehead were the perfect power couple, two beautiful people straddling the wires strung between the tops of the NYC–Washington DC power poles. Frank had seemed besotted by Bernardo's photos. 'Her hair isn't my scene—that dumb bob—but those Angelina Jolie eyes, haunting, and her Salma Hayek lips, wow. No way that gal's a terrorist.'

'You think?' Tori had said, unsure if Frank was serious. 'Someone out there probably thought Osama Bin Laden looked pretty hot—like his wives, for starters—but Barack Obama still authorised the kill.'

Bernardo was an olive beauty but, unlike in the photos, she didn't go for stilettos at work. Today, that was Tori's prerogative. Through the glass-topped table in the meeting room—selected no doubt by a male decorator and presumably the reason Bernardo was wearing slacks—Tori could see that she'd already nudged off her sensible pumps and was unconsciously splaying her toes, as if an already hard day was about to get tougher. The rest of Bernardo's posture was closed, with crossed arms and her face pallid and a little frazzled. If she had put on lipstick that morning, it had already worn off. She was trying not to chew her lips or maybe, Tori thought, it could be an attempt at self-control, perhaps to stop her screaming, *What the fuck do you want? With all this China shit scaring the hell out of the markets, our merger's already falling apart, so I don't need any new crap from you about fucking Iran.*

Tori continued with her approach, trying to be as annoying as a fingernail scraping down a blackboard. She slowly slipped a sheaf of papers out of her satchel, and took time to arrange them neatly in three even piles in front of herself. 'It's a new bag. Do you like it?' she said as she closed the latch, but without looking up. Bernardo didn't answer, but Tori could hear her deeply inhaling to control herself. Then Tori extracted a sheet at random from the middle pile and ran her finger down the margin as if checking an important fact before speaking. She knew the meeting Bernardo had stepped out of was important, but so was a visit from the NY DFS's Chief Auditor, Serious Fraud, and she wanted the banker to know that, and to feel that. As head of risk, Bernardo would be used to juggling crises, but she wouldn't have unending patience—especially not today—and Tori wanted to stretch it, to see if she could make the woman's strings break.

After the coffee was placed in front of Bernardo and the waiter closed the door behind him, Bernardo unleashed. She held up the NY DFS letter she'd been handed. 'What rumours? I've heard of none. Not a single one. Ms Swyft, please make your case … and quickly … I'm in the middle of an important board meeting.'

Bernardo's voice was so controlled, so tight, that her own Australian accent was almost non-existent but, Tori thought, ten years in Paris and New York could do that. 'It's Dr Swyft, actually. But, Dr Bernardo, if you help me I can assure you that you'll get back to your little meeting nice and quickly.'

'Yeah, right,' Tori heard Frank say over her earpiece.

'Dr Bernardo,' Tori continued, 'I'm really here to discuss some other rumours with you, off the grid as it were. You'll have noticed my Australian accent, a tad more pronounced than your own.'

Bernardo sat up even straighter, if that were possible. 'Have we met?'

Tori smiled, and put down the sheet she'd been holding. She crossed her legs and pulled the hem of her skirt down demurely. 'Actually, your husband and I go way back—'

'What?' Bernardo slapped the table, then started to stand. 'Is this one of those other woman things? Jesus fucking Christ, that's the last—'

'Please sit, Dr Bernardo. Yes, sit. Thank you. No, I'm not the other woman coming to break up the picture-perfect couple.'

Bernardo's body remained on guard, and even if Tori weren't staring directly into her eyes to unsettle her further, she could have detected the tension from the sudden pungency of her perfume. Until now it had been subtle, a hint of frangipani, but under the stress it was as if an entire tree had bloomed.

'Oh,' said Tori, shifting her gaze to the window over the other woman's shoulder. 'Don't you love sunset? The pinks are always my favourite. And look, I think I can see … what's that? Staten Island? A bit hard to tell in this failing light.'

Bernardo didn't look around and started twisting a lock of her hair, but when she realised it was a tell, she dropped her hand. 'Dr Swyft, is this about my husband or about Iran?'

'I first met Alan a long time ago … when we were both in Nine Sisters,' Tori said without answering, her eyes glued to Bernardo, watching for a flinch, but apart from a brief expansion of the woman's lungs, there was nothing. She was good, but how good? Tori sat still and waited to find out.

Bernardo took her first sip of coffee, to fill the silence. After an excruciatingly empty minute, she spoke. 'Nine Sisters?' Then she stiffened again. 'Look, why the hell are you here?'

Tori pushed back her chair and stood and, her stilettos click-clacking across the zinc floor tiles, she walked past the phone, mumbling something to Frank that Bernardo wouldn't be able to make out, and went over to the floor-to-ceiling window. With her back to Bernardo, she continued: 'It's a long way to the top, isn't it? Took you ten years to get here, to the soaring heights of one of the world's most important banks. Third biggest by assets, isn't it? Fifth biggest by market capitalisation? This week anyway. It's a perfect tent to be pissing out of, don't you think?' She turned back to see Bernardo reaching for the phone, presumably to call either security or her husband. 'I wouldn't do that, Margy. I'm not here to harm you, or Alan. I'm here to help you. You *were* in Nine Sisters, right? In fact, you introduced young Al to the group, didn't you?'

As Bernardo took her hand back from the phone, her brow furrowed into a vee and she rubbed her forehead. 'I left Nine Sisters. I agreed with Al—and the professor, whatever his name was …'

'Mellor.'

'Whoever. The guy was delusional. Sure, I wanted to save the whales, the planet and all that—who doesn't?—but he entranced me, okay, and when I realised that, I quit. Anyway, it turned out it was just some cockamamie psych experiment we all got conned by. A total sham.'

Tori's hands went to her hips and she laughed. 'Come on, Margy. We both know it was no sham. The train wrecks in China are no sham. Dr eKiller in LA is no sham. My own little crisis in the nuclear plants, though thwarted, is no sham …'

Bernardo's eyes suddenly glazed into the hazy blue of a sky with an incoming storm. 'The trains? Nuclear …?' she said. 'We're lenders to some of … and I've seen the risk reports. You're *that* Swyft?'

Tori bowed. 'One and the same. And by the way, it's also not a sham that, because your husband Alan had been in Nine Sisters, he just got himself suspended from Homeland Security and was frogmarched out the door.'

'What? Alan hasn't done a thing. They wouldn't susp—'

'Then ask him.' She pointed to the phone, hoping that Frank had heard the extension number she'd seen as she walked past it and whispered to him a few moments earlier.

Bernardo dialled her husband's mobile phone and Tori, with the tiny transmitter/receiver lodged deep enough in her ear canal to be invisible, hoped to hear whatever Frank would be saying at the other end.

'Dr Whitehead's cell phone,' he said. 'Roger Daltrey speaking.'

Tori thought he was getting quite good at this, though she wouldn't have chosen the name of The Who's lead singer as an alias, but Frank was a diehard fan, as she'd discovered at the Cipriani when she had to suffer through a screening of the rock opera *Tommy* on the in-room movies.

'Mr Daltrey,' said Bernardo, clearly no music buff. 'I don't believe we've met? It's Alan's wife here, Margy. May I speak to him please?'

'Ma'am, I'm a temp. There's been a bit of a kerfuffle,' he said in his best Oxford accent, knowing it wasn't unusual for Brits to work in Homeland Security if they'd taken US citizenship. 'The official script is that Dr Whitehead is unavailable, but since it's you I guess I can tell you that he has been, shall we say, suspended, though I'm afraid I don't know any more than that.'

She asked to speak to Weiss, her husband's deputy, but 'Daltrey' told her Weiss too was unavailable. She then dialled her New York apartment and this time Frank hammed up an imitation of a recording by a sing-song Pakistani phone operator. He was a perfect mimic after years listening to his parents. 'I am truly sorry, but this phone service is suspended. Please dial 1800 ...' She hung up.

'Swyft, what's going on?'

'Margy, as head of risk of this place you're being a trifle naive, aren't you? Both DHS and the CIA have got the names of every member of Nine Sisters, including Alan's, mine, and yours ... Yours was Quando back then, wasn't it?' She saw the woman blink. 'The reason I'm here is to warn you, as Q/1, that they got onto Alan, who was W/12 of course, and they also got onto me, S/14. In my case, I had to cobble together a story that someone else had fucked over my neutronics model— Oscar Philips, do you remember him, Phi/8? The long and the short of it is I had to play along, just like you still are, saying how I believed the whole Nine Sisters thing was a sham, yadda, yadda. That way, I could buy time and warn the others, like you … Sacrifice my plan for the greater good, although they wouldn't see it that way, would they? I was too late for Alan but I'm not too late for you.'

'But it *was* all crap. At least to me it was. No one would seriously believe—'

'Yeah? And I believe I saw the President of the United States on your boardroom video a little while ago.'

'Shit, how did you …?' But Bernardo didn't finish. Her suit, light grey, was already starting to darken under her arms.

Tori felt good standing near the huge plate-glass window. It still radiated heat from the day, and the sensation she'd experienced earlier emboldened her. 'Margy, they're closing in. Stop fucking around and get moving. Activate your plan. They've got Mellor, too, by the way, not that he's much use. Dementia, but then he always was a bit crazy, right? And do you remember the Russian? Good looking, blond, at least he was back then. Yevtushenko? Y/2? They're onto him. The guy's fled Russia and his Cloud's on a timer. If they haven't stopped him already, he's just leaked every bit of confidential data sitting inside his Cloud network, passwords, bank accounts—probably yours—police records, hospital records, whatever. And in six hours, boom! Massive Cloud bursts all over Europe and the US. A tempest like we've never seen before when everything that's run off his NuAgeCloud grinds to a halt. But, hey, they've got scads of teams trying to stop it. So you, you need to move.' Tori threw Mellor and Yevtushenko into the mix just in case Bernardo had been in touch with the professor or knew anything about the Russian, so it would reinforce the veracity of her fiction. Sprinkling truths onto lies added credence to the deception: Spycraft 101. 'Does EuropaNational use NuAgeCloud?'

As Bernardo leant down to help slide her feet back into her shoes, Frank let Tori know that there'd been no data dump out of NuAgeCloud so far, none that he could see, but that Yevtushenko's leak website had been taken down, and that might be why.

Bernardo stood, drawing herself tall. 'Er, no, we don't use NuAge. But look, I don't know what this is … some weird kind of *Candid Camera* or *Punk'd* or whatever, but I don't bite. I'll tell you this though: I *am* worried about Alan being falsely accused. No way would Alan … His whole job, his career, has been about protecting this nation. How can you dare? How can they—?'

Judging by the pace that the remaining clouds outside were turning to pink and golden wisps, the wind was getting stronger, but not as fierce as the mental storm that Tori hoped was buffeting Bernardo. She did feel a smidgen of guilt; if Bernardo were truly innocent, as Whitehead and now she maintained, this would be a torture, but Tori and Frank felt they had no choice other than to push her to the brink and see if she jumped.

Tori click-clacked back to the table, shuffled and shook all her fake papers into a single neat pile and placed them in her satchel. 'Alan must be a great actor. But that's no surprise, is it? That was the plan all along. For him. For both of you. For me, too. We'd get into positions of high trust, the higher the better, and then boom! Me, close down the nuclear industry for a generation, creating instant havoc and long-lasting power shortages. You two, bring down between you the most prosperous nation as well as the global financial system. Yep, the true power couple. Can't get bigger than that, eh? You guys must have great pillow talk, huh?' she said. 'So, Dr Bernardo, I take it you're not calling security to have me arrested?'

She and Frank had debated that even if Bernardo were clean, the chances she'd raise an alarm were low, knowing that the fuss from accusing someone as smart and unpredictable, or mad, as Tori would cast an immediate spotlight over Alan's situation as well as her own, and worse would probably lead to her own suspension, possibly even derailing the sensitive merger talks. They assumed a clean Bernardo would try to see Alan, to discover the truth and clear the air. They calculated, also, that even if she were still in Nine Sisters, she'd most likely respond in exactly the same way.

The banker placed her hands on the glass table, looked around to check the door was still closed, then glared at her unwanted guest. 'Iran? That was a ruse, right? There's no Iran problem at all is there?'

'There's a big one if you read the papers, but it's not the one I got you out of the meeting for.'

Bernardo cracked. 'Just get yourself the fuck out of here!'

Tori smiled.

'So far, so good,' said Frank through her earpiece, even though neither of them yet knew which side Bernardo stood on. According to Frank, the chances were she'd make some excuse to ditch going back into the board meeting, slip out of the building and head to her apartment in the hope that Whitehead was home or had somehow left her a message.

'Or,' Tori said a few moments later, as she was plummeting to ground level in the elevator, 'with one of the largest banks in the world unwittingly backing her with its $2.56 trillion in assets, she'll unleash a financial hell on earth, making the global economic crisis seem like a backyard BBQ.'

'Either way, we've got to keep close to her.'

Tori looked her reflection up and down and smiled. The stilettos and tight suit had been perfect choices, helping her to ease comfortably into her tough guy role. Once before she'd used 'bitch stilettos', as she called them and, though that was with a male suspect, she was perversely not as successful. It was in Norway in 2012, just before Anders Behring Breivik went to trial. The right-wing extremist had a year before killed seventy-seven people by detonating a bomb in a government quarter in downtown Oslo and going on a shooting rampage at the nearby Utøya island youth camp. Prompted by conspiracy theorists that tagged the deranged killer as a CIA stooge, Davidson had sent her over as a sign of good faith to the PST, Norway's internal security service. Naively, after skimming page after page of Breivik's rambling 1500-page manifesto on the plane, Tori thought that interviewing him in stilettos might throw him, but instead he threw her. Sitting opposite her in the interview cell, the chairs and table bolted down and with his hands and legs restrained, his cold eyes and the downward pull on his mouth oozed with his disgust for her. He spoke only a single word to her: 'Whore!'

It was not Tori's finest hour and she reminded herself that Davidson, listening remotely just as Frank had been today, would probably have enjoyed the sociopath's gibe at her expense.

33

O NE OF WHITEHEAD'S FIRST OUTLAYS IN his DHS role was to upgrade the National Operations Command Centre, including by throwing a sizable chunk of the budget on the massive wall-sized projection screen that Weiss was now striding back and forth in front of in his elevated capacity. As well as acting head of DHS operations command, even greater responsibility rested precariously on his shoulders as point man not just domestically, but in 'coordinating' all the international agencies involved in the joint effort, a moot term when it came to herding the Italians or, at home, the FBI.

Any observer would instantly deduce from his clipped commands, his stiff posture and his buzz cut that John Weiss had a military background, like his suspended boss, but to those who knew him the close-cropped hair also betrayed his vanity, since it wasn't from a career habit or even for nostalgia, but because he'd gone prematurely grey at twenty-three.

The electronic screen completely covered the room's thirty-foot-wide front wall so, for the operatives sitting at their phones and computers in the curved tiers of desks facing it, the screen was perfect for managing the Nine Sisters crisis, providing the entire room with immediate visuals on everything the moment it happened. Weiss had assembled eighty people in the room including the section chief of the FBI's Critical Incident Response Group and five of his top FBI people, plus he'd mobilised several hundred of his own in the field, not including the police, FBI and, after the latest name his team had decoded and tracked down from Mellor's stegas, the US Coast Guard.

As each name was decoded and checked against university doctoral records in Sydney to get a fix on the specific individual, a new section on the screen would begin filling out. The first seven columns had been live for hours: Mellor, of course, and six of his fourteen followers, Whitehead, plus Yuan Li Ming in China, Wilbur Fenton in LA, Tori, Oscar Philips and Yevtushenko. With Masood Baqri, B/13, now up, there were seven names to go, or five if you didn't count the two Tori said had left the group before she joined.

Each column was updated live from sources fed in minute by minute from people out in the field as well as those in the room, and not just from DHS and the FBI, but CIA operatives overseas, as well as Britain's MI5, France's DCRI and, very actively, Russia's FSB. China was less forthcoming, but Weiss wasn't complaining. They were already dealing with a national crisis that had deep international repercussions. According to the screen, the major European and US stock markets were already down between eight and twelve per cent at their closes. The plunges weren't from the tragedy of lost or ruined lives. The markets weren't sentimental. What had caused the rout was the widespread fear of a sharp Chinese economic slowdown.

With the eighth column now headed *Masood Baqri, B/13*, an aerial map below his name showed a slowly blinking GPS positioning signal. It was for the MT *African Colossus*, the giant oil supertanker that Baqri was master of. It showed the vessel approaching the northwestern coastline of the Gulf of Mexico, plying among and past the thousands of oil rigs and platforms that dotted the Gulf. *African Colossus* was headed for Louisiana, where it was due to offload two million barrels of imported Nigerian crude oil, a hefty ten per cent of the entire United States' daily crude consumption. The questions for the group of operatives Weiss had allocated to Baqri were many, and they had little time to answer them. Was Baqri still active in Nine Sisters? If yes, what could he possibly be planning for this huge vessel and her cargo? The Gulf had mostly recovered from the *Deepwater Horizon* incident in 2010, but another massive oil spill would be a kick in the guts to America's South, let alone to the oil industry.

The task for the investigators was immense and complex. Knowing that Oscar Philips and Yevtushenko had used pre-set time fuses, whereas Yuan Li Ming and Fenton had not, told all the agencies that merely apprehending the remaining suspects was not enough. They had to make sure they doused whatever fires they might have remotely set. Like Weiss had said about Yevtushenko: 'That bastard can disappear off the face of the earth, so long as we beat his deadline.'

Weiss, indeed all the agencies, knew that if Yevtushenko's leak, let alone his crash and burn, went live, the fragile European economy—even more enfeebled by the new China crisis—as well as emergency services, would be crippled, cut off at the knees. With the leaks, the strangest aspect of the Russian's plan, at least initially, was that he'd timed the avalanche of information to hit in the middle of the European night, and by the time most criminals wised up to misappropriate it, he would have crashed his system and Europe would already be stuffed. The sense in it was voiced first by MI5's Maria Channells: 'He screws his clients, those who trusted him, and then he screws everyone else who didn't. Brilliant.'

What Yevtushenko was setting in train was not only runs on banks, but power plant shutdowns, so subway and train transport would be frozen in Paris and London, airports closed across Europe, hospitals unable to function, the French and German stock exchanges locked down, and crowd control in many major centres would be next to impossible with police communications in disarray.

When Weiss's eye caught Baqri's entry being filled out on the far right-hand side of the wall screen he shuddered, thinking about the additional pressure on all the teams he and his peers had put in place and were still putting together all across the world, dedicated professionals charged not just with designing multiple emergency and communications plans, but stretching every synapse of ingenuity they collectively possessed to stop the accelerating number of catastrophic fuses being set by a mere handful of well-placed, highly intelligent individuals.

Yevtushenko was one heck of a foe, thought Weiss. To pull off his insane goal of wiping out finance and industry, he was pissing his own billions up against the wall. The Russian had managed to convince some of the biggest, most sophisticated organisations in Europe to trust his firm, its financial and technical strengths being key. None of his clients even for a second contemplated that NuAgeCloud's stability and strength was immaterial to its famous and fabulously wealthy majority owner except as an effective tool to mislead and deceive them. No one had even a clue that all this muscle was the antithesis of what he ultimately desired, that it was an elaborate mirage he'd created merely to seduce them into his lair so he could spring his trap.

London's Metropolitan Police Service, no patsy, was one of them. If Yevtushenko's Cloud did crash and burn, swathes of the Met's activities would be neutered while it scrabbled to get back online and operational, throwing the world's number two financial centre into chaos, and since the Met was also the first line of protection for the royal family and senior members of the British government, MI5's Maria Channells had already agreed secret plans with her Prime Minister that if the crash and burn wasn't stopped by 1.30 am London time—5.30 am Russian time—the monarch and senior ministers would be airlifted out of London.

The FSB's latest news was that Yevtushenko had deleted all the emails in his Aubrey Williamsburgh account. The Russians were hoping to find him by tracking the funds he'd syphoned off to finance his mystery island. Weiss knew they'd eventually get the backups from the server host, but that was going to take time. Meanwhile, Uri Golovanov had told him that to stop Yevtushenko causing any more harm than he'd already set in train, Russia's President had signed an executive order officially confiscating all his stock in NuAgeCloud and every bank account he or his company had within their jurisdiction. If they failed to stop his crash and burn, the shares would be worthless, for sure, but if they did manage to pull the plug in time, Mother Russia would just have earnt itself a cool billion or few—subject to what the shaky markets would separately be doing.

Weiss imagined the FSB chief would also be salivating over the photos of what would probably become his own new *dacha*, the country mansion Yevtushenko owned until now, conveniently positioned close to Vladimir Putin's on the eastern shore of Lake Komsomol'skoye, a quick hop northeast of Saint-Petersburg by helicopter.

But he didn't think Uri would savour it for long. Stopping the midnight leaks would be a heads up to Yevtushenko, they all knew that, potentially prompting him to remotely re-enter his network from wherever he was hiding and shorten the six-hour delay for his crash and burn. So time was even less on their side than they initially thought and, risking a panic with overnight users, the Russians set to work on frantically building an impregnable electronic firewall that would cocoon the NuAgeCloud servers and stop him accessing it. When Golovanov came online to tell them the firewall was in place, the relief in the ops command room was palpable, though brief. They all knew this was a temporary patch, not a fix, and though there were smiles and nods, and hopes the Russians would beat the six am Saint-Petersburg time clock, heads quickly bobbed down again as people got back to their own time-beating tasks.

Apart from the hunt for Yevtushenko, Weiss had got all the agencies to agree that no one would approach any of the suspects until he had given specific clearance. Yet in Italy, the Polizia di Stato had already ignored that protocol.

As if he were the terrorist, Italy's leading expert on dementia was almost yanked off the stage while he was giving his opening address at an international conference in Rome. He was flown to Venice despite his complaints, arriving at close to midnight. Zooming along the canals in an open launch, the night air freezing him in his dinner suit, he fumed about his mistreatment and eventually, disgusted by the police as much as the stench in Mellor's apartment and his daughter's distracting protests from the room where the police were holding her back, he gave the doddery professor the most cursory of examinations. But even a more intensive examination would have yielded the same outcome: that trying to extract anything of substance out of Mellor was a futile exercise, regardless of what time of night it was.

As the gerontologist and the cavalcade of police left as swiftly and as noisily as they arrived, Mellor stood at his apartment window, looking down on Calle del l'Albero as cigarette smoke curled around him, the rumble of police boots on the *masegni di trachite*, Venice's famous paving stones, making him smile though he couldn't recall why. Through a disbelieving gauntlet of local residents in pyjamas and robes rubbing their eyes under the weak yellow streetlamps, the police thundered down the narrow street to the launches waiting for them around the corner, carting with them Mellor's computer and box after box of his papers and books.

When the live, though hardly visible, feed of the raid came up on the ops command screen in New York, Weiss was seething and, in a rare moment of uncontrolled fury, smashed his tablet computer on the floor. Twenty armed shooters barrelling down the cobblestones of a sleepy Venetian street was not his idea of a sneak or a subtle approach.

THE YEVTUSHENKO SECTION of the screen was headed by two clocks, one counting down to Russia's midnight, when the dam was set to break on the biggest leak of high security information in history—a torrent more than a leak, as Weiss saw it. The other was set for Russian six am, when every wisp of Yevtushenko's Cloud was set to disperse into nothingness.

As the minute-hand on the first clock ticked closer and closer to the earlier deadline, Weiss's mood shifted from contained to tight to pent-up, like a panther about to pounce. The temperature in the room didn't rise, but everyone there was sweating. Weiss strode across in front of the screen, looking at the clock, checking his own watch, shouting for his replacement tablet computer, then at two minutes to leak time—2.58 pm New York-time—he stopped in the centre of the room and clapped his hands.

'People! Attention!' His face was grim. 'It looks like we're going to have to—' But he was interrupted when a video window popped open on the screen behind him and a few seconds later, Golovanov appeared. The FSB director now looked as haggard and drawn as Weiss felt. Even a new *dacha* was not enough to cheer him, not tonight. The entire room was hushed, apart from a scattering of uneasy coughs. Everyone froze as Golovanov kept blinking into the room. After a few seconds he nodded, having got the signal that he was live. 'Weiss, Channells, Delacroix, colleagues. With one minute to go I have good news. All data have been secured. There will be no leak.'

When the cheers and whoops died down, Weiss asked his Russian colleague, 'The crash and burn?'

'That is proving harder to crack but we have six hours, *da*? And to save you asking, Weiss, we still cannot find a trace of Yevtushenko's plane.'

'The island? Any clue where that is?'

'*Nyet*.' The video window vanished without more. No one had time for pleasantries.

Hours earlier, the combined security chiefs were in heated debate whether to go public on the NuAgeCloud threat, or the emerging links to Nine Sisters—in other words, Fenton, China, Tori's neutronics model—though Whitehead, of course, was never an option for disclosure. Other security services were only alerted on a need-to-know basis, although affected local emergency services were being told that their computer services might become compromised to an attack so they could start making contingency plans. But going public was a political decision, one they kicked upstairs even though the agencies had good reason to feel that politicians were notoriously unreliable and preferred for as much as possible to be kept under wraps for as long as possible. It would be a tough call for the politicians. If the Russians couldn't stop Yevtushenko's crash and burn, Europe would wake up in chaos, and a few hours later so would the US. But going public would cause a far quicker and more intensive pandemonium when businesspeople, woken from slumber, started to panic, desperately initiating their disaster recovery plans in advance and trying to migrate off the NuAgeCloud system ahead of the deadline.

But far worse, and the key point Weiss had stressed to his superiors, was that going public would be a warning to the remaining members of Nine Sisters, virtually guaranteeing they'd launch their own plans well before the agencies even discovered who they were.

The argument had persuaded his bosses and in US President Isabel Diaz's rapid-fire round of one-on-one calls with her political peers, she cast America's chips toward non-disclosure. Even though the Chinese had their hands full with the relief and rescue operation sprawled all over their enormous country, they were the first Diaz had called and the first to agree with her about keeping quiet, but with secrecy hardly alien to them, she didn't see it as a major victory. They'd already stopped Yuan Li Ming's suicide note from picking up any momentum, not hard since they controlled the social media, in fact all the media. Central control did have its benefits occasionally, President Diaz thought, but not with any sense of envy.

In the US, the only people who knew of Wilbur Fenton's confession so far were the two astonished detectives who'd arrested and continued to interrogate him; their equally disbelieving immediate superiors; the FBI, who they'd in turn reported it to; the people in Weiss's ops command room; and now a handful of politicians. All up, more than a few. But as far as the general public were concerned, Fenton was no more than a crazy doctor who killed his illustrious patients. A serial sicko, yes, but not a politically motivated terrorist who babbled on about nine unidentified sisters saving the planet, and even more weirdly, to those interrogating him, that he was one of them.

34

AS THE LATE AFTERNOON SHADOWS LOOMED over Sixth Avenue and its six lanes, all theoretically heading uptown, clogged with rush-hour traffic, Tori stood near the newsstand light to make her pretence of flicking through magazines credible, yet kept her eyes on The Skewer's entrance. After feeling the daggers of the news vendor's filthy stares at her back for five minutes, she almost whistled with relief when she saw Margy Bernardo stride out of the building. To the vendor's further disgust, Tori replaced the magazine in his rack. She watched Bernardo walk right past the line of limos in the drop-off drive and head for the kerb to put her hand out for a yellow cab. Tori shot her own hand out too and her cab came first. 'See that woman across there … grey suit trying to hail? I want you to wait till she gets a cab, then follow her.'

'Lady, you kidding me?' said the driver spitting bits of burger and placing the rest of it on the seat next to him. He turned around, his expression as incredulous as the plotline in

255

one of the soaps he was addicted to watching. 'This lane's a no-stopper until seven!'

The aroma of barbecue made Tori peckish, but this was no time for food. 'Ah, she's got one. Go! Follow them! And will you turn off that radio, please?' Tori was no fan of techno music and besides, it drowned out everything, including Frank who was reporting over her earpiece that he was halfway up from SoHo in a cab himself, and already monitoring the GPS-tracker Tori had planted on their quarry.

They both expected Bernardo to head to the Upper East Side, where she and Whitehead had their apartment, but instead, her cab swung a left, heading west, and then another left at Seventh, and headed back downtown. 'Frank,' said Tori, needlessly holding her phone up to her ear so the driver wouldn't think she was talking to herself, 'curiously, she's heading—'

'I know, downtown. I've got the signal on my screen, remember? I'm already heading to Seventh, where are you?'

FROM HER CAB window, Tori saw Bernardo's cab pull up outside a battered redbrick walk-up back in SoHo, a few blocks from Thatcher's place, where Frank had started. The cab didn't budge after its passenger got out and entered the building, so Tori instructed her own driver to wait too. Out of her satchel she took the monocular she'd got from Thatcher, a super-zoom day/night optics and thermal scope. After three minutes, Tori's driver started drumming his fingers, and after five was slapping his steering wheel like he thought he was Charlie Watts bashing away on the Rolling Stones' classic, '(I Can't Get No) Satisfaction', which he clearly wasn't getting very much of while he was sitting around, even if his meter was ticking over. Annoyed, Tori threw a fifty into the front of the cab, and when the driver picked it up she said, 'Some quiet, please. If I want a performance, I'll get you to take me to Madison Square Garden. Okay?' He was about to speak but the faded image of President Ulysses S. Grant he held up to the light seemed to placate him. He pocketed the bill and took a tattered copy of *Killing Richard Dawson* from underneath his burger box, tried to wipe the red sauce off the cover before realising it was the cover design, switched on his book light and started reading.

Tori had counted two page-turns and four chuckles by the time Frank arrived in a cab. As he went to open her door, her driver flicked the central locking switch to keep Frank out. 'It's okay, I know the guy,' she said, wondering if the driver would have done the same thing if Frank had been white.

UPSTAIRS, MARGY USED her key to enter Kass Cardozo's apartment and looked around at the familiar but austere furnishings, a long way from the luxury of her own place. Kass had never been interested in material possessions; she was devoted to her work, and to Margy, and that was all she lived for. Kass hardly even stayed in her apartment, which the neighbours would attest to; she was like a ghost, they'd say, no trouble at all. As a senior security analyst, hired by and reporting solely to Margy, Kass roved the world spot-checking EuropaNational's most sensitive facilities for protocol breaches and systems weaknesses. Over time, Margy felt that she and Kass had become very close. Not a single person in head office apart from Margy ever saw Kass or her reports, and the people there even used to joke she was a phantom. Of course, Margy had never mentioned Kass to Alan.

She didn't want to burden either him or their relationship with the knowledge. Given his work, the less he knew the better. If he had secrets, so could she.

She entered the bedroom, stark white like the rest of the apartment. She and Kass had decided early on that white was their colour. Clean, innocent, without sin or stain. As the world should be.

As it would be.

Margy riffled through the closet and pulled out a pair of pants, white corduroy, a blouse of white silk, and her favourite white hoodie. She unzipped her work suit and folded it on the bed, then removed her undergarments and headed for the shower.

Margy needed steam to clear her head, and her body, especially to remove the foul odour of that Swyft woman. Margy never got into a sweat, not even back during the Lehman Brothers crisis which, at the time, she saw as a dress rehearsal for what she had been planning for years. She didn't even sweat when the nation's President had shone a light on her during the board's videolink with the White House, when she asked Margy how her husband Alan was. But with Swyft, she had sweated. Normally, she was Dr Cool, but not then. As she dropped her head back and let the hot water stream over her face, she couldn't get Swyft's audacious stupidity out of her head. No one was supposed to contact anyone, had she forgotten that fundamental rule of Mellor's notwork? The fool could prejudice everything. That was why Margy had sweated. Years of work, of dedication, could easily have been tossed to the wind.

She wondered if Swyft was right, that the trains in China were theirs, that Dr eKiller was one of theirs. She hoped so. And she kept her fingers crossed for Yevtushenko, hoping his plan didn't suffer the same fate as Swyft's. Margy wasn't someone who prayed, but as she thought of making an exception, she laughed, letting the water enter her mouth. Maybe there was a God?

Margy's plan had been to activate her own attack in two days' time, once the board meeting was over, once the fine details of the merger announcement were hammered out and released. The impact would be even greater. Stunning. Shocking. The effects of bankrupting EuropaNational would monster what those Lehman pipsqueaks did back in 2008. This time, it wouldn't just be the world's third largest bank in sudden and rapid free fall but, once the share swap was in place, she would also take the tenth largest down with it. If she played her cards right, or rather her algorithms, the entire global financial system would be taken down and destroyed with them, not merely suffering a body blow and getting to limp along like the last time. Major banks all over the world, but especially in the US and Europe, would drop like dominoes, with their governments simply too broke to guarantee them. Politicians might go on TV and say they'd back the banks, but with the massive debts and deficits the politicians had been racking up, the public wouldn't see their promises as worth a sod. International commerce would dry up. Few would have ready money, and those who did wouldn't part with it. Essential projects would stall. Governments would fall. Employers wouldn't be able to pay their workers or suppliers. No one would cash cheques. Credit cards would be dishonoured. Debit cards would be frozen. Investment would evaporate. Retirement incomes would be shot. Hard assets would be the only things of value; if you couldn't touch it, it wouldn't exist. The world would be jolted back to a simpler lifestyle. China, a little removed from the mainstream, would not be safe either. It was already teetering due to the trains crisis, but Margy would push it right over the edge. She had ensured that EuropaNational's counterparty limits with the top three Chinese banks had been dramatically increased only a week ago and the Chinese had, as she liked to say, already taken it to the limits, exposing themselves in the billions to EuropaNational and thirty of its subsidiaries.

The fast train system, critical to the country's urbanisation and growth story, was facing a shut down pending an investigation that could take months. She'd heard it on the radio in the cab coming over tonight. No transport. No development of new areas. Workers unable to get to their jobs. Slow growth, or better, no growth. Perfect. China was a soft target, and was set for a hard landing.

What was that woman's name in Nine Sisters? Yuan Lee something—or maybe it was Li, she couldn't recall—but she did remember her as Y/6. Could this have been Y/6's doing? She hoped so. What was her name? Ah yes, Yuan Li Ming. She slapped her thigh. How could she forget? They did after all enjoy each other's company rather intimately before she'd left the group, though after she met Alan. The hairs on Margy's skin bristled as if Li Ming's long fingers were once again stroking her. But she stopped the thought. This was not the time.

Li Ming's plan had clearly been brilliant. A precision blow to cut off the blood flowing to the heart of China's growth. Margy's own plan, she felt, was equally masterful in its simplicity. As global head of risk, she had access to the super-user passwords for every critical system inside EuropaNational, as well as the weekly internal audit reports she received from operations all over the world cataloguing all the bank's weaknesses, from the mission-critical to the merely troubling. Last month, she'd run war games across her global team to check how robust the bank's worldwide systems were if they faced her precise style of attack.

Her deputy had complained the war games were a waste of
time; that it was both absurd and an affront to the bank's culture
to contemplate that any EuropaNational insider would even
dream of unleashing the kind of damage she was asking them
to 'hypothesise'. If she thought of Swyft as audacious, Margy
thought of herself as having—what was the word? Yes, chutzpah.
Shameless audacity. Shaking her hair under the water felt good,
like rays of the sun were illuminating her and her alone.

The superb part of last month's dummy run was the
confirmation that EuropaNational's systems were completely
vulnerable to a 'Bernardo-style attack', as she had cheekily
labelled it with her team of ignoramuses. The idiots had happily
identified that eighty-three fixes were needed if they wanted to
stop what Margy was about to do tonight, fixes she made sure
would not even be started until the end of the next quarter. But
even that was too soon for her deputy who ranked the risk as
negligible, complaining there were far more obvious threats in
the queue that needed attention first.

That bitch Swyft had done Margy a favour, she supposed,
by breaking the notwork's code of silence. If Uncle Sam had
come calling before the merger announcement instead of Swyft,
Margy would have been hauled off for interrogation. Once
that happened, Margy's deputy would go into damage control,
assuming that the war game was no joke at all, but a dry run,
that he'd been entirely wrong and that she'd not only been
right, but she'd been right because she was the plant, the corrupt
insider. Corrupt. Such a misunderstood word, she thought. It
was the system that was corrupt, not her. What she and her
fellow Sisters were doing was purging the world of corruption.

Margy had no choice but to act early, to act now. The vile
finance industry and the bloated, overpaid fat cats she'd forced
herself to smile at and pander to all these years would hardly

be very accommodating if there was a hint of a scandal about her before she launched, even if she was married to a national treasure. She'd be suspended, no doubt about it, and even if she was cleared she'd never ascend to such an elevated position of trust again. She bent to pick up the soap and as she stood back up, she became a little lightheaded, and had to steady herself against the glass.

Then it struck her. What if Swyft was lying? What if Swyft were a stooge trying to trick her? Maybe she had followed Margy here tonight? No, that would be crazy; Swyft knew far too much. Surely the authorities would simply have taken Margy in for questioning rather than put Swyft up to such a ridiculous charade. No, Margy decided, she was good to go. She twisted off the hot tap and gave herself a blast of cold. She needed her whole body to be on high alert tonight.

The white towel more caressed the water off her skin than rubbed it. Even the hairdryer was white and when all the moisture was blown away she fitted a wig, the only black item in the place. She had once tried a white wig but it wasn't her, or at least it wasn't her image of Kass Cardozo. Kass's hair had to be black. Yuan Li Ming's had been black, too.

She opened the wall safe and removed Kass's security pass and credit cards, some of the very few pieces of physical evidence that supported her existence, on top of her fake employee records, this apartment and the EuropaNational account Margy had set up to automatically deposit her pay into. Margy's super-user access ensured that Kass passed every one of the bank's threshold checks for accounts and employment. With Margy's unfettered access, essential for a head of risk, creating a ghost employee was easy.

The blast of cold water hadn't done the trick. She wasn't sure if the heat coursing through her was because tonight culminated a decade of relentless elbowing into position or whether it was still the shower so, naked, she sat on one of the sofas to cool down and, despite trying to think of something else, her mind was once again dragged back to the elegance of her plan.

By virtue of EuropaNational's sheer size and geographic spread, it was one of the world's largest players in virtually every financial market. It was already the fourth largest lender and third largest deposit taker in the US. In Europe it was the second in both. Not only was its broking arm second by volume and value on the New York and London stock exchanges and third on NASDAQ, and heavy on commodity and other exchanges like the Chicago Board of Trade and CME's Globex, its other divisions were significant market makers, trading for the bank and its thousands of clients across the world in foreign currencies, exotic credit derivatives, commodities like gold, copper and oil, as well as bonds and T-bills.

If something was traded, EuropaNational traded it.

The bank operated on all the official exchanges, but it traded even more extensively off-market, in what had become known as dark pools, deals done electronically or over the phone, direct with the bank's clients or with other banks. With Margy taking the helm tonight, she would forge all this together into a nuclear warhead. Not only would this missile blow up her own bank but it would blast the entire financial world out of the water.

If anything could stop industry and commerce from continuing to abuse a delicate planet, this would. Professor Mellor would be proud of what she would achieve.

She rested her head back and closed her eyes. There were three parts to her plan, all possible only due to her trusted super-user access codes. None of it would get picked up—except by her—for a few hours, the astonishingly short time she needed.

First, she'd flick off the safety switch and allow customers and other banks to run up unlimited credit on her bank's books, a prescription for disaster in itself.

Next, she'd suck into the bank all customer 'segregated' accounts, funds the bank was legally prohibited from mixing with its own money; but tonight, not only would they be mixed, they'd be syphoned off. Stealing these client funds would double-up on EuropaNational's already gigantic trading firepower. Margy didn't care who owned these accounts—big corporations, small businesses, retirees, even charities and advocacy groups like Greenpeace—her mission to purge the world of excess mattered more.

But her deathblow would come from stuffing this bulging wad of electronic cash into the bank's High-Frequency Trading systems and tricking the HFT computers not just to lose, but to lose catastrophically. That way, she'd break the bank, its customers and virtually every party who was unlucky enough to be trading with it tonight. In other words, almost every major financial institution in the world.

Now she was actually going to do it, the sensation was becoming intense.

What Margy especially loved was that she was using the incredible speeds of HFT trading to destroy the very system that created it in the first place.

People thought lightning strikes moved fast, but HFT trades could travel thousands of times faster.

Using highly complex mathematical algorithms, these HFT super-computers scanned multiple markets at the one time, trawling for the briefest and tiniest trading opportunities. Already, HFT spoke for the majority of trades on some big stock markets, and it was an HFT mantra never to remain exposed to market risk for very long, normally only milliseconds, but Margy was going to turn that right on its head.

She would be tweaking EuropaNational's HFT algorithms to skew their trading in ways their programmers had never intended. She was no 'algo' herself, as the mathematical geniuses who wrote the codes were called, so, for her recent security-testing 'war game', she'd seconded one of the bank's top HFT computer nerds to manipulate the code for her, 'to prove it could be done'. He proved to her that to do what she needed was breathtakingly simple; merely making the code jump some critical lines and creating a dummy confirmation program, changes she'd kept a copy of for tonight.

After making those changes, and all the HFT computers started trading, while they'd definitely be buying, they'd only *think* they were selling. That was because the sell orders wouldn't be transmitted to anybody except a file she planted deep inside the machines themselves, one that in turn would issue fake confirmations to fool the machines into 'thinking' that the matching sell trades had indeed been done. The bank's HFTs would be buying, buying, buying … gorging themselves on risk on top of risk on top of risk. As all the other automated parties it was trading with saw EuropaNational spitting out more and more buy orders, they'd all start chasing prices even further up.

Some markets and parties had built protections to stop this, called circuit breakers after a couple of so-called Flash Crashes when rogue HFTs had caused major market mayhem. But for Margy, the allure of HFT was that very few of the off-market trading pools that she would be getting EuropaNational to swim in tonight had these circuit breakers. Rules never kept pace with technology, and they'd certainly never keep pace with someone like her; someone who didn't break them by accident or stupidity but who worked long and hard to expose their weaknesses and, with the most serious intent, aimed to exploit them.

Her HFTs would pile up a stack of buy orders so high it would almost reach the sun, and when she pressed 'stop', the soaring markets would screech to a momentary halt, stuttering as if in thin air, and then the panic would be on, with prices plummeting like Icarus without his wings. As she kept her HFTs back, out of the markets, all their trading partners would start to freak that EuropaNational might go belly-up owing them sums that dwarfed Lehman Brothers.

EuropaNational wouldn't physically have in its vaults even a fraction of the multibillions that it would owe, and once the market got a whiff of that, regulators would race in, as usual too late, to snap-freeze EuropaNational. The bankruptcy litigation that would explode all over the world would chill the global financial system for months if not longer and meanwhile, with hardly anyone having ready access to their money, financial collapses would become the new, new normal.

Big banks always had millions of transactions open at any moment so, even when things were going fine, they were physically unable to do up-to-the-minute, one hundred per cent accurate calculations of who owed what to whom. They got as close as they could, using sophisticated simulations which, in truth, were only high-probability guesses. Even running these risk models was a massive exercise. At EuropaNational, Margy's risk team notionally closed off the bank's books four times a day: at six am, twelve noon, six pm and twelve midnight. If Margy launched her attack straight after the books closed for the six pm run, she knew she'd have hours before anyone internal twigged that something was wrong, and by then it would be too late. She had a six-hour window for her plan, but she didn't need anywhere near that long.

The clock on Kass's wall had just ticked over 5.15 pm, affording Margy a breather, so she slid down on the sofa and opened her legs a little wider. Yes.

She shifted herself even lower, pulling aside the crotch of her panties with the tip of her finger, then touching herself. At first, lightly. Slowly. She licked her lips at the pleasuring, the luscious, teasing tickling. When she thought she could almost bear it no more, her finger teased even more, lifting away and rising up until it brushed her lower lip, tantalising her tongue out for a taste. She sucked the finger briefly but strongly, then it withdrew, wet with her saliva, slipping itself over her bottom lip and then her chin, drawing a moist thread down her neck and her chest and lingering there, between her breasts, denying them the strokes and the pinches they ached for, before continuing down, where again it wet itself, this time inside her.

Margy didn't need anyone else for anything, and tonight, she would prove it to the whole world.

SHE PADDED BACK into the bathroom. After a light wipe over with a cloth, she dabbed on a few touches of Kass's favourite perfume, and raised both wrists up to her face to sniff the subtle notes of lychee and freshly cut apple. 'Summer in a Bottle' said the box, a curious choice of scent, she thought, for a woman whose life's work was bringing on the winter. She laughed. It was the deep throaty laugh she knew Alan loved, and which he joked, when they first met, that she'd got from sitting at Mellor's feet for too long and breathing in his cigarette smoke.

Then she saw Kass's razor and had an idea.

AFTER FRANK SLID into Tori's cab and sat beside her in the back, they stayed silent, their eyes fixed on the entrance of the building Bernardo had gone into and waiting for her to leave. After hearing eleven page-turns and two guffaws from the front seat, they watched a woman emerge from the building but she was dark-haired and dressed in white and, pausing at the kerb near Bernardo's waiting cab, she looked up and down the street. Tori slipped on her FrensLens, but the woman was too far away and it was too dark to get an inkling of her identity. The hair and the clothes weren't Bernardo's but she carried herself with the same determined posture. Frank picked up the day/night vision monocular, fiddled with the zoom and a couple of seconds later nodded and handed the eyeglass to Tori. Though the streetlight cast a golden glow over the woman's black ponytail, Tori saw Bernardo's defiant face beneath. Her hair was no longer a mousy bob, but her olive skin, broody eyes and voluptuous lips were Bernardo's.

'Damn! Her tracker's still inside the building,' said Frank, looking down at his computer. 'We're going to have to stay close. Shit, I hope she didn't find it.'

'And she's wearing Nikes,' said Tori, squinting, with the viewer still at her eye. 'Maybe she's going for a run?'

'Or a runner,' said Frank as his phone vibrated. It was Thatcher texting him a real estate search on the walk-up, but it was inconclusive, the records showing it was owned by a secretive Liechtenstein anstalt that it would take even the authorities weeks to trace ownership through. Frank put the phone away.

'It's strange she got the cab to wait,' said Tori. 'Everyone changes to go partying, but a hair switch? Surely the driver would get suspicious.'

Their own driver turned off his book light and squinted toward Bernardo. As he laid the book on the seat beside him,

he spat the gum he'd been chewing into his hand and pressed it
into the empty burger wrapping. 'If you don't mind me saying,
happens all the time with them suits. Wanna let their hair
down at night, go where they shouldn't go … you know, get
a bit of anonymous downtime when they go off-piste. I had a
Wall Streeter last week and he got me to wait downstairs for his
"brother", but it was *so* not his brother. For sure it was the same
dude. So hey, you guys private eyes or something?'

Tori took a deep breath and, reaching into her purse, peeled
off another green and tossed it into the front seat. 'Just drive,
okay?'

35

AT JUST AFTER SIX PM, THEIR cab trailed behind Bernardo's as it slid below the iconic Silvercup sign in Long Island City, a part of New York where even neon icons had their Vs blinking on and off.

'If it's someone locked inside there trying to send out a victory signal, I hope it's meant for us,' said Tori as she raised her crotch and zipped up her jeans. With Frank's eyes averted the whole time, she had wriggled out of her chief auditor's clothes when they hit the 59th Street Bridge and had spent the last five minutes squirming her way into the denims, sweater and Reeboks that he had brought along for her. No matter how much of a kick the stilettos had given her, she knew they'd be useless against Bernardo's running shoes, except maybe in toe-to-toe combat, an activity she didn't expect to feature in the evening's activity but still needed to be prepared for.

Their cab passed through a part of the neighbourhood that, judging by the broken windows and spilling dumpsters, even the bargain-hunting gentrifiers had forsaken, then it slowed to a crawl as Bernardo's taxi pulled up a block ahead of them outside a squat, five-storey concrete building that occupied that entire block. Windowless, it was possibly a converted warehouse and Frank immediately texted its address to Thatcher as a steel-grey door halfway along its side released a stream of people into the mild night air. Some of them crossed the street to a bus stand, others scurried to the taxi rank around the far corner and another procession headed, according to their driver, for the Queensboro Plaza subway station a few blocks away.

Inside the building it was changeover time. The night shift must have already clocked on since, apart from Bernardo, the only people outside were those leaving, but Tori and Frank watched as she stayed inside her cab, and even when the river of people exiting the building had become a trickle, she still didn't move. They waited some more, until a bus arrived and loaded up with the thirty or so people who'd been hanging around for it. Although Tori couldn't see the taxi rank, she guessed it too had cleared after two vacant cabs slowed to a crawl as they approached the corner before speeding away still empty.

Bernardo's door swung open and she waited by the kerb until her cab drove off. She began walking up the block, past the steel-grey exit door and continuing until she reached a navy-coloured door at the corner of the building closest to Tori's cab.

From where Tori and Frank were sitting, and despite the lighting that illuminated both doors, the building seemed to be signless. It was as if some overpaid executive had it in his head that a five-storey fortress plonked in a run-down area that breathed hundreds of people in and out three times a day could possibly stay anonymous.

As Tori opened the door of their own cab, she again peeled off some bills for the driver, but this time asked him to swing around the corner and wait there. As the taxi took off she hooked her arm over Frank's, not expecting to feel such an electric frisson from the touch. She took a breath to cool herself and got into step with him, as a tipsy couple swaggering along the street in the dark, with her literally keeping one eye on Bernardo through her eyeglass. When the banker was standing at the entry scanner it was easy to watch her through the monocular's day vision setting; but with the front light above her, her white outfit radiated an almost blinding aura, making her look like the saint they were increasingly sure she wasn't.

Tori stopped, pulling back on Frank, and adjusted the zoom. 'She's put her security pass up to the scanner ... Shit, it's not hers. I mean it's her photo—at least with black hair, but the name ... it's Ka—Kass something. Her finger's covering the rest ... Got it! Cardozo. Kass Cardozo.'

'I don't like this,' said Frank, reading the text he'd just received on his phone from Thatcher. 'That's EuropaNational's American data centre and the head of risk is here posing as somebody else?' He typed a reply back to his friend while Tori watched Bernardo push the door open and step inside. Even from across the street they both heard the door click firmly shut behind her.

'That poor bastard Whitehead,' said Frank, looking up. 'His career's cactus and his one salvation ... the angelic wife he's so desperate to protect ... and the bitch is going to fuck him over, as well as the bank that's doling out a fortune to her to protect it.'

Tori wasn't quite so sure, not about Whitehead. 'I know Weiss said he'd passed the polygraph, but they're hardly foolproof, we both know that.'

When they crossed over and reached the door Bernardo had entered through, Frank shook his head and put his bag of tricks on the ground. 'Damn scanner,' he said. 'You seen one of these babies before?'

Tori shook her head, so Frank took a photo of the entry pad with his phone and sent it to Thatcher. 'It's going to take us a while.'

'Then I'm not such a fan of the porch lights,' said Tori, pointing to the spotlight above them. She reached down into Frank's bag and pulled out one of her stilettos, aimed it way above their heads, drew back and pitched.

'Good swing.' He nodded.

It wasn't just good, it was perfect. The lamp didn't break—Tori didn't want that—but she did dislodge it so that its beam shifted sideways, to light up the pavement several metres away from them and successfully cloak them and the doorway in obliging darkness. Frank leapt for the shoe as it came back down. 'Your *Devil Wears Prada* days are over,' he said, holding it near his face and working the broken heel as if it was a mouth.

'Damn. I was going to wear them to the deal closing party in Athens.'

'Don't hold your breath. If what Bernardo's planning is big enough, there might be no deal and no closing. It's already looking a bit iffy, with the market wobbles over the China thing, and if Yevtushenko's not stopped—' He let it hang.

The entry scanner resisted Frank's first attempt to get past it, a passcode Thatcher had sent through. 'Damn, again,' he said. 'Thatcher says four failed attempts and it trips an alert at the security base.'

'What if we can't get inside?'

'I guess we'll cross—' he started to say, but when a car squealed around the far corner, they both fell back to hug the side of the building and watched as the vehicle tore up the street toward them, dimmed its headlights then switched them off just as it screeched to a stop with one wheel bouncing up onto the kerb only metres from them.

'What the—?' Tori whispered as the driver's door swung open and the inside light briefly lit up Alan Whitehead's face. 'This is getting a bit cosy, don't you think? I doubt he's seen us, so here goes,' and as Whitehead got out of his car she leapt forward, slammed the door back into him, winding him, then dragged him to the ground, simultaneously yanking his arms behind his back just in time for Frank, who had removed his own belt, to bind them together.

'Who the—oomph!—fuck are—?' their captive started as he struggled and jerked his head around in the dark, trying to see, not that it would help him much since, apart from Tori's initial videolink to Langley, he hadn't set eyes on her for ten years and he'd never seen Frank at all.

'It's us, Whitehead,' said Tori. 'Swyft and Chaudry.'

He immediately stopped struggling. 'Jeez, am I glad it's you, at least I would be if I wasn't lying face down in the gutter with your knee in my … oof … back.'

'You're glad?' said Frank.

'Sure,' he huffed as Tori pressed down even harder. She wasn't taking his word for anything, not yet. 'Reach into my left pocket,' he said, but neither of them moved. 'Do it for chrissakes.'

Tori did, and felt several pieces of smooth plastic, like credit cards. She pulled them out slowly and, using her phone as a flashlight, saw they were all EuropaNational security passes. All in different names, and all with the same photo of Bernardo with black hair she'd seen ten minutes ago through her monocular. But none in the names of Kass Cardozo or Margy Bernardo. 'How'd you get these, Whitehead?' Tori didn't give him any slack, keeping her knee firmly in position.

He told them that once he'd passed Weiss's lie detector test and was allowed to clear his desk, he'd gone home to his and Bernardo's apartment. 'I opened our wall safe to double-check I didn't have anything in there that DHS might be worried about—which I didn't—but Margy's EuropaNational emergency wallet was there, like it always was, and given everything that's happened I decided for the first time to open it. It felt like a betrayal, like I was cheating on her, but when I found those four passes for access into the data centre here, I didn't know what to think.'

'Why didn't you call Weiss?' asked Frank.

'Same reason I asked you guys to check out Margy for me. If I told Weiss about the fake passes, her career'd be over in a snap. I wanted to confront her myself. I was hoping you'd be here, to be my witnesses. She'll have a good explanation, I'm sure, like it's part of some shadow security test. Besides, if Weiss is as good as I've trained him to be, he'll have stuck a GPS tracker onto my car, so I'm thinking his boys won't be too far behind me anyhow.'

His story had a ring of plausibility, but it didn't seem right to Tori and she remained wary. His tone was genuine too, but it all seemed too conveniently coincidental. She wasn't the only practitioner of spycraft who sprinkled truths onto lies to enhance the deception. 'How did you know your wife would be here, not tied up in that board meeting you told us about?'

Judging by his grunt when she pressed forward with her knee, Whitehead would have shrugged if he could have. 'It wasn't that hard, Swyft. I used the Find My iPhone app to track her here. My phone's on the front seat. Check it and you'll see ...'

Frank squeezed his arm inside the door—Tori and Whitehead were something of an obstacle to opening it any wider—and he felt around on the front seat until he found the phone and drew it out. The screen was displaying a map with their precise location and a dot was flashing with the text *Margy's iPhone*. 'Tori, he's telling the truth,' he said, typing a text message to Thatcher from Whitehead's phone and then deleting it.

'Fine,' she said, guessing correctly that Whitehead had kept this phone charging inside his safe for times he didn't want to be traced. Like now. She shifted her knee to his side and unbound his hands. They both got to their feet, though he was more unsteady, and he rubbed his hands around his wrists one at a time. 'You tie a pretty tight knot,' he said, Tori noticing a slight smile cracking his face, or perhaps it was a wince.

She swiped one of the cards he'd brought across the scanner and the door clicked open. The lobby was unmanned and a few metres inside stood a line of shoulder-height glass capsules, each fronted by its own security pass scanner, and only big enough for a single person to pass through. She kept one card for herself and handed the others to Frank and Whitehead. 'Here, and bring your phone so we can locate her inside this place.'

SO FAR, THE cards gave them access inside to wherever they wanted to go. No matter which door they tried, they got through. According to Whitehead's phone, Bernardo was in the southwest corner of the building, although he couldn't tell which floor. Pretending to be cleaners, using the mops and brooms and buckets they found in a closet, they searched the ground floor, then the next one up. As they moved, none of the people rushing around challenged them, the working assumption clearly being that if you got inside the fortress, you had the authority to be there.

While they were in the elevator heading to the next floor, Frank's phone vibrated and after he read the message, he pressed the fourth floor button. It wouldn't light up and instead *Access denied* flashed up on the screen. 'Hmm,' he whispered, worrying they might be overheard. 'I asked Thatc—' he started to say, but with Whitehead present he stopped. 'I asked a buddy to hack into the blueprints for the security system here and he's betting she'll be in "The Cage", in the southwest corner of the fourth floor. He says it's the only part of the whole place that requires a super-user passcode to get inside. Once there, he says, you're sitting at a control panel where you can check, run, stop and even change every major computer system the bank's got worldwide.'

'Fuck,' Tori and Whitehead said at the same time but without whispering.

Whitehead pressed his security pass up to the wall panel and touched '4'. This time the button lit up. The lift slowed as it got to level three, and opened on a short, stocky Hispanic-looking man carrying a tablet computer. He entered, but was clearly surprised when the lift car started moving up, not down as he'd expected, and when he noticed that the fourth-floor light was on he also started eyeing them and their cleaning equipment with suspicion. Tori saw from the ID badge pinned to his shirt that he was Eduardo, no surname, Night-Shift Cleaning Supervisor.

'Why don't I know you guys?' he asked.

'We're on day shift,' she said, stifling a yawn. 'We were running a bit behind when some jerk spilled his coffee over a computer, so we're just leaving now.'

'Leaving from level four? I doubt it,' he said and shot his hand toward the alarm button, but Frank was faster, grabbing him and twisting his fingers before they made contact. 'Pleased to make your acquaintance, Eduardo,' he said, mocking a handshake.

After they deprived an unwilling Eduardo of his phone, pager and tablet, tied and gagged him and locked him in a closet, the only sound on the fourth floor was the drone of air-conditioning and computer fans. The air here was chill, cooler than the other floors, with a taint of ammonia suggesting that some of Eduardo's team—or their day shift counterparts—had already been and gone, the reason for his suspicion. As the trio stepped slowly down the corridor, they peeked into room after room, all banked with computer servers that seemed to be running themselves, not a soul to be seen.

'If this be the future, give me the past,' said Frank. For some reason, the building was colour-coded. Maybe, he thought, a trial on rats—or, perhaps, bankers—had proved that different colours made people work harder. The ground level had been decked out in shades of yellow, darker for the walls and doors, paler for the floor and ceilings, and the other floor they'd been on was set in greens. When the elevator doors opened up on Eduardo on level three, it was blues. This fourth floor was white, so the cleaning gear they'd been carrying had come in especially handy when Tori's punch to his kidney finally got Eduardo over the line and willing to cooperate despite the bloodied nose Frank felt forced to give him.

Thatcher had already sorted out the security guards who were watching a wall of monitors in the basement. Listening in via Frank's and Tori's earpieces, he'd heard the commotion with Eduardo in the elevator so, before they exited he told them he'd hacked in to the CCTV system, temporarily killed the signal from the Level 4 cameras and set the relevant screens in the basement so they'd loop over the last few minutes of nothingness while he channelled the real signal to himself so he could monitor his friends' progress. He noticed that someone else had already set the CCTV from The Cage on loop—he guessed Bernardo—so he diverted the true signal to one of his screens and let his colleagues know.

The three inside padded down the corridor, aiming to sneak up to The Cage without alerting Bernardo and hoping to use one of their fake passes to enter it and surprise her. 'Margy's got a thing for white,' said Whitehead under his breath as they continued. 'She decorated our whole apartment in it. Wonder if she had a hand in this place?'

When they reached the last door, through its glass porthole they saw an expanse nearly the size of three tennis courts, a wasteful space completely empty apart from The Cage, a fifteen metre by fifteen metre barred square set right in the middle. From outside the room, the steel bars enclosing The Cage looked to be an inch thick and set three inches apart and were fixed to thick plates at the floor and ceiling. As with the room itself, the bars and plates were white and, according to what Thatcher was telling him over the earpieces, the building's architectural drawings, on file at the city planning department, described them as powder-coated tempered steel.

The Cage's door, also constructed of bars, was on the side of its perimeter facing the intruders, and through it they saw Bernardo, with her back to them and seated inside a C-shaped wall of flashing computer screens that rose halfway to the ceiling. Not slumped but purposeful, her back was straight and her hands were out wide, like an orchestra conductor about to begin.

Tori swiped her card over the security panel and—yes!—the door gave a faint click as she pushed it open but, as soon as the three of them were inside the room, Whitehead broke cover and shouted across the cavernous space, 'Hey, Margy, sweetie, I'm here … I'm here with some, er, friends.'

His wife slowly dropped her hands and swung around in her chair, her eyes like blades of ice, and Tori felt their tips slide shivers down her spine.

'What's with your black wig?' asked Whitehead casually, as if seeing his own wife in disguise while seated at the controls of the bank's global nerve centre was as normal as arriving home to a freshly poured chardonnay.

'What's with your black friend?' she retorted, noticing Frank first, but on recognising Tori her mouth pressed tight, like wire. 'You!' she erupted after a second. 'What the fuck are you doing here? *All* of you.'

Out of the side of his mouth, Whitehead quietly told Tori and Frank that he had this, that they should let him run with it. It wasn't the approach they'd agreed, but they felt they had no choice. 'Margy, you've met Tori Swyft. It was me who, er, asked her to come to The Skewer to warn you. She risked a lot doing that, and she's even convinced DHS I'm clean,' he lied. 'Listen, we don't have much time before they get on to you, too. So let us help you out. Many hands make light work, and all. What's your plan?'

She rocked in her chair, a finger rubbing the last vestiges of lipstick off her lower lip as if she were debating with herself. The others didn't move. They stayed silent. The fingers of Bernardo's other hand began to drum the armrest on her chair. Then suddenly, she reached back, grabbed her ponytail and ripped off her wig.

Whitehead grasped at Frank's arm to steady himself, visibly shocked by his wife's shaved head. She looked up at him and laughed. Again it was the throaty, raspy Marlene Dietrich laugh she knew he loved, even if tonight he didn't seem to. 'I've prettied myself up for the FBI's perp shot, Al, for when I give myself up. As you can see, I've thought of everything, so I don't need your extra hands, okay? All I have to do is press that single key—' she pointed vaguely behind her, '—and the financial world erupts in flames. You got here just in time to help me cheer on a real bonfire of the vanities. This will be beautiful, babe, and we'll have done it ... what we spent ten long years planning. Bring on the winter!' she shouted, unbottling a decade of her self-restraint. '*Fiat justitia*—'

Alan and then the others joined in. '—*et ruant coeli*. Let justice be done, though the heavens fall.'

Bernardo started to spin her chair back around to the keyboard.

'What's the plan, sweetie?' Whitehead asked.

She turned back. 'Hard, direct action, Al. Not like those namby-pamby Occupy Wall Street jerk-offs.' She spat a gob of phlegm onto the floor. 'Why occupy it when you can fucking destroy it?'

'Yeah,' said Whitehead, 'but like I said, sweetie, *how* are you—we—going to do it?'

At first Tori assumed Bernardo's husband was trying to get onside, buying time, stalling, waiting for an opportunity. But there were moments—when Bernardo said 'we' and, with that strange quiver in his voice, when Whitehead repeated it— that her head flashed with the idea that maybe he was excited, aroused even, by what his wife was doing.

Bernardo rubbed a hand over her bare head. 'It feels so right, babe, us doing all this. When I press that one little key back there, it'll alter the approved algorithms for the HFTs.' Suddenly she shifted her eyes to Tori, 'They're the bank's high-frequency trading computers ... After that ... and stupid EuropaNational doesn't know this yet ... we're going to use all the bank's money, and its customers' money, and money it doesn't even have, to buy and buy and buy until there's almost nothing left to buy … currencies, euros, pounds, yen, dollars, renminbi, all of them, and commodities, oil, gas, copper, lead, pork bellies, cotton, whatever. Then derivatives too, and stocks and bonds. You name it and my little computers here and I will be buying it, lots of it, fields of it, warehouses of it, oceans and mountains of it. And we'll be selling none of it. We'll shove so much of every damn-fucking-thing down the bank's greedy throat that we'll burst it apart, and when the others realise they're not going to get paid for what they've sold to us, we'll blow up every other bank and party who trades with us, or who trades with someone who trades with us … in other words, the entire fucking financial world. Babe, this is going to be … beautiful.'

Bernardo paused, drinking in the elegance of the mayhem she was about to unleash, then drew a breath and continued, 'No more money for miners or real estate developers or any of the other grasping bastards out there to keep raping the planet with. None for pathetic obscenities like The Skewer. Nothing for armies and weapons makers. Everything stops dead, sweetie. Everyone goes bust. Banks, oil companies, governments, the works. We'll be back to a simpler world, babe. If we can't grow it or make it ourselves, we won't have it, we can't have it.'

She swivelled around and moved her hand toward one of the many keyboards arrayed around her. 'Tonight,' she shouted over her shoulder, 'the planet gets to start over. And now, it's time … for my big bang!' She was right, but she didn't know how right.

Both Frank and Tori, simultaneously gripping their ID cards, leapt to a sprint toward The Cage, hoping to cross the twenty metres of empty floor to reach it in time. Whitehead held back, they assumed frozen when, suddenly, Thatcher screamed into their earpieces, 'Ankle holster! Gun! Behind you!'

Tori stopped, and swung her head back to see Whitehead's eye coldly aiming a black gun barrel at her—a Glock 26 subcompact?—or maybe he was aiming it at Frank, and before she could think let alone react, she saw him mouth the word *bang* and, in an eerie flash, the bullet whistled toward her and past her, missing her chest by an inch. Finding her voice, she yelled, twisting her head around in time to see the shell flash past Frank's own open mouth, enter The Cage between the bars and blow apart the back of Bernardo's head.

For Whitehead's former wife, red was her new white.

36

'IS THERE ANY OTHER KIND OF journalist?' snapped John Weiss after the DHS operations command's media adviser interrupted him, groaning that a pushy journalist from the UK's *Financial Times* was following up a lead directly linking China's train disaster to both the nuclear plant debacle and Dr eKiller.

'Tell him I'm tied up,' said Weiss, only to be told it was a woman and that since she was threatening to write regardless, being uncooperative was risky. 'And what we're doing here isn't? Jesus, how many times have I heard that line from a hack?' He knew all the classic tricks. 'Put the bitc—er, the reporter on. What's her name? … You kiddin' me, right? Pippa fuckin' Pierpont? Hell, Billy Bob, who'd shackle their kid with a name like that?' He held out his hand for the phone.

'Ms Pierpont, John Weiss here, acting head of ops command. I want you to listen hard, okay? First, the rules of the game: we're off the record and you can't use anything I say as background or any other weasel-word reporter shit. No highly placed sources sayin' this or that. Nothin' unless I okay it word-for-fuckin'-word, you got me?'

'Actually no, sir,' replied Pierpont. 'That's not how we work in London. What I'm sitting on is big and I believe true, so we're posting it on our website in fifteen minutes and gearing up for a late print edition. I'd like a quote from you but, if you don't want to talk on the record, I'll call the White House. Maybe they'll be more helpful.'

Weiss looked at the screen spilling out more and more information as if it was a spawning animal. 'Listen, Ms Pierpont. And this is definitely off the record, okay? You need to give me twenty-four hours before you go live with this.' He knew he was confirming the story for her, but he decided he had no choice. It was probably the only way he could buy the time he needed. 'Otherwise, you'll be shinin' a green light, a heads-up, for a bunch of the craziest crazies since Patty Hearst and the Symbiotic Liberation Army—'

'Symbionese?'

'Whatever. You'll be responsible … you personally, Ms Pierpont … for I don't know how many deaths and untold misery. I'm takin' a risk here in sayin' this, even off the record, but, ma'am, it'll make that disaster in China seem like an elbow itch. If you hold off the twenty-four hours I'm askin' for, I'll give you what you want this same time tomorrow. The whole caboodle.' Weiss knew he might have to break his word to her, but that was the least of his worries.

'Sorry, Mr Weiss. Glad to have you verify my story but right now I've got this as an exclusive and, tomorrow, who knows? So if you won't help me, I'm afraid—'

'Listen, Pip, if—'

'It's Pippa.'

'Right … If I give you what you want, today, will you agree to sit on it for twenty-four hours?'

After several minutes of toing and froing, she agreed, in principle, but had to cover it off with her editor, her one stipulation being that Weiss had to give her the specific information when she called back with his okay, with no hold backs and provided she felt Weiss wasn't giving her the run-around, the *FT* would stick to the deal. 'If you try to screw with us, sir—'

'Screw you? Not likely,' he said, though after he hung up, then returned to his call with Russia's FSB head, Uri Golovanov. 'Uri, I've already got the media pissin' on my back. There's been a leak somewhere so we're riskin' wholesale panic with time runnin' even shorter than we thought. Where are you guys with crackin' Yevtushenko's Cloud open?'

37

HOURS EARLIER IN PARIS, DR CLARE Dupont let her robe slip off her shoulders onto the parquetry floor and stretched her hand out tentatively into the darkness, tingling with the anticipation. Despite the pitch black around her, the sharp, sweet scent of the curtains drew her to them. She hadn't noticed before but the spray of ruby grapefruit and wild raspberry cologne she had blushed them with before going to sleep somehow captured the essence of someone freshly showered and primed for action.

She gently tucked her locks, still slightly damp, back behind her ears, then brushed her fingers down one of the sumptuous velvet folds, so lightly that she wouldn't risk any light peeping in. The touch, so lush, was like a kiss of heaven that beckoned her forward. First her hips swivelled into the soft, voluptuous material, then her arms and shoulders and finally her cheeks, first left and then right, then left again.

She reached for where the drapes fell together and swept them apart, the sparkle of the Paris afternoon bursting in on her, its sun stroking the hairs over her naked skin and casting a welcome glow over her blonde hair so it glowed like a new day. She looked briefly down on those strolling below, people who couldn't see her up on the sixth floor, and then her eyes flicked across the street to Notre Dame Cathedral. Unless Quasimodo was still swinging along the gargoyles and flying buttresses somewhere over there, she thought, her nudity and this private moment were hers to relish alone.

In a ritual toast to Victor Hugo's hunchback, she raised her hand to the window glass, already pleasurably warm, reminding herself how society had sorely misjudged the morally upright, decent man as a monster, just like it would inescapably miscast her. Dupont had chosen this apartment not so much for her affinity with the fictional character but more for its bird's eye view over his home. Apart from her precious collection of maritime memorabilia and first editions, the physical things that delighted Dupont most in the world were here, or close by: Notre Dame's three stained-glass rose windows and, around the corner, Sainte-Chapelle's fifteen tantalisingly delicate walls of glass.

With the sun pouring through her own window, she flung it open, wanting to shout at the top of her voice about the legacy she would tonight bequeath to the world, but a gust of bracing November reality chilled her yearning.

In the maritime world where she worked, Dupont was known as quite a siren, though no one had worked out how treacherous her songs really were. Her libertine charms had seduced many—men and women—but those, and her showy outfits and baby blonde hair were a sideshow, an entertainment for her delight not theirs. Above all, it was her intellect that had vaulted Clare Dupont onto the peak safety committee of the

International Maritime Organisation. If anything, her fashion-plate looks and her flirting had been disadvantages, leading many in positions of power and influence to be sceptical of her ability, but ultimately all she had to do to satisfy them was open her mouth.

Dr Dupont was a world-renowned expert on the technology that powered ECDIS—the Electronic Chart Display and Information System—the shipping world's version of electronic street-mapping but better. Not only did it integrate GPS with traditional maps, like car and smartphone systems did, it integrated multiple radar and sonar operating at different wavelengths, and an array of other critical alert systems and navigation tools that the maritime sector had spent decades developing. With ECDIS bringing all these safety systems together in real-time, vessels knew instantly where they were and what was around them, over them and, most crucially, what was hidden beneath them.

The company she headed had recently taken the slot as the number-one global vendor of ECDIS equipment and software, now widespread navigational aids for large vessels. She had mentally high-fived when SOLAS—the International Convention for the Safety of Life at Sea—had declared that ECDIS would be compulsory on large passenger ships, cargo vessels and tankers, as it had been since mid-2012, a success that was one reason for the award she would be receiving tonight. But even later, at around one am, after all the leading ECDIS professionals from around the globe had pottered back to their homes and hotels after the conference dinner, she would activate her bug. They might all go to bed tired but happy, but they wouldn't sleep well.

She hauled the window closed and turned back to her desk, too busy to dress and not knowing or minding if her shivering was from the cold snap or the thrilled anticipation of what she'd be doing in a few short hours.

Seated at her computer, she entered her password and opened the draft email she had been crafting on and off since she got back to Paris from Geneva two days ago. She read it over, slowly, for possibly the twentieth time and yet again fine-tuned it. Finally, and with almost a pianist's flourish, she typed her name, followed by 'D/5, Nine Sisters'. Finally, it was done. Perfect. Ready.

Explaining her radical action with purpose but not fervour was almost as crucial as the deed itself. But Dupont's was not a wordy 121-page manifesto à la the Unabomber, let alone a 1500-page copycatted opus like Breivik's, the Norwegian nutcase. Hers was a tight, four-paragraph statement explaining who she and Nine Sisters were, what she had done, how she had done it, and why. Those other manifestos were so long, so turgid, so repetitive, that not only did they put potential converts off reading them, they allowed the authorities and vested interests to manipulate the public into believing the authors were sick devils. Well, Breivik was a Satan, true, but that wasn't her point.

She addressed the draft email to her entire contact list—not just friends and family but everyone of stature in the international maritime safety community. She also added the distribution list she'd compiled containing hundreds of addresses for the major news wires and TV networks across Europe, the US and, in Mellor's honour, Australia. *The clucking chooks*, he had told their group, *will help get our message out, so make sure you feed them.*

With her message composed she felt suddenly dizzy and, standing haltingly, her hands splayed flat on her desk, she inhaled slowly and deeply, and when the moment had passed she unlocked her drawer and removed its contents.

The gun barrel, so cold, so hard, felt blissful against her cheek. And as she tickled it down her neck to her chest, she knew that what she would be doing later tonight was right, and it would all be good.

Very good.

38

ROM AFAR, THE MT *AFRICAN COLOSSUS* was like an island plateau daubed with the pigments of autumn, except the reds and browns were painted steel and the trees were cranes and derricks spiked across its topsides. The supertanker was incomprehensibly massive, and for Captain Masood Baqri, this voyage at her helm was set to be the climax of his sea career, of his life. After nineteen days crossing the Atlantic, his martyrdom and that of the thirty-five others on board was only two hours away.

The RMS *Titanic* had fielded a crew of 860 yet the *African Colossus*, at almost twice her size, carried a tiny fraction of that number, and usually only a pair of them in the bridge with Baqri. Tonight the chosen two were his British chief officer and a Filipino seaman, neither of whom he had ever warmed to. Needing so few to navigate, steer and control a floating giant like this was a tribute to man's ingenuity, but to Baqri it was a flawed resourcefulness, fatally flawed, an abuse of the bounty that God had bestowed on mankind, and so he readily accepted that it was up to him and others like him to divert man's abundant creativity and energy back to helping the planet, not destroying it.

For the last nineteen days, his cargo holds, big enough to swallow ten Taj Mahals, swirled with the two million barrels of light sweet crude he'd picked up at Chevron's giant FPSO, a floating production, storage and offloading vessel moored at its Agbami deepwater oilfield off Nigeria's coast. This $200 million shipment was scheduled for offloading tomorrow morning at Louisiana's Offshore Oil Port, still 170 nautical miles away, but that schedule wasn't Baqri's and he had decided that neither the cargo nor the tanker would ever keep it. This oil wasn't destined for fuelling cars or power stations; instead, and with Baqri in command, it was going to choke them dry.

Ten years he'd planned for this day, for this voyage. It had always seemed so far off, so impossible … so idealistic and impractical … but it was now within his grasp.

Suicide bombers merely killed people, but a suicide tanker, especially a supertanker, that was on another scale entirely. His *African Colossus*, travelling the arteries of the international carbon economy, would strike a deathblow to its heart. The Gulf of Mexico's oil and gas industry would be finished. America would be finished. He, Baqri, would behead the snake where so many others had failed.

Baqri was aware that his plan would ruin a stunning, precious, irreplaceable part of the very global ecosystem that he and the Nine Sisters were committed to saving, but for the bigger picture sacrifices had to be made. Excited though saddened, he rubbed his arm through his shirt, reminding himself that his tattoo underneath, an Urdu translation from his beloved *Hamlet*, explained his mission perfectly: *I must be cruel only to be kind. Thus bad begins and worse remains behind.*

Baqri had enjoyed a good life at sea and it showed. One of the perks of three decades plying the oceans was that he got to handpick his chef so, though Baqri was tall—over six foot—his uniforms puffed out a little more broadly these days. One of his wives sometimes pinched at his muffin tops, though he preferred love handles, his second wife's term for them. Yet he wasn't all flab and even against men thirty years younger he held the ship's trophy in arm-wrestling.

He'd taken a year out of sailing when he toyed with a doctorate in maritime law in Sydney, but he quickly discovered that even though the self-possessed city preened itself as a seaside paradise, he couldn't help his nostrils itching and his skin crawling every single day he was stuck on campus, craving for the simple, natural things he missed: the spray of tangy sea salt or the ethereal beauty of the milky sea, those sublime moments in the inkiest blackness of a night-time ocean, when his ship would plough into invisible blooms of bioluminescent plankton causing them to flare up, as if a veil of blue sequins had fluttered across the surface.

Yes, he was more of an ocean addict than he realised but, on top of that, it was in Sydney he opened his eyes to Professor Mellor's revelation, that he could do more to combat piracy— planet piracy—by winning command of a supertanker than he could posturing and waffling on about arcane legal precedents in the stuffy courts of admiralty.

From the moment he flung on the secret cloak of B/13, Baqri included in his prayers five times a day a wish to become master of a supertanker. He had aimed for an LNG tanker—the fires and explosions of liquid natural gas would be exponentially more dramatic and filmic than for an oil tanker—but he'd got stuck in the oil groove. Even so, his prayers were answered sooner than he expected, first with MT *Atlantic Princess*, then

MT *Ocean Goddess*, but both were merely VLCCs—very large crude carriers—and he needed a ULCC, an ultra-large, with more length, tonnage, extra cargo and more impact physically but also, more importantly, psychologically. Eight months ago, the new, gigantic MT *African Colossus* became his. To most people, ships like this carried liquid energy and thus life. But to Baqri, they were poison, and his aim was to transform this one into a torpedo and wipe out the industry most responsible for the planet's woes.

African Colossus stretched so far that even during the daytime Baqri had difficulty seeing the bow from the navigation bridge without the aid of his trusty binoculars or the forward CCTV. At the vessel's launch, an American TV reporter interviewing him told the cameras that if the vessel was tipped on its end, its 415-metre length would even tower above New York's Empire State Building. At the time, Baqri had stifled a giggle, wondering how the reporter would feel when she later learnt she'd interviewed the man who, after that comparison, would surely become known as the sea's King Kong. He'd thought of himself that way ever since, though for his crew he worked hard at a different image: as a firm and decisive commander, of course, yet a decent man, a cultured reader of books, of Shakespeare and poetry, and a man for whom civility and manners were not lost arts.

He wandered over to the push-button espresso machine he'd installed in the bridge at his own expense. His chief officer had a penchant for skim-milk cappuccinos and the seaman with them tonight was a devotee of short blacks, in coffees as well as women, as Baqri had observed when they'd gone ashore in Port Harcourt, Nigeria.

With his back to his men, he unbuttoned his shirt's breast pocket and drew out a small vial. He twisted off the lid and, checking he was not being observed, took a quick sniff of the liquid to check for its telltale aroma of almonds. Originally, he had aimed for an odourless poison but in Port Harcourt, cyanide was so easy to get. He drizzled the toxin into two of the cups then pushed the buttons for the three coffees, finishing them all off with a sprinkling of almond flakes, a Baqri innovation that no one who visited the bridge dared to refuse. Personally, he detested almonds but nineteen days of yet one more pretence was nothing if it served its higher purpose.

39

WITH BERNARDO DEAD BEHIND THEM, TORI and Frank were focused on Whitehead. Standing in a sea of white—the floors, the walls, the ceiling—the black Glock in his hands was as stark as the act he'd just committed. Unsure of his next move, they froze themselves, worried the slightest step might get him to fire again. But he was no longer looking at his wife, not even at them. With his eyes on his pistol, he turned it on himself, and stared into the barrel, its faint tendrils of smoke curling into his nose as if they were threads exploring a path for the next bullet. Tori raised a foot, and he didn't react. She took a step, then another and slowly approached him, fully conscious that the slide of the sub-compact semi-automatic was primed with a cartridge ready to fire. When she was within reach, rather than try to twist his arm and run the chance of a wild stray bullet, she shot out her right hand, pressed the release catch on the gun grip and with her left simultaneously pulled out the magazine, the swiftness of her move disorienting Whitehead into releasing the weapon to her.

Frank, relieved to see Tori with the gun, stepped over the blood oozing out of The Cage and tried his ID card to get entry, but it wouldn't work.

Whitehead didn't look at his wife's body. Freed of the pistol, he stared at his hands, turning them over and over as if wondering whose they were and how they'd got attached to his wrists. They didn't tremble, and neither did he weep; he just stared. Tori stood next to him, at a loss for what to say, unsure how to comfort him, so she settled on silence and, oddly, so did Thatcher, leaving her and Frank's earpieces in silence. Whitehead had done the incredible. What could anyone say?

Seeing Frank struggling to get access to The Cage, it seemed clear to Tori that Whitehead killing his wife had been the only way to prevent a financial crisis of apocalyptic dimensions.

She caught his eye and silently pointed to her phone then to herself, mouthing *Weiss*. When Frank blinked and nodded to confirm he understood, she left the two men in the room alone, the only noise the whirring of the air conditioning.

Before ringing Weiss, she looked back through the portal at Bernardo's body, twisted forward over the desk so Tori could no longer see where the chunk of her skull was missing even though its splatters over the computer screens and bars were sickeningly visible. A stream of blood gushed down the back of her white hoodie, as if a wild man had painted the number one there. One, she reminded herself had been Bernardo's Nine Sisters number: Q/1. The blood flowed down, dripping over her chair to the floor, seeping into the cracks between the white floor tiles, forming a red ladder that no one would ever want to climb.

40

'**O**UR PEOPLE ARE DOWNSTAIRS FROM YOU,' Weiss told Tori, feigning calm and control yet feeling dirty, soiled.

After playing the video clip that Tori had asked Thatcher to send through, watching his boss slip the Glock out of his ankle holster, seeing him shoot Margy, Weiss was overcome but he knew he couldn't let his emotions show, not in the operations room and not on this call. Whitehead had been his mentor, his hero, the man who, seeing Weiss wallowing in the middle of the executive pack, had shown faith and shuffled him to the top.

Tori had just filled him in on her last few hours, starting with the real reason she'd diverted her flight to New York. Weiss couldn't believe any of it at first, that Margy would even think of bringing down the financial system, or that Alan would kill his own wife.

But Weiss had just seen it on the video clip, with his own eyes. Whitehead had done what Weiss was certain he wouldn't have the guts to do: advance the public interest over his own wife's life. Now Weiss had to live with himself, a treacherous shit who had dared to put a tail on this man, this hero, as if he were some grimy suspect.

Weiss didn't know what to say. 'Weiss,' said Tori after a while. 'Are you still there?'

'Sure, sorry. Look, in the circumstances, I'll get NYPD and the FBI to lay off Alan—and you, of course—for tonight anyhow. They can take all the statements they need from the three of you tomorrow. It's unusual, but hey, it's all on the video.' He paused, while he suppressed the choke that came to his throat. 'Meanwhile,' he coughed, 'I'll get my guys to take him home and sit with him.'

It wasn't only the tail, or even Weiss's fondness for Whitehead or his career debt that made him feel like he needed a shower, there was his affair with Margy. It had lasted a full year. She had started it but he'd ended it three months ago when the guilt of betraying Weiss's own wife, Blanche, on top of deceiving his boss and friend, had become too much for him.

Weiss had never known Margy by the surname Quando— her first short-lived marriage had never come up—so when he'd seen the name on the stegas it meant nothing to him and, so far, his team hadn't dug up anything on a Margy Quando either.

She had seduced him, that was for sure, but now he felt even more sickened, wondering if she had done it, not as Margy Bernardo the wife of Alan Whitehead, but as Q/1. Fuck! he thought. He didn't have a clue why Margy had started it, and now he had no way of finding out. That she'd been playing him seemed highly likely. The fuckin' *bitch*! His head was screaming. Each kiss, each 'sweetie', every massage of his, er, ego ... All of it, every single thing she'd ever said, she was toying with him.

The habitually composed, unflappable man was embarrassed by the beads of sweat he felt sure were glazing his forehead and starting to darken his shirt under his armpits. He had a sudden and absurd fear that everyone milling around him would guess why, if they weren't already mocking him behind their hands. His thing with Margy could finish him. It wasn't that he'd made a mistake. In his job he was expected to take calculated risks. But the duplicity? During the affair, a maxim his first boss swore by had clanged inside him: *Betray the bed then betray the Fed*. He'd dismissed it at the time as even more old-school crap from the codger, but whatever Weiss thought about anything anymore wouldn't matter. What mattered was what the director of DHS would think, Whitehead's boss—his own boss now he was acting head of operations command. Acting. How impermanent, how transient a word that really was.

Was he duty-bound to confess the affair to the director? If he did—Jesus! He had no way of knowing where it would end: whether Blanche would stand by him; if he'd get access to the kids. All the words and images on the wall screen were swirling and jumping out at him as if he was wearing 3D glasses. He needed to hold himself together.

'Swyft,' he said, remembering Tori was still on the phone, 'it's a lot to ask given what you and Frank have done already, but I need you both to do one more thing, for me. We're totally stretched here and ...'

EUROPANATIONAL'S DATA CENTRE was swarming with New York cops and FBI and DHS agents, with two from DHS escorting a shattered Whitehead downstairs to their car to drive him home. Still in a daze, he wasn't speaking and, given the circumstances, they didn't push him. As they opened the car door, he held back and despite their prodding and cajoling, he declined to get in.

'Chapman, Manton.' Whitehead seemed to be forcing the words out, as if his tongue was stuck inside a sock. His breathing was laboured, and Chapman wondered if he was an asthmatic. 'Please … I'll be fine … Really,' he added when Chapman took an inhaler out of his pocket. 'My car … It's—' He pointed down the block through the incongruously festive-looking flashes of blue and red lights to where his sedan was sandwiched between a fire truck and an ambulance, its wheels still resting up on the kerb. He gathered himself up, and shook off Manton's arm. 'I can drive myself home. Seriously. No nursemaids. All I need is some alone-time … with a bottle of Jack.'

After getting the okay from Weiss, Chapman and Manton walked Whitehead to his car and, as one closed the door for him, the other surreptitiously moved around to the rear bumper and removed the GPS tracker underneath it.

The pair stood by the side of the road and almost saluted their hero as his wheel bounced down off the kerb as he reversed, then as he slowly drove off.

'Poor damn fucker,' said Chapman, switching off the tracker and slipping it into his pocket while still on the line to Weiss who, at first, thought the pity was meant for him.

WHOOPING ABOVE TORI and Frank's heads on the roof of the data centre, the FBI Tactical Helicopter Unit's Black Hawk UH-60 started lowering its ten tonnes until, like a weightless feather, it briefly swayed and hovered inches above the surface to pick them up. As the sergeant pulled them aboard, Tori suddenly remembered that their cab driver was waiting for them down below, so as soon as she was belted in and had her headset on she asked the pilot to request DHS Officer Chapman to pay him off and release him.

Frank had already jumped onto his laptop and was checking out the profile Weiss had sent through. After he'd skimmed it, he passed it across to Tori to see if she recognised their rather unusual target, a Catholic bishop the stegas had revealed as M/4, Giovanni Marini.

She nodded. 'He's one of your lot,' she shouted back, attempting a smile but too drained from what they'd been through to show any teeth. 'But, hell, what damage can a Vatican prelate really do? Praying a bit harder's hardly going to change anything.'

'I don't know,' replied Frank, turning up the volume in his headset speakers. 'The old Church has caused a fair bit of trouble in its day. Maybe start with the Crusades, then the Inquisition, perhaps their blind eye to Auschwitz, and hey, let's not forget the paedophiles ... Shall I go on?'

'With all that uncritical devotion, say again why you dropped out of priest school?'

His reason had nothing to do with hypocrisy, nor even dogma. Frank was still a believer and though Tori had never noticed, he attended Mass whenever he could, though he drew the line at the confessional. Priests weren't covered by the Official Secrets Act.

THE GALA DINNER program described him as His Excellency, the Most Reverend Monsignor Giovanni Marini, Bishop and Prefect of the Vatican's Secret Archives. Marini was in Philadelphia to open *Lux in Arcana*, an exhibition of one hundred of the priceless treasures he was solemnly charged with preserving. He'd brought them to America after a predecessor had shown them to record crowds in Rome's Capitoline Museums, the first time in centuries that they had been allowed to leave the walls of Vatican City. He'd personally escorted them to Philadelphia and had already spent two weeks curating the display at the city's Museum of Art, a Grecian-style temple in appropriately massive Roman proportions. Marini was secretly excited to see the Museum's celebrated front steps in real life. Until now, he'd only seen them in the *Rocky* movies, which he surreptitiously watched all six of each year after Mass on Easter Sunday, his post-Lent tradition. In fact, if the bishop had been wearing civvies instead of being so encumbered with his robes, and not so fussed about committing the sin of vainglory or drawing attention to himself, he might have been tempted to run up the famous steps himself, raising his arms and spinning around in triumph like so many of the other tourists did.

WEISS'S TEAM WAS so under the gun that he felt he couldn't spare a single man or woman to try to work out how a priestly member of Nine Sisters could do any damage. The best guess someone had voiced so far was that Marini might make his big statement through destroying the treasures but while Weiss knew that would be distressing to many, he wasn't going to lose any sleep over it, even with a mother-in-law who was as Catholic and as offensive as Mel Gibson. Then again, with President Diaz a Catholic, he needed to cover his butt, the reason why he'd leant on Tori and Frank to check Marini out for him.

At this time of night, driving to Philly would have taken them two hours on the Interstate 95 even if he'd given them a sirens-blaring escort, and the quickest train would've been an hour but only after they'd pushed all the way through rush-hour traffic to Penn Station. The chopper Weiss had commandeered for them would be quickest by far, around forty minutes.

One of his researchers had discovered that Marini, lodging at the St Charles Borromeo Seminary while in Philadelphia, was tonight the honoured guest at a Mayoral dinner at the Museum of Art with Sylvester Stallone, somewhat strangely, also attending.

'WEISS, IT'S PIPPA Pierpont, *Financial Times*. My editor okayed our deal, but things have moved on and we're going to have to make a new one. You better switch on CNN.'

'I'll call you back,' he said, and hung up. 'People,' he called out. 'CNN, now. Big screen.'

The TV helicopter was circling an unidentified building itself surrounded by emergency vehicles, and its spotlight beam pinpointed two people on the roof scurrying aboard an FBI Black Hawk in its typical dark livery.

Tonight, in a world exclusive, CNN exposes a new terrorist group and reveals a fatal shooting in Long Island City, New York that, with only seconds to spare, defeated their brazen plot to cut the global financial system to its knees.

Less than thirty minutes ago, in the building directly below our helicopter, the worldwide data centre of the EuropaNational banking giant, a senior Homeland Security officer shot and killed one of the bank's top executives, believed to be a Dr Margy Bernardo.

Bernardo is suspected of being a member of a previously unknown anarcho-environmentalist terrorist group, the Nine Sisters, also called 9S. Senior sources in Washington are also linking this same group to the Chinese fast train catastrophe, which has so far claimed almost 9,000 lives and injured 15,000.

CNN has also received unconfirmed reports connecting the secretive group to Dr Wilbur Fenton, the immunologist being called Dr eKiller—

Just in … Some big questions being asked in Washington … Dr Margy Bernardo, the deceased EuropaNational executive and alleged terrorist, is … was … the wife of Dr Alan Whitehead who, until earlier today, headed up the Department of Homeland Security's counter-terror operation against the 9S group. Dr Whitehead can't be reached …

'Holy fuck,' shouted Weiss. He spun around, almost shouting into his assistant's ear, his usual demeanour of calm and restraint shot. 'Where are these media bastards scroungin' their info? I want you to find out who the fuck is leakin' all this and break their bal—Just find them. If those buzzards get any more before we neutralise 9S, we'll have a global fuckin' stampede on our hands. And get me Uri Golovanov. And Admiral Warner!'

41

TORI AND FRANK'S CHOPPER HURTLED THE hundred miles southwest to Philadelphia at its maximum cruise speed of 151 knots. Just before they'd agreed to board, Tori, knowing she had Weiss over at least a small barrel, asked him for a status update on Yevtushenko's imminent Cloud burst. With time running only a couple of hours short of the six am Saint-Petersburg deadline, the news was not good. Once belted up inside the helicopter, and despite the terrifying possibilities should the Russians fail, she couldn't keep her head from drooping.

Frank nudged her awake. The light from his computer screen was bright and glary, and it took a few seconds before her eyes adjusted to see that he was pointing to a map. He explained that earlier in the evening, when he'd messaged Thatcher from Whitehead's phone, it was to ask him to set up a tracking monitor on the phone's location, exactly what Whitehead had done with his wife's phone. After everything else that had happened, Frank had forgotten about it, but Thatcher had just sent him through this map, mainly because it didn't make sense. Instead of the distressed widower driving himself home to the Upper East Side as he'd said, the map showed a route that cut right across Manhattan from east to west and then under the Hudson River via the Lincoln Tunnel into Union City. Judging by the barred, boarded up windows on the image that Frank now opened up on the screen, again courtesy of Thatcher, Whitehead's phone had now mysteriously found itself inside a derelict two-storey clapboard building whose tired, faded signage indicated it had once hosted a Pentecostal church.

'The next curious thing,' Thatcher typed, 'is that the same offshore entity registered as owning Kass Cardozo's apartment also owns this property. What's more, how come this abandoned building is generating a sky-high power bill, higher even than the rather dizzying usage from my own humble apartment?' The truth was that Thatcher actually didn't receive any bills. His considerable power intake was gratis, a generous courtesy of the local power company except that they weren't aware of their largesse.

'Weiss,' said Tori once he answered her call, 'something weird's just come up. Instead of going home, Whitehead's driven over to some place in Union City.'

'Can't you give the poor guy a break? Fuck it, give *me* a break. I'm up to my eyeballs here. Maybe he's—I don't know— gone to his shrink? Hell, you couldn't blame him. Shoulda thought of it myself, really. So can you just stick to what I asked and check out that damn bishop? Gotta go, I've got the Russkis on the line.' He was about to hang up, when he added, 'Hey, I got my guys to strip the tracker off Whitehead's car. How the hell do *you* know where he is?'

'I used to work for Langley, remember?' Tori turned to Frank as she ended the call. 'What a prick. After all Whitehead's done. The guy could be in some kind of daze ... or trouble ... and Weiss doesn't give a shit. Well, I do.' She patched herself through to the pilot. 'Change of plan,' she said, and gave their new destination, in Union City.

As the chopper swooped into a long right curve, she leant into Frank. 'I'm with Thatcher,' she said. 'Why would an abandoned church be drawing all those kilowatts?'

'Speaking of kilo-stuff,' said Frank, 'we haven't heard from Axel ... like on how they went in Greece today.'

'And we should update him on this, too.' Tori looked at her watch. 'It's two-ish in the morning over there. Maybe we should wait till later?'

'With the chance that Yevtushenko's Cloud is still going down, I think he'll want to be kept in the loop. SIS might need to take some precautions.'

'If he hasn't done it already!'

'OH MY, IT'S noisy where you are. What is that confounded racket?' Axel asked as he switched off the TV with his remote, plumped up his pillows and sat up in bed. 'Hmm, 7.15 pm in New York ... Where *are* you two? Rattling along in some subway?'

'No, we're hitching a ride on an FBI Black Hawk. Axel, this is for your ears only, but Whitehead's wife was—'

'—in Nine Sisters. I know. I caught the story about the shooting on CNN just now and I did wonder if it was you two climbing into that chopper. I was about to call you to find out.'

'How'd they get onto it so fast? Did they say anything about who shot her, or why?'

'Only that it was a senior Homeland Security officer, but no name.'

'It was Whitehead, Axel. Her own husband killed her. Frank and I were there and, for a frightening split second, it looked like he was going to kill *us*. It was—' Tori shook her head, '—gut-wrenching. The woman was about to bring down the entire financial system … one person, one brilliant but crazy person in a position of the highest trust and influence, just like Mellor had planned. I still find it hard to—'

'It's only hard to believe such things if you have no imagination, Tori. The mixture of human ingenuity and passion is the finest yet potentially the most malevolent concoction known to mankind. You of all people—'

'Listen, the Russians haven't sorted out Yevtushenko's Cloud yet and there's less than two hours to go, so we thought we should give you a heads up, in case you need to shift anything, or quietly warn some clients—like Soti, maybe?'

'SIS is fine, but I can't tell anyone else without … Can you imagine if it got out that we were responsible for a panic? My grandfather had one of those in 1929 and it almost … Anyway, thank you for raising it. Soti, by the way, is still partying in the hotel. He was hoping to find you here, especially after our good news.'

Frank took a look across at Tori and cut in, 'Some good news would be extremely welcome.'

'Of course. Soti and I left the PM and his people at one am, oh, an hour ago. It's been a long—'

'And?' said Tori.

'Well, Giorgos—I mean the PM—as we speak, he's discussing the final plan with his Cabinet, to make sure he can get it through the political hoops. He convened an emergency meeting for half past one. If all goes well we'll be signing and announcing formal heads of agreement tomorrow, aiming for it to be ratified as soon as possible by the whole Parliament. Giorgos didn't want to risk any leaks and neither did Soti, so we've decided we need to step out on the front foot … big fanfare but little time, that sort of thing. So well done, Tori. Provided the rest of your 9S friends are kept at bay—'

'They're not friends, Axel.'

'True, but if they are, well, neutered, your little deal is set to become a mighty big deal. The biggest SIS has ever done, by the way.'

Tori tried not to blush anymore as she hung up, but from the curl she observed at the end of Frank's mouth, she was certain she was failing, positive that her reddening skin was visible even in the darkness cloaking them inside the Black Hawk. Then she realised that he could see her, just as she could see him. To avoid further embarrassment, she glanced down at his computer and saw how close they'd got to the indicator flashing the whereabouts of Whitehead's phone, and guessed it was only a couple of minutes.

Her phone rang and, as before, she fed the call through to her and Frank's headsets.

'Tori, this is your happy Greek,' said Soti Skylakakis, slurring as if he'd had one too many of his Metaxa mojitos. 'I'm in your bed, but you're not here.'

Frank made a point of removing his headset and turned his head away so she couldn't see the grin he was struggling to hold back.

Axel must have invited Soti to use her suite, she guessed correctly. 'It's a bit late for you, isn't it, Soti?'

'You can't keep a good Greek down, eh? Especially one who is going to become a president, thanks to you.'

'Thanks to others, too … Besides the deal's not signed up yet, Soti, so—'

'Axel says you're embroiled somehow in this Nine Sisters shit I'm hearing about. I had *three* sisters once. Not mine, of course, but each other's, and all at the same time. Incredible! But *nine*, whew! That would be a handful, even for me.'

'Your point?'

'My point? Exactly.' He sniggered. 'When are you returning to Athens? I would very much like to, er, thank you.'

Frank jabbed his elbow at her and pointed out the window and downwards, signalling that they were hovering above the house. 'Soti, gotta go. Talk soon,' she said, relieved to end the call. It wasn't that she didn't want to see him—on the contrary—but Tori wasn't big on drunken dirty talk, not even with a multibillionaire. Certainly not with Frank sitting next to her and Whitehead in the building under her.

42

'THAT'S WHITEHEAD'S CAR PARKED OUTSIDE,' SAID Frank as the chopper hovered above the house and spotlit the licence plate. 'Thatcher was right, this is the place.' Frank handed Tori another of Thatcher's hot devices he'd brought with him, a radio tomographic imager. Until Thatcher got his hands on this unit, their use inside the US had been reserved for the CIA. RTIs were like X-ray vision devices; they could 'see' through walls, or in this case, a roof and, because they operated with radio waves, it meant that ambient light, for example from the chopper, wouldn't interfere. Likewise, if the streetlights outside the house had actually been working.

'He's in there,' she said, holding the device up to her eye. 'It's a single person, definitely. He's standing up against a wall ... Why's he doing that? No, it must be a door because he's pulling it out, towards himself ... It's very thick ... looks as thick as his arm ... Now he's walking through the doorway ...

I'm guessing it's a doorway ... but I can't get anything inside there. Maybe it's encased? Judging by the thickness of the door, maybe it's steel-lined?'

'If you were really Clark Kent with that thing, it'd be *lead*-lined.' Frank laughed, plugging a cable into the RTI and connecting it to his computer so he could see what she was seeing.

There was no visible movement down below for maybe a minute. 'He's about to come outside ... Kill your lights,' she told the pilot. 'Nav lights, everything. What's he carrying?' The screen showed he was holding a large box in front of himself. 'Look, his head seems to be over the top of it. It's like he's leaning forward. It must be damn heavy. Its size ... it's like an Esky, but what's inside it?'

'It's like a what?'

'An Esky. A picnic cooler? Aha, I got it! The power bills. Where he took it from must be a giant cool room.' They watched as Whitehead put the box down and seemed to run his hands down his body, first shaking his shoulders and then his legs.

'Do you think he's removing his clothes?' said Frank, scratching his head.

They watched as the ghostly figure moved into a small inner room, and started to rub his hands in his hair and then all over his body. 'He's showering, got to be. Tori, I think he's got biohazards stored here. Maybe the avian flu virus or something like it.'

'His wife wanted to destroy Wall Street. *He* wants to wipe out the entire population of New York City.'

'And the rest of the country! It'll spread like—'

'Fuck! I'll get Weiss on the line.'

'Why aren't you guys in Philly?' growled Weiss, the exhaustion and pressure, and the guilt, getting to him. 'Didn't

I make myself clear, that you should forget Whitehead and go see the bishop?'

'Shit, he's looking up. He must have heard the chopper … Lift! Lift!' Frank realised he needed to flick his headset mic back so their pilot could hear him, 'Lift! And shift south two blocks,' he said, realising that Whitehead exiting the house and hearing and then seeing the outline of a blacked-out FBI helicopter hovering directly above him might not be prudent.

'What do you mean lift?' asked Weiss, and Tori explained.

She put down the RTI and switched to the night scope, plugged Frank's cable into it and zoomed it in so they could both see the front door on the computer screen. 'Weiss,' she said, 'this property Whitehead's in is derelict, okay, but it soaks up as much juice as a small factory, and it's owned by the same offshore entity as the place where his wife did her identity switch. We think he's got a bio-safe cool room inside, a shower, the whole deal. He's lugged some sort of heavy box out of the cool room. I'm hoping we're wrong but we're thinking it contains some kind of pathogen—'

'Whoa, Swyft, aren't you jumpin' to a heck of a lot of conclusions from sittin' in the sky and lookin' through the roof? That man, like I told you, is a damn hero.'

'I thought he was, too.'

The front door was kicked open from the inside and a man, wearing a full bodysuit with tight-fitting wrists, gloves, head cover and eye protection and carrying a large, and definitely cool container, lumbered down the stairs and headed toward the car. With the streetlights out, the thermal vision only showed reds and greens but it was clear enough and Frank sent a still image he'd captured to Weiss. 'See that?'

'I need better,' said Weiss. 'Give me a live feed.'

The screen on the ops command room wall now showed exactly the same green/red scene that Tori and Frank saw, although a little jerkier. 'Swyft. The man's my friend, my *mentor*. Fuck!' Weiss slammed his fist down on the first tier of desks he was standing next to so suddenly that the three women working there almost jumped out of their chairs.

'Hey, people,' Weiss shouted to the room, ignoring them. 'Everyone stop the fuck what you're doin'. Stop! Now! That figure up there on the screen? We believe that's Whitehead. Alan Whitehead, suspended director of DHS operations command, the hero we all watched takin' down his own wife to save us all from a financial holocaust. But what we're lookin' at here don't make sense. It's Whitehead live in Union City, comin' out of a derelict house. He looks to be wearin' a biohazard body suit. So someone, anyone, give me an innocent explanation of what the hell he's doin' there dressed like that and carryin' that chill box to his car. Somebody. Please?'

The silence exploded around him. For thirty seconds, no one spoke or even murmured. Whenever a phone rang, it was killed. Everyone just kept switching their nervous eyes from the screen to Weiss and back until he eventually signalled to Oliver Clapin, section chief of the FBI's Critical Incident Response Group, who was standing at the water cooler. All eyes moved to Clapin as he walked back to Weiss carrying two cups.

He held one out to Weiss, but he shook his head. 'Clapin, you know what you—' Weiss began, then his chest started to heave. He closed his eyes, took a deep breath and set his jaw tight, then blinked a few times, putting his fist to his mouth and forcing a cough. 'Clapin, you know what you gotta do, right?' he said, now reaching for the water.

The FBI section chief stared at Weiss. 'But he's a friend of yours, isn't he?'

'I thought so, yes,' he said, taking a sip but averting his eyes.

With a hand free, Clapin tapped the unmute button on his Bluetooth earpiece to turn his mic on. 'Swyft,' he said, 'switch Weiss and me through to your pilot.' He waited until he heard the click and continued, 'Lieutenant, you hear me okay?'

'Sir?'

'Lieutenant, this is Oliver Clapin, section chief of—'

'I know who you are, sir.'

'Then listen up good. The male person exiting that house you've been surveilling is Dr Alan Whitehead who, until earlier today, was head of ops command for DHS. Through the efforts of your passengers, we have every reason to believe that Whitehead is carrying highly virulent pathogens in a chill box and that he's about to release them in a crowded public place somewhere in New York City. We clearly cannot let him do that, lieutenant. So, aim your spot—but don't turn it on—aim it onto the container he's carrying, and when I give the order, switch on the light for two seconds—no more than two seconds—and tell me what you see, okay? But wait for my order.'

'Copy that, sir.

'Swyft, switch your scope from thermal to night vision, I want personal eyeballs on this.' The wall screen went black, as Clapin knew it would with the streetlights out. 'Perfect, ma'am, thank you.'

'Lieutenant, spot him … now! What do you see?'

The pilot saw what they all saw. 'Full body suit, sir. The box is now in his car trunk but I had eyes on a fluoro-orange biohazard symbol on top of it.' As the screen cut back to black, everyone's pupils still burned with the image of Whitehead coldly staring up at them, closing the lid of his trunk as if in a dare.

Clapin looked over to Weiss, his eyebrow raised in question, and Weiss nodded.

'Swyft, back to thermal please, fast. Lieutenant, do you have a door gunner?'

'Two, sir.'

'Then take him down.'

43

WEISS FELT LIKE SHIT, BUT HE knew he had to hold himself together. He'd just got off a private line to the director of DHS and was walking back into the ops command room. Yes, he should have called the director earlier, and yes, there were no ifs or buts that were relevant. Did he know that Whitehead was godfather to the director's son? Did he know that Whitehead had been best man at the director's last wedding? Did he know that—? How the fuck, he was still screaming inside his head, was he supposed to know all that shit if no one fuckin' told him?

'We've got the Russian FSB on hold, sir,' Weiss's assistant told him.

'Don't you think I know where the fuckin' FSB is from?' he yelled. It better be good news, he told himself as he checked the screen clock on top of the Yevtushenko column and saw it ticking down. 'Golovanov, I hope you're callin' to tell me that you folks have done it. I really don't need no disappointment right now.'

'Weiss, what the *góvna* are you playing at? We were making some progress when a—I don't know how to translate this— let's say a wall got erected around Yevtushenko's Cloud. It wasn't there before, and it didn't come from him or his system. My guys tracked it to your country but then the trail went dead. Weiss, we only have eighty minutes left and some *mudak* in your team is playing games with us. If I didn't know better, I'd say you Americans actually want Europe to collapse—'

'Good thing you know better, then.'

44

THE BRIDGE ON THE *AFRICAN COLOSSUS* was securely locked from the inside. Now, with his two shipmates on watch out of the way and the rest of the crew either asleep or in the engine room twelve decks below, Captain Baqri rippled with confidence. He rechecked his route and his array of navigation monitors, reminding himself that he had to make his move at the last possible moment, with the US Coast Guard inconveniently tracking every ship that plied through the hundreds of working oil and gas rigs that dotted this section of the Gulf of Mexico. Routine monitoring was one thing, but Baqri had no clue that tonight there was more than that, with two enormous screens elsewhere displaying specific live aerial satellite feeds of his vessel, and his alone. One screen was inside the DHS's Washington nerve centre and the other was in New Orleans, at operations command for the US Coast Guard's Eighth District. Though Baqri didn't know it, these thermal images of the MT *African Colossus* made it look more like a ghostly torpedo than a ship, an impression nearer to the mark than the authorities yet knew.

'SHE'S PRETTY CLOSE to the Macondo Prospect, isn't she?' asked Weiss down the line from Washington. Macondo was the undersea well that in 2010 became more infamously known as the source of the *Deepwater Horizon* spill.

The Coast Guard district commander, Rear Admiral Alex Warner, checked the charts. 'That's relative, sir. *African Colossus* is sixty nautical miles from MC 252,' she said, meaning Mississippi Canyon block 252 where Macondo was located, 'and she's one-fifty from the LOOP.' The Louisiana Offshore Oil Port was where *African Colossus* was due to offload the following morning. 'So far, the vessel is right on course. But given what you've told us about her captain, I'm mighty prickly.'

Weiss wasn't sure if her discomfort was over Baqri being B/13 in the Nine Sisters, or because he was Muslim. The intelligence on Baqri was that he'd been born in Pakistan close to Abbottabad, the place where US Navy SEALs Team 6 killed Osama bin Laden, an event very personal to Weiss. Not only had he lost his best friend on 9/11—Ali, a Muslim, had been an anti-trust lawyer working in the Twin Towers—but a decade later Weiss was the DHS team leader poring over the folio of personal papers the SEALs had seized from bin Laden's lair. Weiss's specific focus had been on al-Qaeda's plans to seize and detonate US oil tankers, and it was Weiss who wrote the briefly confidential alert to police and the energy industry that highlighted al-Qaeda's aim that this would cause an 'extreme economic crisis' in the West.

Apart from the flimsy thread of Baqri's birthplace, Weiss didn't have a shred of evidence linking the captain to al-Qaeda or similar terrorist organisations but, for him, the stegas he'd got from Tori were enough to unmask Baqri as a deep and radicalised environmentalist, just like Bernardo, who would use any means to achieve his altruistic ends.

'Weiss,' said Admiral Warner, 'there's around four thousand rigs down here in the Gulf—'

'Yeah, but not right where she is.'

'Okay, a few hundred,' said the admiral. 'That make you feel any better? What I was going to say was with the wrong hands at her wheel, this tanker's a potential *Death Star*. If she spills that load or, worse, rams into a platform, it will not only screw the Gulf, this time it'll yank the handbrakes on offshore oil production for a generation at least.'

The *Deepwater Horizon* spill had got close to doing that, but what took precedence that time was President Barack Obama's political pragmatism to help the Democrats win the mid-term elections through trying to kick aside the recession crutches that had been hobbling America. Now, with President Isabel Diaz not even a year into her own term, Warner was far less sure what the White House response would be. 'With the vessel in my jurisdiction, Weiss, I say we can't cross our fingers hoping that Baqri's a Han Solo. We've got to assume he's a Darth Vader.'

Weiss was as much a *Star Wars* fan as the next person, but something didn't gel for him. 'Admiral, here's the thing ... if he's trying to save the planet, and if he does what we think he's doing, sure it'll turn the offshore oil taps off, I get that, but he'll be unleashin' an environmental Armageddon down there. For a greenie, it doesn't make—'

'For fuck's sake, Weiss, what don't you understand about that Latin shit you said these 9S people whisper to themselves? Here, I wrote it down: "Let justice be done, though the heavens fall." Weiss, what these 9S-ers are all about is the greater good. This is nothing short of a suicide ship. A flock of dead birds, a few schools of putrid, stinking fish, some lost lives ... all in all a trivial price if first prize is hauling these great United States to her wobbly knees. Hold a minute,' she said and tapped her phone onto mute as Captain Robert Ambrose, chief of the Coast Guard's Response Division, wheeled himself in.

Three years earlier, Ambrose had survived the crash of his Dolphin MH-65C helicopter off Pensacola, Florida during an attempted rescue when he and his crew braved forty-knot winds to reach a sailboat adrift and violently pitching and rolling in heavy seas. Ambrose could no longer fly but, for Warner, there was no better strategist under her command.

'Admiral, we've done the role-play,' said Ambrose. 'If I was standin' at the helm of *African Colossus* and hopin' to max the kill, what I'd be doin', in say ten—' he checked his watch, '—nine minutes, I'd be turnin' the wheel a notch west of her current course, pushin' the screws right up and lockin' her autopilot so as to aim her bow straight at *Deep Thunder*.'

'Holy—!'

'Yes, ma'am. She'd hit that monster rig in maybe forty minutes flat and given the distance from New Orleans, our boys—er, and girls—they don't have a whole heap of time to get out there and stop her.'

The *Deep Thunder* oil and gas platform, standing hundreds of metres off the Gulf floor, was claimed to be the deepest, tallest freestanding structure in the world. Its steel and reinforced concrete topsides spanned over two football fields and towered eighteen storeys above the waterline. The topsides alone, at 60,000 tonnes, could easily bench press an Iowa class warship, and day in and day out it fed 400,000 barrels of oil and 6.8 million cubic metres of gas into an undersea pipeline that helped keep American industry and transportation alive.

Ambrose checked the page on his lap. '*Deep Thunder*'s 130 miles out from base, so even if we flew out, like, right now we'd be too late. At heat-warp one, our Dolphins'd take the whole forty minutes just to get there, even before a VDEL,' he said, meaning the manoeuvre when a hovering helicopter drops personnel onto a vessel below by a vertical delivery cable drop. 'So we're thinking you might want to scramble the 122nd, ma'am, and get an F-15E Strike Eagle to go take a look-see.'

The 122nd Fighter Squadron was co-located with Admiral Warner's Coast Guard operation on the joint reserve base in Belle Chasse just outside of New Orleans and, as she knew, the Strike Eagles flew ten times faster than one of her Dolphins. But she wanted this operation to be the Coast Guard's glory, not the Air National Guard's. 'Aren't any of our own craft out there on routine surveillance?'

'It's Baker's farewell tonight, ma'am.'

'Damn.' The popular Captain Paul Baker's retirement party was about to kick off, and the admiral shook her head at her folly for agreeing to let the night surveillance team attend it. She'd not been in favour of the leave passes, but Baker was Baker and it was leukaemia, so there would have been hell to pay if she'd said no. 'And our Guardians or Ocean Sentries?' The Coast Guard's planes flew faster than the Dolphin MH-65C helicopters, but they were still nowhere as fast as the mach 2 that Strike Eagles could get to.

'Our closest wings are way over at Corpus Christi.'

'Texas! Shit.'

That was what Ambrose thought of Texas too, but he knew this was not the time for a parochial wise crack.

'I don't know about the F-15s,' said Warner, reflecting. 'I'm thinking maybe Eglin's F-35Bs.'

Eglin Air Force Base was just over in western Florida, not far from her base at Belle Chasse. The extra distance would add maybe eight minutes onto a journey out to *African Colossus*, but unlike the 122nd's F-15s, the F-35B were STOVLs, short takeoff and vertical landing stealth bombers. That meant they could hover and, given the likely task ahead, Warner thought that if she had to go outside the Coast Guard, she might at least trade up to get herself that capability. Her decision-making had nothing to do with the fact that the wing commander of the 122nd had just dumped her after a four-month relationship, nor that the coward had done it via a text message.

BAQRI ROLLED HIS prayer mat out in the bridge, checked his coordinates and headed to the bathroom for *wudu*, his ritual washing before prayer. As he was about to twist open the tap, he heard the buzzer from the engine room, and went back to take the call.

'Captain,' said the vessel's chief engineer, 'just double-checking your last order that we take her up to full throttle, sir.'

'Correct, chief. Is that all?'

'But sir, we're crossing out of the shipping lane—'

Baqri was terse. 'Is that all, chief?'

'That's all, captain,' said the chief engineer, taking the hint.

45

THATCHER PREFERRED TO WORK ALONE SINCE it allowed him to poke around without anyone interfering. For what seemed like an age, he'd been going over Frank's screenshots of Yevtushenko's computer, and he watched as Russia's FSB who, via Weiss were working off exactly the same shots, did everything wrong. These *tovarishchi* needed a new revolution, he thought, his self-confidence boosted just a little by the tiny beads that bubbled into his nose from his flute of Dom Pérignon.

'My dear Chowders,' said Thatcher, 'how goes it, old bean?'

The FBI chopper had left Union City as soon as the emergency vehicles arrived and Frank and Tori were back en route to Philadelphia.

'That Superman scope you gave us was—' Frank started, but stopped. He couldn't bring himself to pander to Thatcher's endless ego by raving about the brilliance of his equipment even though, because of it, they had possibly saved millions of lives.

That would come later, when he felt able to work himself up to another hour of preening, but right now he needed some rest.

The thunderbolt of shock at Whitehead's betrayal plus sheer exhaustion already had Tori slumped and asleep next to him, and Frank could barely keep his own eyes open especially after they'd spent the first fifteen minutes of this leg of the flight trying to figure out what strange game Whitehead, as an active 9S member, had been playing. For one, why did he ask them to scout Margy out when he could have warned her himself? Their best guess was simple paranoia. Years in their secret services had taught both Tori and Frank that it should never be excluded as a possibility and it seemed to fit here, that Whitehead was petrified that either he or Margy had been bugged and that if they talked, they'd both be caught and stopped. Then why kill his own wife when, with Tori and Frank in his sights, he could easily have shot them and let Margy continue? Frank's guess was that it had been even more paranoia; that Whitehead freaked he might not be fast enough to take down both of them, and risked the survivor shooting him and then Margy, and destroying both their plans. But by killing her, he guaranteed that the shattered hero they'd believe him to be would be free to launch his own attack.

By the time Thatcher's next call was vibrating in Frank's pocket, he was dozing. When he saw who it was, he switched it through to his headset. 'First thing's first, Thatcher, did you get into the Russian's Cloud?'

Thatcher held his crystal flute up to the light and slightly rocked the glass so he could enjoy his chandelier twinkling at him through the pale liquid gold. He brought it down to his nose and snuffled in the aroma.

'Thatcher, are you there? Did you get into the Cloud?'

'My friend, I am soaring in them,' he said before taking another sip and letting his tongue toy with the liquid. If Tori had been listening, the combination of Thatcher's speech impediment with his affectation would have had her screaming: *My fwend, I am sawing in them.* But Frank had been hearing Thatcher for so long he didn't notice.

'Thatcher, are you inside it or not?'

'Chaudry, Chaudry, Chaudry … Is your bishop a Catholic? Perhaps a bishopric?' He laughed. 'My dear fellow, don't be so doubting of my prowess. Not only did I get in, I had a very pleasant waltz all around it. I venture to suggest that even you, dear friend, could have beaten those Russian nincompoops to the prize if you hadn't been so busy elsewhere. You wouldn't believe their incompetence. For a start, Chowders, they—'

Frank was far too tired to listen to Thatcher's bluster and was dozing in and out, though he did wake to hear Thatcher insisting that Frank say nothing to DHS about the Cloud crisis being averted.

'But won't it be obvious?'

'Weren't you listening to a word? Attention span, my good fellow. How many times must I …? Let me repeat,' he said, in truth relishing another opportunity to pat himself on his back. 'I popped my little fortress up around their fluffy Cloud not just to keep them out, which they deserved, but to keep Yevtushenko out. The *idioty* didn't even know that he had broken in and was nosing around, as he surely would after his treasured megaleak didn't start at midnight as it was supposed to. Can you believe those …? Ugh.' Thatcher took a comforting but noisy sip of his champagne. 'So,' he said, continuing, 'I did manage to cut off Yevtushenko's prying fingers, but the FSB don't get that for free, my friend.'

'Meaning?'

'They don't get access to my secret passageway into the splendidly intact Cloud until two minutes before the six am deadline when—and you will love this—I have arranged for the majesty of my exertion to reveal itself with the demonic virtuosity of Bach's *Brandenburg Concerto Number 4*. Those moments where you suspect the music is from outside this world … that disaster might strike at any moment … A perfect climax, don't you think?'

'Thatcher—' started Frank, tiring of his friend's ego, charming though it was, and bored with his passion for this one piece of music that Frank had heard so often over the past two decades and, in the early days, which Thatcher had conned him into playing for him until he got sick of it, something he thought was never possible.

'My dear Francis, it will be my finest moment. Well, one of the ever so many.'

'You're saying they won't find out the Cloud's fine until the very moment they think all hell is about to break loose? You can't seriously—'

'The Bolsheviks must pay for their ineptitude, and their turpitude. You do recall our disagreeable little venture into Chechnya, don't you?' He spoke firmly. Thatcher never shouted, not even in anger, but then he softened. 'I know, I know. You keep telling me we should let bygones be bygones. But we can at least let Thatcher enjoy one little pleasure, can't we?'

Frank had spent a lifetime pandering to Thatcher's little pleasures, from as far back as their schooldays. His first was when he learnt that his friend's ethereal world would tremble itself apart if his thirteenth birthday passed without him savouring a particular eighteen-year-old single malt from Islay. Thatcher wasn't Jewish, yet he claimed it was 'a manhood thing'. The prized scotch they snuck into Eton was far too smoky and peaty for Frank, but Thatcher revelled in it for weeks, spending more time sniffing it than drinking it, or rather letting it loll on his tongue. Alcohol for Thatcher had never been for getting drunk, purely for the bliss it afforded his highly tuned senses. Frank had never once seen him even tipsy.

'Thatch,' he said without thinking, risking his friend getting annoyed now that his plastered-down hair was so sparse, 'six am is no good. I know it would be a good tease, perhaps even deserved, but there is so much shit going down tonight we have to give them a break. There's too much hanging off this … thousands of people, support services …' He felt he was getting nowhere so he brought out his big gun. 'Besides, DHS told me that if this isn't sorted by 5.30 am Russian time—that's 8.30 pm here in New York—the Brits are going to evacuate the entire British Cabinet, plus,' and he paused for effect, readying his aim for the bullseye, 'the Royal family. That's in the middle of the goddamn night in London, you know, Thatcher.'

There wasn't a more ardent monarchist on the planet than Thatcher. Frank suspected his friend's underwear had the Union Jack printed on them. As he listened for a reply, he wasn't sure if what he heard coming through his headset was the swishing of liquid or a rattle in the whoop of the helicopter. 'Thatcher? Please? How about Russian time five pm, that's … half an hour from now?'

'How about five-thirty?'

'Five-fifteen?'

'Done. *Spokoynoy nochi*. Goodnight, my friend.'

'I doubt that.'

As Frank terminated the call, he thought about calling Weiss to give him the good news, but a deal was a deal. Besides, he would never betray his friend, no matter how tedious he could sometimes be.

46

'SHOCK TERROR CLAIM AGAINST SOFTWARE KING', declared the newsflash crossing the screen on Auckland's TV One.

The Prime Minister has just told a shocked Parliament that this morning's arrest of computer whizz Dr Tom Major on serious tax charges narrowly stopped Dr Major from launching a cyber-terror attack that was aimed at destroying millions of the world's computers, and bringing New Zealand to a standstill.

He claimed that Dr Major is a key member of a previously unknown radical environmental terrorist group called Nine Sisters or 9S whose credo is to save the planet by destroying consumerism, industry and commerce.

Both the government and the Security Intelligence Service are keeping tight-lipped about the group, refusing to comment on claims made by cable network CNN that plants from 9S occupy some of the most trusted and high-powered positions in business and government around the world.

According to CNN, the top executive of banking giant EuropaNational, a woman shot and killed in New York thirty minutes ago, was also a secret member of 9S. A spokesman for EuropaNational in Auckland has told TV One that all New Zealand depositors' funds with the bank are safe.

CNN and the UK's Financial Times *are also suggesting that 9S is behind the catastrophic fast train crashes in China that have claimed nearly 9,000 lives and injured many thousands more.*

They are also connecting the clandestine group to the notorious serial killer, Dr Wilbur Fenton, who Los Angeles police have charged with the murders of former Apple CEO Steve Jobs and …

The Prime Minister told Parliament that Cabinet today designated 9S under the Terrorism Suppression Act, and that the Security Intelligence Service has applied to the High Court for urgent orders to deny Dr Major all access to electronic devices.

Senior legal sources tell TV One the High Court is likely to reject the application due to the same 'inherent weaknesses' in our country's terror laws that former NZ First leader Winston Peters claimed were shown up in the Urewera case in 2012 and first revealed in the secret US diplomatic cables that WikiLeaks released in 2011.

Director of the Security Service, Kenneth McJames, has refused to comment, but—

47

OR DR OLEV JACKSON, PULLING THE door on his mother's hospital room closed was a respite, shutting out the hideous beeps of the monitors and respirators and the god-awful stench of her piss that he'd accidentally spurted all over the room when one of his damn stupid spasms had knocked her catheter's drainage bag off its hook.

He stood, his fingers touching the handle as if transmitting his lifeblood and energy to his mother. His heart was beating so loudly that he imagined Sarah, the gentle nurse still cleaning up inside, could hear it. Dr Jackson, not a medical doctor, loved his mother, the only woman who had seen him for who he was, whether he was on his drugs or not. She didn't tease him about his tics or poke fun at his other nervous habits. His father, that yellow-bellied scab, had deserted them both when Jackson was four, ashamed of his son's involuntary outbursts and random limb jerking. The snivelling creep began his rejection, apparently, a year earlier when he stopped all family outings, whether to the mall or to the country club, and even to the local playground. According to Jackson's mother, the weak-willed shit-for-brains couldn't bear the idea that onlookers, let alone his precious drinking buddies, might possibly wonder if his own manly genes had fathered a freak. Boo-fucking-hoo.

By the time Jackson made it to university, he had stopped fretting about his spasms, finding they could even be a great pretext for smacking someone he despised with impunity. But his adoring mother never relented, always trying to give her genius of a son a less fractious life, and eventually she tracked down the drugs that mellowed his tics. He popped those square blue pills for sixteen years, right through his undergraduate degree, his doctorate and until they finally helped him get promoted to the plum job he sorely wanted at NERC—the North American Electric Reliability Corporation.

But once he got himself comfortably seated in the NERC's big leather chair in his home town of Atlanta, Georgia, he binned the drug prescription, deciding that all his kowtowing reports as well as his pen-pushing superiors could put up with the real Jackson and, if they mouthed a critical word or pulled any discriminatory funny business, the sticker he'd stuck to his briefcase warned them of the fate they'd suffer: 'Don't Tic With Me!'

From his role at the top of NERC, Jackson knew exactly what he was doing. More critically, he knew what everyone else was doing. Both the US and Canada had certified NERC to design and enforce the reliability standards for North America's bulk-power systems and, under the aegis of both the US Department of Homeland Security and Public Safety Canada, NERC got to operate the power industry's crucial Information Sharing and Analysis Centre. Only last week, Jackson had personally supervised a massive grid security exercise ostensibly to check that power utilities complied with the new 'critical infrastructure protection' program he had been instrumental in designing.

As a result, Jackson had access not just to every smart grid network in North America, but to all their security codes and protocols, crucial to shutting down the power system and freezing to death the world's biggest, most voracious consumer, America.

He'd taken one of Professor Mellor's catchphrases—Bring on the winter!—to heart. The Canadians weren't as bad as the Americans but in a war, and this was truly a war, they were collateral damage. Besides, the last Canuck he'd met really was an eh-hole.

That was Jackson's plan, which he'd originally set to be executed today but, three weeks ago, when Gladys had suffered her stroke, everything changed. Her doctors didn't have a clue how long she might remain in her coma, and he'd almost lost it when he overheard one of them in the corridor saying it could be for months. That time it took him a full six minutes to control his twitches.

As J/10 in Nine Sisters, he was supposed to go live right now, but there was no way this devoted son was cutting off the country's power, his mother's lifeline. However long she needed it, he would make sure she had it, end of story. He didn't care what Professor Mellor or the others might think, just like he didn't care what anyone thought about his tics. Winter would have to wait its turn.

Jackson was so lost in his thoughts he hadn't heard the footfalls down the corridor. But when a large hand touched his shoulder, a shudder shot through him and his leg lashed out violently. Suddenly the gesture he imagined was meant as a comfort turned itself rogue and was wrapping itself around his neck, twisting him into a headlock and pulling him down onto the floor.

'Dr Olev Jackson, you're under arrest. You have the right ...'

48

'MADAM PRESIDENT, THE FIRST F-35B
LIGHTNING II was wheels up fifteen minutes
ago,' said Weiss, aware his every word and blink
was being beamed by videolink across town into the prickly
nerve centre of national crisis management, the Situation Room
on the ground floor of the West Wing of the White House. He
scanned the image of the room on his screen, noting that while
all members of the National Security Council were assembled
around the long table, embarrassingly, his own director had not
yet arrived so Weiss would be flying solo. Ah! Finally his boss
walked in. The director nodded to the room and to Weiss,
undid his tuxedo button and sat directly behind the Secretary
of Homeland Security. Weiss continued his briefing, running
through the day's events so far, the Nine Sisters targets dealt with,
those still outstanding and the one they had yet to identify.

When he first mentioned the full extent of Nine Sisters'
tentacles as he knew them so far—all of them sleepers, all of

them people who had insinuated themselves into positions of the highest trust—the President audibly gasped. And when he spoke about Margy Bernardo's and Alan Whitehead's deaths, he watched her hand rise to cover her eyes, a brief yet revealing gesture.

Bernardo's death was already public, courtesy of those media cretins at CNN, but President Diaz had not yet heard that Whitehead had been killed until Weiss told her and the assembled group. He paused, watching her olive skin blanch, and certain he knew why: that she felt the betrayal personally.

It was superficially personal in that Whitehead himself had frequently boasted to Weiss over beers about his relationship with Diaz, claiming to have made 'a mighty big impression' back when she was still a senator and sat on the Hookergate Joint Congressional hearings, the in-camera enquiry into the Secret Service following the infamous prostitute scandal during an Obama visit to Colombia. Weiss had thought it was his boss's usual harmless bluster, but merely days after Diaz had taken office she had asked for Whitehead personally, for him to cast his eyes over her own presidential security.

But at the deeper level was President Diaz's very public and breathtaking experience of personal treachery by a man she trusted more than any other, her own husband. Many in the nation were still coming to grips with that scandal even these ten months later.

And still it was even more than that for Diaz. Neither Weiss nor anyone in the room, apart from Diaz's chief of staff, had any idea that during the President's call with the EuropaNational board only that afternoon she had made brief chit-chat with Margy Bernardo and specifically asked after her husband.

Until now, the White House had been content to let Weiss and the coordinated agencies get on with their urgent and multipronged work unhindered, albeit with hourly reporting, but when the Gulf of Mexico came under direct threat—America's energy lifeline—and Gregory Samson, the President's chief of staff, had explicitly reminded Diaz how former President Obama's reputation almost took a direct hit over his initial bumbling of the *Deepwater Horizon* spill in 2010, she assembled the National Security Council.

Weiss waited for Diaz to sip her water and he noticed that, even over the videolink, the trademark sparkle in her green eyes was dimmed by the gravity of everything he'd just hurled at her. Her eyes seemed troubled and dark, almost as black as her hair. Without seeming to care that it would reveal the infamous scar across her throat, she took a moment to rotate her head to crack her neck, then squared the papers in front of her and placed them under her tablet computer.

'Mr Weiss,' she said, 'first may I offer my condolences. I expect Dr Whitehead was a friend of yours as well as your former superior.'

'Correct, Madam President.'

'This must have been an exceedingly difficult decision for you, but you have my thanks, and those of a grateful nation.' She paused for a moment. 'What's the timing, Mr Weiss? How long till the planes reach MT *African Colossus*?'

'Lieutenant Colonel Moore has given us one, two minutes from now for the fighters, ma'am.' Moore was commanding officer of the Warlords, Marine Fighter Attack Training Squadron 501 that flew the F-35Bs out of Eglin air base. 'And Admiral Warner now estimates fourteen minutes all up before the vessel's possible first impact with the oilrig, but I still emphasise it's only *possible*.'

Isabel Diaz cast her gaze around the NSC, aware she sat in the same chair as Barack Obama when he authorised the killing of Osama bin Laden. 'Possible? Do we think it's only possible when the vessel's radio hasn't been responding to urgent Coast Guard requests for … for how long?'

'For far too long,' the chairman of the Joint Chiefs answered, 'but there could be many reasons for that, Madam President. It's uncommon but …'

None of the buts that the aged general rattled off hit the true mark, which was that Captain Baqri had shot out the speakers in the vessel's bridge. The last thing he wanted was to risk unnerving his own resolve with the Coast Guard sending him increasingly plaintive and urgent calls.

The President tapped on her tablet. 'I see that *Deep Thunder*'s working crew is 236 personnel—'

'Less by now, ma'am,' said Weiss. 'Coast Guard has already contacted the platform and ordered an immediate power down and evac. I'm hopin' those folks will either be in lifeboats or helicopters from nearby rigs and gettin' away from there super quick.'

'I just got a confirm,' said Admiral Warner, her voice activating the screen that popped her face into the Situation Room as well as Weiss's command centre. 'We've got a QRF on the way and yes, evac has commenced. The lifeboats will head for a supply ship tethered 200 feet away and I'm told that when they're all aboard—and it'll be a cram—she'll be steaming out of there at balls to—er, full throttle.' The military personnel on the call understood she had been about to say *balls to the wall*.

President Diaz knew the slang term too but she let it pass and ignored the muffled sniggers around her. 'What's a QRF?' she asked Warner, choosing also not to notice the colour rising in the admiral's cheeks.

'Quick response force, ma'am. A number of rigs out there share specialist maritime security teams and this one is manned by retired SEALs and FAST professionals out of theatres like Iraq and Afghanistan. They've got a dedicated helicopter kept on top of evac needs, so we've requested they take a flyover of the *African Colossus* for us.' Everyone in the room knew SEALs were the US Navy's principal special operations force, but the President hadn't heard of FAST before.

'FAST?' she asked.

'Sorry, ma'am. The Marine Corp's Fleet Anti-terrorist Security Team.'

'Impressive.'

Admiral Warner continued: 'We've imposed an extra-wide fifteen-mile exclusion zone for shipping and aircraft around *Deep Thunder* and we've ordered evacs on all nearby rigs. It's mighty busy out in the Gulf tonight, ma'am. If Captain Baqri isn't listening to his radio and picking up the chatter, the nav lights in the sky might get him a bit excited.'

'Let's pray it's a false alarm, admiral, but good work,' said Diaz. 'Maybe Baqri will heed the exclusion zone and change course.'

'I doubt it, Madam President,' said Lieutenant Colonel Moore, appearing in a separate window onscreen. 'One of our F-35Bs has just given a visual confirm of the vessel's course and speed, and basically, ma'am, she's a 400,000 tonne torpedo aimed straight for the heart of the platform. If she hits, what we'll have on our hands'll make both *Deepwater Horizon* and *Piper Alpha* look like Sunday barbecues.'

Piper Alpha? Her chief of staff, always at the ready, handed her his tablet computer. She skimmed it and saw that in 1988 an explosive fire had not only destroyed the North Sea platform but killed 167 men. *Deepwater Horizon*, where eleven had died, was horrendous, but *Piper Alpha* had been way worse. 'Please continue.'

'If she hits, ma'am,' said Weiss, trying to retake charge, 'we'll be lookin' at the biggest man-made environmental disaster in human history outside of wartime. The vessel's tanks will rupture for sure, so yes, those two million barrels on board will escape and possibly catch fire, setting the sea alight, but that's not the worst of it. At 400,000 tonnes fully laden, as the colonel has said, and travellin' full steam at nineteen knots—'

'If you'd let me,' said a man seated in one of the chairs around the wall, right next to the Director of Homeland Security. Though fiftyish and balding, his thick biceps and rounded shoulders suggested Douglas Frost was a gym junkie as well as the Director of Washington's GMCC, the Global Maritime Operational Threat Response Coordination Centre. 'Ma'am, our engineers have run a scenario that shows her snapping the platform clean off its pegs. This rig ain't no floater or semi-submersible—' he looked down at his computer, '—the topsides alone come in at 60,000 tonnes of reinforced concrete and steel, but all that's sitting on top of a 700,000-tonne gravity-base structure—more steel, more concrete—with 1.2 million barrels of crude swilling around in the caisson storage tanks halfway down. If she takes a direct hit from MT *African Colossus*, ma'am, she'll collapse down on herself with all that mass crushing everything in its way as it crumples hundreds of feet to the ocean floor. The derricks, flare boom, pumps, pipelines, wellheads, power plant, everything'll go down and she'll start spewing oil and gas out into the Gulf waters and up to fuel the surface fire and, ma'am, there'll be no ways to get through all that metal and debris to turn it off like we did at *Deepwater Horizon*. Simply put, ma'am, the Gulf of Mexico will become a blazing bubbling cauldron of oil and gas and we won't be dousing it anytime soon. The fire, the smoke, the toxicity … this would kill the Gulf, ma'am—everything in it and everything round it.'

President Diaz didn't want to believe what she'd just heard, but these were the experts and several other heads were nodding, including, she noticed, Weiss's, albeit he was clearly peeved by the attempts at one-upmanship. Her mind was spinning. Apart from the utter destruction and the lives and habitats lost, she had also to consider the financial quake that would rattle America's and Mexico's economies, let alone the world's, as well as the deep psychological trauma. Isabel knew about scarring and the time it took for healing. This crisis could easily be worse than Hurricane Katrina, perhaps even 9/11, let alone the terrorist plot only last year against New York. 'My God!' she whispered, the weight of all those events piling up to conspire against her.

IN PARIS, CLARE Dupont once more wiped the pistol and placed it on her desk, using the same cloth to dab the sweat off her face. It was 1.30 am and she was done celebrating after the conference dinner. She'd known she was getting an award, but not the big one. Her entry into the International Maritime Organisation's Safety Hall of Fame was completely out of the blue and her plan to stay off the booze at the party afterwards had dissolved in the euphoria. 'The irony and the ecstasy,' was what she felt like trumpeting in her acceptance speech, but as she stood at the award lectern she reminded herself to stick to the humble, studious monotone that had been her public and trustworthy image for so long.

But now that it was time, she clicked on her radio transmitter. Thousands of tankers and other working vessels were already at work, plying harbours, seas and oceans, avoiding wharves, islands, coastlines and other known hazards such as reefs and oilrigs, even icebergs. Hundreds of passenger cruise ships would be leaving or entering port, not so much in Europe and Africa given the time of night, but more in the Americas and Asia.

All she had to do was press 'Go' on her computer and her latitude shift program would be transmitted to every ECDIS loaded with her software and primed to receive it. Vessel captains and navigators who happened to be watching the screen at that split second would notice it flash blank but before they could worry they would see it restore, few of them noticing that their reported latitude had changed slightly with every ECDIS sold by her company now out of whack by half a mile.

She'd rigged it so that the radar system display would mimic the ECDIS, confirming a ship's positioning even though it was half a mile out of skew. Vessels in enclosed waters, rivers and harbours, would notice the error quite quickly but in open sea there were no landmarks to judge against.

She had tried to think through how it would pan out, but every scenario she came up with led to another, and she concluded that different captains would react in different ways, some saving the day and others blind to the danger till it was too late. The spate of wrecks on reefs and oil spills would overwhelm port authorities, coast guards and naval fleets around the world but, however it turned out, and whatever evasive action the old salts took once they grasped there was a problem, the reality would see hundreds of crashes and thousands of scrapes and near-misses.

It was true, sadly, that her plan would cause environmental damage but Dupont rationalised it knowing that to save a body, you sometimes had to amputate a limb. Cutting global maritime transport off at its knees and gutting the vacuous vacation cruise industry were worthy prizes to her. Thousands of voracious fossil fuel-guzzling environmental vandals would be left in limbo, floating or anchored or reefed, with a worldwide crisis of panicked passengers and crew demanding lift-offs, seeing both commerce and tourism grinding to a halt. Longer term, she was confident the oceans would return to normal, just as the Gulf of Mexico had after BP's *Deepwater Horizon* disaster, so yes, some birds and fish would have to die, as would those people who had to be sacrificed for the greater good.

At 1.35 am Paris time, she pressed 'Go'.

She had expected to be exhilarated by this action, and her skin did tingle, but having now taken the step she'd toiled and prepared so long for, the sensation wasn't the sweet shiver of ecstasy but more a deep sigh of exhaustion.

There'd be a massive investigation, she knew that, and also that they would eventually fix her bug, but her email message would leave the shipping world in lasting tatters, especially after the new paragraph she'd inserted tonight at the end of her draft. She'd got excited about adding it when the news reports on the hotel bar TV alerted her to the stunning successes of her Nine Sisters colleagues in China and LA and the more equivocal reports from New York and Auckland. Dupont's new words over-egged it just a little, but history was replete with cases of productive disinformation so she forgave herself, yawning once more, and hoping that Professor Mellor would forgive her too. She reread the text she'd added:

Authorities will soon tell you they have fixed my bug but they will be lying, and sea travel will remain at peril. I look down from the wall of the Maritime Safety Hall of Fame proud to reveal myself as a member of Nine Sisters and proud of my fellow members Margy Bernardo, Tom Major and especially Wilbur Fenton and Yuan Li Ming. But we are only the vanguard. There are more, many more of us. Each of us has worked hard to infiltrate the highest echelons of government and business and seat ourselves in positions of great trust where we can take genuine, effective and lasting steps to save our planet. The president of your company, or even your country ... how do you know that he or she is not one of us? Remember, we Nine Sisters give no advance warnings. Fiat justitia et ruant coeli. We Nine Sisters will bring on the winter, so a new spring for our planet can follow.

Dr Clare Dupont,

D/5, member of Nine Sissssss

Dupont's eyes kept closing, and finally she fell asleep at her desk.

49

THE F-35B BUZZED LOW NEAR THE *African Colossus*'s bridge. 'The lights are switched on inside the bridge and I see the captain clearly, ma'am. He's standing at the helm,' said the pilot, knowing he was transmitting direct into the White House Situation Room. 'I'll take another swing past.'

A minute later he added, 'He's giving me a thumbs up, ma'am, and from here he looks to be in fine spirits. Now he's waving a can of Diet Coke at me.'

Coast Guard Admiral Warner, still linked into the Situation Room from New Orleans, spoke to the pilot. 'Corporal McNeilly, how many people are located in the bridge with him? I would expect at least two.'

'I'm hovering, ma'am, just a moment … There's none that I can see … Wait! I think I see two pairs of legs on the floor sticking out from under a table. Ma'am, I think there are two men down in there.'

Corporal McNeilly was now flying directly above the bridge of the *African Colossus* at precisely the same speed as the vessel, his plane's nose pointing in line with the bow 400 metres ahead. The second jet was flying a little astern when McNeilly radioed back in. 'Instruments confirm *Deep Thunder* is ahead of *African Colossus*, at twelve o'clock precisely. It will be a direct hit in … ah, thirteen minutes twenty seconds.' His instruments also showed a small aircraft approaching, still two miles away. He waited till he had a visual on it before reporting it in.

'Unmarked helo approaching, violating airspace exclusion zone … looks like the Huey. Awaiting orders,' he said, expecting the incoming to be the quick response force helicopter but taking no chances, not with the President, the NSC and his own commander listening in.

'I confirm they're the friendlies,' said Colonel Moore. 'Let 'em approach and board.' Moore turned to the camera and looked into the Situation Room. 'Madam President, I've authorised the QRF to board, attempt to seize control and change her course. The two men on assault duty are former SEALs, ma'am. I have total trust in them.'

'I'm not sure who we can trust these days, colonel,' said Diaz without thinking, instantly regretting her comment. 'Do we have a plan B?' she asked quickly, knowing that even if the QRF were as trained and trusted as she'd been told, failure was always an option and the consequences of that tonight were horrifyingly imaginable.

'Yes, ma'am. It's not guaranteed either, but it's for one of the F-35Bs to fire on the engine—'

'Bomb the ship, colonel? Won't that risk an oil spill and a fire?' she asked, her concern evident as she grabbed the table and pushed back her chair.

'A minor spill, yes, and possibly an engine room fire but a sea fire is unlikely, ma'am. The heavy fuel oil she's burning doesn't easily ignite, and it'll be sitting in segregated tanks in the engine room, behind the accommodation block. With tight targeting, all the cargo tanks will remain intact.'

President Diaz stood and arched her back, trying to ease out some of the stress. 'But shooting out her engine won't stop her,' she said. 'It'll slow her, but all that momentum … won't she keep going?'

'True, ma'am,' said Frost, stepping forward this time to stand next to her, too close and too familiar for her liking and her scowl as she looked around told him so. If she'd been a man, she thought, no way would he have tried that. Their eyes met briefly, hers sharp and steely, and he took a step back. 'Ma'am,' he said, 'to give you a flavour of how far she could travel fully laden without power, even if we did get control of her and did a crash stop manoeuvre—that's bringing her back from full ahead to full reverse as fast as we can—she'd take seven, maybe eight miles and, say, thirty-five minutes to bring to a complete stop and—'

'We don't have that time,' said Diaz, sitting back down and running her hands through her hair. She looked up at the clock and saw it was already 7.45 pm. The cookies that she and her little boy, Davey, had started baking before dinner would be toast by now, and there was no way she'd be getting back to the Residence even to read him a goodnight story. The way things were looking she doubted that even she would be getting one tonight.

'Plan B, ma'am?' said Colonel Moore. 'One of our F–35Bs takes out her engine while the other blasts some wing ballast tanks in her bow from the side so we can try to shift her off course by just enough to miss the rig—'

This time it was Admiral Warner who interrupted. 'Ma'am, if I might say, plan B is a work in progress.' Meaning she disagreed entirely with what both Moore and Frost had proposed. 'Before we decide to blast a single thing to kingdom come, another scenario we're running is that once the QRF are on board, they get the vessel's chief engineer to place the engine on emergency stop, then take the crew aft into the steering gear flat, manually operate the hydraulic rams and turn the rudder hard over.'

THE TWO F-35Bs pulled back as the Huey, a UH-1 Iroquois, approached, manoeuvred carefully around the funnel and the exhaust updraft from the propulsion diesel, then hovered briefly high above the bridge, dropping two cables into the darkness. Two men clad in black leathers and helmets slid down, narrowly missing the vessel's main mast and radio antenna, smooth and fast stopping just short of the monkey island, the deck above the navigating bridge, to avoid Baqri below hearing any telltale boot crunch. The second their rubberised soles did touch, the Huey retracted the cables and pulled back, heading for the helo-winching area on the upper deck, port side, a little forward of the midship manifolds.

One of the men drew his weapon, an M11 Sig Sauer P-228—a SEALs' favourite—just 7.1 inches long and 1.5 inches wide, a recoil-operated, semi-automatic that fired a 9mm NATO round in both single- and double-action modes from thirteen-round magazines. He sat himself down at the very edge of the monkey island. With his back to the vessel's bow, he adjusted his protective goggles and pulled up his facemask and, as soon as his colleague planted himself firmly across his legs to hold them down, he twisted back and dropped his torso down across the front of the bridgehouse. Seeing Captain Baqri aiming his own pistol at him through the glass, he fired three quick rounds, swung himself back up, took the hands offered to him and both men jumped to their feet and sprang to either side in case of enemy fire from below through the deck. They waited, scanning around themselves searching for hazards—something they should have done first—when the shooter suddenly fired two rounds at the beam above his colleague's head and took out a CCTV camera. Immediately, they both shifted position again, a split second before a bullet ripped up through the deck, precisely where the shooter had been standing.

'Where that was aimed, you could have been the butt of every joke under the sun,' the other man cackled through his helmet mic.

'We'll see about that.' The shooter unzipped a coil of cable that had been velcroed to his leg, hooked one end onto the stainless steel karabiner on his belt and tossed the other end upwards, looping it over the beam above his head and throwing the other end of it to his colleague after it dropped back to his hand. As soon as the second QRF member caught it and secured it to his own karabiner, the shooter took a backward jump over the edge, shooting repeatedly into the bridge as he plunged past the glass. As he passed, firing his weapon, he saw little inside but smoke and flames. As soon as he shuddered to a stop at the end of the cable, he started swinging himself side to side and upwards onto the starboard wing bridge. When his feet hit the deck there, his number two, after disconnecting the cable joining them, jumped down from the roof to meet him at the steel door that blocked their entry into the navigation bridge.

The second man pointed out to sea, beyond the bow, to where in the distance they could both see a blaze of light getting brighter and brighter: *Deep Thunder.* He circled his finger near his ear, as if something was amiss, or crazy.

At that moment, Corporal McNeilly radioed into operations command from his F-35B. Once the Huey had dropped the rest of the assault team on the winch pad he had taken his jet back up above the bridge and, through his undercarriage thermal cameras, had been watching the two men with heart-pounding admiration, sending eyes on the assault transmission direct into Coast Guard operations, who relayed it into the White House Situation Room. 'Colonel, something's not right here. *Deep Thunder* is no longer at twelve o'clock. She's starting to point away to … ah, closer to one o'clock.'

'Not right? Depending on the distance, that sounds mighty alright to me, corporal,' said President Diaz. She noticed that Weiss, on one of the video screens, had muted himself but was gesticulating and talking heatedly to someone off-camera. 'Weiss,' she said. 'What's happening there?'

50

WEISS LOOKED INTO THE CAMERA AS if surprised, like his mind had been somewhere else. 'Sorry, ma'am. It doesn't rain but it—you know what I mean. I've just heard that a new 9S attack has just been launched and we, or rather the French, are about to arrest the perpetrator. It's a woman … name of Clare Dupont … Dr Clare Dupont. She heads up a company that sells ECDIS systems—that's the maritime equivalent of GPS. It stands for, ah, Electronic Chart Display and Information System. The French have just alerted me that, via a satellite transmission, she's tricked thousands of ECDIS receivers worldwide into misreading their latitude coordinates. This is an incredibly grave development, a major risk to shipping, human life and the marine environment, ma'am, and we—'

'Weiss,' said the President, 'I can only imagine the horrific scale of this, and the consequences, but while you were busy talking to the French I think we just learnt that, ironically,

Dr Dupont's efforts may in fact have saved *Deep Thunder*.'
She speculated that before Dupont had initiated her shift in
coordinates, Baqri must have locked *African Colossus*'s rudder on
automatic pilot, fixed onto *Deep Thunder*'s bearings, and that it
was due to Dupont's 'trick' that the floating bomb they'd been
worrying about had started to veer away from its aim at the rig.
'Weiss,' said President Diaz, 'there's something you need to do,
and you need to do it right now.'

DUPONT WOKE IN a daze, lifting her head off her desk as
she heard the violent crunches of her door being kicked in. Her
email! She immediately pressed 'Send', unaware that it wouldn't
be going anywhere except her outbox since DCRI, France's
internal security agency, had remotely taken control of her
computer thirty seconds before the commander authorised the
physical raid to commence. With the ramming of her door and an
ear-splitting sound being directed into her apartment from two
men who'd been airlifted onto the roof of Notre Dame opposite,
she knew her time was short. She pressed the 'Kill' button on her
screen so the authorities would never be able to undo what she
had done, let alone work out how she'd done it.

As she raised the barrel of her pistol to her mouth, her front
door burst open, slamming itself back onto the mythical sea
monsters crawling all over her priceless Sebastian Münster map
of the world, the glass smashing and shards slicing into the
sixteenth-century parchment. The first member of the assault
team launched himself across the room and crash tackled her
so the bullet she managed to fire shot out both her cheeks,
blowing her tongue apart and shattering half her teeth, leaving
her alive though no longer conscious. The capitaine smacked

the gun from her hand and reported back through his helmet mic, '*Appartement sécurisé. Agresseur neutralisé.*'

Back at headquarters, one of the DCRI analysts was listening to the raid through headphones at the same time as he was remotely viewing the ECDIS transmission screen he had taken control over. He sat tapping his fingers on his desk while thinking about the trio of Dupont's buttons displayed in front of him, 'Go', 'Reset' and especially 'Kill', a button that due to his fast work hadn't worked when Dupont had pressed it on her own computer.

Visualising the French President awarding him a Légion d'honneur or some such award for saving the maritime world, he was about to show his initiative by pressing 'Reset' and restoring ECDIS to its accurate glory, when his commanding officer suddenly appeared, shouted 'Stop!' and knocked his hand away from his mouse.

WEISS AND DELACROIX from France's DCRI were immediately joined on a conference call by their security service counterparts so Weiss didn't get to thank him for personally ordering the hold back on hitting the 'Reset' switch, as requested by President Diaz.

Uri Golovanov, frustrated over his people still being unable to crack Yevtushenko's Cloud and with all of Europe breathing down his neck, came out punching, demanding the ECDIS be reset immediately. 'Hang *Deep Thunder*,' he shouted.

It was unspoken but the others on the call were wary, not just that Golovanov was under pressure and not thinking clearly, but that he might be thinking very clearly, knowing that with Russia sitting on more than double America's oil reserves, his bosses in Moscow might congratulate him if the US and the West went into an oil tailspin tonight.

After ten heated, tense minutes of wrangling, Golovanov caved in, agreeing with the others that DCRI should continue to keep their fingers off the 'Reset' switch, at least until the moment that *Deep Thunder* was in the clear.

To minimise global maritime mayhem, the group agreed to the broadcast of immediate and detailed 'All Ships' alerts, for everywhere except the Gulf of Mexico, in case Baqri was listening and where the US Coast Guard had already been mobilising everyone under its command.

51

THE TWO EX-SEALS STOOD BACK FROM the door to Baqri's bridge and between them fired two magazine clips into the lock and the hinges, then reloaded from the multiple spares clipped to their belts. Before the door eventually fell in, smoke started to curl out of the bullet holes and when the door did drop, they stepped back and hit the deck just as a fireball rushed out, hungry for fresh air. As it subsided, the first sprays from the bridge's fixed-sprinkler fire-fighting system hit them outside and, springing to their feet, they ducked their heads and entered.

It took a few minutes before the smoke cleared enough for them to see that next to Baqri on the floor was a twisted jerry can, but even under the thick stench of smoke in the air they had already smelled the unmistakable odour of gasoline. One of the men pointed to the rear of the bridge where, in red hull paint, Baqri's message dripped down the wall: '*9S fights for the planet.*'

The junior of the two men took a snap of the slogan on his phone and sent it through to Coast Guard operations command. The leader radioed in, mentioned the image was coming and continued: 'Whatever controls and instruments the captain didn't smash have melted. We can't do anything from up here, so we'll try to contact the engine room … Nope, the phone's out, too … We're leaving the bridge and heading down there.'

By the time they found their way to the machinery control room adjacent to the engine room and took command, *African Colossus* was bearing down on *Deep Thunder*. After calming the chief engineer and five crew, they persuaded the chief to stop the engine, sound the emergency alarms and direct all personnel to the lifeboats to abandon ship, except for the chief and two of the crew in the control room who vowed to stay but only once they were assured the QRF's Huey had enough room for them if they all needed to make a quick escape.

In the White House Situation Room, everyone had eyes on the vessel courtesy of the cameras from the two F-35Bs, one of which was positioned above and about twenty metres back from the bow, the second plane trailing behind the stern. The Huey, as promised by the QRF team to the engineers below, was flying above midships in readiness for a last-minute rescue, and from these vantage points the pilots watched as the rest of the crew assembled at various mustering posts and entered the lifeboats. Launching lifeboats with a mothership going full throttle at nineteen knots would normally be highly risky, but equipped with the latest in vertical-launched freefall capsules, the crew at least had a chance.

Up ahead, the topsides of *Deep Thunder* lit up the Gulf skies like a stadium on Super Bowl night. From the moment the bow of the *African Colossus* had started to veer slightly to starboard, drawing away from the trajectory that Baqri had programmed into the automatic pilot, the Situation Room became still, apart from various occupants subconsciously squirming or edging sideways in their chairs as their minds willed and nudged the vessel to shift just a little bit wider and a little more quickly. The room was silent, too, apart from the drone of static from the lead jet's open radio transmission and occasional jumpy hiccups of breath.

As the yawning distance between the two gargantuan man-made objects began to close in, the question that was biting most of the lips in the room was whether the *African Colossus* would draw to starboard far enough and fast enough to allow the entire 415 metres of her length to clear the rig. At the nineteen knots that Baqri had taken her speed to, Admiral Warner had calculated it would take close to forty-three long seconds for the whole ship to pass a single point on *Deep Thunder* but, allowing for the massive platform's own length, it would take up to sixty-three nerve-racking seconds before they'd know if the stern had cleared it too. The crisis wouldn't be over if it did; they still had to stop *African Colossus* from either crashing into another rig or grounding herself, so the plan was that once she was back in open water, the QRF team would direct the remaining crew to execute a crash stop manoeuvre.

It was now clear from the visuals that the bow would clear the corner of the topsides by quite a wide berth and, when it actually did, everyone except Isabel leapt to their feet and cheered. When the others noticed the President unmoved, her eyes mesmerised by the screen, they sheepishly sat back down, fixing their ties or jackets as if nothing had happened. Inwardly, Isabel had been cheering with them but knew she needed to hold back any overt emotion till the end. She was used to tension after ten months in office, especially given how she won it, but nothing she'd experienced was like the long, drawn out torture of these chilling, deadening seconds and she needed to keep tight control of herself. She suddenly understood how Sisyphus must have felt, spending an eternity trying to push a huge boulder uphill only for it to keep rolling back down but she knew, unlike the mythical king, that her rock would have an end. She just didn't know what it would be.

Fifteen seconds after the bow had passed by the topsides with forty-eight seconds to go, Weiss's assistant shook his arm and told him that a New Orleans *Times-Picayune* reporter was demanding a comment on a story about a rogue tanker in the Gulf. 'Tell her to fuck off,' he erupted, a snap like a fifty-cent firecracker, then reverted to watching the screen not realising he'd left his mic on. Off-camera, his assistant pointed to his earpiece and to the raised eyebrows on his director's face that was showing on the video screen from the Situation Room. Weiss almost apologised, but decided silence was his best option. If this did turn to shit, he didn't want the books that would be written about it recording him as a groveller.

With the bow well clear of the platform, the forward F–35B stealth bomber switched position with the Huey and, as the vessel continued to ply ahead, Corporal McNeilly kept his jet hovering directly above the point where the collision would occur, assuming it did, giving the Situation Room a moment by moment aerial view as the aft of the moving tanker yawed closer and closer to the edge of the platform. He manipulated his scanner so the images they were receiving displayed a superimposed hairline grid of precision measures, showing both length and time.

At midships, the vessel was still clear, but the gap had narrowed to twenty metres.

By the time 330 of the 415-metre length had passed, with

only eleven metres of air and water separating tanker from platform, all the moisture in Isabel's mouth seemed to have moved to her hands, and she moved them to below the table so no one could detect her wiping them on her slacks.

But at the 365-metre mark, with only an eight-metre gap and five seconds to go, the President's hands, the least experienced in the room, were no more white-knuckled than those of the most veteran general.

At 390 metres and with 2.55 seconds left, the gap had narrowed to two metres. Not a single person in the room was blinking, or moving.

'Are we going to do this?' Diaz asked into the thick air, but no one knew and no one answered.

With twenty metres of the ship left to pass, the gap shrunk to a fissure and then to a crack and finally the two giants touched. Metal started scraping on metal and such a crackling gush of sparks sprayed into the night sky it looked like 4th of July but to the ears in the Situation Room, the squealing and screeching of slowly twisting steel and the rasping crunches of splitting, crumbling and exploding concrete were like howls from the depths of a tortured hell. Despite the room's thermostat being designed to keep these bodies, and heads, cool in times of high tension, nothing could stop the rank odour of sweat welling in the room and tainting the air.

Suddenly, the screen distorted and blurred. To Isabel, it felt like plunging into an abyss in reverse, a dizzying, bilious nausea rising from a fist pounding inside her gut up into the gorge of her throat as Corporal McNeilly executed an abrupt vertical lift to escape the sparks and flying debris.

'Will they explode?' Diaz asked, her hands gripping her thighs, and her muscles almost in spasm she'd been sitting so tight for so long.

'No idea, ma'am,' said Admiral Warner, blinking and somewhat dazed as her face popped up on the sound-activated screen.

WHEN THE CAMERAS refocused on the collision zone, *Deep Thunder*'s emergency sprinklers were doing their best to douse the fires and, via a transmission from the QRF down below in *African Colossus*, they heard the chief engineer shouting, 'We've ruptured the side shell-plating to the steering gear flat—' The gash was fortunately above the water line, but no one in the Situation Room knew that.

52

B Y THE TIME THOSE IN PARIS managed to reverse Clare Dupont's ECDIS latitude shift, taking as short a time as was safe to verify it, a dozen Mayday distress calls had come in. Four vessels had suffered loss of life, MV *Polar Majesty* in Antarctica being the most catastrophic, with 183 passengers and crew dead.

Polar Majesty hadn't had a hope. One minute prior to Dupont's launching, a gale-force whiteout whipped up off the southern glaciers without warning, instantly blotting out the utopian blue skies that the cruise ship had been sailing under for the last six days. On its maiden voyage, the ice-breaking vessel was suddenly in lockdown, totally reliant on its electronics as well as the massive fog lights that the bridge snapped on to try to illuminate the towers of ice they knew would soon be looming at them out of the blizzard.

The highly experienced crew knew that nothing would stay as it had looked before the storm, with icebergs known to move rapidly in high winds. But they had no idea that, with eerie echoes of the tragic 1979 Mount Erebus aviation disaster, the electronic instruments they were now completely beholden to had repositioned their ship on all the screens they were monitoring. Their equipment was worse than useless; it was utterly and dangerously deceptive.

As soon as the Chilean navy's Rescue Coordination Centre received the *Polar Majesty*'s Mayday, they dispatched their nearest vessel to the rescue, but even at full steam the ATF *Lautaro* was eighteen deadly hours away.

The moment they eventually located the cruise ship, the rescue crew knew it was too late. The elite upper-deck cabins were listing only metres above the waters their occupants had paid to be so far above, and their windows were jerking closer and closer to the water line as thousands of gallons kept gushing into the vessel, probing through every aperture their icy fingers could find.

According to the bridge's last radio broadcast, a series of huge rogue waves from a calving glacier—at least that was the captain's blind guess—hit the *Polar Majesty* from the side, smashing five bridge windows and three officers' quarters plus the starboard wing bridge and undoubtedly many passenger cabins.

Knocked sideways by the wave, a hungry pack of icebergs began their ravenous gorging, first puncturing two of the *Polar Majesty*'s diesel fuel tanks, the oil drooling onto the icebergs like dark blood on a predator's teeth.

SOTI SKYLAKAKIS SOBERED up the instant he took the distressing call that the MV *Polar Majesty*, the vessel Simone

Lucas, his head of IT security, had been cruising on, had broadcast a Mayday only seconds before its radio went dead.

Tori called Soti a few minutes later. 'Soti, I know it's late in Athens but—'

'My dear Tori, I've had the most shocking news. Simone Lucas and Athena—'

'That's why I'm call—'

The raucous din of the helicopter made it hard for the Greek to hear. 'Where the hell are you calling from? I can't—'

'Soti, please try. Frank and I are in the US in an FBI helicopter. We're assisting Homeland Security and it's through them we just heard about Simone.'

'Why would they—?'

'Soti, I didn't realise it when Simone joined those meetings on your yacht by satellite phone, but I knew her, not as Lucas but Barr, Simone Barr.'

'She was a friend to you, too?'

'Er, no. Actually, she was no friend to you either.'

'Tori, how dare you! She could be floating face down in glacial waters and—'

Tori spoke over him as best she could and, as soon as she mentioned Nine Sisters and that both she and Simone had been members, Soti exploded into the phone. 'Those *poutánes*, whores! I heard about them on CNN. What the fuck, Tori. You? You're saying that even *you* are one of them … a fucking sleeper terrorist? Ha, sleeper! I guess that's not so funny, eh?'

Axel, who Tori had taken the precaution of linking into the call, spoke up to cover what he expected would be Tori's embarrassment. 'Soti, drop it. You have my personal guarantee of Tori's integrity, but we're calling to alert you that Simone has become our—your Achilles heel.'

'Careful, my old friend. There's not a soul inside my company I trust more than Simo—'

'With what you've heard already about Nine Sisters, why is that a comfort? Soti, this could be an existential threat. It could ruin you. Everything … gone. You need to bring in your cleaners. These Nine Sisters people are smart, Soti. Simone is—was—I don't know—*is* brilliant. We've got to find out if she somehow infected or compromised your products and if she did, how we can reverse it before anyone outside gets a whisper.'

'The deal with Greece?'

'Soti, until we know what she's done or not done, there can be no deal. If Simone's name gets linked to Nine Sisters—and we'll do our best to delay that for as long as possible—your business will evaporate in a snap of your terrified customers' fingers … unless you've already got reassuring answers, and plenty of proof. So go get the proof. Please?'

'What are we going to tell Giorgos? I can't just ring the Prime Minister and say I'm gone, the whole thing was a joke. Shit, Axel, I need a reason and—'

'—and it can't include even a whisper about Nine Sisters.'

'So what do I tell him?'

Tori imagined she could hear Axel's beads clicking. Finally he responded, 'I'll think of something.'

53

AS THE FBI HELICOPTER WHOOPED IN close to the Philadelphia Museum of Art, Tori looked down at the crowd, rugged up and milling around the foot of the famous Rocky steps, waving placards with *We love you, Sly* and *Go Rocky*. On the way here, she and Frank had both watched a news clip on Frank's computer of Sylvester Stallone's stretch limo arriving an hour earlier. After a few gloved hand-slaps with fans, he had turned to the steps and, to a rising cheer, ran up two at a time, his fake fur coat flapping behind him. At the top, he hoisted his arms above his head just like in his movie and twirled around, punching the air.

'Why are they all still there?' Tori said, peering down. 'It's not the warmest evening to be out.'

'Desperate to see him leave? I don't know, not much else to do round these parts except clog your arteries with that disgusting Philly cheesesteak,' said Frank, and he handed her the suit she'd crammed into his bag earlier in the evening. 'Crushed black linen, madame! The latest couture, I hear.'

If Tori hadn't been so tired she would have cracked a smile, but instead she conserved her emotional energy and got busy untying her trainers, squirming out of her jeans and sweater and stretching into her suit just in time for the police below, pre-briefed by Weiss's people, to haul the crowd back off the roadway and clear their chopper for landing.

Frank hopped out first and Tori followed, carrying her stilettos so she didn't re-snap the heel that she had stuck together with superglue, courtesy of the helicopter pilot's stash. As she leant on Frank to put them on, the shower of camera flashes almost blinded them, so with their forearms up in front of their faces, they followed the police through the throng and up the steps to the museum entrance.

'The redhead,' someone shouted from behind. 'It's Scarlett Johansson!'

'Who the fuck's the Indian dude? He's wearing jeans and a hoodie, for fuck's sake. No respect.'

At the top, out of sight of the fans below, Tori did her best to fix her hair using the mirror app on Frank's phone. 'Here goes,' she said, straightening her suit, and they entered the museum.

An officer was in the Great Stair Hall, holding a waiter's outfit on a hanger ready for Frank. He checked the size—XL—and took it behind a pillar to change.

'Pretty schmick-looking waiter,' said Tori, peering around and giving him the eye. 'If the help gets to wear a tux, what do the guests wear?'

She handed Frank her pair of FrensLens so he'd be able to spy the bishop easily inside the crowded hall, but he waved them away. 'You kidding? Our special guest will be rather obvious in his black cassock with purple trim.' He took the clip-on bowtie off the hanger.

'Axel would have a fit,' she said moving behind him to fasten the bowtie.

With Thatcher again listening in via their earpieces, she didn't mention the tie or he too would get overwrought. Between the British dandy and her boss there was only so much sartorial sacrilege she was willing to be accused of being party to.

'Actually,' said the officer, coming up behind both of them, 'the old bish is wearing bright purple with red trim. He looks a bit like this rapper my kid likes.'

The bish? The irreverence didn't fuss Tori but she felt Frank stiffen. 'Purple, eh?' she said as she fixed his collar. 'That'll mask the bloodstains pretty well. Okay, Frank, let's do this.'

As they entered the hall, with Frank balancing a large tray of sliced rare beef along the length of his arm, the Philadelphia Baroque Orchestra was playing. 'It's Bach's *Brandenburg Number 4*,' hummed Thatcher into their ears. Tori heard it as *Bwandenburg* but said nothing whereas Frank rolled his eyes and said, 'As if I didn't know,' while begrudgingly swinging to the rhythm as he walked.

One of my all-time favourites, Frank mouthed as Thatcher said those exact words.

'Tori,' said Thatcher, 'hear those violins ... ah, those recorders. My God. Those musicians are playing like angels. Is it live?'

Over their earpieces, they heard what sounded like the phsst of a champagne cork. 'Such synchronicity,' said Thatcher, not waiting for an answer. 'At this very moment you get to enjoy the bliss of a Brandenburg and so do the Russkis. If you, ah, focus on the time, you'll notice it is 5.15 am in the land of the Cossacks and right now the FSB, just as we agreed young Chowders, will be discovering that Yevtushenko's Cloud is and will remain intact, so yes, my friends, Europe can rest easy, at least due to that little crisis being over.'

Frank smiled, and made a beeline through the grand Saint-Laurent Gallery for the bishop, an easy mark among the hundred guests and seated with the movie star under the Romanesque abbey portal. Tori stayed back just a little, fussing at this table and that one, trying her best to look officious, checking flower arrangements as if she knew what she was doing, and starting to pick up an old matron's napkin for her.

'A little more beef, Your Excellency?' Frank said, leaning into the bishop's ear, just before he allowed some of the blood swilling in the platter to drizzle over the metal lip and onto the prelate's lap. 'Oh my, I'm so, so sorry—'

'Your Excellency,' said Tori rushing over, 'on behalf of the museum and—' she paused, noticing the mayor's icy glare, '—on behalf of our fair city, please accept our sincere apologies. This should never have happened.' She proceeded to mop up some of the spreading stain with the old lady's napkin.

'Too damn right!' growled the mayor, suddenly drawing his hand to his mouth when he realised his profanity. 'Heavens,' he quickly added, 'I'm sorry, Your Excellency, I didn't mean—'

'It is fine. Really,' said the bishop, smiling. 'You know, turn the other cheek.'

Tori took his elbow. 'Your Excellency, please come with me and we'll clean you up faster than, ah, the mayor can kiss a baby.' She said the last part very quietly, so only the bishop and apparently Thatcher could hear her, and was surprised when both laughed.

Despite the mess on the bishop's lap, he seemed to enjoy the attention. This hadn't been his most scintillating evening so far, even with the mayor on one side and Stallone on the other and a wine glass or two too many, plus if Tori could have read his mind, she'd know he'd welcome any excuse to evade yet one more Brandenburg Concerto and save himself yanking out the rest of the thinning strands curling around his purple zucchetto. Before leaving the table, he leant over to Stallone and nudged him. In a deep voice, he said, 'I'll be back!' and laughed, but the affronted actor simply glowered at him.

Tori led the bishop to an anteroom being used by the waiters as a cool room for the function. There were crates filled with ice and drinks lined up along one wall, and glass-fronted refrigerators containing racks of the desserts along another. As they entered, Frank continued to apologise until the policeman securing the room closed the door behind them as arranged.

'Your Excellency,' said Tori, 'may I call you Giovanni?'

'Excuse me? That is somewhat irregular, signorina.'

Tori's smile beamed at him. 'Giovanni, you don't remember me? Tori Swyft? Sydney? Nine Sis—'

As soon as she started to say the words, he placed his soft hand over her mouth. 'You …? Yes, I think I do recall. Your red hair and those eyes of yours. They are still filled with passion, yes? But Signor Clumsy here?'

The original plan they'd discussed in the helicopter had been to approach him the same way as Margy Bernardo, pretending to warn him, to act onside. But now Tori was here, she was drained, and putting on yet another act was too much, so without any warning to her two sidekicks she went for the jugular with honesty.

'Giovanni, your jig is up, if you understand me.' He nodded, so she continued. 'Let me introduce you to, er, Signor Clumsy. He is Francis Xavier Chaudry. He is not a waiter and nor am I the functions manager here.'

The bishop held out his hand and Tori passed but watched with a wry smile as Frank took it and kissed his ring. 'Boys, are we done with the churchy stuff? Giovanni, like you, I was in Nine Sisters but unlike you, I left. The US Government knows everything I know and more, and we, that is Frank and I, have been working with them to locate and then neutralise—'

'You are going to kill me?'

As he raised his hand, Tori thought he was going to cross himself, so she reached out and held it. 'I dearly hope not, but be warned. An hour ago—' she checked the clock on the wall, '—we were sadly involved in the deaths of two members of Nine Sisters.'

'May I ask who?'

She told Marini about Bernardo and Whitehead. When she got to Whitehead pulling the gun on his wife, she hesitated but pushed on. It had to be told, and as she did so the emotion poured out of her exhausted body. She blinked away her tears, and saw Bishop Marini pale and start to sway on his feet.

'Are you okay, Your Excellency?' Frank asked, putting his arm around the prelate and pulling a chair in behind him. 'Please, sit.' He took a bottle of water from one of the crates, twisted it open and handed it to him. 'Here.'

The bishop threw his head back and guzzled the contents in one draught and Tori dabbed her own eyes with the stained napkin. Marini handed the empty bottle back to Frank and wiped his mouth with his sleeve. 'So, Margy Bernardo,' he said. 'I do remember a Margy but she had a different surname then. It was—'

'Quando.'

'Yes, Quando. Italian for *when*. I remember now. She was Q/1, right?'

'And you were, still are, M/4. Is that right?'

He leant forward and put his head in his hands. 'How could they even contemplate those things? The economic damage? And a biological plague? I don't—Look, I thought—I imagined Nine Sisters would do many, many things but not such evils.'

'Do you remember Yuan Li Ming?'

He turned his face toward Tori and strained his brow. 'Ah, yes … the Chinese girl. She seemed, er, very keen.' So keen she had tried to seduce him, despite the bishop even then being a priest. 'What about her?'

'You've heard about the train crashes in China?'

'Surely not!'

Tori's eyes answered him. 'We need you to tell us what you are proposing, Giovanni, or what you've already set in motion.'

He sat back up and shrugged. 'I will cause only one death, one deeply deserved death.'

Tori and Frank both stiffened. The Pope? They heard Thatcher having the same idea.

'The Church,' said the bishop. 'The Church as she has become. A mendacious, scheming, secretive Church. A Church aloof from the needs of her flock. What I have planned, what M/4 has planned, is not violent but it will herald a new dawn in Christendom. When I return to my room tonight at the seminary, I plan to fire up a revolt in the Church that will tear it inside out.' The bishop's eyes were drawn to Tori's foot tapping on the parquetry. 'You don't believe me?'

She was fuming. Outside this room, good people were struggling to stop a bunch of crazies, and she was stuck with a guy in a dress giving her a flatulent, clichéd sermon.

Frank saw her shoulders tightening and her mouth thinning into a hot filament of high voltage current. 'Your Excellency,' he said, conflicted between his deference to a man of the cloth who felt the weight of words, and his own sense of the greater morality, 'we don't have much time. Please get to your point.'

Marini didn't look up but instead focused on his ring. He hadn't gone for a sparkling amethyst in a rich gold setting, he reminded himself; his was a cheap two-tone silver cross with a signet spiral he had bought from an aged artisan at a village fair. He slid his hand into his pocket and pulled out the key he had been carrying ever since he became prefect. 'This key, metaphorically, will be the start to repairing the many, many wrongs my beloved Church has perpetrated over centuries.'

It unlocked, he explained, a single wire cage located at the furthest reaches of the sprawling eighty-five kilometres of shelving inside the Archivum Secretum Vaticanum. The archives were in a fireproof, two-storey reinforced concrete structure known as the Bunker, a vault buried beneath the Cortile della Pigna of the Vatican Museums, and this was the only key to that cage.

He told them of his abuse as a child at the hands of Padre Luigi and his discovery, after he became prefect of the archives, that thirty-two other children of both sexes had been abused by the same priest as he was moved from parish to parish, six in all. 'Add me, and it makes thirty-three souls. That's the number we know of,' he said and turned his face to Tori. 'Count the buttons on my cassock, my dear.'

'She doesn't need to,' said Frank. 'There are thirty-three, Tori, the number of years that our Lord Jesus Christ lived on this earth.'

Marini closed his eyes, and placed his hand on Frank's. 'Thank you, young man. To me, that there were thirty-three of us was a sign. How do you say it? Yes, a wake-up call. Thirty-three children's lives altered, in most cases ruined, and in three cases cut short by their own twisted, tormented hands. I read it all in the section of the archives that is kept truly secret.' He held up the key. Thatcher babbled in their ears that the bishop was referring to the widespread misconception that the Archivum Secretum were the Vatican's 'secret' archives, when the correct idiomatic translation was 'private'. Yet as Marini explained, there *was* a section—this single wire cage—a section so secret that he, the prefect, was the only person trusted with access to it.

'Those files revealed I was the last of Padre Luigi's victims. If the Church had acted, had removed him when the first, perhaps the second complaint was made, many families, many lives—my own life—would have been different. But they left him there unmasked and unhindered for decades. Yes, they shifted him around, but this foul devil was permitted to walk tall, swishing his priest's cassock inside homes and hearts and—'

Tori interrupted. 'Please?'

He wiped his forehead with his sleeve. Marini had never discussed this, any of it, with a single soul, not even his own confessors over the years. 'As I spent night after tortured night locked inside this sealed cage, reading and sobbing, I discovered there were hundreds more Padre Luigis. All over the world and with thousands of little Giovanni Marinis whose innocence, whose trust, whose faith were sullied. All of it covered up, hundreds of victims paid off with many, many millions, money the Church, my Church, took from the devoted who believed they were helping the needy. It never crossed their generous minds that the bread they took off their own barren tables was being sold off to buy silence to protect the Church's wealth and hierarchy.'

Tori was going to speak, but Frank held up his hand. 'These abusers,' he said, 'they weren't the hierarchy, they were individ—'

'Mr Chaudry, I am the hapless guardian of files that sheet the blame, the institutional blame, up to the highest levels … the highest level, if you understand me? But for their cover-up, this grotesque, filthy stain would have been removed a long time ago.' He laughed, a strained, difficult laugh. 'Do you think that when the Italians returned sovereign status to the Holy See in the 1920s they understood the real reason why the Vatican so sorely wanted it? It's in these files. The prize was sovereign immunity, so that the laws of man could no longer touch those who committed the sins of man. And then in the 1930s, as a further protection, prescient Vatican lawyers started persuading pliant or naive governments around the world to pass laws letting the Church shoehorn its assets into trusts so that, if the Church ever did get unlucky and was ordered to pay any actual damages out of its assets, it could say, "Assets? What assets?" With everything locked inside these trusts, the Church technically had no assets to pay any damages with. Brilliant, yes?'

Tori was stunned. The Vatican had not only come up with her 'little idea' of becoming a sovereign itself almost a century ago, it had actually done it, and done it effectively. Yet until now, no one truly understood the scandalous implications. The conversations she'd had with Soti, and the ones she'd had with Frank and then Axel about possibly extending the same idea for the beleaguered tobacco industry—

Suddenly, her 'little idea' sickened her, and all the more because she realised for the first time that it always should have.

'You're saying they did all this to evade liability?' said Frank.

'At first, it was to evade disclosure more than anything else. If nobody knows, there's nobody to sue. But all this opened my eyes to how aloof ... how far the Church has strayed from its true mission and, with Nine Sisters, my mind went far beyond this ... to how the Church teaches our flock to be supine, to accept their lot, when we should teach the opposite. The once benign yet now malignant bans on contraception and abortion! Through the population growth it fosters, it has become a cancer eating up sparse resources in destitute countries, yet all the Church does is sprinkle holy water over pop stars who prattle on about feeding the poor, rather than working to humanely stem the upsurge in their numbers.'

Tori saw that the blue in Marini's eyes was like crystal, sharp and clear. 'Look, Giovanni. I get it, okay. You want to save the Church and the planet. Don't we all? The planet, anyhow. But saying your three Hail Marys won't cut it.'

He looked up at her and without taking his eyes off hers, stood up so they were only inches apart and she could smell the bile, and a little alcohol, on his breath.

'Ms Swyft, or perhaps it is doctor, I will tell you. After what WikiLeaks, that Australian fellow did, I got the idea of digitising the entire contents of my wire cage. It took some time, as you might imagine but it is all done and, when I get back to my room after dinner this evening, I will send the files out into the world like butterflies to land wherever they might.'

Frank took a step back, clearly agitated. 'Nuclear bombs more likely.'

'My son, the truth is the truth. Yes, this will gut the Church morally and then the lawyers will gut it physically, bankrupting the Church, undoing the trusts, forcing us to sell off our gold, our art, even our cathedrals and returning us to humble sackcloth to pray with our flock in their homes and halls and fields. So … that is all. Meanwhile, if you don't mind, I will now return to my table to finish my meal and pay respect to my hosts.' He turned and left them, not waiting for a response.

'His last supper,' said Frank, his eyes wider than Tori had ever seen them. 'Tori, what he's planning … we've got to stop him.'

She stood silent for a moment. 'Why?'

54

TEN DAYS LATER, SOTI WAS BACK on his yacht, this time rocking off the coast of Muscat in Oman and mixing sun with business, as usual. He wasn't on his route to Dubai as he'd previously scheduled but was instead heading to the Seychelles, an archipelago paradise off the East African coast.

So far he'd found no evidence that Simone Lucas had infected any Ólympos or Delphi products yet, despite his empire seeming immune, solid proof would take a few more weeks of testing. Axel had been quick to anticipate this when he advised him to slam the brakes on the Greek deal.

Soti knew it was good advice but it was hardly his finest moment; the furore that his sudden withdrawal ignited in his friend Giorgos's cabinet room that night and which, by breakfast, had spilled out into the media, looked like costing Giorgos his prime ministership as well as throwing Greece into yet another political crisis.

By noon, Axel had manufactured the excuse. He'd spent the intervening hours trading favours with a less complicated client, creating a mini-clone of the Greek deal with the Seychelles.

SIS's connections to the island nation went back to 1943, when his father built the first international standard hotel on Beau Vallon Beach. The current President was a longstanding friend of Axel's, having enjoyed the Schönberg family hospitality while studying at Harvard at the same time as Axel himself. With the Seychelles limping into recovery after an earlier government's default on a substantial Euro loan, Axel knew they'd be a willing target when he called, offering his old friend a chunk of Soti's FrensLens plus a few hundred million—which he knew would be easy money for Soti— to help lift the tiny country out of its debt pickle and allow Soti to tell an unhappy Giorgos that this was a prudent trial run, a toe in the water, for one of these never-before-tried 'corpocracy' deals.

More than that, and despite revelations about Nine Sisters going viral and filling every front page and news bulletin, Simone Lucas's name never got connected to 9S, except as one of its victims. Soti had no idea how Axel secured that but he did know that his own major clients—Apple, IBM, Samsung, Dell, Sony and more—would have pulled the plug on him at the merest whiff of a scandal. Due to Axel's fine work, he still had a tomorrow, even if Giorgos didn't.

Tomorrow, yes. He picked up his poolside phone and dialled. 'Tori my dear, congratulations,' he said before she even spoke.

'For my Presidential Medal?' she asked, sitting up and setting her copy of Proust on the sand, leaving the pages open. She'd only heard the news herself that morning when the White House phoned to let her know she'd be awarded the high honour in a ceremony in Washington DC in two weeks.

'That crass bauble?' spluttered Soti. 'Heavens, no ... I meant well done for getting rehired by Axel ... Hey, what's that noise? Where the hell are you?'

She took a deep breath, inhaling the salty, kelpy air she'd grown up with and shook her head, smiling. 'It's the surf, Soti. I'm in Sydney,' she said and flipped her book closed with a finger, suspecting even her new plans were about to change.

'Another thing ... this Dominican deal? Axel called me, of course. But your damn little idea's given him a licence to print some very big money. You'll be getting a wallop of a bonus—'

'Soti, why are you calling?' she cut in, remembering she was still furious at Axel. It was one thing he'd pulled the Seychelles rabbit out of his hat without asking her, but that was necessity. The Dominican Republic deal, on the other hand, he'd negotiated even after she'd asked him not to.

'I need to, ah, see you. I'll send over my jet.'

'To take me where?'

'The Seychelles, of course. After all, I'm king there.'

'Not quite,' she said, a smile breaking through.

'Whatever. By the way, I've got them to name the capital "Victoria" ... after you!'

She let it pass, aware it had been Victoria for years. 'So why do you want to see me?' she asked.

'Trust me.'

She laughed. Sometimes, she thought, you have to trust somebody.

EPILOGUE

ABC NEWS:

BREATHTAKING CARIBBEAN MOVE:

'MARLBORO COUNTRY'

Anti-Tobacco Laws Up In Smoke.

TO HOWLS OF protest from international sporting, government and health circles, Dominican President Luis Miguel Rodrigues announced his nation's new name— 'Marlboro'—following the signing of a ground-breaking agreement with tobacco giant, Philip Morris.

In front of a shocked media, Mr Rodrigues unfurled his country's new flag, the red and white logo of the famous cigarette brand, with a small band behind him striking up the nation's new anthem, the catchy tune the public still associates with Marlboro, the theme from *The Magnificent Seven* movie.

Waving aside criticism that the deal will overturn decades of international efforts to choke off cigarette advertising, Mr Rodrigues said, 'This is a new dawn for my country. With Philip Morris's generous backing, our new nation of Marlboro will become sports and tourism capital of the world, generating hundreds of thousands of skilled permanent jobs for our citizens, exciting new opportunities for our youth, and giving pleasure to millions of visitors.'

After it formally amends its constitution to ratify the deal, Dominica will acquire the Marlboro brand and all of Philip Morris's production facilities worldwide … In return, the company will immediately start pumping billions of dollars into local schools, hospitals, sporting facilities and other needed infrastructure, and has already set aside a billion dollars in global tourism advertising that will explicitly feature the country's new name, flag and anthem.

In Geneva Switzerland, the Director-General of the World Health Organisation, Dr Pamela Hudson said, 'It's a pact with the devil. This outrageous "flag for fags" deal must be stopped in its tracks.'

…

Thumbing his nose at international sporting bodies, Mr Rodrigues said, 'As of today, we open our doors to the world's top athletes, inviting them here as citizens of our new nation of Marlboro.' He added that all athletes competing under the new Marlboro flag, including future Olympics, will enjoy tax-free status, world-class training facilities, five-star accommodation in new beach resorts and free first-class travel.

In Lausanne Switzerland, officials from the International Olympic Committee went into emergency session …

US tobacco trial lawyer, Harley P. Hearst, slammed the deal as a ruse to chop compensation to tobacco victims. 'This scandalous deal opens up unparalleled global advertising and marketing for Big Tobacco, and at the same time will rip food and medicine out of the mouths of cancer victims and their families,' Mr Hearst said. 'While the country of Marlboro's new tobacco activities won't gain full sovereign immunity in American courts, a little known loophole may exempt them from punitive damages. This could let Big Tobacco off a very big hook.'

Following the announcement, the stock price of Philip Morris rocketed 64 per cent, and stocks on Dominica's stock exchange also surged, closing 43 per cent higher.

IN A HAZE of foul-smelling cigarette smoke whose tentacles poked into every reach of his daughter's apartment in Venice, Professor Mellor sat hunched in front of a BBC TV news channel. He'd been propped there by Signora della Scala who, despite everything he was supposed to have done, still dragged herself downstairs to care for him. At least that way, she thought, his dutiful daughter could keep her job at the art museum and scrimp enough to buy this ungrateful *brutto figlio di puttana bastardo* his food and his expensive, filthy smokes.

The old woman tossed a fraying blanket over his lap before pinching her nose and readying herself to leave him to his TV while she tidied up his dismal bedroom, a task she detested almost as much as she now despised him.

If it wasn't for her pity over the disgrace he had heaped on his daughter's shoulders, she would have stopped coming. Mellor had only yesterday been carted back from Rome where—once the Nine Sisters had exploded into world headlines—the police had whisked him away for intensive examination and interrogation.

Over the last ten days he was put through batteries of tests and third degrees that last night's TV had said proved no more than what the original gerontologist had determined, namely that he was non compos mentis. So what did the authorities do? she fumed. They washed their hands of him, dumping him back on his poor, humiliated daughter.

He seemed to be comfortable watching TV, although it was clear to her now, after the experts' tests, that for his empty, watery eyes 'watching' was a misnomer, with him officially clueless that the channel screeching in front of him was breaking even more stories about his now infamous 'notwork', especially the endless personal tragedies coming out of China. Even worse, to her, was this outrage closer to home.

It wasn't enough that her beloved Church was suddenly under assault from new class actions all over the world and all emanating from the crazed, irresponsible actions of a single bishop, a traitor who did not do the bidding of God but of this evil man Mellor, a decrepit old man who couldn't wipe himself let alone cross himself.

And now, she slapped her forehead as she listened, there on TV was another man she reviled, the Italian Prime Minister, preening himself with the audacious proposal that Italy tear up the 1920s treaty that granted sovereignty to her beloved Vatican. She crossed herself, muttered 'Holy Mary, Mother of God', and left the room.

As she stomped down the corridor, a reporter wearing a biohazard bodysuit came onscreen and was speaking from outside what he described as Alan Whitehead's biochemical hideaway in Union City. Suddenly, the professor sat up straightening out a wrinkle in the rug on his lap, and a lustre flickered in his eye. The side of his mouth without the cigarette hanging from it curled up a little and he coughed, his throat thick.

'You win some, you lose some,' Mellor said, his voice a raspy whisper and, reaching for the glass of water on the side table, he took a sip. 'Bad luck, Nine Sisters. Better luck, Ten Brothers.'

His eyes went dead and the glass tipped over, spilling the water onto his lap.

AUTHOR'S NOTE

P EOPLE IN HIGH PLACES BETRAYING THE trust placed in them is no freak event: Judas gave up Jesus to the Romans; the Cambridge Five, recruited at university as Soviet KGB spies, infiltrated the highest echelons of the British intelligence services.

Back in 1641, philosopher René Descartes called people like these 'the evil genius … as clever and deceitful as they are powerful, and who direct their entire effort to misleading us'. Today, they'll scrupulously wear the uniform of their peers, camouflaging their zealotry beneath pricey business suits, salon haircuts, academic letters and a work ethic façade so industrious they'll be extolled as icons. Like the Nine Sisters in *The Trusted*.

Almost all the 9S stratagems are possible today though, for ethical reasons, the book is hazy on the mechanics. The missing ingredient has been the evil genius who has nudged herself into position so she's able to flick that switch, or bypass it. But perhaps she's already there, simply waiting for her moment.

To give rigour to 9S methods, I travelled to most places in the story and consulted with relevant experts who, over weeks and in some cases months, helped me come to grips with the technical hurdles. If you think I've erred anywhere, it may be due to an innocent mistranslation of my experts but it might also be an intentional blind.

My thanks to: Gordon Maddern and Gilbert Verdian, for advice on hacking, computers and IT, to ensure that what various characters do with computers, Clouds and assorted IT technology is credible. Gordon is a professional ethical hacker, a senior security consultant at Pure Hacking in Sydney, where he gets to break into companies and tell them how to fix the holes. Gilbert lives in London and also secures enterprises and governments to protect them from threats. Gilbert's completing his PhD on cutting edge information security and his first book, *Enterprise Security*, is soon due for release. JCG and JDV— who asked for anonymity—are veteran nuclear power plant experts in the US. Without them, Tori might not have won her PhD, nor would the nuclear power plants have gone haywire in the way they do. John Manning, a nautical engineer and global expert in floating production systems, gave extensive help on ultra large crude carriers, oil rigs and maritime practices. In Norway, Atle Falk from Umoe Schat-Harding Equipment on vertical-launched freefall lifeboat capsules. In Melbourne, Chris Killmore on steel production. In Singapore, Satish Chetty on smart grid power industry technology. For how banks operate, I stretched my memory as an ex-banker and conducted extra research, but Allan Moss AO and Steve Allen also helped. Johan Sallfors, a fund manager in Sweden, and his algo colleagues for detailed technical advice on high-frequency trading (HFT) and algorithms. In Sydney, Stephen Hanson, fund manager and asset consultant, on some other financial aspects. On wheat genetics, in Sydney, Dr Geoffrey Gordon and, at ANU in Canberra, doctoral fellow Hugh French. On steganography, an especially helpful technical paper was: *Secure steganographic communication algorithm based on self-organizing patterns*, Loreta Saunoriene and Minvydas Ragulskis. Phys. Rev. E 84, 056213 (2011). For a couple of tips on the CIA, former Agency veteran Glenn Carle and his book, *The Interrogator, a CIA agent's true story*. The idea to redact—black out—parts of *The Trusted* came from Glenn's book. Sarah Dunn, a nurse in Sydney (and my niece) for some hospital expertise. Andrew Frankland, trusts and estates lawyer at Bartier Perry for checking and improving Professor Mellor's Will. Electronics engineer Ronald Ross (my cousin) for fine details on the Antarctic. Ronald designs, builds and deploys scientific instruments in the Antarctic, working with the US National Science Foundation and the Korean Polar Research Program, and has collaborated on Antarctic projects with Chicago University, Stanford University and the US National Snow & Ice Data Centre in Colorado.

Thanks also for these other contributions to *The Trusted*: The idea for FrensLens came out of a chat with David Gonski AC. For the surf rock instrumentals I played while dreaming up Tori's exploits (just as she would have), Rob Hirst from *Midnight Oil*, *The Break* and *Backsliders*, as well as Martin Cilia and *The Atlantics*. From Batlow, in the magic foothills of Australia's Snowy Mountains, Sulari Gentill, her husband Michael and their boys Edmund and Atticus, for keeping Thatcher (and me) supplied with their delectable truffles. Dee Leopold, Harvard Business School's head of MBA admissions, helped me get Tori Swyft's sojourn at Harvard right. The General Sir John Monash Foundation for awarding Tori the scholarship to attend Harvard. (I once sat on the Foundation's board and selection panel so I was relieved Tori upheld the Foundation's values and returned the money after she dropped out.) P. Hatfield, Eton College's archivist, for confirming that Frank Chaudry, with his Pakistani Catholic heritage, could have won a King's scholarship at the time. Midget Farrelly, Australian surfing icon, Jeff Ryan from Misfit Aid, and Tommy Herschell from Triple M's Surf Report for giving the nod to my surfing chapters. Simon McKeon AO and Guido Belgiorno-Nettis AM for some nautical fine-tuning. Craig Chapman in New York and Eric Grinbaum in Paris for titbits of local knowledge, and Peter Sotiriou for some Greek profanity. The staffs of the Grande Bretagne Hotel in Athens and the Hotel Cipriani in Venice for assistance. (Readers, there were no freebies, just hospitality.) Various people for some characters' names, including Maria Channells who won a competition to be named as the head of MI5. John Grill, Ron McNeilly, Helen Johnstone, Russell Staley, Loucineh Mardirossian and Alison Green for putting me in touch with some of my experts.

An apology. Even though the crimes alleged against Dr Wilbur Fenton are entirely fictitious, I apologise if that slim part of the story offends anyone, not least any doctors and family of the former Apple CEO, Steve Jobs.

Producing a book from a manuscript is the work of many skilled hands and minds, so my thanks to *Pantera Press*'s wonderful team, especially Alison Green, editor Kylie Mason, designer Luke Causby, proofreader Desanka Vukelich, typesetter Graeme Jones, Karen Young for production, as well as the team at *Simon & Schuster*.

Last, people advise writers, 'Never ask for your family's opinions,' mainly because they tend to be indulgent or ignorant. My family's are neither. I thank them for that, and for all the things that matter far more.

About John M. Green

WHEN IT DAWNED ON JOHN that what got him up in the morning was writing, not his day job, he quit the job. That was after two careers spanning 30 years, first in law and then banking. His wife was his role model, earlier tossing in her own successful business career to chase her creative passion. She is now an award-winning sculptor.

The Trusted is John's third novel, but the first Tori Swyft thriller. It follows *Nowhere Man*, a financial thriller with a futuristic twist, and *Born to Run*, a political thriller.

John is also a well-known business writer, his articles having appeared in *The Australian*, *The Australian Financial Review*, *Company Director*, *Business Spectator*, *The Age* and the UK's *Financial Times*.

As well as writing, he's active in business as a leading public company director and has a variety of non-profit and philanthropic interests. He is a co-founder of *Pantera Press*.

John and his wife live in Sydney. They have two adult children who share their passions for the arts, books, business and philanthropy.

Praise for John M. Green's Novels

'A spectacular thriller ... it kept me up nights ...
John M. Green is the new Michael Crichton ... but better!'
– P.J. O'ROURKE, INTERNATIONAL BEST-SELLING AUTHOR

'Well-crafted as it is eminently believable. With the
sophistication of John le Carré and the pace of Jeffrey Archer'
– ABC RADIO

'An atmospheric thriller' – THE AGE

'... the best tradition of thriller writing, with knife-edge
moments and arresting prose' – THE AUSTRALIAN

'... one of those *pick it up and can't put it down* reads'
– SYDNEY MORNING HERALD

'... gripping ... moves at a cracking pace and is impossible
to put down ... a compelling writer of master thrillers'
– AUSTRALIAN FINANCIAL REVIEW

'A cracking thriller ... meticulously researched ... the
action is relentless as the past-paced plot heats up
... a terrific climax' – DAILY TELEGRAPH

'One of the most surprising thrillers of the year'
– CANBERRA TIMES

'Unputdownable' – THE WEST AUSTRALIAN

'... conjuring a bewildering landscape of betrayals'
– COURIER MAIL

'... well delivered, tight and paced ... an entertaining style
... "James Bond" at times' – AUST CRIME

'WARNING: Fasten your seatbelts & please remain seated for
the duration of this thrilling ride ... impossible to put down'
– THE READING ROOM

'... thrill-a-minute saga ... Green keeps you guessing'
– THE ADVERTISER